Those Pearly Gates

***Also by Julie Cannon
in Large Print:***

Truelove & Homegrown Tomatoes

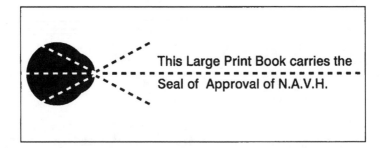

This Large Print Book carries the
Seal of Approval of N.A.V.H.

Those Pearly Gates

A Homegrown Novel

Julie Cannon

Published in 2005 by arrangement with Simon & Schuster, Inc.

Wheeler Large Print Hardcover.

The text of this Large Print edition is unabridged.
Other aspects of the book may vary from the original edition.

Set in 16 pt. Plantin by Liana M. Walker.

Printed in the United States on permanent paper.

Library of Congress Cataloging-in-Publication Data

Cannon, Julie, 1962–
    Those pearly gates : a homegrown novel / by Julie Cannon.
        p. cm.
    ISBN 1-59722-115-5 (lg. print : hc : alk. paper)
    1. Mothers and daughters — Fiction. 2. Spouses of clergy — Fiction. 3. Remarried people — Fiction.
4. Georgia — Fiction. 5. Domestic fiction. 6. Large type books. I. Title.
PS3603.A55T48 2005b
    813'.6—dc22   2005020420

This one's for my folks,
Bob and Gloria Lowrey

As the Founder/CEO of NAVH, the only national health agency solely devoted to those who, although not totally blind, have an eye disease which could lead to serious visual impairment, I am pleased to recognize Thorndike Press* as one of the leading publishers in the large print field.

Founded in 1954 in San Francisco to prepare large print textbooks for partially seeing children, NAVH became the pioneer and standard setting agency in the preparation of large type.

Today, those publishers who meet our standards carry the prestigious "Seal of Approval" indicating high quality large print. We are delighted that Thorndike Press is one of the publishers whose titles meet these standards. We are also pleased to recognize the significant contribution Thorndike Press is making in this important and growing field.

Lorraine H. Marchi, L.H.D.
Founder/CEO
NAVH

* Thorndike Press encompasses the following imprints: Thorndike, Wheeler, Walker and Large Print Press.

Contents

Prologue
Lou

The hardest lessons of my life always seemed to sneak up on me like the nests the dirt daubers built out in the barn. I'd figured on some smooth sailing, at least for a while, after Aunt Imogene married the Reverend Lemuel Peddigrew, and Jeanette turned her life over to Jesus.

But I remember well that fateful day, and being so troubled in my heart over the goings-on that come evening I paced up and down the hallway and through the kitchen in my nightgown, finally pausing impatiently at Imo and the Rev's bedroom door. Mostly they went to bed with the chickens, right after the supper dishes were washed and put away, but occasionally

11

they'd wrap up in robes and mosey out to sit in the den to thumb through old issues of *Reader's Digest* and the *Guideposts*, or to look at television for a spell.

That night their snores were a beautiful sound as I headed out to the back porch. Grateful for the solitude, I sank onto a damp pew gleaned from the old chapel at Calvary Baptist and spread my notebook open across my thighs. In a pool of lamplight, my stomach a fluttery knot, I sat tapping my pen on a clean sheet of paper.

Intimately familiar with both the dark and light sides of Jeanette, I had this feeling she'd somehow got herself back on a slippery slope, but I wasn't exactly sure yet what to make of her latest escapade. My heart began beating double time as Lavonia Fullard's quavery voice ran through my mind; "I ain't a gone make no bones about it," she'd said as she waggled one gnarled finger at the previous Wednesday night's prayer meeting. "You give old Slewfoot a ride and he'll always want to drive!" She was an ancient woman, one of the founding members of Calvary Baptist, who claimed she got regular words from the Lord, and who felt it her calling to share the revelations.

I began to entertain visions of Jeanette

backsliding from the faith, running around with married men, and getting a job dancing topless at the Honky Tonk Tavern.

C'mon Loutishie, I remember trying desperately to reassure myself, *let those words spill on out. It'll help you calm down.* The notebooks had become a way for me to release emotion, and many times I'd write like a crazy person, not stopping till I could draw a deep breath, look my scribblings over and say, "I get it now!" That anxious night, I whispered a short prayer that even if I couldn't figure everything out right away, I could at least clear my mind, maybe even allow myself to get a little bit of sleep.

I started out by writing "April the First" at the top of a clean page. That right there made me stop and laugh out loud. I wondered if I oughtn't be too surprised at what I'd seen and heard in Cartersville that afternoon. Maybe it was only a big cosmic April Fools' joke! Maybe I was overreacting and being a Miss Goody Two-shoes. Was it wrong to do the thing Jeanette was planning to? While wearing clothes that showed all a woman had to show?

Wait a minute! Anybody who'd been there and seen her face would know I wasn't getting worked up over nothing.

Pondering all this I looked up from my notebook to peer out into the settling darkness. The smell of wet earth filled the air as water dripped and ran from the swollen creek at the side of the farmhouse down into the Etowah River.

It was one of the earliest, wettest springs on record in Euharlee, Georgia, the kind where the rain hangs a cool, low mist over everything. The songs of spring peepers, joyous over the season, rang out from the creek. There were other froggy sounds, too, various croaks and husky trills calling for mates.

Down in the lower hundred acres of the farm, called the bottoms, the Etowah River sliced through what used to be a field full of Silver Queen corn that was my Uncle Silas's pride and joy. That land had grown fallow at his death and stayed that way, as the Reverend's hands were full tending to the needs of his flock.

On the top two hundred acres, there was nothing left but the farmhouse, Imo's little quarter acre of a vegetable garden, assorted barn cats, and Dusty Red, our fearless yard rooster. Oh, and Bingo, but he felt more like one of the family than a dog.

In her prime, Imo had been a hardworking farm wife who cultivated a huge garden, cleaned the house, cooked, canned, sewed, gathered the eggs, milked the cow, and thought nothing of jumping out of bed in the dark of night to chase down an escaped bull. And during those two years between when Uncle Silas passed away, and before her marriage to the Reverend, she still kept her big garden as well as a small herd of Angus.

But the day Imo said "I do" again, all this fell by the wayside. Imo took the job of pastor's wife seriously and she was gone from the farm practically all day: sitting with shut-ins, comforting sick and bereaved folks, and tending to things at Calvary Baptist.

I was ten the first time I was ever away from the homeplace more than a night. I went off to stay with a buddy at her granny's house in Atlanta for a week that summer, and she lived smack dab in the middle of that big city, in a fancy condominium with thick carpets and gold mirrors. The only animals around were little featherweight dogs that folks carried out to the sidewalk on leashes.

The first couple of days were exciting — going to art galleries, strange restaurants, and fashion malls. I'd barely given a thought to Imo, Uncle Silas, Jeanette, or the farm, but by that third day I thought I would bust if I couldn't see some wide open spaces, and I couldn't get back home fast enough. When I did, I told Imo I was never leaving again, and she just looked at me, nodding and laughing.

Though Imo wasn't my birth mother, she raised me from my first cry in this world, and I became the shadow of someone who loved to garden, who knew the connection we humans need to the earth. If she felt the need to see the world, she never let on. She seemed more than content right there on the farm.

While Imo and I were both country girls at heart, Jeanette called the farm, and Euharlee, Georgia, for that matter, Dullsville. When she finally moved away to Cartersville, she was beside herself.

My trip to Cartersville that day started out innocently enough. Jeanette called and put Little Silas on the phone. "Auntie Lou," he said, his breath laced with wonder, "I can ride my bike without wheels!" Of course, he really meant without training wheels, so I said to him, "I'm going to come see what a big boy you are."

When I got there, the front door was

standing open and I walked on in. Jeanette, Little Silas, and Reverend Montgomery Pike were sitting at the dinette table in the kitchen eating macaroni and cheese for lunch.

Jeanette's hair was piled in a big pouf on top of her head, above eyes made up in glittery blue eye shadow and long swoops of black eye liner. She wore jeans and a clingy pink shirt that said "Princess," and she was holding a can of Fresca, laughing a little too hard, excited or maybe nervous about something. I guess I was frowning, because when she spied me, she laughed and hollered out, "Git on in here, Loutishie. You look like you been sucking on a lemon."

I never took personal offense at anything Jeanette said to me like that. It was just our relationship, had been since the day Imo and Uncle Silas adopted her when I was three and she was six.

Little Silas dropped his fork and half-danced over to where I stood in the doorway. "Auntie Lou!" he said, grabbing my hand and looking behind me. "Mi-moo?"

"No, sweetie," I said. "Imo's busy at the church right now and then she's got to pick Tiffany up from cheerleading."

17

"Tiffany?" Jeanette's lip curled. "Mama picked the *Reverend's* grandchild over her own?" She slammed her Fresca can down, sending a small spray of droplets on the table.

"Tiffany's her grandchild, too, now, Jeannie," I said in a pleading tone.

"*Step*-grandchild. Ain't the same thing and you know it!"

"How are ya, Lou?" the Reverend Montgomery Pike asked as he stroked Jeanette's forearm. "What's shakin' down on the farm?"

"Oh, nothing much," I said, grateful for the change in subject. "Imo's hardening off the tomato seedlings."

I was fourteen and Jeanette was seventeen when we first laid eyes on Reverend Montgomery Pike. He was preaching at Imo's fiancé Fenton Mabry's funeral, though when it came to preachers, the Reverend Pike was not your run-of-the-mill. For one thing, he was younger than most, and covered up with tattoos and piercings on account of the fact that before he got the call to be a man of God, he sang with a rock 'n' roll band. He looked like a rock 'n' roll star, too, with his dimples and this dark swoop of hair that reminded me of Elvis.

"Hungry?" he asked, pulling out a chair for me.

"No, thanks."

"Cain't believe Mama didn't come with you, Lou." Jeanette stabbed some macaroni and popped it into her mouth, and began chewing so hard her jaw muscles quivered.

"Jeannie, sweetheart," the Reverend Pike said, "you know how busy your ma stays."

"Hmphh." Now Jeanette crossed her arms and thrust out her bottom lip. "She acts like Reverend Peddigrew's family is more important than us."

"You know that's not true," Montgomery said as he scooped Little Silas up and placed him on his knees. "This boy right here is the apple of her eye." He bounced Little Silas up and down. "Mine, too."

One thing I always marveled at was how taken Montgomery was with Little Silas. Acted like he sprung from his very own loins, though Little Silas had dark brown skin, like a walnut, on account of Jeanette's fling with the married India-Indian who used to run the Dairy Queen.

The day Montgomery and Jeanette were married, he got things in motion to legally adopt Little Silas, and then gave him his

19

own last name. To me, that was God answering Imo's prayer that there would be a man around for Little Silas to learn from. Montgomery carried Little Silas hunting, fishing, to the monster truck shows, and just about everywhere else he went, too. That was most likely the easy part of marrying Jeanette, because she stayed in a huff about something almost all the time. I looked hard at her face now, her pouty lip and scowling brow.

"C'mon," I said, prodding her playfully in the shoulder. "Let's all go outside and see this boy ride!" Little Silas hopped up and grabbed my hand, pulling me from the kitchen to the back porch, through the creaky screen door, and down the steps out into a slight breeze and a clover-covered yard buzzing with fat bumblebees. He danced impatiently underneath a pear tree covered in lacy blooms, waiting as Montgomery emerged from the house carrying a bike helmet and as Jeanette sashayed across the yard to perch sulkily on top of the picnic table.

She glanced down at her watch, crossed her arms, and then squinted through the bright sunshine at Little Silas.

"Alrighty, darlin'," she hollered, "show Aunt Lou how smart you are." She bit her lip, then added, "So *she* can go home and tell Mi-moo what Mi-moo missed!" She patted the table. "C'mere, Lou, sit right up here beside me. I need to ask you a favor."

I moved to the table, wondering about the strange tone in Jeanette's voice and watching a hawk circling overhead. After a bit, she drummed her fingers nervously on her thigh, leaned over real close to me and in a breathless voice whispered, "Lou, sweetie, I need you to do me a huge favor and keep an eye on Little Silas this afternoon."

"Sure," I said, watching Montgomery push a little green bike with plastic streamers hanging from the handlebars up to the top of the sloping backyard. He held it steady as Little Silas, face serious, swung his leg over the seat.

"Got a friend coming over who needs to talk to me," Jeanette said, still whispering, "privately." I nodded, clapping and cheering as Little Silas pedaled wobbily along, with Montgomery's outstretched hand always at the ready. Jeanette checked her watch constantly and finally she called out to Montgomery that it was 1:15 and wasn't it time for him to skedaddle?

He looked surprised.

"Don't you have that important meeting about the new parking lot?" Jeanette said.

21

He nodded. "Guess I'd better run. Good-bye, sport, ladies. Nice to see you, Lou."

"Whew." Jeanette blew out a long whoosh of air soon as she heard his truck pulling onto the highway. I looked at her hard. "Don't you like it when he comes home for lunch?"

"Adore it," she said, stretching out her leg and letting it dangle off the short end of the picnic table. "I love the man to bits, Lou, but like I told you, someone's coming over. April and I are . . ."

She kept talking but I tuned out at the sound of that name. There was only one April I knew of. Her younger sister, Dawn, was in eleventh grade with me. Dawn had a sullen face and she hung out in the back parking lot of Euharlee High, cutting classes and smoking like a chimney. There were five or maybe six sisters total, girls commonly known as "hussies" around Euharlee. All the sisters were daring and compelling females, who could draw men, even married ones, with only a slit-eyed, come-hither look. The talk was that April worked as a stripper at a nightclub in the sleazy part of Atlanta.

My mouth dropped open. "You talking about April Horton?"

She nodded and that was when I knew why she wanted Montgomery out of there.

"You got a problem with her?" Jeanette's voice rose.

"Problem?" I said stupidly.

"Yeah," she said, narrowing her eyes. "What's the matter with April Horton?"

"Bad company corrupts good morals?" I said weakly.

"Well, it just so happens I didn't ask your opinion, Saint Loutishie. And anyway, even if she was, and I said *was* bad, then it would be my job as a fine upstanding church lady to point her to the straight and narrow path, now wouldn't it?"

Hurt, I answered, "Well, I only meant . . ."

"You were being judgmental, Loutishie Lavender."

"But, I heard that she —"

"The Bible says not to judge folks. The Bible also says even Jesus receiveth sinners. He eateth with them, too." Jeanette turned on her heel. She had me there, I thought, sitting in the sun and watching her huff back into the house. But still, I felt something was up. And what it was was not Jeanette's intention to proselytize a wayward April.

I followed Little Silas to the sandbox, plopping down cross legged in the grass, wondering what Jeanette was getting herself tangled up in this time. If anyone knew what a long and rocky road it had been for her to make it this far — to get a high school equivalency diploma, graduate from beauty college, find a job working part time at the Kuntry Kut 'n' Kurl, to be raising this beautiful child, and being a minister's wife to boot, a minister's wife, I may add, who was supposedly walking with Jesus — then they would probably be holding their breath, too.

I had been there through all of the juiciest episodes of Jeanette's past, and I was only just getting to the point where I could relax regarding her eternal destiny. I'm not saying that Jeanette having April Horton over was a sin. Or that it was a sure-fire signpost on the road to backsliding from the faith either, but like I said, I had this *feeling.*

I could smell trouble like a skillet full of bacon frying.

Nervous, I kept glancing over my shoulder at the house and before long this baby blue Trans Am zipped up the driveway. A youngish woman stepped out, with frizzy bleached blond hair to her shoulders, wearing a black tube top over a faded blue-jean miniskirt. She was tall, made taller by some platform sandals that also made her hips wiggle as she climbed the brick steps, her elbow bent against her waist with a cigarette between her fingers. I got even more nervous when I saw she was smoking, because it wasn't long ago that Jeanette had given it up.

April Horton nudged the door open with her hip and after a minute or two, I heard them both screeching with laughter — sounded like a couple of hyenas. Across from me, Little Silas looked up at the house. In his black eyes there was a question. "Your mama has a friend over," I said.

He nodded and bent back over a plastic dumptruck, his face screwed up in concentration. Trying to make lighthearted play, I patted up a mound of damp sand with one hand, and with the other bored out a hole in it. "Hide in here, buddy," I instructed, "hide from the bad guys."

"The bad guys are big," Little Silas said, thrusting his hand inside the cave and smiling up at me. In the sunny backyard we listened to the purr of a distant lawn mower and moved from the sandbox to the tire swing and then to the slide. Somehow

I managed to play enough to distract my-self and to satisfy Little Silas. "I'm hungry," he said at last, putting his grimy hand in mine.

Jeanette and April were in the den with the TV on. When I peeped around the doorway they stopped talking. Jeanette sat on the couch with a couple of hair-styling magazines open on her lap, eating from a bag of Doritos, and April was leaning over her shoulder with a Pepsi in one hand and a cigarette in the other. Jeanette caught my eye. "Hey April," she said. "You remember Loutishie."

"Nice to see ya, kiddo," April said.

"Nice to see you, too," I said, staring at her glossy red lips. I felt my neck growing warm as I pictured her dancing naked on-stage, strutting her stuff up and down as men eagerly reached their hands toward her bare flesh. "Uhm," I said, "we came in to get us a snack."

"There's some oatmeal cream pies on top of the Frigidaire," Jeanette said. "Me and April are going outside."

Little Silas and I plopped down at the dinette with milk and oatmeal pies, but I was too distracted to answer his constant questions. My curiosity got the better of me and I crept across the hallway, through the tiny den, to a window facing the back-yard.

Holding my breath, I watched Jeanette as she literally squatted in air, smiling over at April, and holding her hands up with her forearms parallel to the ground. What a funny position, I thought, like she's riding an invisible horse. April was leaning forward in the air, too, pushing her behind out and swiveling it around.

I witnessed pure devilment in their faces as they nodded at one another, rose up higher, keeping their feet planted in the grass, and in the craziest way you ever saw, rocked their pelvises forward and to the side, still holding their hands out. Their tongues slithered out to slowly lick their lips in a sensual way. Then they opened their mouths into ovals, threw back their heads, and rolled their eyes upward; bucking, twisting, and writhing their hips wildly.

Then I stared with my mouth hanging open as April cupped her bosoms with both hands, bit her bottom lip, threw back her head and pursed her lips in mock ec-stasy. Jeanette watched, then mimicked this entire move.

"What in heaven's name," I uttered into the chintz curtains. I turned away, to Little

Silas who was behind me then, licking the cellophane wrapper of his oatmeal pie. "What you doing?" he asked, and I knelt to press his face against my neck, a raw impulse to shield him from what I called the forbidden fruit of the hussies.

In front of the television, we sat watching Grover sing his ABCs. You could be overreacting, reading it all wrong, I told myself, maybe it's only a couple of girls having a light and passing fit of spring fever.

But Jeanette's and April's faces when they came into the house a good half hour later held conspiratorial smirks and all my doubts flew right out the window.

When April left, I found Jeanette standing in the hallway rifling through the mail. "What were y'all doing out there, Jeannie?" I asked in a tight, high-pitched voice I could not help.

"Oh, playing around," she said offhandedly.

"What?" I insisted. "What were y'all playing?"

"Nothing really."

I followed her into the sunny yellow kitchen and stood while she scraped congealed macaroni into the trash. I knew enough not to back Jeanette into a corner, so I decided to let her stew a while, think I'd forgotten all about it. Then, perhaps she'd let it slip out. Or maybe it wouldn't be a slip at all. She'd come right out and tell me because she'd intended to all along. She'd never been a shrinking violet. You just had to know the technique to draw things out of her.

I sat down at the table as Little Silas varoomed through the kitchen pushing a plastic car. I would be patient, I would be shrewd. Soon as Jeanette cleaned up the lunch dishes, she went into the den, sank down onto the couch and grabbed the remote. I was right on her heels. "Pretty day out, don't you think?" I said.

She shrugged, flipping through the channels.

"Little Silas rides his bike like a pro," I said. "I bet Imo'll be sad she missed being here to see him today."

She scowled.

Shameless, I kept on, though mostly it felt like I was betraying Imo. "She sure stays busy looking after the Reverend and his family," I said. "Busy all the time going and doing for them."

Jeanette reared back and snorted in disgust. "Makes me so mad I could spit!"

I nodded.

"Heading up Bible studies and prayer chains and chasing the Reverend's grand-young'uns all over kingdom come." Jeanette folded her arms. "Probably even irons his underwear."

"She does take a lot of care of him," I affirmed. "She was out gathering pokeweed this morning. For his spring tonic."

Jeanette's eyes blazed. "Ain't seen hide nor hair of Mama for four whole days. Four days!" She slapped the armrest. "And she's got time to go hunting pokeweed, but she ain't got time to come see her only real grandchild ride his bike? Huh!"

Knowing Jeanette and her self-igniting ways, I sat back to wait. "Mmm-mmm-mmm," she moaned, shaking her head slowly with her eyes shut in disgust. Little Silas, sensing his mama's agitation, climbed into her lap, stroking her face in a delicate, tentative gesture.

"Probably too busy at the Reverend's church and seeing about the Reverend's pile of family to even *notice* anything here in Cartersville!" she fumed. "Wouldn't even realize it if we all fell in a hole over here in Cartersville."

Directly, the scowl still on her forehead, Jeanette turned the channel to cartoons, set Little Silas down, and stood to stretch. "Hey, it's almost four," she said, walking over and playfully bumping my knees with hers.

I shrugged. I would starve her for interaction.

She nudged my knees again. "Hey," she said, "wanta see my new shorts?"

"Sure," I said offhandedly.

Soon we were in her bedroom and she was fishing around through mounds of clothes on the floor.

"Really, Jeannie," I said, "what were you and April doing?"

"Hmm?" She was playing dumb.

"You and April. What were y'all doing?"

Jeanette turned to me then, and her face looked almost relieved as she began. "It ain't bad, Lou. Just having a little fun. April's going to enter the erotic bull-riding contest Friday night at the Honky Tonk Tavern, and she invited me to come watch her. It's one of those mechanical bulls. Cash prizes. Afterward, they've got a live band for dancing. It's Ladies' Night."

My insides shriveled. Jeanette was in spiritual quicksand! She would forget Jesus, stray off the narrow path, and start running with the hussies of Bartow County again.

"These here are what I'm wearing," Jeanette said, poking her feet into the legs

31

of some denim shorts no bigger than swim-suit bottoms, so bleached out they were al-most white. She sucked in her stomach to snap the shorts, and twirled to show off her long, tanned legs. "They're tens," she said, "but this brand is sized small."

Standing there, Jeanette had a look of eager searching, with her flyaway hair and her darting eyes. Like a child in front of a candy store. She laughed and began chat-tering on about a fight April was having with her landlord, and about how April was two weeks behind on her rent, and how if the man threatened to put her stuff out on the sidewalk again, that she was going to tell his wife he was a regular at the Paperdoll, where she worked as a naked dancer. "That ought to buy her some time, huh?" Jeanette said, smiling. "Least till Saturday. April figures she's gonna win this contest and she's giving me forty bucks for doing her hair and makeup. That's real im-portant, you know, Lou. The presentation part is." Jeanette nudged me with her foot and I nodded, saying nothing. "April was just showing me the moves today, Lou. I wanted to see what you do for a mechan-ical bull-riding contest." She dug around in her closet and came up with a pair of pink suede boots that had three-inch heels.

"How do you think these look with the shorts?" she asked as she slipped them on and spun. "Did I mention first place is five hundred bucks?"

I shrugged, struggling to look indifferent. Then I gathered up my courage. "You really think the Honky Tonk is a good place for a mama and a preacher's wife to be going, Jeannie?"

She met my eyes with her blue-green ones and she said, "Ain't one thing wrong with it, Loutishie. Everyone'll have all their clothes on. Plus, it's in Fulton County. Don't nobody from around here go to the joints in Fulton County, and anyway, Montgomery and Little Silas'll be sawing logs while I'm watching April ride the bull."

I decided then and there not to say another word about it. I turned on my heel and strode to the door. "Bye-bye, buddy," I said to Little Silas, who was under the coffee table playing with some plastic dinosaurs.

I was still fastening my seat belt when Jeanette came galloping outside in the shorts and boots. She stuck her head inside the passenger window. "Relax, Lu-lu," she said, laughing. "Okay? Thanks for watching Little Silas, and be sure and tell

33

Imo what she missed." All of a sudden her grin faded. She held up her pointer finger and swished it side to side. "But don't you dare tell her about the Honky Tonk. Some folks happen to be real narrow-minded."

I didn't say yes or no, just hightailed it home with my brain racing. I figured it was way too early to tell if I *was* being the Little Miss Righteous that Jeanette always accused me of, or if I was just keeping alert to the wiles of the devil, as Reverend Peddigrew says we're supposed to do.

Sitting glumly on the back steps at home, I tried to pray but could not. So I whistled for Bingo, and when he came loping up from the barn, we took off for the bottoms.

Usually the Etowah was unhurried, running along like drips of sorghum syrup down the side of a knife, but the spring rains had swollen the waters, and we had to pick our way carefully upriver to a sandy spot where it was relatively broad and a bit shallower. Save for Bingo's panting, all was silence and reflection. I sat down, wrapped my arms around my legs, and rested my chin on my knees. "Purty, ain't it, boy?" I said, ruffling the smelly fur at his neck.

An image suddenly flashed across my

mind; Jeanette and me as young girls, our bare legs finely scratched from the blackberries we gathered along the river's edge, wading out into the muddy, slick-bottomed river, the churning of our feet turning the water into a color like Imo's coffee-milk in the mornings.

When we were at the river, Jeanette and I entered a play world of immense proportions. We fished and hunted for arrowheads. We bobbed and floated in a couple of Uncle Silas's huge tractor tire inner tubes till our bodies were tawny as the Cherokees. We became like blood sisters, and now I recalled the innocent part of me that thought things would never change.

Then Jeanette turned twelve, thirteen, and she discovered boys. From her first crush, she was a goner. At times she would still come down to the river with me — but it was never the same.

Gone were our carefree days in the summers — days spent playing school, helping Imo in the garden, setting watermelons into the cold water of the spring for a treat late in the day.

Jeanette became a wild-eyed young woman who spit in the face of authority, sneaking off at night to run with a fast crowd. I witnessed all this with my heart in my throat, praying without ceasing that she would return to the straight and narrow path.

What I saw in Imo then was denial where Jeanette was concerned. She simply did not want to face reality, but when Jeanette got pregnant, Imo could ignore it no longer.

I suppose Imo never relaxed again until after the shock waves wore off on the day that Jeanette — who had fallen in love with Montgomery Pike — turned her heart over to Jesus at the altar just after Imo'd said her wedding vows there with the Reverend Lemuel Peddigrew.

I laid my head on Bingo's warm stomach and I worried that we had seen the last of clear, blue skies. I worried that a storm might be on the horizon. Knowing Jeanette and the pull that worldly delights and trinkets held for her, knowing her tendencies, I imagined the erotic bull-riding deal escalating into another full-blown walk on the wild side.

One

❧

Classics

Imo

They were on the weathered front porch of the farmhouse, waiting for Miss Cathy and Brownie Troop number eighty-six to arrive. Lemuel sat arrow straight on the swing. Imogene was in a rocker facing him, so she could see their visitors come around the bend in the drive.

Though it was a Thursday he wore his Sunday best, a crisp gray suit with a thin navy pinstripe. His shirt was spotless white and over that lay a vest and a scarlet tie fastened with a gold clip. A fancy telescope and a tall tripod lay propped against the porch railing.

Imogene wore a milk-blue shirtwaist dress to match her Keds and a cream-colored crocheted vest to give it some pizzazz. She fingered her earbobs — large enamel pearls, a wedding gift from the Garden Club girls just two short years ago.

At a quarter till seven, Lemuel pulled his pocket watch from his trousers. Peering at it, he frowned and sat up even straighter. "Let's hope she didn't forget," he said.

"Cathy wouldn't forget," said Imo.

"Might," he said.

"Maybe you got mixed up on the day, Lemuel."

"No, ma'am." He crossed his arms. "I did not."

"Maybe it's tomorrow evening instead. A Friday night would make more sense. It's not a school night."

"No, ma'am, it is not Friday that they are coming. It is tonight and it was to be at six-thirty p.m." He leaned back against the swing.

They were quiet for a spell. Imo glanced over her shoulder at the sagging barn. Bingo was fastened up inside one of the stalls. Though he would not hurt a fly, she knew some small children were scared of dogs and she didn't want anything to ruin Lemuel's evening of talking with the Brownies about astronomy, a recent fascination of his. Now she just hoped he had the date correct.

As if he could read her thoughts, Lemuel uncrossed his ankles, planted his heels on the porch, and straightened his knees to start the swing rocking. Imo could see the muscles tightening in his jaw.

Except for the creaking coming from the swing's rusty chain, it was a quiet evening. Loutishie was gone off with some friends from the high school. Imo took a deep breath; every now and then she caught a feel of the coming season. A bud on the dogwood trees or a dab of purple from an early crocus, and all around the sounds of birds and bees, trembling in the air to celebrate spring's arrival. As the days grew milder and brighter, and the sun slowly warmed her patch of southern soil, she felt the familiar restlessness over getting outside into her garden. No amount of staring wistfully at the glossy pages of her garden catalogs or even starting her tomato and pepper plants from seed (since February) could satisfy her.

She watched late sunlight fall across a rusted pickup sitting on cinder blocks beside the shed. "Might come a rain," she said, looking beyond the shed, "I see dark clouds yonder a ways."

Lem scowled. "Hope it holds off till

we've had a chance to look at the stars."

"You're sure it's tonight?" she asked him gently.

"Yessum. I am positive it is tonight. It is tonight at six-thirty sharp." Now he swung steadily, gripping the swing's armrest with one large white-knuckled hand.

"Thursday? You're sure? Six-thirty?"

"They'll be here, Imogene."

"Well, it's ten till seven now."

"You can imagine how hard it is to round up six little girls and settle them down, now can't you?"

"But you know how Cathy is. I figured she'd be here at six if you told her six-thirty. Maybe you did get mixed up, Lem, dear. It could happen."

He fished his pocket watch out again, flipped it open and peered hard at its face. "I'm not mixed up," he said in a voice that said *don't ask again.* Frowning, he kept the swing moving in a steady rhythm.

"I'll just run in the kitchen and check the calendar," Imo said after a bit, rising.

He held out an impatient hand to motion her back down. "Keep your seat. It's on the calendar. I already checked."

"Let me call Cathy then. Maybe you wrote it down wrong. Maybe you wrote it down on Thursday's square by mistake

40

and it's really tomorrow."

"I did not."

"Maybe you recollected the wrong date, then. That could happen. She said one thing and you remembered it wrong."

"I remember talking to Cathy about it like it was yesterday."

"But Lemuel, it *was* last week when y'all talked about it. Anyway, everybody makes mistakes. It's almost seven now. Go in and call her."

"I didn't make a mistake, Imogene! I didn't forget! Maybe they've had a flat tire." He stood up sharply and dug in his pocket for his keys. "I'll drive down the road a piece and check."

"Call first." She grabbed the crease of his trousers and tugged.

He shook his head, pulled away. "They've gotten in a fix and I need to go help them. Could be a flat tire, the battery . . ."

"Please, Lem, dear. Dial Cathy's number first. What would it hurt?"

"Well . . ."

"You could be wrong. Last Saturday morning, for instance," she added cheerily, patting his leg, "you missed your haircut appointment. You remember Wanda calling you to say you missed it? You had

41

to run over there after we ate a bite of lunch. Had to go to her house since she closes the salon at noon on Saturdays."

"What?" He scowled. "Oh, that. I know I did. You've got to realize, Imo, that was because of Miz Pritchett's grandson. The mess he was in over at the dirt track."

"Well, you're not a spring chicken anymore, Lemuel. All I'm saying —"

"I'm not a spring chicken anymore? What's that supposed to mean? I am on the ball. I am holding everything together."

Imo closed her eyes to gather her thoughts. "It's not a sign of weakness if you did get mixed up or forget, dear. It's only human. You said to me the other day, you said, 'Imo, now tell me why in the wide world did I come in here?' We were standing in the kitchen. I was making some slaw and I said maybe you were after a glass of tea. And then you remembered. You came in there for a spoon of peanut butter. Don't you remember that?"

"Remember the peanut butter?"

"Remember coming into the kitchen for something and forgetting it."

He turned and clumsily fiddled with the head of a walking stick he kept leaning against the porch railing. He looked out over the lawn, whistling under his breath.

Imo saved him. "Going to lead them out into the upper pasture?"

"Yessum. Figured I'd walk them to the clearing and show them Polaris and Ursa Major. Talk to them about the Milky Way, show them the Big Dipper."

The sight of his rigid back told Imo to let it go, not to rub it in. She settled down to wait, to let time reveal to them the verdict. She wasn't exactly used to being a preacher's wife yet, though two years could sometimes feel like an eternity. There seemed to be a very fine line between showing reverence for him as a man of God, and being his earthly helpmeet, which sometimes meant pointing out his human frailties.

Life had been much simpler being Mrs. Silas Lavender. For forty-eight years her place on this earth was secure with Silas beside her. She knew just what each day held. She knew exactly where she stood in the community, and also what was expected of her in regard to his side of the family. She and Silas had married when she was sixteen and she figured they would be together until the end. The end of what, she didn't know, but until his diagnosis with cancer she hadn't fathomed a life without him. Now, at sixty-seven, Imo was starting all over again.

She stole a sideways glance at Lemuel Peddigrew, seventy-five. Being married to him was like being kin to half of Euharlee. Not only was she the Reverend's wife, which was very close to being the mother of a congregation of one hundred and thirty-four folks, but the number of his literal blood kin was staggering. Not just brothers and sisters and sons and daughters and grandchildren, either. There were aunts and great-aunts and uncles and great-uncles and a vast number of cousins and second cousins and second cousins twice removed. All required attention and sometimes Imo felt like she barely made it from day to day, tending to birthdays, anniversaries, sickbeds, recitals, and baseball games.

This had indeed been the busiest two years of her life and now she had a new, almost reverential awe and respect for her dear friend Martha, the former Mrs. Lemuel Peddigrew. There was not a single day that Imo did not miss Martha or have questions she wished to ask her. Along with questions about being the tireless mother figure and pillar of the church and the president of the Garden Club, Imo would ask Martha how in heaven's name she had managed this man.

Aside from the matter of this stubbornness tonight, he could be as messy as a teenager, was particularly unhandy when it came to fixing things around the house, and even worse when it came to things around the farm or in the vegetable garden. He was all thumbs with the rototiller and could hardly tell a squash seedling from a cucumber. The man was clueless about composting and mulching and pulling suckers from the tomato vines. These things did not come naturally to him and though he was a willing companion, it took more time for Imo to explain it all than to just do it herself.

Of course, he had his fine points as well. Many of them. He was generous to a fault, he served his Lord with a pure heart, had a wonderful sense of humor, and could fish with the best of them. Though theirs had been an arranged marriage — namely, a death-bed promise to care for each other that Martha extracted from the both of them — he seemed to love her. The fact was that he would do just about anything for her. He thought nothing of getting up in the dark on Sundays, starting the coffee, and bringing her a cup in bed.

Often he spoke sweet words to her and

told her she was beautiful. Sometimes it made Imo feel guilty when he said she was beautiful. Martha had been stout, and she had a broad, plain face with twinkling blue eyes that gave the impression of country-fresh honesty. Beautiful in the classic sense of the word, Martha was not. Still, she always managed to look neat. Whether she wore an old house dress to work outside in her flower patch or was all gussied up for church, she looked her best. Two things you never caught Martha without were her smile and her eagerness to help another soul in need.

Though Imo might beat Martha in the looks department, she obviously lacked a lot in the pastor's wife department. When Martha was Mrs. Lemuel Peddigrew, she was a font of Biblical wisdom, a one-woman task force. Committees formed effortlessly, folks were raised up from their sickbeds, flower arrangements appeared almost by magic, clothes and food were rounded up for the needy, pancake suppers were griddled to perfection — all from Martha's indefatigable hand.

These things did not come as easily to Imo. While she went about her life as Mrs. Lemuel Peddigrew and performed her duties as the pastor's wife of Calvary Baptist, she often had the feeling that Martha was watching. She sensed that if she turned her head in a quick jerk, she would see Martha with her hands clasped in front, her lips in a soft smile as she gazed at Imo's life.

Was it a critical smile? Imo wondered. Most likely not, given Martha's sweet spirit. But it should be. There did not seem to be one tiny thing that Imo could do as well as Martha had. Though Imo reckoned that if she'd had to move into the parsonage, these feelings would be much worse. She'd have run into Martha everywhere she turned. What a blessing that Lemuel had agreed to move out to the farm with her and Loutishie.

Now, that was proof of real love if anything was! To indulge Imo in her request to stay on the farm. The very land where she came into this world, that held all of her memories and the garden where she spent her finest moments. A place that helped salve her heart and boost her spirits.

For a while in the early months of their marriage, Imo discovered just how much she needed the comfort of her homeplace. The Reverend had closed himself off romantically and physically from her, and this made her feel hurt and confused.

There had been so many emotions running through Imo on the day that they married she still could not say to this day if it was relief or disappointment on that first night together as man and wife when he exited the bathroom of their tiny cabin in the Great Smoky Mountains clothed in plaid flannel pajamas, socks, slippers, and a plush green terry-cloth robe with a belt securely fastened at his waist.

It being winter, he stayed in the robe as they drank Sanka and discussed their plans for the coming day. He wouldn't look directly at Imo that entire night. He looked all around the edges of her. He looked at a print of Monet's *Sunflowers* hanging above the bed, at a table which held the telephone and a glossy magazine of area attractions.

Imo began to feel even more self-conscious, practically naked, as she reclined against the headboard of the bed, tugging at the short hemline of a red diaphanous negligee. The negligee had been Maimee Harris's idea. "It's your wedding night, girl," Maimee said, shaking her head, "I can't believe you are planning to wear *that*." She scowled at a floor-length high-necked nightgown with long sleeves made of thick muslin that was draped over Imo's bed with the rest of her trousseau.

"Why not? I think it's just perfect."

"Perfect, my foot," Maimee said. "Looks like something a nun would wear."

Imo's thoughts whirled. She did not know what a lady should wear for the wedding night of her second marriage, let alone a pastor's wife. She would, she decided, make the drive to JoAnne's Fashion Corner, and let an expert give her opinion. JoAnne herself directed Imo to a circular rack of frothy confections in colors like seafoam and shrimp and jonquil.

Imo didn't exactly know what she expected the Reverend to do that first night together, but her chest flushed hot and pink as she pictured his hands lifting the negligee. She pulled the spread over her bare legs as he continued to wear his robe. All while they sat there talking she kept hoping he would at least do something.

Even a chaste kiss would be nice, she thought, something to seal the deal.

As ten o'clock came, he said, "Well, looks like it's time to hit the hay" and scuffed off to the bathroom to brush his teeth. He returned to bed, still wearing the robe, sat on the edge of the mattress with his back to her to remove his slippers, slid his sock-clad feet into the covers, and pulled the covers up to his waist. Only then did he remove the robe, draping it across the foot of the bed and lying back quietly, pulling his side of the sheet and then the blanket up to his chin.

She lay on her side, facing him expectantly. He snaked his hand out from the covers and she tensed, waiting for the warmth of his touch, but his hand went up and through the air above her to turn off the wall lamp. Then he lay with his arms folded across his chest in the dark and the minutes passed in perfect silence until at last his snores filled the cabin. Imo lay awake till past two a.m., feeling silly in the negligee. For as little as he had touched her that night, Imo wondered that he hadn't gotten a cabin with two single beds.

There certainly wouldn't be much to tell the Garden Club girls. This was just as well, she tried to convince herself. It would give her a bit more time to adjust to thoughts of making love with her pastor.

She'd wondered many times if being intimate with a man of God was on a higher plane than with an ordinary man. Imo herself liked to keep God out of the bedroom when she and Silas had made love. It just did not seem very Christian to be doing something so naked and earthy, so human.

So *physical.* All the pulsing and throaty moaning.

Surely Lemuel will get around to the act in his own sweet time, she reassured herself as several days passed with no intimacy. She kept reassuring herself with the memory that she herself was barely able to function right after Silas passed away. It had been all she could do to put one foot in front of the other. The fact of the matter was that she'd had more time to heal, and Lemuel's grief-stricken heart was probably not ready for intimacy with Imo yet as Martha'd not been in the ground a whole year. This salved Imo's wounded pride as the days turned into weeks.

But when six solid months had passed without more than a friendly pat on the shoulder or an occasional squeeze to the knee while they looked at TV together, Imo began to fret. It felt like a bald-faced lie to say they were married.

You should not be complaining, Imo, she told herself often, *it is wonderful to have a life companion. Lemuel is good to you and you two enjoy each other's company. You know your life as man and wife was a purely practical arrangement, namely so Martha could leave this earth in peace. Don't expect to have passion. You just*

51

need to learn to be satisfied with things the way they are.

She almost had herself convinced when one day things began to change. It was a Saturday, early evening, and Imo was cleaning up after supper. She was at the stove, scraping leftovers into a skillet full of bacon drippings.

The late sun threw a pale rectangle on the linoleum and the radio on the window-sill was playing "My Better Years" by the Johnson Mountain Boys. She stirred the shiny mixture in the skillet with a long wooden spoon, took a sip of her tea, and moved to the rhythm of a wailing fiddle.

When the skillet's contents were warm, she stepped out on the back porch to scrape it into Bingo's bowl, and he came running eagerly, his tongue lolling out and to one side. He wolfed the food in one giant gulp and she ruffled his rib cage, saying, "I don't know why I even bother sometimes, Bingo. I don't believe you had time to taste it." Smiling, she brought the skillet in and set it on the counter beside the sink. She laid a flap of rubber over the drain and turned on the hot water full blast. A short squirt of Palmolive and the scent of lemons filled the air. At the sound of footsteps behind her, she turned.

There he was, standing so close she could feel the warmth of him, an expression on his face she'd never seen before. His cheeks were pink and smooth, the spicy scent of freshly applied Old Spice mingled with dish liquid. "More tea?" she asked cautiously. "Can I fix you some dessert?"

"You," he whispered, "I want *you,*" and Imo stood frozen at the sink.

He turned the faucet off, spun her around to face him, and grasped her waist, pulling her against him roughly. She was trembling all over as he leaned in to nuzzle her neck.

"Let's make love," he breathed into her ear so hotly it left wetness.

Nodding, Imo wrapped her arms around his rigid body, but strangely enough, what flew into her mind at that particular moment was not passion, it was the memory of them at Martha's funeral, standing amid the cloying fragrance of hundreds of roses; their frightened and stunned faces whenever their eyes met. She looked hurriedly to the left and the right, feeling vaguely guilty, as if she were being watched, as if she were cheating with her best friend's husband.

"In the bedroom," he said huskily, pulling back and peering into the very depths of her soul. She noted how huge his pupils were, how rapid his breathing, and she willed the specter of Martha away so she could connect with that stirring of her own desire. All these long months she had dreamed of this moment and here it was!

"You make me feel like I'm eighteen again!" he kept saying when it was all over. He was pleased with himself, Imo could tell. He had a smile on his face and heavy-lidded, complacent eyes. She studied her hands, laced together on top of the quilt, the gold of her wedding band reflecting a sliver of light from the bedside lamp.

After a bit, she closed her eyes. They had become one flesh at last and she didn't know whether to laugh or cry. Intercourse with Lemuel, other than his grateful utterance to the Lord as he spilled his seed, was on no higher spiritual plane. It was still the same earthly sensual act of the masses.

With this first impassioned union, it was like some wall had been knocked down. Lemuel began to parade around in their bedroom wearing only his boxer shorts. He nestled nude against Imo as they slept. When Tuesdays and Saturdays rolled around, he combed fresh Vitalis through his hair, shaved and slapped on Old Spice, brushed and flossed his teeth, and got that amorous look in his eyes once again.

Each time, Imo was pleased. They quickly learned to read each other's bodies, to move and caress in just the right ways, and after their trysts they lay spent and intertwined, their hearts thudding in unison. Their love making was all the more special to Imo as she'd never figured on such passion with her pastor.

Musing on this, Imo leaned her head back against the rocker and studied Lemuel's face. What a dear man he was! This lover of hers. A strong man, too. Letting her stay here on her beloved farm. If he were any lesser, he'd have dug in his heels and insisted she move to the parsonage. This act seemed so great to her now — the concession of a man secure in the sense of who he was.

This realization made an uneasiness settle over Imo. Ten after seven. Possibly *she* was the one who was wrong about the time for the Brownies' visit! Who had made her sovereign over Lemuel? Cathy could very well have had a flat tire. Or worse!

Imo's heart bounded up into her chest as

she stood to go fetch her purse. She would say she was sorry to Lemuel as they drove along Flat Shoals Road searching for Cathy. But even before she could utter a word, Cathy's van came around the bend and Lem let out a sharp "ah!" She looked at him and he nodded in one satisfied dip as he rose and gripped the stair rails to help himself down to meet the girls.

Cathy lowered the window of her blue van before it came to a stop beside the birdbath. "Howdy, Reverend and the Missus!" she called. "We're a wee bit early, I know, but the girls were so excited I couldn't hold 'em back a second longer."

Lemuel was unruffled at Miss Cathy's words. When the car stopped, he gallantly opened her door. "I *like* an early start!" he said.

This was interesting, Imo thought, this disconnect from reality. She told herself that once she got him alone she would try and get to the bottom of things. Please, Lord, she breathed, let this be an isolated incident, keep my beloved's mind sound. But if he really were as clueless as he seemed sometimes lately, she'd simply have to carry him in to talk to Dr. Perkins.

She walked around to slide the side door open and release the Brownies. Six girls tumbled out. Girls with shiny full hair beneath brown felt beanies, wearing sashes with glinting gold stars sprinkled across them. Laughing and jumping, they scrambled around the van to Miss Cathy's side.

"Shhh. Settle down now, girls," Miss Cathy said, calming them with high eyebrows and the hand signal of two fingers raised. "Listen up now. The Reverend here has planned a special treat for us. He's going to show us the Milky Way."

"I love Milky Ways!" the smallest blond-haired, pink-cheeked wisp of a Brownie exclaimed.

Miss Cathy giggled and held up her fingers once again. "Now, ladies, hold your comments. Reverend P has got us a star-gazing tour planned, then Missus P has some refreshments here at the house where we can all ask our questions about stars and stuff." She turned to the Reverend. "Ready, sir?"

A smile spread across his face. "I surely am. Reckon we ought to head to the upper pasture, to the wide clearing." Miss Cathy and the girls fell into step behind him, and he ushered the group past an old hand-plow which served as the mailbox post, past the well house, the springhouse, the garden shed, the rusty pickup truck on cinder blocks and the tractor shed. The girls remarked on everything with vibrant gestures.

"Astronomy," the Reverend began in a deep voice as they strolled along a dirt path and between an opening in the barbed-wire fence, "that's the scientific study of the universe beyond our earth, dealing with heavenly bodies, their motions, magnitudes, distances, and physical constitutions. What we can see this time of year, in early spring, will be Ursa Major, also called the Great Bear, but more commonly known as the Big Dipper. This is the best-known group of stars in the sky! We'll also take us a look at Polaris, the North Star."

As the last shred of sunlight faded, Imo trudged along at the end of the procession, her heart still troubled by Lemuel's confusion about the time. *What a pity if the Reverend's mind was slipping,* she thought. This was worse than anything she could imagine! Worse than losing a limb, eyesight, or hearing. It was so terrible she was determined to do something about it immediately. Try and stop it, staunch it, make it disappear. But what could she do? How could she help her dear Lemuel? She knew that he worked entirely too hard tending to his flock and that he poured himself out too completely in his sermons. Why, he should be retired at his age!

He was using himself up was what it was. If she could have, she would have made him retire yesterday, while his mind was still sharp. But she could convince him to retire now, couldn't she? Yes, there was no question about it. She'd have to.

The group came to a stop and the Reverend fumbled with assembling the tripod. While he was tediously affixing the telescope to the tripod, Miss Cathy led the girls in a vigorous rendition of the song "Make New Friends." Imo eyed the low canopy of clouds above them, but didn't open her mouth. At last he released a long sigh and patted the telescope. He bent his knee and cocked his head to peer through it at the sky. He scowled. "Can't see a blessed thing!"

In the meantime, fat raindrops began to fall and Miss Cathy gave him a polite, pitiable smile. "We'll get our uniforms all soggy out here," one Brownie wailed.

"Well," he said gloomily, "reckon there's nothing I can do about the weather. We'll just have to reschedule our stargazing for a clearer night. Let's head to the barn to talk about our Milky Way till this rain eases enough to get on back to the house."

It was dark as night inside the barn and Lemuel grasped the string dangling from a 40-watt bulb. He perched himself on a dusty bale of hay. "Have a seat, ladies." He gestured toward more hay bales scattered across the dirt floor in front of him.

Bingo whimpered, straining against his tether. Imo hushed him, then leaned against the rough boards behind Miss Cathy, whose perfume was so strong it made her eyes water.

"Okay, ladies, let's talk about our Milky Way," Lemuel said, rubbing his chin. "Our galaxy is called the Milky Way. Now, don't get confused. You'd have a hard time getting your mouth around this Milky Way." He laughed and the girls laughed with him. "The Milky Way I am referring to contains roughly four hundred billion stars. Each star is a sun, with its own family of planets. Our nearest star is twenty-six trillion miles away —"

"How old are you, sir?" a tiny girl asked, touching his wrist, which appeared to be a solid mass of wrinkles under the 40-watt lightbulb.

There was a pause. "Well, little lady," he chuckled, "I was born in 1927. So that makes me seventy-five years young."

"We're studying the olden days in Miss Warman's class!" another Brownie chimed in. "They didn't have no TVs or computers back in the olden days."

"Girls, girls, hush up," Miss Cathy said. "It is not polite to ask folks how old they are."

"It's all right," he said. "When I was a little feller, we couldn't even do things like this." He reached up and yanked the lightbulb string once more and the barn was dark. There was a collective squeal from the girls, and he pulled it on again. "We couldn't pull a string and get us some light. We didn't get electricity until the middle of the 1930s. I was about eight years old before we had our house wired for electricity. There were no lightbulbs. No electric ranges. No refrigerators. No washing machines or clothes dryers. We didn't have tub baths like you do today. We didn't have hot running water."

A gasp from the girls.

"That's right," Imo chimed in. "Most folks just stayed right where they were their entire lives. Bartow County was a rural county, and my folks were farmers right on this very land and my daddy grew or raised most of our own food. We were what you call self-sufficient. Most farm folks back then were. I can remember my granny, Eula Mae Bryars, saying all the time, 'I just think it's a disgrace for a farming family to live out of a paper bag.' That meant only the things you couldn't grow on the farm should be bought at the store. We had us a milk cow, a couple of hogs, chickens, and Momma kept a big backyard vegetable garden."

A young hand shot up, waving vibrantly. "Y'all didn't have any *stores?*"

"Oh, we had us a store all right," she said. "Bought a few things in there — things like sugar, salt, coffee, shoes, matches, tobacco, and snuff. Things we couldn't grow on our own."

Miss Cathy nodded at the Reverend. "Tell 'em about how hard folks used to work."

"In my day," the Reverend said, "growing up in a tiny rural town down in South Georgia, young'uns had to go to work soon as possible to help support the family. Farmers' kids would carry water to the folks working in the field — to the cotton pickers, the plowers, whatever they had to do to help harvest the crops. The schools closed down during cotton-picking time."

"Did y'all ever have any fun?" a serious dark-eyed Brownie sitting next to Miss Cathy whispered.

The Reverend whispered right back. "Had some of the best times of my life. Didn't have no TV, but my daddy could tell some of the best stories of anybody alive. Unbelievable stories that he swore till the day he died were true."

A boom of thunder rattled the roof of the barn and all were quiet a moment. "I'll tell you something we loved come summertime, 'sides swimmin' in the creek," the Reverend said. "That was when the ice man came. Remember I told you we didn't have anything like a refrigerator? Well, we had us a ice man and he made his rounds in a truck loaded with big ole blocks of ice weighing a hundred pounds apiece, insulated with cotton hulls and jute bags. He traveled through the countryside and he had this ice pick he used to break those blocks into chunks, and while he was busy chippin', us children would gather around to pick up the ice chips that flew out. Then that feller'd grab his ice tongs and tote a block of ice into our kitchen and set it into our icebox. That's what kept our food from spoiling." The Reverend smiled and placed his hands on his knees.

The girls sat with their mouths hanging open.

Miss Cathy giggled a bit to fill the silence. "I bet y'all couldn't just run off to McDonald's for a Happy Meal, could you?"

Imo's eyes sparkled. "Couldn't do any such thing," she said. "We lived on cornbread and beans. Maybe a little bit of fatback, streak-o-lean, or grease gravy if we were lucky. Sometimes Momma'd send me out to grab a nice fat frier from the chickenyard. Then she'd build a fire in the cookstove and wring that chicken's neck. We'd scald it in hot water, and I'd pluck the feathers out and she'd cut it up for frying. Mmm mmm. That was some good eatin'!"

Now the Brownies' noses were wrinkling in disgust.

There was another rumble of thunder and the Reverend said he reckoned they'd be stuck a while longer.

"Any of you girls have a question about life the way it used to be here?" Miss Cathy urged.

One small arm shot up and a girl with sparkling green eyes asked did they have telephones way back then.

"Naw," the Reverend answered, "all the

way through the thirties and the forties there weren't hardly any telephones, maybe a few in the rich folks' houses. Weren't none in the rural areas like this. If you wanted to call somebody or if somebody called you, in my little town the Sullivan Country Store was the place you had to go. All the livelong day Mr. Sullivan was sending for someone to come to the phone for a message."

More silence, except for a gentle rain falling on the roof and the muffled sound of spring peepers. Imo wondered if it was time to make a dash up to the house for snacks. "Are there any more questions?" she asked.

"Tell us about the schools in the olden days," said Lara Lee, who was in Miss Cathy's lap. "My pepaw said they didn't used to have school buses when he was little."

"Nope, boys and girls had to walk to school from near and far," the Reverend said. "I had to walk two miles there and two miles back, even in the wintertime. You know the little wooden building down on Jessamine Street? One they use for the cotton museum? That was the Bartow County schoolhouse. Weren't no desks like you have today. Had benches. In my school we had to take turns bringing water up from the spring every day. Had to cut fire-wood in the winter for the pot-bellied stove sitting in the middle of the classroom.

"We studied the three R's — Readin', Writin', and 'rithmetic. The teacher'd call roll and the first thing we did after that was listen to her read a verse out of the Good Book. Memorized a Bible verse every day, we sure did. Can't even *pray* at schools nowadays."

A few solemn nods and then Miss Cathy said, "Sounds like the storm's passed."

They dashed through the drizzle toward the house, and as they went Imo's mind spun. She'd heard so much more than just the words back there in the barn. Now he would see that he was a true dyed-in-the-wool product of the olden days, even if he didn't like to admit it. This whole talk to the Brownies should enable him to realize just how old he was, and how the time had come to slow down.

Back inside the house Imo led everyone into the bright yellow kitchen and handed out dish towels to the huddle of Brownies so they could dry themselves. By the oven's clock it was eight p.m. and she figured everyone was ready for a snack and bed. She would wrap things up quickly and powerfully. She set out a line of paper napkins and paper cups with tiny blue ducks marching around the rims, stirred a pitcher of pink lemonade, and unclipped a bag of Pecan Sandies to sprinkle in assembly-line fashion. As Miss Cathy served the lemonade Imo poured three cups of water into the top of the Mr. Coffee machine and took great comfort in the rich, nutty aroma of chicory coffee and the gurgle of hot water down through the filter.

The little girls ate and she positioned herself at the head of the table, took a long slug of steaming coffee and a buttery bite of a Pecan Sandy, and searched Lem's face. "I bet these girls have just about decided that you and I lived in the dinosaur ages, don't you, dear?" He did not answer and she addressed the girls. "When you all are through with your refreshments," she said, "we can take a quick look at some real old-timey things out on the porch. Things Reverend Peddigrew had when he was growing up."

She led the way to the back porch. Dim and cool, with a scuffed wooden floor, the back porch actually seemed more like an attic these days. When he'd left the parsonage to move in with Imo, the Reverend had left much of his family furniture sitting there to collect dust, but some things he'd wanted to carry along with him. Sentimental things that were his dear mother's, along with some old toys and lots of books.

Right away one of the Brownies discovered the wooden handle of a butter churn which sat next to an icebox. "It's so smooth!" she cried.

"It's worn down from years and years of hands churning butter," the Reverend said. "See?" He covered her small firm hand with his wrinkled one. "Momma'd hold it right about here and go up and down, up and down."

"Look at this!" another girl crowed. She held up a thick Sears catalog, circa 1937. "Look at these weird people!"

The rest of the troop clustered around as she flipped the brittle pages. "Look at this man's hair! Check out this pair of shoes!" There was a great commotion as the group pored over pages of clothes and gadgets modern for their time.

When they settled down, Imo proceeded to show them a chair with absurdly short legs. "The Reverend's folks used this for riding in the back of horse-drawn wagons," she told the group. "They sawed the legs off so the chair wouldn't tip over while they were sitting in the back of the wagon as it rolled over bumpy spots."

"That must be *ancient*," breathed one of the girls.

"It's a antique all right," said the girl at her elbow. "This whole place is like a antiques shop!" She was twirling her finger in the dial of a dusty black rotary phone.

"The Reverend and I are antiques, too!" Imo said, with a smile.

"I have a better idea," the Reverend interjected with a twinkle in his eye. "I don't like the way 'antique' sounds. Don't care for senior or old-timey neither." He laughed. "We're classics!"

Before long they all moseyed back into the kitchen, across the den, and toward the front door. It was pitch-black outside and Imo turned on the front porch light to help them see to get down the steps. Miss Cathy instructed the girls to say their thank-yous.

"We were proud to do it," said the Reverend as he followed the group down. "Next time we'll pick us a clearer night to look at the stars."

Imo stood up on the porch to say her good-byes. She looked down on the Reverend's bald spot and the sparse gray hairs he swept over it, at the slight stoop to his shoulders.

"Allow me to get the door, ladies,

and . . ." he was saying, but the chatter from the girls caught the rest of his words. Imo kept watching him. For a while he and Miss Cathy spoke through the van's window, laughing and gesturing about who knew what.

Finally, Miss Cathy cranked up, and the Reverend stepped back and stood on the grass beside the van, smiling and waving extra hard as if to prove something.

Two

&

Store Up Your Treasures in Heaven
Imo

Morning sun fell across the sideboard, illuminating a thick layer of dust. Imo paused and ran a finger through the gray fuzz, blew it into the air, and glanced around. Funny, the mess the house seemed to stay in with just the three of them. Why, they were hardly even there during their waking hours.

Loutishie was either off at school or outdoors and Lemuel kept busy at Calvary tending to his flock all the livelong day. He requested Imo as his sidekick, and she guessed she should be flattered that he wanted her companionship the way he did, but she certainly couldn't tend to housework or the garden the way she needed to. She literally had to *steal* moments to get out in her garden patch!

The walls of the church, the funeral home, the interior of the Reverend's truck, the homes of the bereaved congregation members; these sometimes drew in around Imo like a prison. She ached to be out in her garden, her little bit of heaven on earth as Silas used to call it. She stood at the parlor window, her cheek against a windowpane and her hands gripping the sill. It was a warm day in mid-April, the sky so blue it clutched at her heart. Gazing at a robin hopping along under the pecan tree, her mind took her back to those early months of their marriage.

A December wedding it was, the soil rock hard. This was fortunate, because when it finally sunk in that Lemuel expected her to travel around with him as his "earthly helpmeet," her brain began to buzz with little worries about the coming spring. What would she do when it was time to drag out the rototiller? To plant and tend? To weed and keep the critters out? Lord knew these alone were a fulltime job. And what about harvesting and putting-by?

She was expected to do so much as the pastor's wife; she visited the sick, organized prayer chains, received many calls from beleaguered members of the congregation. She felt like Lemuel's secretary. These constant requirements frustrated Imo and whenever she tried to shuck out of some duty she felt guilty.

Today was their visiting day at the hospital in Rome, and also, the Reverend's ninety-four-year-old Aunt Fannie had invited, no, ordered, them to stop by her house for some afternoon coffee and pie.

Imo sighed deeply. She wished she could hit a pause button on the Reverend. Slow him, slow life down a bit. But here it was, barely seven o'clock and he was at the breakfast table, guzzling black coffee.

Like clockwork, he rolled out of bed each morning at six a.m., took a tub bath, shaved, combed his sparse hair across the top of his head with a comb full of Vitalis, and then slid his dentures in. Next, wearing only his boxers he performed one hundred toe-touches and one hundred overhead reaches. Once his exercises were done, he selected a fresh pair of overalls with a coordinating set of suspenders and a neatly pressed chambray shirt, which he laid out in flat-person style across the bed.

73

He sat in a chair to strap garters below his bony knees and pull on a pair of nylon knee socks, fastening these to the garters. Then he slipped a shirt on and waited while Imo buttoned it (his hands ached so badly, particularly on cool mornings) before he stepped inside his overalls, into which he dropped his wallet, pocket watch, a hankie, and a small silver cross.

After all this was accomplished, the Reverend winced as he slid his feet into a pair of highly polished wingtips. The wingtips, once only a part of his Sunday preaching ensemble, had become his statement after Martha's death, and though they were incongruous with his weekly hayseed farmboy image, he stubbornly insisted on wearing them. Each time he put them on, without fail, he remarked that everyone in heaven surely went barefoot. Whenever Imo replied that perhaps it would help his bunions *down here* to wear some of those soft athletic shoes they sold at the Wal-Mart, he reminded her of the apostle Paul's thorn in the flesh, which God allowed to keep him humble.

"Plus," he'd say, "just because my dogs are hurtin' me is no reason to let my image slip. Folks count on me to look a certain way, Imogene. I can suffer these aggravatin' bunions in the name of spreading the Gospel."

Once the wingtips were tied, again Imo's job, he sat on the edge of the bed and did what he called his deep breathing for several minutes, inhaling and exhaling loudly. "Alrighty, sweetie," he bellowed when he was done, rising to stretch exaggeratedly. "Time for my morning tonic."

At this point, Imo would be in the kitchen, stirring a tablespoon of Certo fruit pectin into a cup of grape juice. This morning tonic was a venerable home remedy for the Reverend's painful stiff joints; especially his knees, hips, and hands.

She would watch his Adam's apple bob up and down as he drank it. After a satisfied "aahh," he would sink into his chair at the kitchen table to await biscuits and coffee, this from Imo's hand as well.

"Jackson Turner died last night," he announced that morning. This meant more visits for their day. There would be food to be delivered to helpless family members, and hurting folks to be comforted. Imo felt her fingernails pressing into her palms and she was visited by one of those grumpy, irritable feelings that she was sure got her blood pressure up.

She had never pictured herself as a fussy, selfish old curmudgeon like she was behaving now. She knew it was much harder to be the family of the dead, those wounded folks having to put together a funeral and getting on with life. She'd been there, too many times in fact. Dealing with the grief was much worse than having to go and offer comfort as the minister's wife.

Mr. Coffee gave a sort of burp after Imo filled it with water and hit the switch. On automatic she mixed lard, flour, and buttermilk, rolled it out in a thin layer of flour on the countertop, and cut biscuit circles. Her hands had done this so many times she did not even have to think about it. Instead she fought to push her ugly thoughts down. She glanced over at Lemuel, his bowed head looked so vulnerable in the early light.

He did not flinch when she slid the golden biscuits from the oven into a basket which she placed on the table. She poured their coffee, set out preserves, cream, and sugar, and sank down across from him. He was quiet as she stirred sugar into his coffee. When he commenced to eat, it seemed he was having a bit of trouble chewing his biscuit.

"What's wrong, dear?" Imo took another sip of her coffee-milk and reached across the table to touch his forearm. "Taste bad?"

"Mighty good." He garbled around a gummy bite still in his mouth. "Can't find my dadgummed dentures."

"Your teeth?" Imo exclaimed. "Why, they're in the glass in the bathroom where you always keep them."

He shook his head.

Imo stood. He was just mistaken. They were surely there, and she would go and fetch them. She trotted to the bathroom and even before she lifted the glass she saw it was indeed empty. Her eyes combed the bathroom. Nothing. She stood with her hands on her hips. It's not like he could swallow the dentures. He'd had them in his mouth at supper yesterday evening, and they hadn't left the house after that. Where in heaven's name could they be?

He *had* to have them. Having his teeth in was important for getting out in public. Imo searched the bedroom floor, his dresser, the closet. Hmmm, she wondered, smiling as she glanced into the waste basket and found it empty, would they even have to go and do their tending to the sick and bereaved and visit Aunt Fannie if he couldn't find them?

A thought struck her. Perhaps the Lord was intervening here. Maybe He was showing Lemuel that it was time to rest. What would it hurt? The world would go right on spinning.

Maybe she'd have herself a day out in the garden! Such a pretty day it was going to be, too. Not a cloud in the sky.

She nearly jogged back to the kitchen. "You were right, dear," she smiled, "not there. While you eat and think about where they might be, I'm going outside for a spell." She would ponder matters as she worked. Many times she had remarked to the Garden Club girls that one minute in her garden was surely worth many times more than an hour with a psychiatrist.

It was seven forty-five as she fastened on her straw hat and slipped into an old nylon windbreaker of Lou's to head out the back door — time for the Reverend to enter into what he called his "prayer closet," which was actually him just sitting there in that same chair, in a meditative repose with his eyes closed and his lips moving silently. That would go on until eight-thirty or so, and from then till nine o'clock sharp, he would work on his Sunday sermon. After which he stood, stretched, and summoned

Imo to his side to "commence our plan for the day."

This meant she had a bit over an hour till then, but maybe even the whole day if he couldn't find his dentures. The dusting, the laundry, the breakfast dishes, and making the bed could just wait. This was her window of opportunity to get started on the satisfying job of cultivation. The wetness had been a perfect breeding ground for a lush crop of weeds and she intended to remove them before they gobbled up the fertilizer and choked out her young plants.

Imo paused to stroke the silky brush of Bingo's fur before collecting her hoe from the shed. The thought of a whole day in the garden, at home, satisfied her on some deep level and for the moment all her troubles fell away.

When she reached the midst of the garden, she stood a moment to ponder. Her early spring restlessness was growing now, since the previous Saturday when she'd risen before dawn to put the rototiller into high gear and broken ground for the bulk of the garden. She'd even managed to steal the time to seed some collards directly into the garden and to risk planting out her "frost-tender" crop of cucumbers. She'd felt daring as she tamped soil gently around the ranks of tiny cucumber seedlings. Her plan was a bumper crop this year, enough for making oodles of pickles, and she determined to trellis her plants to increase the yield and to protect the fruits from soil rots.

Where there was a will there was a way! Now all that was left to get outside were the tomatoes, peppers, okra, squash, sweet corn, and her Kentucky Wonder snap beans. This put her in mind of the marigolds and sunflowers. This year she had chosen African marigolds again, mostly on account of their huge lionlike heads staring at her from the pages of her garden catalog. The sunflowers she was going to put in with the Kentucky Wonder snap beans to serve as their supports for climbing.

She bent to inspect a tiny dew-covered cucumber seedling. Coming along nicely. She took the flat blade of her hoe to firm the soil around the plant.

Suddenly she was stricken with a sobering thought. Was it wrong to love the place the way she did? Could that count as idolatry? She knew all about storing up riches in heaven. Still, she felt that she had to be terribly careful in this case, and she wrestled a moment with the knowledge that she preferred time in her garden to being a pastor's wife.

Why, certainly she could keep things in perspective here and do both! Love the farm and the garden, and at the same time love folks. There was time and energy to do both, wasn't there? Imo's heart swelled with thoughts of doing for others. She calculated the days till Good Friday. She had two weeks. Two weeks before she would allow herself to set out the remainder of her garden. She would sew baby quilts for the poor mothers at the homeless center in Rome, work at the soup kitchen in Cartersville, and scrub walls at Calvary's nursery.

Then another thought surged in; after Easter would be the ideal time for Lemuel to retire! Or at least cut his hours down to half and take a breather. Thinking of Good Friday also put Imo in mind of Easter Sunday. A chime went off in her brain to remind her of her intentions of making Easter dresses for Lou and Jeanette, and a white Easter suit for Little Silas. She'd have to get by Mozelle's Fabrics soon for patterns and cloth.

She walked toward the shed for the garden cart and a pitchfork, then wheeled over to the barn to get straw for mulching the cucumbers. The sun was moving up in the sky and a few scattered puffy clouds sliced it into rays that looked like a child's watercolor — a round yellow ball shooting stripes of yellow down to the earth.

Imo turned her face up like a daisy, marveling at something as ordinary as the sun, and then she set off, wheeling the cart along the fence toward the garden's edge. As she passed by the corner of the side pasture which flanked the garden, she spied it.

Pokeweed. Tender green leaves of pokeweed springing up in the neglected corner. Reluctantly Imo brought the cart to a standstill. She should stop and gather some of it, carry it inside, and make Lemuel more spring tonic.

"But I've made the stuff for him twice this spring already," she said aloud, lifting the cart's handles and wheeling forward determinedly. "Plus, it surely takes a while to prepare, and I really need to work out here in my garden patch while I've got the opportunity."

She stopped short. "But then again, Imo," she reminded herself. "The man *did* say it makes him feel better than his vitamin B_{12} shots." She glanced down at the golden straw in her cart, then to the garden straight in front of her, then over her right shoulder at the house.

She bit her lip; this was hard. She found herself arguing aloud once more; "C'mon, Imogene, you don't get many chances or sunny days to garden like this," and then, just as clearly she heard another voice saying *Store up your treasures in heaven.*

But still she hesitated, and Bingo sauntered over to her side. He sat and peered up at her till she met his eyes, liquid brown eyes under shaggy dark eyebrows which were raised up at their centers like he was pleading with Imo to go inside and make the spring tonic for Lemuel.

"Oh, all right! All right!" she said, throwing up her hands suddenly and dropping the garden cart so that Bingo dipped his head.

In the kitchen, Imo removed stems and old leaves from the pokeweed, thoroughly washing a sinkful of the tender greenery.

There he sat, with his yellow legal pad alongside his Bible on the table, working away on his sermon, so intent he'd barely acknowledged her back in the house. She rummaged through the Frigidaire for some fat-pork to flavor the pokeweed.

Wrangling the stew pot out from under

the sink, she filled it with water, plopped the fat-pork into it, and clattered it up onto the stove top. None of this disturbed him. He could surely focus well. When the water was to a rolling boil, Imo added the pokeweed. It would take thirty minutes of boiling, with occasional stirring, till it was tender and Imo reckoned she might as well tend to the breakfast dishes and straighten up the bedroom as she waited.

As Imo scrubbed sediments of biscuits from a cookie sheet, she glanced briefly at Lem's serious face. His lips were all puckered inward where the teeth were missing, but look at how he concentrated on his sermon! Surely once it got to be nine o'clock and he summoned her to his side to commence their daily plan, he'd realize that they couldn't take a step outside the house without his teeth. Then she would return to the garden and lay the mulch around her cucumbers! Surely the Lord was preparing her way, blessing her because she was making the pokeweed tonic, putting Lem first.

She moved around the kitchen, wiping countertops, stirring the pokeweed, drying and putting all the dishes away. As she worked she tried to imagine what he'd do stuck around the farm all day. He wasn't much of one for looking at TV in the day-time. Perhaps he could nap, put his feet up and relax. They could spend some time visiting together out on the front porch. It was going to be warm and dry enough for that.

She would fix a special lunch; vegetable soup, cornbread, and some slaw. Open the last jar of bread-and-butter pickles from the pantry. Make a fresh pitcher of sweet tea, maybe even a pecan pie from the nuts in the freezer.

Imo sure did wish she could talk to Martha. Get a few pointers on how to deal with this man. But Imo didn't believe in those people on TV who said you could communicate with the dead. They got on there and gave all kinds of messages from departed loved ones and made entire families into believers.

Imo didn't know their trick, but she did know that the closest thing she'd have to communicating with Martha was Wanda, Martha's sister. Wanda might know a few things Martha used to do to get her way. Perhaps she'd give a call down the Kuntry Kut 'n' Kurl in a bit, catch Wanda between sets and perms. See if she couldn't get any information out of her.

Sometime lately, Imo realized that she'd

begun to view Martha as a sort of rival. She wouldn't be missing her as a friend so much as trying to outdo her, to one-up her on caring for the needs of the congregation at Calvary and for the Reverend, as well as heading up the Garden Club.

Was it jealousy? Envy? It surprised her so much to feel this way, particularly since she knew these feelings to be grave sins in the Lord's eyes. She tried to reason them away, to rationalize that it wasn't jealousy — that instead it was only her yearning to measure up, to serve the Lord as best she could.

Imo strode into the bedroom, savoring a clear view of herself outside tending the garden. Sunshine fell across the rumpled bedclothes and she was drawn to sit in the puddle of warmth lying across the bunched quilt. She sat for just a spell, turning her face toward the window, closing her eyes and smiling.

What a lovely day it was turning out to be. Spring, her favorite season, and sadly the shortest, was honestly here. Spring was also birthday time for Loutishie. She'd be turning seventeen! Hard to imagine that the child was almost grown, Imo mused; next school year she'd be a senior. Stretching first the sheet, and then the woolen blanket up over the pillows, Imo let her gaze wander out the window to the yellow heads of some early jonquils blooming by the septic tank.

At last she managed to pull her eyes back inside to give a final approving glance back at the tidy room, and when she did, she noticed a small lump near the foot-board.

Could it be?

Well, she thought, it could not be. Could be a sock. She wore socks to bed and occasionally one rubbed off, but her memory of crawling out of bed offered nothing. Nobody would blame her if she just left the lump there, unchecked, she reasoned, and went on about her business. Why, even if it *was* his teeth, that just proved the poor man could use some time off. It would be one more solid example of why he needed rest and relaxation.

She laid a hand on the cool doorknob. Nobody would even know if she didn't inspect that lump there. Well, actually, she considered a minute as she glanced heavenward, *Somebody* would know. It was this thought that sent her back to the foot of the bed to pat the lump. Definitely not a sock.

Imo hoped against hope as she threaded

her hand between the bedclothes and closed it around the object. She winced as she felt Lemuel's smooth porcelain teeth. Sighing from the depths of her soul she ran them under the faucet in the bathroom, and carried them as an offering on her outstretched palm.

"Found your teeth," she said. "They were in the bedclothes."

Lemuel's face lit up as he reached for the teeth and settled them into his mouth. "Thank you kindly, dear," he said after he had positioned them with his tongue. The teeth filled his face back out and he smiled a Cheshire cat grin, running his tongue across the teeth. "Ah, the marvels of modern dentistry," he said, standing up. "Time to commence our plan for the day."

"Isn't it strange that they were in the bed?" she pressed him.

"Not that strange." He shrugged. "Could happen to anybody. Folks do strange things at night when they're plumb tuckered out. You've heard of sleepwalking, I know. I've heard of folks who walk to the Frigidaire, fix themselves a seven-layer sandwich, eat it, clean up, get back to bed, and don't know a thing about it in the morning."

"But you don't sleepwalk, Lemuel."

He sniffed the air. "Something sure smells good in here."

"Pokeweed tonic," she said.

His eyes lit up. "Got cornbread?"

"Got a tat left over from last night's supper."

"Well, praise God. Can't wait to sink my teeth into it. Now that you've found them, that is!" He laughed as he touched his mouth. "Stuff you make is delicious."

She waved his compliment away. "Anyway, Lemuel, if you don't sleepwalk, it must mean you're wore out. You need to slow down and take it easy."

"I'm fine. Just fine. No need to worry about me. Like I always say, I'm spry as I was in my thirties!" He stood and slapped his thigh with a loud *whack,* bent his knees, and did a few sudden dips, up and down, up and down.

Imo cleared her throat, she ground her teeth till they ached, fighting the urge to rattle off a list of his foibles of late. Simmering inside, she hurried to the stove to stir the pokeweed, inhaling its acrid odor. Listen at that man! Stubborn as the day was long. Or blind, one. Apparently he had no intentions of ever admitting his faults or slowing down.

What would it take for him to see? Lord,

it was as plain as the nose on his face that he was slipping. She turned to the cabinet for a plate and plopped some pokeweed onto it. Holding this aloft, she turned toward the Reverend, searching his face. Could he not remember the Brownies incident? Missing his haircut? All this forgetfulness of late?

But maybe that was just it! Possibly he couldn't remember.

"Surely do appreciate this, Imogene." He sat smiling, holding a fork, with a dish towel tucked into his collar. "Just what the doctor ordered."

Imo placed the steaming platter in front of him and watched as he gobbled it down. He wiped his mouth with the end of the dish towel, patted a small spiral notebook on the table. "Got our day all planned out for us." He looked up at her and cocked his head. "Aren't you going to go get yourself ready?" He waved his fork and the tines caught the sunlight from the window, sending a blinding flash directly at Imo's eyes.

"Oh!" she said, startled. Back in the bedroom, she flung open her closet doors and sat down on the edge of the bed. Staring numbly at the row of slacks, blouses, and dresses, she twisted her hands together.

Oh, she may as well just give on up and go with the flow today. It did no good to try and convince the man. He was going to do just as he pleased anyhow.

Finally she rose to pull out a bright floral dress. Too much for visiting a grieving household and then a sickbed in? Or good to cheer folks up? She closed her eyes to picture herself entering a hospital room wearing the dress. Too blousy, she decided, and wearily returned it to the closet. She fingered a red skirt, pushed that away, too. Pulling a potato-colored frock from its hanger, she sighed and laid it across the bed to select a pair of shoes.

She freshened up the plain dress with a paisley scarf at her neck and combed her hair neatly over her ears. As she applied red lipstick, her hopes of gardening today seemed pathetic. No one had to work so hard at sixty-seven. Everyone else was re-tired. Relaxing. Traveling. Visiting with friends and family. Everyone but her, who was working enough for three women. Three *young* women.

She smiled into the mirror. She certainly looked eager and capable on the outside, but inside she was fixing to crumple. She swallowed her tears and when she reached Lemuel's chair she managed a cheerful enough "Ready, dear."

He jumped to his feet, straightened his tie, and waited at the door while she collected her handbag from the pantry. The man looked supremely happy, as though he might dance out to the pickup, whistling a tune to boot.

For the next week, Imo spent what seemed a lifetime being Lemuel's shadow. Today the glare of the sun on the pickup's hood was almost blinding and she wished she'd thought to bring her clip-on sunglasses. It was nine o'clock sharp and Lemuel drove along purposefully, bound for the old mill to call on Toby Outz.

It was their habit on Fridays, after making the morning rounds, to visit Boss Hawg's Barbecue Shack in Flat Shoals Community, a good forty-five minutes from Euharlee, and fairly close to Mozelle's Fabrics, where she needed to get the fabric for Easter outfits.

Since the denture incident, Lem had also misplaced his eyeglasses, his wallet, and his car keys. Yet, still the man showed no inclination to acknowledge these shortcomings. Imo was not any better at accepting the situation, she was just bearing with it better. She was wrangling her schedule to spend more time in her garden even if it meant turning a blind eye to housecleaning. Dusting seemed senseless anyhow, as it just fell again immediately, and it was the same way with vacuuming and scrubbing the bathroom.

She could let the laundry pile up to an extent, but meals were the one thing she couldn't ignore. Last night she had served a quick supper of tuna melts and apple sauce on paper plates. This was so that she could set in marigolds, tomatoes, and peppers and tend to the fledgling cucumbers. By the waning light of dusk, she'd also managed to put down some straw mulch and apply a nitrate top dressing over them. She worked in the dark to water it in and when she'd come back into the house Lemuel was on the phone with someone.

Imo overheard enough to know that Toby Outz, a crotchety octogenarian who lived out in the old abandoned mill, had a bad case of walking pneumonia. Toby did not cotton to doctors or to modern medicine for that matter, and Imo knew he would be stubbornly resisting all offers to carry him to the clinic in Rome. "We'll look in on him in the morning early," the Reverend was saying as Imo brushed her teeth to get ready for bed.

Imo's only hope as she fell asleep was that they'd finish with him and have time for her to pop into Mozelle's after lunch at Boss Hawg's, and before all their other appointments.

The Reverend climbed out of the car, carrying a little plastic pot of Vick's VapoRub in one hand and some old towels in the other.

Toby Outz must have been watching from behind one of the dusty windows of the mill because as soon as they reached the cement slab in front of the door, he swung it open, standing there all stooped over with a ratty blanket draped across his shoulders.

"Reverend," he said, shuffling back a few steps to admit them. Lemuel stuck out his hand and Toby clasped it feebly.

"Heard you were ailin'," Lemuel said. "The missus here brought you some soup." Imo extended her hands with the soup, but Toby gave no acknowledgment.

"It's bad sick this time," Toby said. "Bones hurt."

"Well, you need to be resting then." The Reverend steered him by the elbow toward an old recliner with tufts of stuffing oozing out. "Sit yourself on down." Toby frowned, but allowed himself to be lowered.

"Let's see here now," the Reverend said as he knelt beside the chair and held the back of his hand against Toby's forehead. "You're burning up." Toby nodded as he bent forward in a breathless coughing spasm of rattly phlegm. Imo shuddered when eventually he hocked up a sizable green wad and spat it out onto a hankie, collapsing backward with the effort.

Lemuel cast a concerned look toward Imo. "Why don't you go heat that soup up, dear?"

"Surely," she said, smiling, relieved to have something she could be doing. In what seemed to be a makeshift kitchen there was the kind of refrigerator kids carried off to college dorm rooms and a hot plate with two burners; both of which were connected to the long snake of an extension cord. A motley assortment of utensils sat in a coffee can in one corner.

She found a dented boiler hanging on a nail above the hot plate. A waft of garlic and onion rose as she emptied her Tupperware full of chicken soup into this and settled it on a burner. She turned around, bewildered by the sparseness of the kitchen, but in time located a chipped bowl, a spoon, and a washrag to use as a napkin. Positioning these on a metal TV tray which she spied leaning against the tiny fridge, she hurried back to check on the Reverend and Toby.

Toby lay pale and prostrate on the recliner. She didn't know what she'd expected, but the sight of his purple eyelids and sunken eye sockets alarmed her. "He's not getting much breath in him," Lemuel told her. "We need to open up his airways."

He rolled Toby slightly to his side, the man gasping as he squeezed the armrests, his mouth puckering open and closed. "Fetch me the Vick's, Imo, and put the towels yonder in some boiling water."

She scrambled to the door of the mill and collected the items, wondering in the back of her mind, in a strange sort of way, if he might die on them. And in an even stranger way, deciding this might be a blessing for him if he did, old and pitiful as he was.

And in the half minute it took to yank a skillet from the wall, pour some murky water from a cedar bucket into it, and set it on the burner beside the chicken soup, she had another thought. One that she declared wicked and pure-T sinful even before it was fully formed.

This thought was that Toby Outz was selfish. Selfish to be sick, and especially if he were to die on them today. The reason for this was that Imo was hungry and she had really been looking forward to a basket of delicious fried chicken at Boss Hawg's. Plus, when Lemuel was seated at the restaurant, in a pleasant mood as he awaited his grub, she planned on sweetly asking him to take a detour to Mozelle's Fabrics.

If Toby were to die, then they surely would not make it to Boss Hawg's or Mozelle's, either one. For a moment she just stood there, shocked at her ugly thoughts, and then she scrambled back to the men, carrying the blue pot of Vick's. "Here," she offered, suddenly all business, as if this could stave off other thoughts.

A hymn fluttered through her mind like a warning: *Lord, I want to be like Jesus in my heart.* Was it her repentant heart that had breathed this into her mind? That brought to her consciousness the popular bracelets with WWJD on them that the young people wore. She'd asked Lou once what WWJD stood for.

"What would Jesus do," answered Lou. "Supposed to make you stop and think, when you get in the middle of life's troubling situations. Makes you stop and think about what Jesus would do if He were in your shoes."

What would Jesus do here? Imo asked herself then, only somehow she transposed Martha's name for Jesus'.

WWMD. What would Martha do?

Martha Peddigrew, the saint. The perfect pastor's wife. She'd probably be in there selflessly washing Toby's feet with her tears and drying them with her hair while she quoted comforting Scripture verses and fed him a seven-course meal.

Cut to the heart at thoughts of Martha's generous spirit, Imo sucked in a deep breath. She ought to go in there and do her Christian duty, without a single thought to her growling stomach and Boss Hawg's crispy golden fried chicken, their puffy clouds of biscuits, and creamy mashed potatoes with a puddle of brown gravy on top. Squaring her shoulders, Imo returned to the recliner. Lemuel had unbuttoned Toby's shirt and he was scooping up thick fingerfuls of Vick's Mentholatum salve, which looked just like Crisco. She watched as he slathered this onto Toby's puny chest covered in a tangle of hoary hairs.

A strong jab of Mentholatum opened up Imo's sinuses and the world became sharp and clear as air whistled up her nostrils and made her eyes water.

"Run fetch the towels," Lemuel said.

She returned to the hot plate and dipped a towel into the boiling water of the skillet. Wincing, she fished it up with a bent fork and held it aloft until it was just bearable enough to wring out and scurry back to Lemuel with. "Alrighty," she said as she reached his side.

If this would only work! Get the life back into Toby Outz! He looked about gone to her as she prepared to lay it over him, but the Reverend grasped it, waved her off, and gently positioned it himself, all the while praying aloud. For a moment she stood there stupidly, at a loss of what to do, and then she realized, why, I should pray, too, and she began to beseech the Lord. There was then an interminable five minutes or so of stingy, strained sucking noises on Toby's part, his eyes still closed, until at last he gave what was like a high-pitched dog's yelp and sucked in a deeper breath, shook his head, and opened his eyes to slits.

With a humble nod, Lemuel patted Toby's callused hand. Imo felt a flood of tender compassion for him and a respect for his confident assurance, his faith. There was a healing touch in his hands.

Something supernatural, a gift, not something he conjured up on his own. Immediately she stood. "Shall I feed him now?" she asked, and without waiting went into the kitchen where she used a coffee mug to ladle soup into the bowl.

She set the TV tray at Toby's side, knelt and gingerly spooned up broth, holding it alight over the steaming bowl. He moved his head her way, sniffing, searching. His eyes were pleading — hungry?

The Reverend gently pulled a wooden lever on the recliner's side and sat him up in a fashion. She raised her eyebrows to ask and almost imperceptibly those eyes of Toby's, with their transparent films, moved to her face. She aimed the spoon at his mouth.

"More?" she asked tentatively as he swallowed, and she dabbed the wet corners of his mouth with a towel. *Yes,* he mouthed and she spooned and balanced broth again and again, bringing it to his eager lips. He ate every drop and sipped sweet tea from a Mason jar.

"Done!" she reported when the soup was gone and the tea was drained. His eyes were noticeably brighter, a bit of color in his cheeks.

A dog barked outside. "Lucy," Toby

rasped and strained to sit up more. "Let Lucy in."

Imo toted the tray back to the kitchen. "Reckon I'll wash these things up now," she crowed to Lemuel from in front of a barrel sliced in half lengthways and anchored with several big flat stones from the river. Toby's sink.

She scrubbed the dishes and listened to the men talking and a dog whining. The Reverend spoke in low and reverent tones, relieved, she knew. She breathed deeply, satisfied to be a part of it all. She bent her wrist to see the time. Eleven-thirty. She praised herself for not even thinking of her own needs as she ministered to Toby. *Bet Martha's proud now.* She finished with washing the spoon and peered around the door frame at the men. Toby was sitting all the way up now, his hand on a dog's head and his feet on the floor, drawing breaths with a scowl.

He was fussing at Lemuel about the county's decision to let Perkin's Mountain be developed. He slapped at the armrests of the recliner, his eyebrows in such an animated scowl it was hard to imagine him as the same man who couldn't get his breath just a short half hour ago. He sure wasn't saying thanks in there. It seemed to Imo that he ought to be grateful.

Generally, she avoided Toby Outz, as did most. He was the kind that loved to enumerate every evil in the world as he perceived it. He'd never married, had no family left to speak of, maybe a distant cousin in a nearby county and a niece up north. Kept to himself at the mill. Never set foot in Calvary Baptist but once that Imo could remember, and that was for his brother's funeral over twenty years ago.

Anyone could see why he lived alone. Imogene put one hand on her hip, collected her empty Tupperware, and went to stand at his feet. "It was so nice to see you, Toby," she said in an extra syrupy voice. "Glad you enjoyed my soup."

He eyed her, but didn't even blink. "Well, toodle-oo and take care," she added as she scooped up the Vick's and the limp towels. Her heels made sharp raps as she headed across the rough floorboards toward the door.

Easing along mile after mile of pastureland, Imo had her mind on lunch. "Reckon I'm still a fit vessel for the Lord's use," Lemuel said, disrupting her thoughts.

"Seems like Mr. Outz could've used the

mouth part of *his* vessel to thank us!" Imo snapped.

"Now, now." He chuckled. "Toby's never been real handy with the niceties of life."

"Niceties? What does it have to do with niceties? What must the man think? That the world *owes* him something? Took a lot of doing to cook soup, and us to come out and tend to him."

"Imo, Imo," Lemuel said, rounding a bend. "What thank have we if we only do for those who are pleasant and thankful toward us?"

Stung, Imo turned her gaze out the window. She twisted the handle of her purse. She reckoned he was right about it. Well, it was lunchtime anyway, time to put away such somber thinking. "We're here!" she said to Lemuel in a tone of eagerness mixed with repentance.

He swung the pickup off the main road onto a deep gravel lot and coasted to a stop in front of Boss Hawg's Barbecue Shack. Boss Hawg's looked more like a pool hall/juke joint than an eating establishment. It was a long cinder-block building, flanked on one side by a Laundromat and on the other by a tanning parlor. Outside, a dozen pickup trucks, along with several old-model sedans were nosed up to the narrow walkway.

Lemuel held the door for Imo, and they walked together past a standing human-sized plastic pig wearing a policeman's cap and holding a sign which said SEAT YO'SELF.

Settling into a booth with red Naugahyde benches, she reached for the menus and presented one to Lemuel. "No need for that," he said, plunking it back behind the napkin holder, "I'm having my usual. You?"

"Chicken basket," she replied, "with mashed potatoes, gravy, slaw, and a biscuit." Chicken! She'd smelled the chicken when they pulled into the lot and on several nearby tables she saw a golden breast or a leg jutting up out of red plastic baskets lined with wax paper. She noted, too, the tables groaning under steaming bowls of Brunswick stew and platters of cole slaw. She patted her skirt band, thankful for the elastic there.

The inside of Boss Hawg's was cozy with its dark paneling and red-checkered café curtains. Here and there hung a poster-sized picture of a covered bridge scene. Against one wall were shelves full of sauces and preserves and honeys for sale, along with dolls in bright crocheted antebellum skirts, holding tiny fans.

A waitress appeared at their table to take drink orders. Her flame-shaped name tag read Dawn. She combed long lavender nails through frosted blond hair and turned to Imo. "What can I bring you to drink, hon?"

Being called hon by Dawn, who was half her age at least, did not seem disrespectful to Imo. Instead it made her feel young and part of the scene. "I'll have sweet tea," Imo said, "with lemon, please."

"You got it, darlin'," Dawn said, turning to Lemuel.

"I'll have the sweet tea, too," he said.

"Well, aren't *y'all* the sweetest!" Dawn giggled. "Be right back with your drinks."

When they were alone, Imo said, "What else is on our agenda for today?"

"Hope Haven in Oak Grove. Then we need to stop by Calvary to pick up a few things, see Aunt Fannie, and go by to check on Kenneth Freeman."

"Kenneth Freeman!" she said, momentarily stunned.

He nodded as Dawn set down their drinks. "Ready to order, folks?"

Imo shook her head. "Give me just one more little minute here," she said, feeling a sudden rush of panic. If it took them half an hour to eat, then they drove to Hope Haven in Oak Grove, visited with several of the elderly residents there, and had to get by Calvary, Aunt Fannie's, and then Kenneth Freeman's, there'd be no time to stop in at Mozelle's Fabrics. They'd barely get home by dark. And she'd planned to sew on the girls' Easter dresses tomorrow. With Easter Sunday just nine days away, she had to get started.

"Listen, Lem, you could drop me off at Mozelle's Fabrics on your way to Hope Haven! I can get the things I need for my sewing while you visit, and then you can pick me up on your way back by."

He considered this a moment. Creased his paper napkin, frowned, rubbed his chin, and then ever so slowly he solemnly nodded. Imo felt a sudden rush of pleasure. Things would work out after all! Tomorrow she would sew and garden. On Saturdays, Lemuel's brother, Felder, came for breakfast and then carried Lemuel fishing or out for a visit at his farm. She hated to feel so jubilant at the prospect of time without Lemuel.

Dawn was back, tapping her order pad. "Y'all ready?"

"I'll have the chicken basket," Imo said, fairly glowing. "Some honey, too, please."

Dawn turned to Lemuel. "I'll have the Boss Hawg's Deluxe Pork Plate," he said, "with loaf bread *and* saltines."

Alone again, Imo turned to Lemuel. He looked like he was pondering some deep thought. She wondered if he minded going to Hope Haven by himself. She wished he would share his feelings with her more. He rarely spoke what was on his mind and she knew he'd feel better if he would learn to talk things out. She figured he thought it was weak to discuss things like that with her. He probably figured talking to the Lord about it was enough. "I'm thinking of doing something simple, something real easy for Easter dinner," she said after a spell.

"Oh, really?" he asked, his eyes wide in alarm. "Not the ham and the coconut pie and everything?"

"Why, silly me!" Imo said, startled at his reaction. "Of course I'll make all that. I'll fix us up a nice spread the way I always have. The way I did us last Easter. I'll do ham, and scalloped potatoes, and early peas, and glazed carrots, and angel biscuits, and, and . . . a coconut pie, too." She paused for a breath.

Lemuel let out a big relieved sigh. "You had me going there for a minute, dear." He smiled.

Their food arrived. "Careful, hon," Dawn warned Imo as she set the basket down. "It's just come out of the grease."

She nodded, trying to keep a look of disappointment at bay. *Take heart, Imogene,* she scolded herself, *you can't expect everything to go your way. You've got tomorrow. You've got today in Mozelle's Fabrics.* She spooned up a bite of creamy potatoes and blew the steam cap away, settling the morsel on her tongue. Then she poked a finger down into the side of a large cakey biscuit and squirted honey in.

Oh, this was living! The slaw was just right, too — a fibrous blend of tart-sweet cabbage with mayonnaise and pickle relish. She was saving the chicken for last, a leg and a breast in the perfect shade of golden. Funny, she mused as she ate. Not more than a year ago, she was all excited about preparing their first Easter Sunday dinner together, and she was disappointed that it felt more like a chore this year. Her thoughts flew to last Easter like it was just yesterday; she was making elaborate shopping lists, setting out her best recipes two weeks ahead of time. Lemuel was all excited, too, standing around in the kitchen and rocking back and forth on his heels as she grated lemon rinds and glazed the ham. She'd worked two solid days on that meal, but what he'd said at the dinner table that Sunday had made it all worthwhile.

"Mmm-mmm-mmm, Imogene," he'd said, a contented smile on his face. "I don't know when I've ever eaten a finer Easter Sunday meal!"

"You mean that?" she'd asked, a warm glow suffusing her soul. Surely he didn't mean she cooked better than Martha, did he? But what else could he mean? She floated along through the rest of that day, feeling simultaneously proud and guilty for cooking better than Martha.

In the next moment Imo's warm memory vanished.

"I invited Toby Outz to join us for Easter." Lemuel rubbed his chin. "Him so alone and ailin'. He'll get to meet Aunt Fannie and Buzzie and all the others."

She lowered her tea glass, closed her eyes to sigh. "You're not serious."

" 'Course I am," he said.

"How many folks total does this make it?" she asked through her teeth.

He shrugged. She twisted her wedding band around her finger. Wasn't life strange? Sometimes the memory of being Silas's wife and those simpler times seemed like a dream. In her mind's eye she saw herself, Silas, Jeanette, and Loutishie sitting around the table for Easter dinner. Just the four of them. Nice and simple and cozy. But marrying Lemuel Peddigrew made her kin, and now cook, it looked like, to half of Euharlee. He called many of the very old folk in town "aunt" or "uncle" though they were not related by blood. He made sure these had an invitation to Easter dinner and he could not resist asking any down-and-out member of Calvary Baptist to come, too.

"Listen," she said. "I'll cook us up the big, fancy feast like last year's, but could we please just keep it to close family? Say, fifteen or so folks?"

"How come?" he asked, dipping his head toward his right shoulder and wrinkling his brow. Imo knew that look by now. He just didn't get it.

Before she could answer Dawn was back. "Pie and coffee for y'all today?"

"Bring us two banana puddings," Lemuel said, "and two coffees. Better make them Sankas."

Imo stared, a napkin raised halfway to her mouth. "Sanka?" she said, startling herself. "Make mine a regular!"

This time when Dawn left for the kitchen Imo squared her shoulders and sat up tall. "Lemuel, you could use some real coffee, too. You like to never got perking this morning. I caught you nodding off over your biscuit."

There was a pause.

"Not coffee I need," Lemuel said. "Reckon what I need is to carry myself into Dr. Perkins's office for another one of those vitamin B$_{12}$ shots."

Imo closed her eyes a moment. "Listen, I've got an even better idea. Why don't you just take a while off? After Easter? Start with a week. One week of doing nothing would be just what the doctor ordered! Seven days off'd be *better* than a vitamin B shot."

"Take a week off?"

"Surely. Slow down. Relax and put your feet up."

"What?" His eyes widened.

"The world will keep right on going, dear, and you'll be better for it." His bewildered face was touching, but Imo had had enough. *"You're seventy-five years old, Lemuel, and no one expects you to keep on the way you do!"*

"That's not true!" he yelped. "Well, I mean, it is true that I'm seventy-five years old, Imogene, but that has nothing to do with it. I have folks I've got to tend to.

111

Folks who depend on me."

"Wearing yourself out won't be good for you *or* them," Imo said. "Take your bunions, for instance. You limp around the house every single morning hollering 'My dogs are hurting me!' but just as sure as the sun comes up, you go out that door, wearing those stiff old wingtips."

"Well, I will not wear play shoes to do my job. I've already explained that to you."

"Lemuel, Lemuel. It's time for you to start taking it easy."

His face was puzzled. He reached for her hands across the table and Imo couldn't think of any other way to tell him. She was saved by two banana puddings plunked down in front of them and a steaming cup of coffee at her elbow.

"Doesn't this look tasty," she trilled, opening a tiny cup of half-and-half and emptying it into her coffee. She cast a look at Lemuel. He was just sitting there, staring at his Sanka.

She scooped up a fluff of meringue and settled it on her tongue, a split second of sweetness and it dissolved, followed by a scalding gulp of coffee and a deeply dug bite of pudding with a banana chunk. "Mmm-mmm-mmm," she said with much enthusiasm.

Lemuel was quiet, barely picking at his pudding, and she wished he'd say something, anything. She felt as if the whole world was on pause. She kept eating and smiling, however, not knowing what else to do. At last she scraped up the remnants of her pudding with a spoon, drained her coffee, and sat quietly, arranging the salt and pepper shakers and the little plastic rectangle full of sugar and Sweet'N Low packets till Dawn appeared with the bill.

They moved toward the cash register and she stood beside Lemuel while he paid. As a peace offering she depressed the faux wood lid of a toothpick dispenser and gathered two slim picks for the ride to Mozelle's Fabrics.

Stepping back outside into the blinding sunlight Imo held a flat hand above her eyes. "Almost feels like summer!" she chirped. He did not say a word, and they climbed into the suffocatingly hot truck. "Woo-wee," Imo breathed, lifting her skirt to fan her legs a bit. "We could surely use to spread a few towels out across this sweltering vinyl, now couldn't we?"

Still, he did not respond. Didn't even remove his suit coat or loosen his tie or crack his window as they scrunched across the gravel lot. When they got out onto the highway, Lemuel drove like he was in slow motion. Imo glanced at the speedometer.

Thirty-five miles an hour!

She searched his face. His lips were moving out and in in a strange sucking fashion, his tongue rolling over his teeth, back and forth. "Pork stuck?" she asked.

"Mmm-hmm," he replied.

Well, at least he was still talking to her. "I got us both a toothpick," she said.

He shook his head, working his tongue back up and over his top teeth and sucked so hard that the cords of his neck stood out. Imo gritted her teeth and stayed quiet. After several more miles at thirty-five miles per hour, she pointed out that the speed limit was fifty-five.

He nodded, driving steadily and slowly along. For a minute Imo was silent, and then she turned toward him slightly. "Are you *okay*, Lemuel?" she asked.

"Just a mite sleepy is all."

"I could drive, then. Why don't you let me drive? To Mozelle's at least, while you rest a spell. A full stomach'll do you that way."

"I'm fine." He waved her words away.

"You could pull over there, into that filling station, and buy you a Co-cola. That ought to wake you up. We could switch seats. You could close your eyes a spell while I drive."

He scowled. "Told you I'm fine."

"I should drive because you're liable to fall asleep," she persisted, "and endanger someone. Endanger us."

"I have been driving for sixty-two years and never had so much as a fender bender!" He scowled. "I used to say to Martha, whenever she tried to be a backseat driver, I said to her 'Martha, I've been driving just about as long as you've been alive! Do you think you can tell me how to drive?' " He roused himself up so much that the speedometer zipped up to seventy.

Imo clutched at the dashboard. This was worse than puttering! Her heart raced as trees and telephone poles zipped by. All she could do was pray that the road stayed this bare of other drivers and that he stayed *on* the road. Yet, even with all this going on, a small ripple of delight made its way across her mind as they barreled along the highway closer to Mozelle's.

She hated to admit it, but she was pleased to hear about Martha's backseat driving flaw. But wait a minute, Imogene, she told herself. Wait just one doggone minute! Maybe it wasn't a flaw atall.

Maybe being a backseat driver was necessary, a kind of societal obligation when you rode with certain folks at certain times. Surely Martha had only fussed at him because she realized the danger they were in, that others might be in because of them. Martha with her saintly heart would never nag or scold if it weren't absolutely necessary. Martha never stumbled along Life's path. Was never selfish, the way Imo was.

Her voice quavered a bit as she spoke this time. "Slow down, dear. You're going way too fast."

"Thought you said I was too slow."

"I did, and you were. But now you're speeding. You need to slow down, Lemuel." And then, after a pause, "Like I've been saying, you could slow down in life, too."

He drew his eyebrows into a scowl as he raced along at seventy miles per hour. They did not speak or look at one another, and after a few minutes came in sight of the Ingles grocery store, which meant that the one stoplight in the tiny town was just a short stretch away and beyond that was Mozelle's Fabrics.

There was a nice sprinkling of businesses at this junction of two highways, and traffic was surprisingly sparse for a Friday afternoon. They zoomed by a video rental store, a tractor dealership, and a short stretch beyond that a filling station mixed with a tiny convenience store. It would be nice to get inside Mozelle's and pull up a chair in front of a pattern book. Then she could relax.

"We're fixing to come to the light, Lemuel," she warned.

"I know that!"

"Well, with the sun so bright you might not make out what color it is. Better be slowing down now. Better get ready to stop if need be."

For a moment it seemed that Lemuel planned to just speed on through the light no matter what color it was, but then he did slow down a bit, to forty, mainly because an ancient white Dodge had pulled out in front of them from a side street and was creeping along. The sun shone fiercely, and Imo strained to see the light up ahead. Still too far away yet to tell the color.

When they were close enough to the Dodge, Imo could see the blinker on the passenger side blinking rapidly. They passed two streets to the right and still the Dodge did not turn. Lemuel pulled closer, a few feet from the bumper. Now Imo could clearly see the tiny white-haired head barely above the headrest. There were two hands in white gloves on the steering wheel at precisely ten and two o'clock, and Imo pictured the driver as one of those dried apple dolls they sold at the county fair; with an old, shriveled face holding two bright raisin eyes and wearing a voluminous dress fashioned out of corn husks.

Poor little old woman was almost to the light now, and Lord have mercy, Imo wished Lemuel would back off of her just a bit. The light turned yellow just as the Dodge approached it and Imo kept her eyes fastened on the Dodge's trunk, willing the old lady on through the light. But in her next breath, Imo knew what was going to transpire.

Before she could even holler "Merciful heavens!" or "Stop!" the hair follicles all over her body drew up tight, and the joints in her knees and elbows turned liquid. The pickup lurched forward in a leap like a panther on its prey and collided with the Dodge in a sickening *crunch!* All the breath flew out of Imo in a sharp "ha!" as she grabbed the dash. Only after all that had transpired did Lemuel shake his head in a dazed fashion and mash the brake pedal.

"Goodness gracious me," she cried. "We've had a wreck!"

They sat there stunned a moment, Lemuel squinting out into the sun's glare, groaning and rubbing the back of his neck. When Imo caught her breath again, she told him, "Maybe you ought to get out and go check on the other driver."

"What? What?"

"Go see about that little old lady in the car you wrecked into."

Feebly Lemuel's left hand hunted the door handle. With slow reflexes he eased the door open and set out a hesitant foot. Immediately he winced and both hands sprang up to grab the back of his neck.

"Hurt?" Imo reached over and laid a hand on his knee.

He nodded, eyes shut.

"Well, I'm okay," she declared, looking out the window. All up and down the road cars appeared out of nowhere, stopping. She didn't dare look in any of them to make eye contact. "I'll go see about her," she said at last.

She crept out and up to the passenger side of the Dodge, where thankfully the windows were down. She laid both hands on the warm metal of the door and stuck her head inside. She peered at the woman, who was indeed wrinkled and bent, ninety or even a hundred years old. "Are you all right, ma'am?" Imo asked.

"Why, I believe I am," she said slowly, patting her sparse white hair and then lifting her legs and flexing her feet in their orthopedic shoes.

Imogene waited, noting the spotless floorboard of the Dodge and the single box of tissues alongside the black umbrella on the backseat.

The old lady pursed her lips. "Yes, yes. I still seem to be in one piece."

Imo breathed a huge sigh of relief. Of course, the lady's *car* was not in one piece. That much Imo knew, but she was afraid to go around and inspect the back closely. Also, there was Lemuel, who seemed to be in a good bit of pain in his neck region.

Now the old lady put her hands on her hips. "What happened here, missy?" she demanded, her blue eyes peering at Imo. The wreck was Lemuel's fault, but perhaps if she mentioned that he was a minister, was hurt, even, it would help things. She smiled sweetly, searching for words. Maybe she should blame it on the blinding sunlight. Of course, that wouldn't relieve them of the responsibility, but it might offer some sympathy.

"My husband was driving. He's a minister, a *Baptist* minister, and he's hurt," she said, testing the waters. "Might have whiplash. You see, the sun was so bright and he really couldn't see very well . . ." Imo straightened and glanced through the windshield concernedly at Lemuel, who was blinking and still holding his neck. She couldn't think of any more to say, but just then a police car slid alongside, lights flashing and siren wailing.

Clouds had moved in, softening the sun's glare as Imogene drove cautiously toward home, thinking of the scene they'd left behind, and conscious of Lemuel beside her holding the back of his neck.

Lemuel looked out the windshield quietly for most of the journey, but as they passed the Dairy Queen in Euharlee, he slapped the dash. "Could've happened to anybody. Woman was driving like a little mouse!" he said. "Didn't you think she was driving like a mouse?"

Imogene stiffened. "Lemuel, dear. She's lived right here all her life. Eighty-nine years, she said. This is her town. She stopped at the one little traffic light in her little town and you bumped into her. You got the citation. Officer says she's not at fault one tiny bit. Eyewitness at the filling station said she was stopping for a yellow light."

"Light had *just turned* yellow!" He looked over at Imo with a pink face. "And since her blinker was on to turn right, I figured that there not being anybody else atall at that intersection, she'd just go on and . . ."

Imogene smiled at him then. "You *figured* she was going to turn, dear. You made a wrong call. Her blinker had been on ever since she pulled out. Maybe she's never heard of right on red. You just weren't paying attention. You should be glad she wasn't hurt." She watched him out of the corner of her eye.

"It's all right," she said after a long uncomfortable silence, "accidents happen. At least both vehicles are still drivable." But the thought was in her mind that he'd been sleepy, unfit to drive. Dull reflexes. A ripple of relief ran through her as she decided that Dr. Perkins, when she carried Lemuel in this afternoon to see about his neck, would tell him exactly that. "We could go directly downtown now if you'd like. See Dr. Perkins before we head back to the farm."

Lemuel smiled. "Maybe he can go ahead

122

and give me my vitamin B$_{12}$ shot!"

Imo said nothing, sure the matter would be settled shortly. Lemuel Peddigrew was no match for the schedule he tried to keep.

That evening, as they sat on the front porch, Lemuel said he'd come to a decision. Imo smiled what she hoped was an understanding and sympathetic smile at his serious face above the bone-colored neck collar that Dr. Perkins had prescribed.

Dear Dr. Perkins, she thought, *he must've spoken some sense into her husband.* She folded her hands in her lap and looked compassionately at Lem's profile, bracing herself to hear the good news. She watched his eyes dart from left to right. He was stalling, she knew. It would not be easy for him to say what he had to.

"Dr. Perkins said I shouldn't drive for a spell."

Imo felt a pang for the poor man sitting there. "Well," she said, "he certainly knows his medicine. What's best."

The Reverend nodded. He lowered his voice so low she had to lean over to hear him. "I know it won't be the easiest thing in the world," he said.

"Of course not, dear. But we'll manage.

We can sleep in, spend us some time relaxing around the farm. In time you'll get used to your new schedule."

A long silence, then he said: "Reckon we'll go on and put my truck in the repair shop, then, and you can drive me around in your car."

"What?!" Imo's skin tightened for the second time that day.

"You know, we're going to have to start using the Impala for my visiting rounds. You like driving it better anyway. You said so."

"Well, I do, but — listen, Lemuel, you've got to just *stop* for a while. Don't you tell me you're planning to keep on at this pace. I figured you'd take this wreck today as a sign and you'd slow down. Start to think about retiring at least."

He winced and shook his head. "There's work to be done, Imogene. Folks to tend to and souls to harvest. No rest for the weary."

"But Lemuel, can't you see —" Imo stopped and sank back against the warm swing. If Dr. Perkins hadn't seen the truth, or maybe he did, and he had just failed to convey it to Lemuel, she was going to have her work cut out for her.

She peered out into the dusky evening,

vaguely aware of the solitary cry of a bull-frog searching for a mate and a banjo twanging on Lou's radio in the house. Her lone comfort was that both her girls were okay. Most thankfully, Jeanette was settled down and heading in the right direction at last. Her stubborn wild streak only a terrible memory.

Three

❧

Dreaming of Shoney's
Lou

On Easter Sunday morning Imo was running around like a chicken with its head cut off, getting things ready for the big dinner we were having after church. She'd been up since dawn, counting out plastic cups and Chinette plates, baking two hams, four cookie sheets full of angel biscuits, and plopping a good half cup of bacon drippings into her humongous pot of string beans. I slipped out to the front porch to stay out of the way. There was a pile of kids coming from the sound of things and my job would be hiding the eggs.

That was fine by me. The day was turning out to be absolutely gorgeous, and I wanted nothing more than to get outside and stay there. If it was anything like last year's Easter dinner, once all those aunts, uncles, brothers, sisters, cousins, and stray folks the Reverend invited showed up, it would be so packed inside the house that a person wouldn't even be able to think straight.

I peered toward the birdbath and the surrounding flower patch, hunting good spots to hide eggs. Imo's money plants were blooming; rosy-purple flowers which would turn into coins of translucent pearly-white seedpods. I was enjoying listening to the *cheer-up, cheerily* of a robin waking up in the crepe myrtles and before long I heard Imo talking to the Reverend as they ate breakfast.

" 'Bout time for me to run get dressed for church," she told him. I looked at my watch. Eight sharp. I reckoned I ought to go get myself fixed up for church, too.

While I was brushing my teeth I saw Imo in the mirror, coming down the hallway behind me, holding a hanger with a lemon yellow dress on it. She waited till I'd rinsed, spit, and turned around to lean against the counter.

"How do you like your new Easter frock, Lou?" She beamed, holding the dress out.

I eyed it hard. Butterfly sleeves, a scoop

neck, and a full skirt which appeared to be about midcalf in length. White ricrac sewn around the neckline and hem. "It sure is bright. Very Eastery. Pretty," I said to please her. But the truth was I thought it looked more like something a twelve-year-old would wear. "You didn't have to go to all that trouble, Imo, what with everything else you've got to tend to."

Imo smiled, a genuinely pleased smile that reached her eyes. "I *wanted* to do it, Loutishie, dear. It was my pleasure," she said. "Took an act of Congress, but finally I wrangled myself a time to get over to Mozelle's and then I sat up late and rose up early to sew. Like I've always said, a body will find time for the things that are important. I made one just like it for Jeanette, too, in robin's egg blue, and a precious tiny white suit for Little Silas."

I guess I shouldn't have been surprised. Every Easter as far back as I could remember Imo had sewed new dresses for me and Jeanette. Here I was a junior in high school and Jeanette a married woman, and she was still doing it. During her wild teenage years Jeanette always shook her head derisively, muttering to me later about the "hideous, homespun, high-necked, low-ankle frocks" Imo made for her and tossing them on the floor of her side of the closet. Mine were hung in an orderly row, and I wore them reverently, proud of all the compliments from the women of Calvary. It was not till Jeanette finally settled down that she would wear the dresses, and I felt that this was even more evidence of her new walk with the Lord.

Slipping into the dress brought to my mind that disturbing fashion show of Jeanette's barely there shorts; I could feel anxiety swirling in the pit of my stomach and I wondered if she would wear the new blue dress to Easter service. The erotic bull-riding contest had been the previous Friday night, and I had not talked to Jeanette since. I planned to corner her sometime at Easter dinner to find out all the details.

I wondered if Jeanette would feel the hand of God, of conviction, on her as she sat today in the pew at the Church of God in Rockmart, Georgia, listening to her husband preach the sermon. Almost every waking second of those two weeks since the afternoon in Jeanette's backyard, I'd wondered if she'd been able to resist the fleshly urges at war with her eternal soul while she danced at the Honky Tonk Tavern.

The Reverend Peddigrew preached over-time, and I watched all the ladies in the sanctuary getting restless, checking their watches. I reckoned they were worried about hams and roasts they'd left in the oven.

The service went even longer when Dusty Puckett went up to the altar rail right after the final hymn. "Lord, I have stumbled," he wailed, hands raised up, tears wetting his cheeks, "and I have fallen. Save me again by Thy infinite grace." The Reverend pushed up his coat sleeves, leapt down from the pulpit, and knelt with Dusty for the longest time.

"Reckon Dusty's took to drankin' again," Miz Clemmons turned and whispered to Imo from the pew ahead of ours. She frowned and shook her head.

"I imagine so," Imo whispered back, hands folded on top of a hymnal.

I felt for Dusty. His face was repentant, so sincere. I don't think I was alone, either. There were sniffles here and there and I suspected there were many who identified with his weakness, if not with drinking then with other demons they battled.

Dusty's propensity for falling from grace over the years had made an impression on my tender brain and I worried maybe it was *easy* to fall like that, that maybe each one of us was only one step away from eternal hell, from separation from God. If I failed to continue in the Lord's commandments, I, too, might find myself tough and callused and careless about my walk of faith.

I used to long for Jeanette to share these convictions. I needed for her to acknowledge the stricken look in Dusty Puckett's eyes as he rushed to the altar rail on so many Sundays. Instead she had snickered at him all those years, at his lank blond hair falling over his shoulders, into his eyes as he bent his head in front of the congregation.

I remembered her irreverent snort during conversations about salvation. She walked so close to the edge back then, laughing in the face of warning. I hated to think of her with April at the Honky Tonk Tavern, taking another walk so dangerously close to the edge after the turnaround she'd made.

I was sitting in the backseat of the Impala as Imo pulled underneath the shed at home. The Reverend rode shotgun, eyeing a yard full of the cars and trucks of our guests. "Boy hidey," he slapped his thigh, chuckling. "Place looks like a used car lot." The church van was parked in the drive, and I was sure Mr. Arnold Beecher, a distant cousin of the Reverend's, had driven it around till it was stuffed with all the random strays the Reverend invited.

When we climbed the back steps and put our feet on the porch, I saw Tiffany, the Reverend's granddaughter, prancing around like a show pony, tossing jelly beans up into the air and catching them with her mouth as a flock of the younger children watched. My Easter basket lay on the floor in their midst. Desecrated.

"This is mine!" I said sharply, scooping it up and sailing into the kitchen. Jeanette was there with a bunch of the younger women. A leopard-print blouse clung to her shape atop a black miniskirt and tall, strappy black sandals. Dangly gold earrings almost brushed her shoulders. I stood there, blinking, holding my basket. It was one thing for her to dress sexy to go to the Honky Tonk, but for church on Easter Sunday?

" 'Bout time y'all showed up, Lou," Jeanette said.

"Dusty Puckett got saved."

Out of the corner of my eye, I saw Jeanette rolling her eyes. "So kind of him to do that on Easter when everybody's starving half to death!" she said.

"Jeannie!" I cried. "You should have seen him! He was really sorry."

"What was it this time? Drinking or wild women?" She put her hands on her hips, cocking a plucked eyebrow.

Before I could answer, I was bumped out of the way by Sharon Anne, one of the Reverend's bossy daughters who wanted to get into the silverware drawer so she could stick spoons in all the side dishes folks had brought. The countertops were crammed full of Jell-O salads, casseroles, and desserts. There was a plate or two of carrot sticks, a jar of bread-and-butter pickles, and a huge tray of cupcakes topped with green coconut and jelly beans.

I looked around at all the folks, dressed in their Easter finery; the females in frilly floral numbers with corsages and patent leather pumps, a bonnet and gloves here and there on the little bitty girls and the old women. The men in gray pinstriped suits, lapel pins, and cuff links. I was captivated by the sight of Little Silas's brown skin against his spotless white linen suit.

Imo stood in front of the stove, turning on the burner to warm the beans. She set the oven to brown the angel biscuits and arranged the hams onto one big platter. Grunting, she carried the hams over to the sideboard and laid a carving knife and serving fork alongside.

Wanda came through the kitchen door. "I swannee, Imogene, hon, you got enough food here to feed all Euharlee." She set down a hash-brown casserole with little bits of bacon and green onions on top.

"Surely is," Imo said. "How are things at the Kuntry Kut 'n' Kurl?"

"Well, you know, we're mighty busy this time of year. Everybody and his brother wanted something special done for today. I worked till eleven p.m. last night. Jeanette, too."

"My stars!" Imo said, "why don't you go on in yonder and put your feet up? You, too, Jeannie."

I watched as Jeanette sashayed on off into the den. She wasn't doing anything helpful anyway, only picking all the french-fried onions off the top of a green bean casserole.

Wanda shook her head fiercely. "Nothing doing," she said. "I always helped Sister with our Easter feast." The way Wanda said *our Easter feast* made it sound like she was claiming Imo and the Reverend's Easter dinner as her own. Imo's eyebrows went up and her mouth opened like she was stunned, but she didn't say a word. She hadn't said a word about Jeanette not wearing her Easter dress, either.

Wanda was in high gear, filling cups with ice and yanking tinfoil and cellophane covers off of food. I'd watched Wanda from afar for years and I always marveled at the way she took over everything and everybody.

She'd started the Kuntry Kut 'n' Kurl when she was just seventeen, running Prelle's Beauty Boutique, a long-standing salon, out of business. She'd managed to get herself elected president of the Bartow Bowlers even before she knew the difference between a strike and a spare, and though she had no children she was on the PTO board at Euharlee High.

Another thing I marveled at every time I saw Wanda was the way she got around, so smoothly and effortlessly, in tight clothes, on four-inch heels, and with her massive chest. I myself would never have been able to maneuver all that stuff. And her hair. I guess on account of being the owner of a beauty salon she felt compelled to try everything. You just never knew what color Wanda's hair would be on any given day. But one thing you could be sure of, it was going to be *big.* Real tall or else volumized out on the sides. Today it was blond and it was teased up so high on top it reminded me of a hat. She wore frosted pink lipstick and denim blue eye shadow that seemed more like something one of my classmates would wear rather than this fifty-plus-year-old woman.

Wanda flung open the Frigidaire and rooted around inside. "Tell me you've got some pickled okra in here somewhere, Imogene. Sister always put out the pickled okra at *our Easter feast.*"

Imo smiled in the friendliest way you ever saw. "Sorry, dear. I surely don't. Got some chowchow down there on the bottom shelf, to the back behind the mayonnaise."

Wanda plunked this down on the counter and sailed out to the front porch so she could holler at everyone to come on in and eat.

"Let's ask the Lord's blessing on our repast," the Reverend said when a line had formed from the sideboard down the hallway and out across the back porch. After a prayer blessing God and blessing all the many hands that had prepared our feast, the Reverend called for the food to be "to the nursing of our bodies and our lives nursing to Thy service." Aunt Fannie looped her arm through Toby Outz's and hauled him to the head of the line to fetch a plate. Aunt Fannie was the Reverend's mama's oldest sister and she believed in honoring the elderly. Had herself a sharp tongue, too, and I knew if she got herself a good gander at Jeanette and Wanda, she would give them a good tongue-lashing over their shameful clothing. I'd heard her call Wanda a floozy to her face before.

For a moment I was torn. Should I sit with the young'uns or the grown-ups? Seemed like I was somewhere between a woman and a child at seventeen. Adults were stationed at the long table in the dining room, the round oak table in the kitchen, two card tables dragged in from the back porch and along the sofa where they could set their plates on a big trunk which served as the coffee table. Young'uns were outside on the picnic table, the back of an old flatbed pickup, the glider, and anywhere else they could find a seat.

I found a place at the kitchen table, beside Jeanette. We were joined by Wanda and Tiffany. Boy, did I feel like a plain Jane

137

sitting amongst those three. Tiffany, though just thirteen, looked older than me. She had a very womanly body and that same slit-eyed smugness Jeanette was born with. She was a cheerleader at the middle school, a buxom girl with a buxom personality and long auburn hair cut into a loopy shag. Generally I avoided her as she used a condescending tone whenever she talked to me. I nodded her way and smiled, but she did not respond.

As we ate I heard talk at the dining table about the Reverend's neck. Shirley June, some type of relative of the Reverend, was asking had he been to a chiropractor yet. "A chiropractor could take care of that pain," Shirley June said. "Line you right up, Lemuel. Line your whole body up straight as a arrow and cure all that ails you."

"I don't trust them quacks," said a man's voice I was unfamiliar with. "Liable to screw you up good. It just takes time to heal up a case of the whiplash. Why, I remember when my Darla run up underneath a chicken truck. Girl was multitasking's what it was — eating on a Big Mac and drinking a Co-coler and smoking and looking at the map and who knows what all else, in her little old T-ota wagon, and she just run right up under this poor man's truck. He was hauling chickens. Took Darla a good year to get over the whiplash. Took four hours for the county to gather up all them stray chickens."

Laughter.

"Land sakes," came Aunt Fannie's voice a bit later, "a year? Imogene, you going to keep on driving him around that long?"

"Well," the Reverend answered shortly, "there's no other way. The Lord's work must go on." He chuckled.

I turned to Jeanette. "You're not wearing your new Easter dress Imo made," I said.

Jeanette shot me an exasperated look, a you've-got-to-be-kidding look. "Ha," she said. "Ha ha."

"What's so funny?" Tiffany asked, tossing an auburn wing out of her eyes.

"You're serious, aren't you, Lou?" Jeanette said. "You're serious as a heart attack!"

"Well, sure I am," I mumbled.

"Seriously," said Jeanette, shaking her head and spooning up some of Aunt Fannie's famous Jell-O salad. "You get a load of the dress she made for me?"

"I'm wearing mine," I said. "Imo really worked hard on them."

Jeanette shook her head, smiling. "I can see you're wearing yours, Lou," she said, "and that makes me see I really need to learn you some things. Some life lessons." She crossed her arms. "Now what would happen to me if I *did* wear that dress?" She crossed her arms and raised her eyebrows. "Think real hard."

I was completely baffled. There I was, the top of my class in school and I could not fathom what she was getting at. Finally I shrugged.

"If I start wearing things like that now," she snorted, "then I'm just one step away from a frump! I'll turn into a church lady! A church lady with sensible low-heeled pumps and polyester satin blouses that tie at the neck and blah skirts for Sunday-go-to-meeting, and Keds or SAS for every day, with pastel-colored pantsuits and a little doodle-bug hairdo, and some white-pressed powder in a compact and maybe, just maybe, some red lipstick. Oh yeah, and I'd have me those big old clunky earbobs and a shawl I'd crocheted and a handbag I'd macraméd." She paused for a breath. "And Lou, that's probably all part of Mama's plan when she sews us those little innocent church dresses."

Tiffany's mauve lips spread into a smile,

and I sat there in silence like a ninny, shifting uncomfortably in my yellow dress. I was an unsophisticated, backwoods hick in her eyes. Country as a turnip green. I must've looked close to tears after that thought sunk in because Wanda stuck up for me.

"Lay off her, Jeannie," Wanda said. "I've always thought Lou looks real sweet, and like I always say, variety is the spice of life. That's what make the world go round."

"Yeah," Jeannette said, looking down at her plate, "I guess you're right. Sorry, kiddo. Reckon I'm just tired. Had me a long, hard night last night at the Kuntry Kut 'n' Kurl. Forgive?"

"Sure," I mumbled. But Tiffany shot me a superior look and I couldn't stand one more minute of things. I dropped my fork, sailed through the house, grabbed the bag full of plastic eggs off the back porch, and headed outside with Bingo right on my heels.

I dragged the eggs along the path toward the birdbath, looking down at my yellow hem and feeling sorry for myself. Was I really so out of it? I considered things; maybe I was a dud, a hopeless fashion don't. I certainly didn't put much thought into my clothes or my hair. Then I wondered what Montgomery thought of his wife's choice of clothing for Easter Sunday. I'd barely spoken to him in line for food and then he'd gone out to the front porch to sit with the younger menfolk.

My thoughts wandered to school and boys. There I was, a junior, and never been asked out on a date. The Junior-Senior Prom was coming up soon, in May, and there wasn't a chance I was going, unless I went stag or with a group of dateless girls.

Pathetic.

I worked myself up into such a state the grass wavered as my eyes filled. It turned into one of those private moments and I squatted down in the grass, pretending to hide an egg, profoundly aware of all the people scattered outside, till Bingo began lapping the salty tears off my chin with his rough, tickly tongue. "Stop it!" I shrieked, laughing and hiccuping at the same time. He finished and sat back with a wide panting grin.

"Reckon I ought to start hiding these eggs, huh, boy?" I said, looking out across the lawn. Probably I wasn't beyond hope. Often Jeanette told me how gorgeous I could be if I let her fix my hair and put some makeup on me.

The idea of this fired my imagination

and before I knew it, I was envisioning myself in a salon chair at the Kuntry Kut 'n' Kurl as Jeanette hovered around me, gushing "Look, Lu-lu, you're stunning, just like I knew you'd be." And in my dream I didn't look like a floozy. I looked pure and glamorous, like this Cinderella Barbie from my youth.

My tears and the decision to ask Jeanette for a makeover were like a cleansing shower. And for the first time that Sunday, I felt the Easter spirit, of new life risen up. I even let myself entertain the virtual impossibility of having a date to the Junior-Senior Prom.

There was this one particular fellow, Hank Dollar, a classmate, who I thought about anytime a romantic notion crossed my mind. We were both in Euharlee High's FFA club, and he was handsome and very popular. Way out of my league. I knew such a thing was virtually impossible, but as I moseyed along, tucking eggs in amongst money plants and daffodils, I felt comforted, giddy almost with thoughts of Hank Dollar.

I still had a handful of eggs left to hide when here came the stampede of young'uns out the back door, swinging baskets from their hands and shrieking with delight. Bingo and I moved out of the way as a dozen little kids plowed through Imo's flower beds, hollering "There's one!" and "That's mine!"

I headed for the house to find Jeanette. Only Imo was in the kitchen, standing at the sink, in her apron, scrubbing dishes.

"Where is everybody?" I asked.

"Well," Imo said, "one of Lem's adopted relatives is providing us some entertainment."

I heard excited voices in the front parlor, followed by a congregational indrawn breath of awe and the pattering of applause. When I got to the parlor there was a crowd standing around the ancient Buzzie. She sat on the piano bench, grinning proudly, her Easter corsage barely clinging to the shawl draped around her shoulders, her long floral skirt hiked up to midthigh and her legs in their dark stockings splayed out to the sides so that they reminded me of string beans.

"Alrighty, let's see, can you do it with your other laig!" someone dared. Buzzie nodded, bent forward, and grabbed her left thigh with both gnarled hands. I watched, shocked and fascinated, as with a grunt, she hefted her ropey leg up and slung her foot all the way behind her head so that

144

her ankle rested on her neck. More clapping and laughter.

"You're sure enough spry, Buzzie, to be ninety-five," Mr. Toby Outz praised her. "I know I cain't do that." He shook his head in wonder. "Miss Fannie, can you do that?"

The Reverend's aunt scowled, she turned red as a radish. "Indeed I would not! Showing my bloomers that way! You ought to be ashamed of yourself, Buzzie Wigham, and on Easter Sunday, no less! Go home and repent! All you street people are like a bunch of circus folk!"

"Least we ain't walking around like folks at a funeral! I thought we was celebrating the Lord's rising from the grave!" Buzzie rolled up one sleeve and closed her fingers into a fist. "C'mon, Frances, want to go outside? I'll take you on back of the well house!"

The crowd grew quiet as the Reverend stepped between the women. "Now, now," he said, "let's all go back and finish our desserts."

I scanned the room for Jeanette. She was off in the corner, sitting on our old faded camelback sofa.

"Hey, Jeannie," I said, sinking down next to her. She was holding Imo's most recent issue of the *Ladies' Home Journal*. On the cover was a picture of the tallest chocolate layer cake I'd ever seen, featuring an inch of mahogany frosting and strewn all about with pansies. Alongside the cake glared thick red headlines, among them "Our Biggest Diet Issue Ever! Slim Down with Our Amazing Secrets!"

"Listen, Jeannie," I said, "I —"

"Later." She waved me off, holding the magazine at nose level. "I want to finish this."

Her lap was full of jelly beans and I craned my neck to read over her shoulder. It was a page that said Fat-Blasting Menus. Day one's breakfast was dry wheat toast, half a grapefruit, and black coffee. Lunch was water-packed tuna on whole wheat bread and an apple.

"Boring food," I said to get her attention.

She didn't answer.

"I don't see how a person could live on that," I added.

Jeanette began tapping her foot.

"I mean, steamed broccoli and unbuttered rice and broiled chicken for supper?"

"You mind?" she said, turning her shoulder away from me.

I figured I'd start with the question

weighing most heavy on my heart and I leaned in closer, smelling stale cigarettes mixed with fruity scents from the jelly beans. "So what happened at the Honky Tonk, Jeannie?" I whispered. "It's a nasty place, right?"

She frowned. "I'm trying to read here."

"Well, what happened at the Honky Tonk?"

"Hush!" she hissed, looking rapidly to her left and right. Then all of a sudden her expression changed. She laid the magazine facedown on her lap and started plucking at her neck directly below her chin. "Listen, Lou, am I getting a wattle? You've got to promise me you're telling the truth."

I looked hard at her neck and shook my head.

"You promise?"

I nodded. "About the contest," I said.

"Let me tell you something —"

Before Jeanette could finish her sentence Montgomery came over and draped his arm around her and with her eyes she warned me to zip my lips.

Out the window I watched a group of the smaller kids playing freeze tag all around the house and Imo leading the women out to look at a purple clematis twining around a pole at the shed. I heard the wail of a fiddle and caught a glimpse of Mr. Toby Outz standing beneath the pecan tree playing a tune while some of the men stood in their suitcoats, nodding their heads and tapping their toes in the grass.

I sat for the longest time till folks began gathering their dishes and ambling out into the yard. Behind them the Reverend followed to say his farewells. Generally on Sunday afternoons he was reclined in the La-Z-Boy, all wore out from preaching, with his eyes closed and his mouth open. I wondered if he would have to hit the hay early that night.

He sometimes fell asleep during meals, though he would deny it. Imo was trying to make him aware of this. She'd been sneaking around with the Polaroid, taking his picture while he was asleep and then putting the pictures on the Frigidaire. He didn't act bothered by them atall. She also tried to point out his forgetfulness and it tickled me no end when I'd hear her reminding him to remove his teeth before he got into bed, to set his eyeglasses on the bedside table and to hang his house key on the nail beside the door. He'd even taken to misplacing his Bible, of all things, but most annoying to him and what really made me laugh the hardest was when he misplaced his coffee cup. This happened daily, sometimes several times a day, and Imo kept threatening to buy him a flashing mug with a beeper. I knew without a doubt he'd be lost without her.

She got put out with the man, but she loved him and she'd never in a million years say one bad thing to me about him. Lately I'd been watching them backing out of the shed and starting down the drive, with Imo setting up behind the Impala's steering wheel, wearing her clip-on sunglasses and her Cherries Jubilee lipstick and looking like *Lord, just help me to endure.*

Finally Montgomery glanced at his watch. "Better go hunt Little Silas," he said. "Getting late." When he was gone, I turned back to Jeanette.

"You've got to tell me, Jeannie," I whispered, "I'm dying to hear."

Jeanette cut her eyes over at me. "Dying to hear what?"

"About, you know, April and the contest."

"Don't ask," said Jeanette, her gaze back on the magazine.

"Aw, come on. What about April's rent money?" I looked as concerned as I could manage, but in my heart I was singing hallelujah on account of how bummed Jeanette seemed to be about the whole episode. Clearly it had not gone well.

"She did not," Jeanette spat finally, snatching up a handful of her skirt's fabric. "She lost, and I decided that I am fat as all get out! I'm disgusting."

I shook my head. "No you're not."

"Am too," said Jeanette, indignant. "This eighteen-year-old girl from Shorter College won. A real skinny-minny. Me and April called her Stickwoman." She sighed, then shook her head slowly back and forth. In the leopard-print blouse and those dangling earrings, she looked almost feral, less like a woman and more like some creature possessed. I sat there beside her, sad for her in a weird sort of way, but relieved she wasn't happy about the evening at the Honky Tonk.

"Place was pretty bad, huh?" I asked.

"Naw, it was cool," she said, her eyes taking on that faraway look as her lips spread into a grin. "You know, music and lights and dancing, lots of men. I'm gonna lose me twenty pounds in three weeks with this diet and then I'm gonna enter! I know I'm sexier than old Stickwoman."

"You're joking, right?" I tried to smile.

"Nope," she said, eyeing me hard, "I

ain't joking and it ain't a sin. All the girls are fully clothed. Listen, I *know* I can win. I've got the moves."

"They're not very fully clothed," I said. "Plus, you're a *preacher's* wife. And Imo would just die if she found out about it."

"Listen up, and listen hard, Lou." She leaned toward me, " 'Cause I am getting tired of explaining all this to you. Do not breathe a word about this to nobody. But that still don't mean it's wrong. Mama's just from a different time. She's set in her ways."

"Her ways are fine ways!" I said, turning away from Jeanette, crossing my arms and staring at the wall.

"Lou," she said in exasperation. "Get it through your thick head. It ain't striptease. I don't get nekkid. I'm just gonna earn me five hundred bucks. Heck, I'll even give a tithe on it. Let's see — ten percent of that . . . that would be how much?"

"Fifty dollars," I said through my teeth.

"See? That's a heap of money for the Lord to use, now, ain't it? Think what He could do with fifty bucks!"

I shook my head. "Think about what Montgomery would say if he knew, Jeanette. He would just *die* if he found out." I had something on her then. I knew it and she knew it.

"But, Lou, darlin'," she said in such a soft, pathetic voice that I had to look at her face. "Last night I had this terrible dream . . ."

"Tell me," I said, patting her knee.

She cleared her throat and ran one hand through her hair. "Okay, in this dream, Lou, I am *humongous.* I mean, I'm not just plump, or fat, even. I'm a whopping hawg, and I'm stomping along through the Shoney's. Like I said, I look just like a friggin' elephant. I mean it, somebody ought to shoot me I'm so disgusting." Jeanette paused, shook her head, and closed her eyes.

"So, I get up to the breakfast bar, see it's morning, and I start piling up my plate with these mountains of French toast sticks, bacon, ham, waffles, eggs, and grits, and hash browns, and all this stuff is just dripping off my plate."

She paused for a breath. It didn't sound all that terrible to me, not as bad as she was acting like. Anyway, it was only a dream. "So?" I said. "That's not awful."

She gave me an incredulous look. "Oh yeah?" she said. "Listen to the rest of it. I'm wearing these disgusting shiny green polyester pants and my arse is bigger than the Grand Canyon, and I'm waddling away from the food bar. And my arms, Lou, I've got these huge arms, with long jiggles of fat hangin' down, just a-flappin' like wings, and I've got a wattle so long it brushes my collarbone. So, there I am, Loutishie, stomping along, licking up all that dripping food with my fat just jiggling, and up in one corner of the Shoney's, along the front window, I see this table of fine women.

"They look like, you know, the grown-up cheerleader types. All sleek and tan, sipping black coffee and forking up shiny wedges of fresh fruit. And they're just smoking away, looking so classy, you know? Like they have it all together? And I'm trying to get over to their table, to show them I'm not really that big old elephant I look like. But I can't squeeze through the tables!" Jeanette's hands were clenched into fists.

"So?"

"What do you mean, *so?*" she cried, slapping the armrest. "I can't think of anything *worse* than that. I swear, Lou, it's an omen."

"You shouldn't swear, Jeannie. And we don't believe in omens." Plus, though I didn't say it, I could think of plenty of dreams I'd had that were far worse than that. Like the times I'd dreamed Imo was dead. Or the one I'd had about Jeanette being down in everlasting hellfire. I could still feel the bone-dissolving fear of that dream if I let myself, and at that moment I could easily picture Jeanette strutting down the wide path to hell, arm in arm with the old devil hisself.

I searched her face. "Listen, Jeannie," I said, pausing to gather up what she called my Holy Rolling religiosity. "Even if y'all are keeping your clothes on for the contest, I just know it's bad. I can feel it. First of all, it takes place in a liquor bar, and second of all, it's, what's the word I'm hunting for? I learned it last week in social studies . . . now, I've got it. It's *prurient* behavior. Arousing or appealing to an obsessive interest in sex."

Jeanette ignored me. She gripped her thigh with both hands and set her teeth together. "I'm gonna lose my whopping arse, Lou," she spat. "And I'm gonna win!"

I frowned.

"I got to be careful or Montgomery is liable to get bored with me." Her voice now was sulky. "You gotta remember, Lou, he's had his share of hot babes in his life. Back when he was in that band he had groupies, women falling at his feet. Gorgeous girls like you would not believe." She slapped the sofa cushion. "But know what, Lou?" she added after a bit, smiling a little, "I did get myself a few whistles at the Honky Tonk. So, I reckon I ain't totally frumped out yet. There's still hope."

"Jeannie," I pled with her, "April's not a good influence."

"Listen, Little Miss Goody Two-shoes," her voice rose. "Maybe April'll turn into a Christian on account of being around me."

"Like Dusty Puckett shows all those bartenders the right way?"

"How many times do I have to say this to you? Jesus hung out with sinners!"

"Yeah. But he didn't *do* what they did."

"Hmphh," went Jeanette.

"Well, you're fooling yourself, Jeanette Lavender Pike!" I crossed my arms.

Jeanette stuffed the magazine into the corner of the couch, jumped up with a red face, and jabbed her finger into my chest. "I don't need you preachin' at me, kiddo! I will dern well do what I please and you better not breathe a word about it to anybody!" She turned on her heel and left that warning sitting on my shoulders. So much for asking for that makeover, I thought.

Four

❧

Lost That Lovin' Feeling

Imo

In mid-May, the air was already getting that muggy summertime feel. Queen Anne's lace and brown-eyed Susans, flowers usually associated with summer, were filling the roadsides. With everything in the garden coming along nicely, Imo had begun to serve early suppers, at five p.m., followed by a speedy, halfhearted kitchen cleanup and then a dash for the garden.

She was thankful to have Lemuel's blessings with this shift in their schedule. Careful not to take a single thing for granted, she had kissed him sweetly that first time and said, "Mind if I leave you with the paper while I go outside awhile?" And she'd been doing the same thing every evening since.

Tonight dusk was threatening and Imo stood knee-deep in the gourds for a quick moment, watching a swallowtail butterfly balance its slender legs on a blossom in order to dip its proboscis into the center. She walked down several rows to check the Kentucky Wonder pole beans. Happily, they were starting to run and soon she could attach them to their sunflowers. She hurriedly glanced over several rows to the Brandywine tomatoes. It would soon be time to start removing suckers from them. The marigolds circling the garden almost made her pause, but she smiled and marched right through the okra and the peppers to the cucumbers.

Her obsession of late was fear that squash bugs were preying on her cucumbers, and this evening she was intent on hand crushing any pests. (Insecticides were a no-no as bees were needed to pollinate her coddled crop.)

Squatting down, she searched each leaf and spotting the ominous shape of a squash bug she prepared her right thumbnail. "Oh, no you don't, buster!" she fussed as she pulled the creature off to mash him. "I've worked too long and hard and I've got my pickles to think of!" There were plenty of squash bugs and at length she finished her unpleasant task and walked back toward the house under the pink-purple hues of the evening sky.

Pausing a moment, she studied Lemuel's truck beneath the shed, good as new now that it was back from the repair shop. The man was literally chomping at the bit to get back behind the wheel. At moments, when she caught him rubbing his neck and shoulders and wincing in pain, or dozing off in the car or at the kitchen table, she mentioned the notion of him taking a little vacation with her. Perhaps to the Georgia coast, or even closer, the mountains in their own backyard. "A little cabin for a week would be so romantic," she urged.

But the mere thought of time off upset him and Imo's patience stretched so thin at times it literally ached. Her only hope was his next visit to Dr. Perkins in mid-June. Surely wise, old Dr. Perkins would tell him that his neck had not mended totally, would probably never be as good as before.

"Going to be a real humdinger tomorrow," Lemuel told Imo gleefully when she stepped into the kitchen. He was sitting at the table barefoot, rubbing his hands together. "Got a luncheon with the deacons at eleven forty-five at Calvary, and Emmit Spinks went into the hospital in Rome, and I need to go by the Bible Bookstore in Cartersville for some materials and then we need to stop in and check on Wallisha Roby. Wallisha's done broke her hip."

Having spoken all this he was now bending down and rubbing his feet, wincing, saying, "Mind fetching me my Epsom salts, sweetie?"

"If your feet are bothering you, I think you'd better take it easy tomorrow," she said sharply as she headed to the cabinet for a bucket and the salts. "Anyhow, I've got my monthly Garden Club meeting from eleven to noon, and then after that us girls have a potluck. You call the deacons and tell them you'll have to postpone your meeting. Emmit and Wallisha will just have to wait. Your feet need a break and that's that."

Lemuel crossed his arms. "I have a higher purpose than to sit here idle and coddle myself."

"It's not a sin to rest," Imo said.

"Tell you what, love," he said in a pleading voice, "tomorrow we'll go to Boss Hawg's, even though it'll only be a

159

Wednesday. That's a promise you can count on."

"But I just told you, Lemuel, don't you remember? Tomorrow's my Garden Club meeting. And potluck."

"Well," Lemuel smiled, "you'll have to choose then." But just as suddenly he winced, "Wait a minute! What am I supposed to do tomorrow?!"

"I should be home by one-thirty or so," she said resignedly.

"One-thirty!" he cried. "The day's almost gone by one-thirty!"

Imo whirled around, looking at Lemuel with a martyred sigh. "I have responsibilities, too, dear," she proclaimed. "You don't even seem to realize I have a life of my own, my own schedule and obligations! I am the president of the Garden Club. The president! And I *am* the president because your dear, departed wife, Martha, was the president and she died, went off, and left *me* all her responsibilities!"

At first, standing there, Imo felt mean, then this changed to a profound sadness which bubbled up from her inner core. She sagged against the counter and buried her face in her hands. "I'm sorry, Lem," she murmured, "so, so sorry I said that." But she didn't know if she was saying this to

160

Lemuel or to God or to Martha.

The room grew deathly quiet and when she had recovered a bit, Imo turned her face to look at him. He ambled over and gave her a feeble pat on the back.

Only minutes later, when she overheard Lemuel talking to his brother Felder on the phone, matter-of-factly asking him for the favor of a ride the next morning, saying, "Oh, Imogene. She's got herself one of them women's obligations, but she'll be back at it come one-thirty p.m.," did she realize that, in fact, her frustration did not even register with him.

Imo spent the next morning fixing dev-iled eggs and stuffed celery for the potluck. Lou was off at school and Lemuel was gone, too, having been picked up at eight o'clock sharp by his brother. The house felt so empty.

She scrubbed the boiler and the mixing bowl, turned them upside down into the sink to dry and wiped the counter clean, all the while her conscience pulsing like a sore thumb. She had fussed at her friend. Her *dead* friend, that is. Poor Martha wasn't even there to defend herself — to say that Imogene had been given a choice and had accepted her lot in life willingly.

161

But then again, though she'd accepted Martha's request to marry Lemuel, it wasn't as easy as it had sounded. There were so many obligations in their relationship and some days lately, it took an enormous act of her will, a decision really, to get out of bed in the morning.

What was especially hard was the knowledge that those warm, fuzzy feelings that had grown between her and Lemuel were getting harder and harder to find. For example, if Lemuel was asking her to carry him into town to Calvary for something when she'd made up her mind to work in her garden, well, she got some ugly feelings toward him she didn't even like to admit to herself.

Sometimes she reckoned that she'd gotten spoiled living the single life after Silas passed. She'd been able to make her own schedule then, have everything her own way. Now she felt out of control in life, out of control of her own emotions. Surely, she mused, there must be some sort of way to achieve a balance here.

She'd wrestled with this all last night, and come today she felt exhausted, both mentally and physically. Leaning against the kitchen window frame, gazing vacantly out toward the barn, she spied a familiar shape sliding by. It was Inez, an old cat Loutishie had rescued from the dump years ago.

When Lou had carried the skeletal kitten in to Dr. Livesay, he said it would be a miracle if she even lived past twenty-four hours. Said she had probably already used up more than her nine lives.

Imo's face softened. But leave it to Loutishie! That child was a regular Dr. Doolittle. She had made a pallet on the floor beside that mangy collection of bones and spent three whole days there, nursing Inez back to life. Though Inez had never plumped up and achieved that sleek, glossy superior look of most cats, she was sturdy enough, and seemed to realize she'd been plucked from the jaws of death, and so was extraordinarily affectionate.

What was strange about her outline today, however, was that she was carrying a bundle in her mouth. Imo reckoned it was a vole or a barn rat. She's earning her keep, Imo smiled to herself. But then Inez slipped inside the well house and just as quickly pranced back outside without her burden. She repeated this same maneuver five times, carrying more bundles. Imo blinked. These were not rats, Inez was a new mother!

Six babies! Oh, you poor soul, Imo thought. She felt like running outside to comfort Inez, wrapping the cat in her arms and murmuring, "There, there. You so old and having to bear this burden. No one to help you."

But Imo consoled herself, wasn't Loutishie going to be beside herself when she found out about the kittens after school today? She'd been moping around lately. Even on her birthday, the girl had barely cracked a smile, though Imo had fixed her favorite supper of chicken tetrazzini, along with an ice-cream cake for dessert.

Six bundles of fur might be just the thing to cheer her up!

Imo dressed in a butter yellow pantsuit and sat on the couch till time to leave. Her smile vanished when her gaze fell upon a picture of Jeanette above the television. She was troubled now, at the memory of a phone call from last evening. Apparently Jeanette had been having massive head-aches accompanied by dizzy spells, and just the admission of this, by someone as private as Jeanette, told Imogene it was serious.

Cradling the celery and eggs Imo made her way out to the shed and the Impala. It would be good to see the Garden Club girls, take her mind off things for a bit, she mused, to hear about all their individual troubles.

She stopped short, nodding and smiling. Just imagine the wisdom thirteen girls could offer on the subject of her frustrations with the Reverend! She tried to compute the sum total of their married years. Even thirteen by forty would be a huge number, and some were past fifty years married. Well, now she had her answer.

Imo pulled to a stop on the road in front of Maimee Harris's home. She stepped out of the car and between a profusion of shrimp-colored azaleas which flanked the road, and wobbled along a meandering cobblestone walkway that led to Maimee's front door.

Maimee stood on her stoop. "Imogene!" she hollered. "What a lovely day you brought along!"

Imo said hello and walked into Maimee's spotless kitchen to set her dishes down. She loved it when it was Maimee's turn to be the hostess; her house was a real log cabin, full of early American antiques, and it was like stepping back in time, to a simpler time.

All the food was lined up on a wooden

countertop beside the sink. Imo lifted wax paper and tinfoil and hand towels to peek at biscuits, sausage balls, fruit cup, and pickled beans. At the dessert section, there was something lemony-coconut, her favorite combination. A large glass pitcher of tea with mint leaves floating in it sat on a round pine table, and alongside that was the ever-present silver coffee urn with a sugar bowl and cream pitcher at its base.

When she returned to the front room, Brenda was stepping inside and Maimee was pulling the log door firmly closed. Slowly they all filed into the kitchen for coffee and tea, then returned to the great room where they found chairs, said their hellos, and settled in. Next came the usual chatter about vegetable gardens, flowers, and families.

When it came time for Viola, the chaplain, to give the devotional, she began by asking if there were any prayer requests to be lifted up. Vulice mentioned her sciatica and Florence told the club about her dog Earl's arthritic hips. Glennis asked prayer for her son and his wife whose marriage was on the rocks.

Viola nodded solemnly at Glennis. "I've heard of more marriages in trouble than ever before," she said. "The Shakletts are divorcing."

There was an indrawn breath from Winnie. "You're not serious."

"Perfectly," Glennis said.

"Seems like they've been married forever. Forty years or so," Viola said. "Longer than me and James anyway."

"Forty-six years this August," said Glennis.

"Reckon why they're splitting up?" Johnnie asked, her coffee cup frozen in midair. "Seems like if you make it that far, you'd go on and stick it out."

"What I hear," Viola said, "is that she just got fed up. Said life was too short to keep messing with someone so disagreeable."

Words began to fly out of everyone. Astonishment here, judgment there, empathy all around.

"Well," said Doris, "everyone in this room knows a marriage takes a lot of work. No matter how young or old it is."

Heads nodded vigorously.

Dear Lord, here was Imo's cue. It was time to open up and lay her heart out on the line. Still, a cautious little voice spoke up inside to say *just wait, Imo. Call Maimee from home tomorrow and talk to her privately.* But just as quickly she remembered something Martha always said: Tomorrow never comes.

It took all of her nerve to say what she said next. She drew a deep breath and squeezed it out between her teeth. "Girls, I'm having some trouble in the marriage department myself."

Twenty-four eyes zeroed in on Imo. She laughed out a nervous breath. "It's just that, well, I don't . . . I . . . sometimes I wish . . . well, it's hard for me to put into words, lately I just don't *feel* as loving toward Lemuel as I used to, what with having to tote him around everywhere, and I wondered . . ." There, she'd started it anyway and that was all she could manage until one of the girls picked up a thread of it and helped her out.

Irma slapped her thigh. "Honey, I know what you mean. I could half kill Fred most of the time!" There was much laughter on that one and plenty of knowing nods. But she'd said it in such a playful way that Imo knew it was no comparison to what she herself was getting at.

Myrtice said, "I'm sure you'll wake up and feel differently in the morning, Imo. We all have bad days."

"No," Imo said, "it's not just how I'm

168

feeling today. This has been going on for weeks now." Imo stared straight ahead and Myrtice reached over and patted her shoulder. This was encouraging and Imo continued, "Sometimes I feel those warm fuzzies for him, when he's doing what I want him to do. But lately, I don't feel too many of them. I believe I'd be happier living all by myself. Well, just with my Loutishie, that is."

Annie Mae said, "What y'all need is a romantic getaway, Imogene. Some reconnecting time away from your responsibilities. The two of you should pack up your bags and head up to Gatlinburg for a week. They got hotels up there with heart-shaped bathtubs."

"That wouldn't happen in a zillion years, Annie Mae," Imo said. "I've tried to get him on a vacation and he won't go anywhere, has to be working all the time. Well, he does go to his brother Felder's place to fish and whatnot on Saturdays, but on the way he stops off and does his preacherly visiting. It was like pulling hen's teeth to get him to slow down the day he crashed into that poor woman's car."

"You'll just have to kidnap him, then, hon," Barbara said. "Make some reservations and pack up his clothes and kidnap him."

Imo's mind raced over a mental image of herself kidnapping Lemuel, and it was not a pretty picture. He would be so angry with her. "Trust me, Barb," she said, "that definitely wouldn't work."

After a while, Myrtice said, "Well, just give it some time. Pray about it. Shoot! We'll all pray about it, won't we, girls?"

Imo took a sip of her coffee. "Thank you, Myrtice."

Viola's eyes swept the room. "Anymore prayer requests?" she asked.

Imo felt her hand go up. "I don't mean to be greedy," she said, "but Jeanette called me last night and she's been having severe headaches and a dizzy spell now and then."

Viola frowned. "That's awful, isn't it? My dear mother used to take the sick headache every single month. She'd go to bed for the entire day. I can remember her just crying and crying with the headache."

"Jeanette's never had headaches before," Imo said. "Never in her life. Strong as an ox."

Maimee leaned forward. "Reckon it's all those chemicals she works with at the Kuntry Kut 'n' Kurl? All that hairspray and those perm kits couldn't be good for you to be breathing in all the time." Imo shrugged. Her mind was elsewhere as

170

Viola delivered the devotional, followed by a prayer, and then Myrtice launched into a discussion on perennials suitable for drought.

The girls all seemed to think a romantic getaway was the answer. Imo sank back against a pillow that looked like a tiny quilt. What would Lemuel think was romantic? What did he love to do the most?

Besides preaching and tending his flock, Lemuel loved fishing! By the time the Garden Club meeting was breaking for lunch, Imo had decided to kidnap Lemuel and carry him off on a romantic fishing trip. Just a day trip, however. One day at a time, sweet Jesus.

Five

%

First Kiss

Lou

I didn't breathe a word to anyone about Jeanette's trip to the Honky Tonk Tavern. She and I were virtually incommunicado as I had sure enough blown it on Easter Sunday when I'd preached at her. Yep, she'd shut up like a clamshell and all I could do was pray hard she would see the light and settle back down.

I was still daydreaming about my missed opportunity for a beauty makeover, but this was just as well as I got not even so much as a glance from Hank Dollar. I got no attention from any other males, either. I might as well have been invisible, and I wondered if, as the years went by, I would always be alone.

"You're just a late bloomer is all, darlin' ": this is what Imo told me when I moped around, complaining about not having a date to the upcoming Junior-Senior. "Enjoy being young," she liked to add. "Believe me, the single life is underrated."

I was so bummed by the way Hank Dollar ignored me that I might have actually broken through that wall I'd unwittingly put up between me and Jeanette, to ask her help on a beauty makeover, except for the fact that I had a partner in my misery. My best friend, Tara, an avowed tomboy like me, laughed every day with me during Honors Lit. We made great plans about how we were going to crash the prom together wearing overalls and boots. This camaraderie and our plan kept me moving forward, somehow able to stave off the gloomy clouds of desperation and depression.

All that month of May I kept extra busy with school, getting ready for my final exams. Summer was right on our heels; I could see it in the faces of friends from school and feel it in the balmy afternoons I spent out at the barn with Inez and her passel of kittens.

Today Inez lay stretched out on her side

in a sunny patch of grass. She slept soundly as the kittens pounced and tumbled all around her, stopping to nurse every now and then. Bingo lounged nearby, a veteran of so many litters of kittens that all they aroused in him was an occasional raised eyebrow.

It was a lovely Friday afternoon. A mild sun washed the landscape and a slight breeze blew my hair softly into my face. I sat up on the seat of Uncle Silas's old tractor, feeling a little melancholy, a cold Pepsi between my thighs. Normally a Friday afternoon with no agenda filled me with delight, it was one of my favorite times. But tonight was the Junior-Senior. As the days leading up to the prom were fewer and fewer, I tried to convince myself that I didn't care.

I chose to ignore the enthrallment on my classmates' faces as they talked of the dance, their dresses, and their dates. I told myself that I was setting my sights on higher things, loftier goals. My senior year was fast approaching and I determined that I would ace my way through it and apply to the University of Georgia, with the hopes of getting into vet school there in later years. I also entertained visions of receiving the coveted honor of being Dr.

174

Livesay's summer intern that next summer, between high school and college.

I tried to view the prom, my crush on Hank Dollar, even, as a silly and extraneous matter. One not worthy of my emotional energies. Yet now, the day of the dance, I sulked. What added insult to injury was the fact that Jeff Hutchins had asked Tara to the prom and she said yes! Hank was going with Lacey Whitcomb, a senior cheerleader for the varsity football team.

Lacey had startling green eyes, a long sheet of dishwater blond hair, and an upturned little nose. She bounced perkily down the corridors of Euharlee High; her lipgloss dazzlingly shiny and her conversation intertwined with breathless cascades of giggles. I knew Lacey had never had an insecure or lonely moment in her life. I was invisible to girls like her.

I took a long, slow swallow of my Pepsi, contemplating what would salve my wounded spirit, take my mind off things. I didn't know whether to head down to the Etowah on a solitary pilgrimage or seek out a sympathetic ear. I slipped down from the tractor, went over to Bingo, and crouched beside him to put my arm across his back. We watched two of the kittens pouncing on a grasshopper.

Bingo's chin lay flat on the ground, his eyes at half-mast. He was relaxed and full of peace while I was tense and wistful. I don't know what I wanted from him, but it wasn't hard to realize that being a dog was a relatively simple job and that I was expecting too much if I thought Bingo could commiserate.

I ruffled his ribs and found myself heading toward the backyard where Imo was hanging out sheets. I slumped down in the glider, watching Imo give each pillowcase a fierce snap before clipping it to the line.

She spied me over her shoulder. "Well, hey there, sugar foot. Lovely afternoon, isn't it?"

"It's okay," I mumbled.

"Are *you* okay, Lou?"

"All right, I reckon," I said.

"Well, you certainly don't look all right. Sitting there with that long old face." She walked over to cup my chin in her hands and I smelled the flowery scent of the laundry powder. "You sad about that dance tonight?"

I shook my head.

She searched my face hard. "You sure? Maybe you've been studying too hard these past weeks. All work and no play . . .”

“Maybe,” I said.

“I know what,” Imo said. “You ought to go do something fun.” She crouched down beside me, her eyes rolled up and to the right in their sockets, like she was thinking hard. “Lemuel and I are driving into Rome to the Wal-Mart tonight. Want to come along? We’re going to get us a milkshake afterwards.”

“Uhm, no thanks,” I said, picturing myself following a buggy loaded with denture cream and All-Bran cereal.

“Maybe you ought to go see a movie or something.” She patted my knee.

“Something,” I said, nodding.

“Okay, let’s see . . . there’s also the skating rink, bowling, and . . .”

I didn’t tell her that all those things would be fine if I had a companion, that I was probably the only soul in the entire eleventh grade not going to the Junior-Senior prom. In as cheerful a tone as I could manage, I said that I was thinking of driving to Cartersville — to see Little Silas.

“I know Jeannie’d love to see you, dear,” Imo said. “But I’m afraid the boys won’t be there. Montgomery carried Little Silas off camping up to Blowing Rock till late tomorrow afternoon, and Jeanette told me she didn't want to go with them."

"I bet she didn't," I said, smiling at a mental picture of Jeanette in a tent, with no TV, radio, curling iron, or light-up makeup mirror.

I drove toward Cartersville with the windows down, the soft air brushing my skin, lifting the hair from my neck. Four-fifty air-conditioning, Uncle Silas always called it. "You roll down four windows and you go fifty miles an hour," he liked to say with a grin. This memory made me smile.

I was musing on this, trying to keep my thoughts off of the actual moment I'd see Jeanette face-to-face. I was hesitant, of course, vaguely uneasy, as if I was next in line to deliver an oral report in history class. I imagined Jeanette slamming the door in my face, perhaps laughing and hollering something rude, or worse, inviting me in to sit in stony silence. I had misgivings, but any of this was better than the misery of being alone during the prom.

I turned into the driveway, cut the engine, and sat there a moment thinking how it was five o'clock, three hours till prom time, and how soon it would be but a memory for everyone.

"Food makes anything better." I couldn't help smiling as I recalled another of Uncle Silas's favorite sayings and suddenly I was starving. I had skipped breakfast and had only picked at my lunch. I decided to invite Jeanette to go out for hamburgers, onion rings, and Cokes. Before I even knew it, I was up those steps, standing at the front door, knocking with my face plastered into a grin like a hound dog wears when he's begging for a bone.

Jeanette opened the door and she was barefoot, in a faded pink bathrobe. "Lou," she said, not exactly startled. It didn't surprise me that on the coffee table I saw a saucer piled high with cigarette butts.

I stared at them pointedly. "I know, I know," Jeanette said, throwing up her hands in a surrender pose strange for her. "I thought I had done swore off 'em, too. But it ain't an easy thing to do, and anyway, I've lost eight pounds in the past two weeks. Keep me from eating." She smiled and patted her behind.

"But they're so bad for you —"

"Lou, babe, Wanda smokes, just like a chimney, and it seems like I can't even get within spittin' distance of a cig without having to have one myself."

I realized then that the ice was broken

between us. Before long we were sitting at the kitchen table and Jeanette was kicking her long legs free of the robe, crossing them at the ankles. She lifted her chin to inhale deeply and blow smoke out, her eyelids dreamy. "What's going on at the old homeplace?" she asked.

"Not much," I said, leaning back and crossing my arms. "Same old, same old."

"Hot Friday night, I bet. Kegs out on the back porch, radio tuned to 106 Rock, and Mama and the Reverend playing strip poker." Jeanette threw back her head, slapped her thigh, and laughed like she'd just told the funniest joke in the world.

Despite myself, I had to smile. "Listen, Jeannie, run get dressed and let's go to the Burger Barn. My treat."

She shook her head. "Nah. Can't."

"Why not?"

"I have done declared this to be my spa night."

"What?"

"You know. A beauty spa. Put on a mud pack, pluck my brows, touch up my roots, do a manicure, pedicure, whatever."

"Oh. I was hoping we could go out somewhere together. Have some fun."

"You can join me and we'll both have a spa night," she said.

"But I'm hungry. Please let me buy you a burger and a ring at the Burger Barn."

"You know I can't go anywhere looking like this, Lou. Plus, I'm trying to lose me some weight. Planning to have a diet shake for supper. Maybe some lite microwave popcorn with it."

"You need to eat some real food," I said, poking my bottom lip out.

"I *need* to get my figure back." She slapped at her thighs and shook her head. "Lou, baby, I have got to firm up my legs and I have got to tighten up the backs of these flabby arms. I found this exercise in last month's *Cosmopolitan* called the back-of-arm-beautifier and I'm going to start doing it. I really am. What you do is," she said, setting her cigarette on the edge of the table and standing up, "you hold your arms out at your sides like this, parallel to the floor, and you twist your arms so your thumbs point behind you and then you swing your arms back behind yourself far as they'll go, and you just kind of pulse them. See?" She looked very serious and determined as she pulsed her arms. "Firms up them saddlebags."

"That's great, Jeannie," I said.

"So what do you say," she asked, "about a beauty spa night for us sisters?"

I didn't hesitate for a minute, it felt so good to be invited back into Jeanette's good graces. She hurried to the kitchen to whir up chocolate Dexatrim shakes and put a flat package of popcorn into the microwave. "Now," she said, turning toward me with her hands on her hips as she waited for the popcorn, "we'll start with those brows."

"What's wrong with my brows?"

"They're shaggy as all get out. We'll clean them up and that'll open up your eyes. It'll be incredible, the difference will, and we'll just go from there."

We sat in the den, watching TV as we ate our supper. I said my own private blessing over the food, but it was a very unsatisfying meal.

"What's happening at school these days?" Jeanette asked as we were carrying our glasses to the kitchen sink.

"Oh, not much," I replied. "Be out for summer soon."

"That's nice, huh? What then?"

"Well, I want to work at Dr. Livesay's office," I said. "He needs people for his summer boarding kennel."

"That figures," she said, patting my shoulder. "Shoveling dog turds. What a fabulous summer."

I didn't say a word back. I knew she was only teasing me.

She ran a hand through her hair. "What I'm going to have to do is, I'm going to touch up my roots. I look like a dern skunk with this dark stripe." She laughed.

I followed Jeanette into the bathroom off the master bedroom. "Now," she said, "first thing we gotta do is get your hair off your face so we can shape your brows."

Almost before I realized it she had swept my long brown hair up and back, twisted it tight, and fastened it with a plastic clip. As she studied my eyebrows, I took a look around. The counter was chock-full of nail polishes, lipsticks, eye shadows, and perfume body mists. On the mirror was taped a picture of Jeanette's backside as she bent over to get clothes out of the dryer. Scrawled beside that, on a tiny Post-it were the words "One moment on the lips, years on the hips."

A tattered shoe box she pulled from underneath the sink was full of silver appliances; eyelash curlers, nail scissors, tweezers. Jeanette dug through the contents, biting her bottom lip and scowling at me. "Wax or pluck?" she wondered aloud.

"Which hurts worse?" I said.

"Don't neither of 'em hurt too bad."

I drew a deep breath. "I don't know about this," I said.

"Gotta suffer for beauty, girl," she teased. "How long were you planning on concealing yourself like this?"

I shrugged.

"You really don't give a fig, do you? Bet you wouldn't care if all you had to wear was a feed sack and didn't even own a mirror."

"Uhm, I don't know," I said, "sometimes . . . sometimes at school I wish I were the kind of girl that gets looked at."

"Then why not? You've got the raw material. I'm going to highlight your hair, do your brows, and teach you how to put makeup on. When I pluck your brows and contour your cheekbones, it'll really bring out those eyes. You'll be the hottest chick in eleventh grade."

"Bet I wouldn't either."

"Sure you would. Listen, Lou, looks are twenty-five percent what God gives you and seventy-five percent what you can do with a little makeup and hairspray." She patted my shoulder. "Plus, darlin', once I do you over, you'll be stunning, with those liquid brown eyes and that chestnut hair and your flawless skin, and then that's gonna make you *feel* gorgeous, and then that positive attitude will show. So much is in the attitude. When I get through with you, you'll totally flip out. You'll think you're God's gift to men."

I waved off her words.

"Hey, got a crush on anybody?" she asked.

I tensed. "What?"

"You heard me. Who you got a crush on, girl?"

I looked down at my feet, my dusty leather loafers with squatty heels, then looked up at Jeanette. She could see it in my face. "Hank Dollar," I said finally.

She smiled. "He got a girlfriend?"

"Well, he's taking Lacey Whitcomb to the Junior-Senior tonight," I said, before I could catch myself.

"That's *tonight*?" Jeanette practically danced a little jig. "Oh, this is so great, Lou!" she gushed, and she squinched her eyes shut tight a second before she tapped a fresh Virginia Slims Menthol Light out on the counter.

I hated the way the conversation went after that. "Well, you are going to that dance tonight, girl," Jeanette said. "Screw my roots touch-up. We're going to doll you up big-time, I'll drop you off, and we'll really give Hank Dollar something to look at."

185

This was not in my plans, but all of a sudden she was headed to the kitchen to microwave some wax, saying "We've got to make haste here," while I felt totally lost, the way I did when I woke up from some crazy half-real dream. Oh, I loved Jeannie for believing in me the way she did, for offering her skill, and her enthusiasm, but I knew I could never do it.

"Look like you've seen a ghost," Jeanette laughed as she came hustling back in. She tapped a cigarette ash into the toilet. "Now, turn around and sit up here on the counter. I'm going to need you to be real still for me."

She was serious as a surgeon as she laid the pot of wax, a thing that looked like a big wooden tongue depressor, and a pair of tweezers out on a washcloth. I sat motionless on the cool countertop, silent while Jeanette steadied my chin, going "hmmm," as she dabbed blistering hot wax around my eyebrows. She pressed skinny strips of a material like cheesecloth onto the wax. My only explanation for not flinching during the whole process is that I was too numb to feel it.

Finally my brain kicked in. "I can't go," I pronounced. "I don't have a dress with me, and by the time I drove home and then

186

back to Euharlee High, the prom'd be over."

"Keep still," Jeanette said, scowling as she ripped the long strips of cloth away. She stroked the tingling skin underneath my eyebrows. "Don't worry about looking pink here. I've got some concealer for that. Now for your hair. There won't be time to highlight, but we'll pump up the volume and curl it."

"Did you hear me?!" I cried.

"You're gonna wear one of mine," Jeanette was telling me matter-of-factly while she bent my head forward and brushed my hair so hard my scalp tingled. "Got a little black number that's made out of this really stretchy fabric. It'll fit you." She plugged a curling iron into the base of a makeup mirror.

"I'm not going," I breathed.

Her shoulders stiffened. "Yes ma'am, you most certainly are going. I ain't going to let you live like a hermit, hiding out at the farm with Mama and the Reverend and Bingo and all them cats and chickens and whatever else it is you collect. You listening? Do you understand?" Jeanette looked as if she might like to grab me and shake me till my teeth rattled, but instead she laid a gentle hand on my shoulder.

"You'll regret it forever if you don't go, Lou," she added softly.

She went to work in earnest, winding strands of my hair around a curling iron, finger-fluffing each steaming ringlet before she moved to the next, finally grabbing a pump bottle of Aqua Net, and ordering, "Close your eyes!" while she baptized the whole do with a cool mist.

"Yep," she said, stepping back, delicately touching my hair as a ribbon of smoke from her forgotten cigarette perched on the edge of the sink spiraled upward. "I knew it. You look totally awesome."

Next Jeanette held my face in her hands, staring at it for a long time. She seemed possessed as she rummaged crazily through a big fishing tackle box full of cosmetics. "All right, Lou," she said, "let's get your face done and if we've got time we'll do something about those nails. They're truly pathetic."

I looked down at my hands. My gnawed-on fingernails had permanent stripes of red Georgia clay wedged up underneath. When we were younger, Jeanette took great delight in calling me a country bumpkin because of this. I recalled one particular morning as we were eating breakfast, when she told me that I looked like somebody off of the show *Hee Haw.* What was funny was that I took that as a compliment. I felt great all that day in Miss Reba's fifth-grade classroom.

Imo always told me it was what was inside a girl that made her beautiful and I took her word on the subject. I knew what beauty meant to Jeanette, however, and I told myself that she was just wired different. As she liked to say, you have to look good on the outside before they'll even *want* to see your beautiful insides. And I realized, that day, that she was right, too.

"Alrighty now, Lou, I need you to hold real still," Jeanette said, and I felt her warm fingers stroking some kind of sludge into my face. The massaging sensation was not unpleasant, but my skin felt like it was suffocating when she finished. Next I felt a soft brush dusting powder over my forehead, cheeks, and chin.

Then she stroked blush on my cheeks and gummy mascara onto my lashes, followed by eyeliner and eyeshadow, finally this lipstick which felt as thick as wax and smelled like bubblegum.

"Done!" she cried exuberantly. "You look gorgeous, Lu-lu. Drop-dead gorgeous. Just wait'll you see yourself!"

Hesitantly, I turned to face the mirror.

What I saw literally took my breath away. The hair was a glamorous arrangement of chestnut curls, full at the crown and then swooping to lie like amulets on my shoulders.

I was terrified as I turned this way and that, and on its surface saw a faint sprinkling of lavender-colored glitter that winked and twinkled when I moved my head. It looked like a movie star's hair. It did not look like me at all.

The face was not mine, either. There were eyes lined in smoky black, sweeping upward at their outside corners like a softer Cleopatra. Cheeks and lips the tender pink of Cherokee roses that bloomed along our fence.

"Told you," Jeanette said, her words sandwiched between two streams of smoke. "Told you you'd be a knockout. Hank Dollar will not be able to keep his eyes off you."

Partly on account of being in awe and partly because of the butterflies circling in my stomach at the mention of Hank Dollar, I just stood there mute as a rag doll. "Well, what do you think, babe?" Jeanette prodded, happily making her way out of the bathroom to her closet door and rustling through the clothes.

"I don't look a thing like myself," I confessed at last.

"You're right and that's the point. You're hot now. Going to be even hotter when you slip this on." She held up a slinky black dress with a plunging neckline and spaghetti straps. "Isn't this sensational? I wore it to a New Year's party back when I was a size six." She had a wistful look in her eyes. "Come on, Lou, you have to hurry so we can get you out the door."

I stood transfixed there in the doorway of the bathroom.

"Hurry," sang Jeanette, holding the hook end of a hanger and bouncing the dress.

In the next split second that dress slid from her hands as she sunk to the floor and suddenly I was out of my stupor, down on my knees at her side. "Are you okay? Are you okay, Jeannie?" I pled as I held her by the shoulders.

It wasn't long at all, thirty seconds maybe, when her eyes fluttered open again. "Man, oh, man, Lou," she said, then let out a long sigh. "Another one of them dizzy spells. I hate it when I do that. Sorry if I freaked you out." Then she scowled and swept her arms across the carpet like she was making a snow angel. "I didn't have no cigarette in my hand, did I?"

I shook my head.

"Well, that's a relief. Last time I fainted I dropped a cigarette and put a hole in the linoleum."

"Last time?"

"Couple of days ago. Had a spell while I was cooking supper."

"Did you faint then, too?"

"I reckon. Got all swimmy-headed. Lost my cigarette, like I said. Probably haven't been eating enough, but I've got to lose me some weight." She sat up, laughed, and pushed her hair out of her eyes.

I jumped up to get Jeanette some water from the kitchen and when I returned, she gripped my forearm hard. "Listen, Lu-lu," she said. "I want you to walk through that door at the gym, looking so hot you make everybody's teeth fall out." She paused. " 'Specially Lacey Whitcomb's. But if she takes after that old momma of hers, her teeth and her looks'll be gone by the time she's forty, anyway."

She laughed, and I laughed too, even though it occurred to me that Jeanette was acting way too glib after such a fainting spell. But that was the way Jeanette had always buried her fears. At that point, I felt I needed to reward her for all her work and so I slid into that little black dress and sidled over to the full-length mirror on the back of the door. A stranger peered back at me.

"Okay, Cinderella," Jeanette said, "slip into your glass slippers and we'll jump in our pumpkin and burn some rubber to get you to the ball." She held out a pair of black sandals with three-inch stiletto heels.

"I'd fall off those."

"No you won't. You'll make out fine. Sit down here and I'll put 'em on for you." She patted the bed. "Just takes a little getting used to is all."

"Are you sure you're okay?" I asked, staring at the shoes on my feet.

"I'm fine, Lou. Just need me a cigarette. And you have a dance to get to!"

A few minutes later I was underneath the blue-black, cloudless sky, teetering precariously toward Jeanette's Monte Carlo.

"Now, remember, girl, you've got to shake your thing," Jeanette said as she turned into the gravel lot beside the gym at Euharlee High.

I was so nervous about the whole experience that I might have broken out in hives, or fainted, but Jeanette was like this superanimated director. "Don't you go in there and just *slump* into a chair along the wall! This is your chance!"

"I'll do my best," I said, "but I don't really know how to dance."

"Move your hips, thrust out your chest!" Jeanette slapped the dash.

I looked down at the flat plane below my chin. I felt the popcorn and the Dexatrim shake doing a rumba in my stomach at the idea of strutting my stuff. Jeanette popped a cassette into the console and music pulsed into my feet and up through the seats. Beside me, Jeanette started shaking her thing and for a moment I was convinced I should push her, in her bathrobe, out the door to go to the dance. Eventually, though, she pushed me, laughing crazily and then burning rubber as she squealed out of the parking lot. I watched the red glow of her cigarette till she was too far.

I stood frozen just inside the door of the gym for a long minute, my hands clasped in front of me, feeling unsure and unsteady on Jeanette's tall heels and marveling at how a bunch of crepe paper streamers, balloons, and plastic flowers could transform the place.

The basketball goals were retracted into the ceiling for the dance, and a prismed glass ball threw polka dots of light everywhere. Bass notes from the music made the walls of the gym literally throb, feeling something like a large heartbeat as they surged through me.

Though I knew if I stayed along the dark perimeters of the gym, I would not easily be seen, I also knew the inexorable nature of my mission. I had promised Jeanette and I had promised myself, and two emotions I did not want to wrangle with were guilt and disappointment. I scanned the crowd, taking in the corsages, the sparkly, shiny high heels on the concrete floor, and the surreptitious swigs taken from brown paper bags.

With an act of my will I launched myself out and into their midst, holding my breath against the sharp odor of Jack Daniel's and sweat. I wound my way through the laughter and excited voices, teetering in and out amongst the shadows, unseen yet by the circles of dancers with their enraptured faces. Across the dance floor, at a long table hauled in from the lunchroom I got a cup of frothy punch and sat down unobtrusively on a chair against the wall. I watched the bodies of my classmates shimmying. I was mesmerized as I witnessed the other sides of Alli and Dina and Jennifer as they twisted to the beat. Rachel, a fat girl who smelled like onions, and her quiet friend Freda stood in a corner talking and I considered that maybe I'd join them later. Several guys from Beta Club were awkwardly perched along the wall.

I felt very removed from all of them. I've made a mistake in coming, I don't fit in anywhere, I decided as I munched on Fritos with onion dip. Mr. Gruner, the ag-tech teacher, stood at the other end of the table, with a dutiful, long-suffering look on his face, no doubt ensuring that the punch would not be spiked. I searched the tangle of bodies for Hank's, finally spotting him against the far wall. I was startled to see his tan face above a ruffled white tux shirt and bow tie. His dark curls caught glints of shine from the swirling strobe. In awe, I sat, not breathing, sending up this absurd and dual-sided prayer that he would notice me, and at the same time, that I could slip quietly away, savoring that particular vision of him.

Beside Hank, hip jutting out in a sassy stance, stood Lacey Whitcomb. With the back of her hand she flipped a long sheet of her shining hair over her shoulder and smiled coyly at Hank. I had a fleeting vision of myself heading over to them and then her turning to look at me and her teeth falling out. Forgetting myself for a moment, I laughed aloud. That was when Tara's face, rouged and grinning, caught sight of me. Her mouth dropped open, then she waved with both hands, gallivanting over and shouting, "Loutishie Lavender! I can't hardly believe what I'm seeing! Is that really you?! You look like a movie star!" Her date elbowed a senior boy, and they both stared at me, shaking their heads, smiling goofily.

Tara draped a scratchy plastic lei around my neck, grabbed both my wrists, and pulled me to my feet and out a ways into the crowd, boogying her hips, saying, "C'mon, Lou, dance!" Whispers melted into approving whoops and I felt my cheeks flush hot with all the attention. At last Tara's ebullient face and the pulsing beat of the song compelled me to move my hips a bit.

Catcalls and whistles erupted at this. Closing my eyes I could hear scattered bits of conversation with my name in them. I was being discussed and approved of, and I fairly glowed. Somehow this infused me with a confidence foreign to me, and I managed to maneuver myself in Hank and Lacey's direction, my heart pounding in anticipation.

I sidled up close to them, making eye contact with Hank, and he smiled and mouthed "hello," though from his face it seemed more like "wow."

Then came a slow dance, and as Lacey pulled Hank to her I returned to the concessions table. I recovered my punch and took a deep breath. I felt worldly and sensual, and I figured I ought to have gone with Imo and the Reverend to the Wal-Mart. But I didn't get the chance to dwell on this for long.

"Hey there, Lou," Hank's voice called from the shadows behind me. His fingers were icy hot on my bare shoulders and I jumped a bit. "You sure look purty tonight," he said in that long honey drawl of his. "About didn't recognize you. Don't look nothing like you do at the FFA meetings."

I didn't know what to say to that, but finally I managed a humble thank you, my eyes downcast, twirling the ends of my hair around my fingers. "Where's Lacey?" I asked stupidly.

"Aw, she said she was going off with some girls to the powder room, but I saw her with Tommy Stanton."

I nodded and Hank sat down in the

chair beside me. He didn't seem all that bothered by the idea of his girlfriend stepping out on him and I wondered if things with them were not as they appeared. We sat quietly, my heartbeat pulsing through every cell of my body. I'd turn my head slightly every so often and see Hank flashing me his hundred-watt grin.

The next song was so loud it made my eardrums hurt. "Outside?" Hank leaned over and said hotly into my ear, gesturing toward the side door. I don't know what surprised me more, hearing him ask me that or me leaping up the way I did and brazenly following him out into the parking lot.

That's when I knew Hank Dollar really had a hold on me. Being around him changed me into someone else, a person who took risks. At that moment I would not have cared if Lacey wanted to punch me out.

The moon was unbearably luminous and melting off to one side, the air so cool it raised goose bumps on my arms. "Couldn't even hear myself think in there," Hank said. I nodded and we walked side by side to the far end of the parking lot, where he leaned back against the door panel of an ancient Chevrolet Celebrity that appeared to be held together with duct tape. I stroked a strip of the silvery tape, tongue-tied.

"Alabama chrome," he quipped with a twinkle in his eye. "That's what Daddy calls it anyway."

I laughed.

"I swear I didn't expect you to be here, Lou," he said, turning me around to face him. "I didn't figure you to be a girl who cared about dancing."

"Me neither."

"Want to dance?"

"Lacey?" I asked.

"Aw, she's all right. She's with Tommy and they can have each other."

"They can?"

"Sure," he said softly, leaning forward with his hands on his knees, looking into my eyes. I wanted desperately to put my mouth against his. It would be my first kiss if I did, but I couldn't summon the nerve to do it.

"Could I Have This Dance for the Rest of My Life?" a throaty song by Anne Murray, floated from the high windows of the gym. "Let's dance out here," he said, and I nodded as his arm encircled my waist, sending tingles up my spine.

From an out-of-body perspective, as I

imagine must happen to shock victims, I watched myself holding on to Hank as he held me close to him in the night air, my heels snagging on the pits and ridges of the gravel parking lot. I held on to the brilliance of that moonlight in the trees overhead, and I held most tightly to the tender kiss he placed on my bare shoulder. He *could* have this dance for the rest of his life, as far as I was concerned.

Six

❧

Romantic Fishing
Imo

The first Saturday morning in June, before daylight, Imo stood in her housecoat holding the phone. She'd just finished talking to Lem's brother Felder.

She had a doozy of a time convincing Felder not to come by for Lem for their usual day together, explaining that she was kidnapping him and carrying him off to Dillard's Lake for a romantic fishing date.

"Romantic fishing?!" Felder's voice rose to an unappealing nasal whine. "Ain't nothing romantic about fishing. Anyways, ain't kidnapping illegal?"

"My word," said Imo, "we are married." She told Felder good-bye and went to the back porch to rummage around for the big cooler. She found it underneath a stack of yellowed newspapers, then glanced quickly at the garden. Lord knows, this would be a lovely day to get some work done out there.

She scolded herself; if she wanted to rekindle the warm fuzzies of their marriage, she would have to turn a blind eye to some things. She carried the cooler to the kitchen, and opened the Frigidaire. Stacked neatly against the back on the bottom shelf were three Tupperware containers. One held an exotic chicken salad, studded with tiny mandarin oranges and pecans, the next contained some purple seedless grapes big as muscadines, and the last was full of tiny cubes of Gruyère cheese. These she nestled into the cooler, along with some tender brown croissants, Perrier, and creamy triangles of mocha cheesecake.

She was certain all this was a romantic spread. Standing among the deli items at the super Kroger in Cauthen yesterday, she must've looked lost, for a vivacious young lady in a bright smock came out from behind the cheese counter to ask if she needed help.

"Yes, please," Imo said, "I'd like some

things for a romantic picnic. An outdoor sort of private shindig for two."

"I see. Well, now, let me think romance here." The lady led Imo to the wine and spirits aisle.

"No, no, no, dear." Imo shook her head. "He's a preacher. A *Baptist* preacher."

"Ohhh, now I got you," she said, and she plunked a green bottle of Perrier into Imo's buggy and wheeled it back to the deli, where she pointed out the chicken salad and the croissants. Imo felt a tickly fluttering in her stomach as the cashier rung up her purchases. She had a secret. She would prove to Lemuel how nice it was to relax out there underneath God's blue sky. Possibly being outside would be as romantic to him as it was to her and so she decided to wear a matching lacy black bra and panty set from the bottom of her underwear drawer.

Halfway toward home, she turned down a little dirt road toward Velma and Zeb's Bait & Tackle.

"Imogene!" Velma practically shouted out as the cowbell hooked to the front door clattered a warning. She jumped down from a stool in front of a tiny television set and hustled over to Imo's side.

"How are you, dear? What are you doing in here?"

Imogene smiled. "Got me some fishing to do."

Velma cocked her head in a questioning pose.

"Now tell me what I need to get."

"Well, that depends," Velma said. "You really going fishing?"

"Mmm-hm."

"What are you wanting to catch?"

"I don't know," Imo said. "I'm not in it for the fish. I'm just going along to be with Lemuel. Romantic fishing trip."

"Aren't you a living doll!" Velma said. "That's just about the sweetest thing I ever heard."

"I hope *he* thinks so."

"Let me run stub this out," Velma said as she held up her cigarette, "and we'll get you all fixed up."

Imo'd sat out in the parking lot a zillion times when Silas was alive, and several times lately, behind the wheel waiting for Lem, but she'd never been inside before. Velma always got herself out to the parking lot so they could visit.

The walls of the shop were rough two-by-fours. Various counters, made from the same, jutted out at odd angles, giving the place the feel of a maze. The floor had a luster left from constant foot traffic down the center of various cabinets and displays. Three white refrigerators, speckled with rust, lined the far wall, along with a wide wooden chest covered in screen mesh. Really, you could call it a big shack, but charming in a way, with its exposed rafters underneath a tin roof.

"Alrighty, dear," Velma said. "I imagine the Reverend has got all the tackle he needs. Do you have a fishing rod for yourself?"

"Yes, somewhere out at the barn. A Zebco 33 combo Silas bought for my birthday one year, but I've hardly ever used it."

"Reckon all you need is some bait then. We got night crawlers that'll catch about anything. Bass, catfish . . ."

Imo shrugged.

"We got some minnows over yonder," Velma said. "Got some Southern gray crickets in this here case. You ever fish with crickets before?"

"No."

"Some women prefer the worms. Don't like to stick a hook through the crickets."

"Oh, uhm, yes," Imo said vaguely. "Worms will be just fine."

Velma grabbed a white Styrofoam cup and a lid from a shelf above the register and walked to the back to scoop up a tangle of worms and dirt from a huge chest. She presented this to Imo, who stood gazing down at the punctured holes on its top.

Imo followed Velma to the cash register and set the worms down beside a jar where you could drop in coins to support Mrs. Eunice Jackson's liver transplant. "Well, I know Lem'll be real tickled," Velma said. "I don't recollect Martha ever going along with him."

As she climbed back into the car, Velma's words were still jouncing around in Imo's brain. Hearing that Martha never went fishing with Lem both comforted and disturbed her, and she had a fleeting impulse to call the whole thing off. If Saint Martha hadn't ever done it, then maybe it wasn't such a great idea after all. But then again, think how memorable it would be when she carried him fishing.

In the wee hours of the morning of the trip, Imo dreamed Martha woke her and asked if she had put an extra rod and reel in the trunk for her. "I most certainly did not," Imo said. "I thought you were dead."

"What does that have to do with any-thing?" Martha said sternly. "I want to fish, too. You can't leave me here by my-self."

"But it's supposed to be a relaxing, ro-mantic type outing for just the two of us."

Martha was pouting. She folded her arms across her chest and Imo noticed the gleam of a tiny golden cross on a chain there, a cross that Lemuel had presented to Martha as a wedding gift. A cross she'd been buried in.

"Well, I reckon you could come on with us," Imo said finally, and she began gath-ering up supplies for the trip and stuffing them into a tote bag.

"I'll be in charge of the packing!" Martha said, yanking the tote bag away from Imo and turning it over to dump the contents out. "You forgot something im-portant. You didn't pack the Mercurochrome and the sandpaper." She looked piercingly at Imo. "And you ought to know we'll need rubber bands if we're going to catch a catfish! Lemuel's got to have rubber bands to keep the fish's mouth shut. If you forget those, he's liable to get bitten to death!" Suddenly Martha pulled a large blubbery-mouthed catfish from the tote bag and plopped it into Imo's arms.

"See? See the teeth on that monster?"

Imo wrenched herself from sleep. It was still dark. The luminous face on her bedside clock read 5:45. She nestled down and over toward the center of the bed till she felt Lemuel's warm hip. But there was a fuzzy feeling of Martha around her. Her tendency to take over a project wasn't something that Imo had altogether forgotten. Imo hadn't minded this atall way back when. It was rather nice to have such a confident person to follow. A born leader.

Imo got up and shuffled to the kitchen for a cup of coffee. Was the dream a warning from Martha in heaven? Could departed spirits do that?

Oh, surely not. That would make things too confusing for the folks on earth. But then again, dreams had meaning sometimes. Look at Joseph in the Bible, when he'd interpreted those dreams that the palace baker and the pharaoh had . . . Oh, surely this dream meant nothing but nerves on her part. Soon she would mention the dream to Lemuel and they'd laugh over it.

Imo heard the melodious trills of a sparrow and she crept outside through the dew-covered grass to check the cucumbers.

The trellising had been a good idea, she decided; the long green fruits looked healthy and free from soil rot.

This boosted her spirits and by eight o'clock, she had everything packed in the trunk of the Impala. Soon after she heard Lemuel stirring, and before long he entered the kitchen rubbing his whiskery face.

"Felder here yet?"

"Nope." She flashed what she hoped was a fetching grin at him.

"Seriously?" His eyes darted toward the front porch where Felder generally sat enjoying a biscuit and coffee as he waited for Lemuel. "Reckon I'd better call him then. It's not like Felder to be late." He lifted the phone's receiver and Imo laid a hand on his wrist.

"He's not coming, dear."

"What? He sick?"

"No. He just said he's mighty busy. Can't spare the time."

Lemuel looked at her in amazement.

It was close to nine when they pulled out from underneath the shed. Lem wore a floppy rolled brim hat and his fishing vest, both of them studded with colorful flies and lures. Imogene tugged and wiggled to find a comfortable position in the scratchy bra and panty underneath her poplin pants and knit top.

When they turned in the opposite direction from Felder's, Lemuel grabbed at the steering wheel. "Whoa!" he said. "Wrong way!"

She clutched the wheel firmly and locked her eyes on the road, smiling.

"Imogene! Didn't you hear me? I said —"

Imogene smiled at her cleverness. "I'm kidnapping you!" She chuckled at his puzzled face.

"What?!"

"Well, see, I've packed us up a nice little romantic picnic, got all your poles and your tackle in the trunk, got some worms from Velma and I figured we could drive out to Dillard's and make a nice relaxing day of it."

He looked hard at Imo.

"Okay?" she coaxed. "It'll be fun. Just you and me." She leaned toward him, urging him to agree, to see them together at the edge of Dillard's Lake, or laughing and tumbling about on top of the quilt she had placed in the backseat.

"Don't worry," she said, "I called Felder and told him I was kidnapping you. I know it's short notice, but —"

"But you don't care for fishing," Lemuel said after a long spell, his face unreadable.

"Well, folks can change, can't they? Anyway, I care for *you*. We'll have fun," she said, patting his arm. "The weather's purty and I packed us up a special lunch."

They drove through the middle of downtown Euharlee, and then alongside Calvary Baptist. "Mighty quiet around here today," Imo said, dipping her head toward the church.

"Yep," he said. "What do you think of the new saying on the marquee there? Eugene Sinkley submitted that one."

Imo slowed to read the white sign on wheels stretched across the sidewalk:

DON'T GIVE UP.
MOSES WAS ONCE A BASKET CASE.

"Catchy," she said to Lem, "very catchy." And it was indeed an encouraging thought.

"Yep," Lem said. "He also submitted one that goes: 'Read the Bible. It'll scare the hell out of you,' but I figured we oughtn't to put a cuss word up on our marquee."

Imo's mouth curved into a smile. "I

212

think it's funny. The word hell is in the Bible, after all."

"It'd offend some. The Bible says if something offends our brother, we shouldn't do it."

"Well," she said, noting the stubborn set of Lem's jaw and feeling a bone-deep need to lighten things up, "I cannot wait to land myself a fish!"

"Want to catch a fish, eh?" He flashed his first smile of the day.

"You'll have to teach me how."

"First, gotta learn to cast."

"Alrighty. I just think it sounds so romantic to fish together. To have something, some hobby we share."

"There's not a lot of talking if you're a serious fisherman," Lem said, glancing over at her.

"We'll just have to make up for that over lunch, now won't we, angel?" She'd never called him angel before and she glanced over to see his reaction, but she could read nothing. "Sure is a nice day out," she added, lifting one hand from the steering wheel and waving it toward the sky. "How about putting us on some music. That'd be fun."

They were traveling along a gravel road at the back side of Bartow County as

Lemuel fiddled with the little knob on the radio and tuned in to some show on car repair. She didn't say a word about it, however, when Lemuel cocked his head in a thoughtful, interested pose at a conversation about a worn-out CV joint. She tuned the show out and at last they turned down a rutted dirt road. Around the first curve, Dillard's Lake appeared, a greenish-brown body of water surrounded by cow pastures. Imogene felt her heartbeat quicken as she pulled into a spot of shade to park. She peered around. No other cars or trucks or people that she could see. That was good. "Time to get fishing," she announced, unbuckling her seat belt. "Let me get our equipment out."

"I can do it," Lem protested. "May not can drive again yet, but I can unload the trunk." His eyes grew wide as he set two folding lawn chairs, the picnic hamper, a cooler, a thermos, a radio, a bucket, the poles, the tackle box, the worms, and a canvas tote bag onto the grass. "What's all this stuff for? Don't need but a pole and some bait."

Imo was bending over into the backseat to fetch the quilt and a daisy-sprigged sheet for a ground cover. She straightened, smiled, and said, "Lem, dear, I wanted to make sure you had everything your heart desires today."

All she got was a perplexed stare, and she realized this was going to take a little work. Lemuel had been hauled away from the comfortable routine of his life, from the security of being in control, and he didn't quite know what to do with himself. "What I desire right now," Imo said, "is for you to impart your fishing wisdom to me." She did her best job at batting her eyelashes. "Now, let's go down yonder to the edge of the lake and you stand behind me and wrap your arms around me and show me how to catch a fish."

"Casting takes lots of practice, Imogene . . ."

"I'm a fast learner."

There was a long uncomfortable moment or two in which it seemed they were going to be stuck in that scene forever, him standing ramrod straight, holding his pole, chin thrust out, eyes narrowed in thought. Finally he said, "Let's give it a shot then."

"I'm ready," Imo answered, careful not to act too excited. She grabbed her fishing rod to walk to the edge of the water. The air there had the rich, musky fragrance of decaying vegetation. A dragonfly hovered close and the loud, electric buzz of cicadas was a comforting sound. Imogene felt a sense of peace as she leaned out over the water to gaze at the still reflections of the pine trees.

"Now, the first thing you want to do is mash this right here down," he said, pointing seriously at a small button on her Zebco. "Then you want to bring the rod back and, now listen up good, as you cast it forward make sure you release the button."

"Cast it forward and release at the same time?" Imo asked, momentarily tensing all her muscles. Stiffly she swung the Zebco behind her, and then flung it forward while mashing the button. But the rod released only a tiny bit of line and this snarled into a knot of sorts. "I'm sorry," she said, both hands clutching the handle. "I really flubbed that one."

"Takes practice," he said, "to get it down in one smooth stroke."

"Show me again," she said.

Unhurried, he smoothed the line and wound it back in. He pointed the rod backward over his right shoulder and snapped it forward with one crisp flick of his wrist. His line arced gracefully through the air and landed like a whisper on the lake.

"Real pretty," she said.

"Now you." He held the rod out to her. "Try and relax a little bit this time."

She stepped to the edge of the water once again, fingering the button lightly as she bit her bottom lip, willing the tension to flow out of her arms and neck. "Alrighty," she said in her most confident voice, and she felt her arm rear back, her thumb pressing the button as she brought it forward.

Again, all she produced was a stunted tangle of fishing line. She tried again, three more times. After the last she paused and shook her head sorrowfully. "I'm sorry, dear," she said. "It'll be fun just to sit and watch you fish. It looks like art when you cast."

He said nothing at first and so she glanced over her shoulder at his face. His floppy hat sat askew over a face she still could not read. Disappointed perhaps?

"So," she said cheerily. "I'll run back toward the car and fetch something to set on. You go right on ahead. Don't you worry a thing about me. I'll be happy as a pig in mud just to watch and keep you company."

Maybe this would work out to her advantage, she mused, stepping over tufts of fescue. He could get in the mood by doing something he loved, and she could relax on the quilt and work up some warm, fuzzy thoughts.

She lugged everything from the Impala to a tree near where he was, unfurled the quilt, and sat down to fiddle with the radio's knob. She found a station, set the volume on extra low, and leaned back on her elbows, tilting her head up and peering at the soft blue sky through branches of the tall sweet gum.

Had she even chosen the right bait for today? She'd flubbed at fishing and now what she had left for luring him to the quilt was the black lace bra and panty set and the fancy food. Well, all she could do was give it a whirl. She stretched out to bide her time.

Several hours later, Lemuel came tromping up to the edge of the quilt. Before he could say a word she gave him a seductive smile and dipped her torso forward to give him a better view of the bra.

His right hand in his pants pocket jingled change and he swallowed loudly as her eyes swept his length. "Come here, darlin'," she said, patting the quilt.

"Hm?" He looked away, toward the lake.

"Bet you're wore out from fishing," Imo said. "Bet you're hungry, too."

"Thirsty's more like it," he said.

She sat up and rummaged around in the hamper for two plastic champagne glasses. "Well, you come right on over here. I've got a nice, cool drink for us to share." She grabbed the Perrier and struggled with the cap till the tension gave way and icy froth spewed out. "Here it is!" she proclaimed.

"That champagne?" he asked, eyebrows raised high. "You know I don't cotton to —"

"No, no, dear," she said, stifling a laugh. "It's a sparkly nonalcoholic beverage."

Tentatively he reached out to accept a cup, sniffed its rim, and took a tiny sip.

"Like it?"

"Got any sweet tea?"

"Really?"

He nodded.

"I didn't pack any sweet tea, Lemuel."

"Co-coler?"

"Didn't pack any Coke, either."

Lemuel got to his feet, adjusted his hat and then his vest. "Reckon I'll go back and fish s'more," he said.

Imo gulped some Perrier straight from the bottle and the bubbles made her eyes sting. She smiled her sweetest. "Stay a while with me right here, angel. It's close enough to lunch. Please?" She reached for the crease of his trousers. "Pretty please, with sugar on top."

"Reckon I might be a touch hungry."

Imogene opened the cooler and set all the various Tupperware on a folded towel along the edge of the quilt. "Catch anything?" she asked.

"Mmm-hmm, got three nice catfish," he said.

"Where are they?"

"Tossed 'em back."

"And I couldn't even get my bobber out on the water good!" she let herself praise him. "I am so impressed with you."

"It's nothing," he said. "Three catfish is nothing, really."

"Why, of course it is!" she exclaimed as she set croissants onto china plates. She folded two freshly ironed linen napkins and tucked them underneath the plate's rims. Next she apportioned out the chicken salad, grapes, and Gruyère cheese cubes, then set a sterling silver fork at the side of each plate.

"Mighty fancy lookin' vittles," he said.

"Come right on over here next to me, angel," she said with a playful smile, holding up a single grape between her thumb and pointer finger.

He eased on over beside Imo, smiling

shyly back at her. His pupils were huge as he looked into her eyes. This was a good sign. On impulse she popped the grape between his surprised lips.

Startled, he took in a gasp of air that sucked the grape down into his windpipe. "Hunh!" he grunted, scrambling to his feet and flailing his arms wildly. He commenced to stomping his right foot as he slapped at his chest. "Hunh! Hunh!" he went on, bending over double.

Terrified, Imo noted his face turning purple. "My goodness. Lord help me," she breathed as she floundered toward him, stumbling over the lumpy quilt. She stood paralyzed, until in her mind flashed an illustration hanging behind the counter in Wooten's Fish House entitled "The Heimlich Maneuver."

She moved behind Lem and snaked her shaking fist up into the spot between his paunch and his chest. She gave a fierce grunt and pressed her knuckles up. Still he clawed at the air with both hands. "Oh, gracious Lord in heaven, help me," Imo breathed as she thrust yet again, harder. This time the grape popped forth and hit the ground with a satisfying thud, rolling along on top of the red Georgia clay. She released Lemuel.

At length he straightened up, drawing gallons of air in and out, in and out, shaking his head like a wet dog. "Good gosh amighty!" he hollered when his color finally returned.

Imo stood near him, hugging herself and feeling totally devoid of bones. "Oh, hallelujah! Thank you, Jesus," she whispered, then, "You scared the living daylights out of me, Lemuel. Us out here all alone the way we are."

"Scared *you?* My life was flashing before my eyes!"

"I know, I know," Imo said as she sagged onto the quilt. "Forgive me. I'm sorry I fed you that grape. I'll let you feed yourself the rest of this." She placed his lunch across his thighs when he sat down.

"I shouldn't fuss," he said, chewing solemnly as they watched the reflection of the clouds on the lake's placid surface.

"How'd you like the chicken salad croissant and the cheese?" asked Imo as they reclined on the quilt when they'd finished.

" 'Twas mighty rich," he said, and then, after a pause, "Martha, now, she used to pack me up a stack of sody crackers, a tin of sardines, and one of them little cans of Vienna sausages. Along with some sweet tea, of course." He closed his eyes as a smile spread across his face.

Imo felt a wistful tightening, like a clenched fist, inside of her chest about where her heart sat. The mood was totally blown as far as she was concerned, and the closeness she'd wanted so desperately seemed about as much a possibility of them walking on water. Here he had all but come right out and said that Martha's Vienna sausages were superior to her carefully prepared lunch. He could forget about a piece of the cheesecake still waiting in the cooler! "Probably rather have Martha's apple cobbler anyway," she muttered under her breath.

"What'd you say?" Lem opened his eye closest to Imo.

"Oh, nothing," she said.

"You sure? I thought I heard you saying something over there."

There was a moment of awkwardness — two bodies lying side by side in the warm afternoon, each entirely removed from one another. Before long they were both asleep.

Imo roused herself first, with a little jump, to discover a thin crust of dried drool on the corner of her mouth. "Oh, my lands!" she fussed. "I must've fell out."

She hadn't expected to do that; she never slept during the day unless she was sick. She turned her head to see Lemuel, his head thrown back, still in the depths of slumber. It was a pity she couldn't let him sleep on, but it was late and the insects were getting bad. She touched his shoulder and he did not flinch. She shook his arm — nothing but a mangled snore. "Lemuel Peddigrew!" she said loudly into his face, holding both his shoulders and rattling him a bit.

"Pfftttpt," he spluttered as he came awake. "What?! Where in tarnation am I?" he asked, patting the quilt with a puzzled look.

"We're fishing, darlin'," she said. "Don't you remember? You were off in dreamland. I reckon we better tote ourselves on home before long." She would not confess to her own nap.

He nodded in a dazed fashion, grunting as he struggled to a sitting position. "This just shows you need some more rest," she pressed.

He frowned down at his lap.

Imogene felt a pang for the man. "Look," she said, "I know it's not easy for you and I can respect that. But I care about you, and I want us to have some years together where we just relax and have us some fun while we've still got our minds and our mobility left."

He sighed deeply.

"Don't you understand?" She found herself twisting a corner of the quilt. "Wasn't this nice today? A little R and R?"

"Imogene," Lemuel said, his voice very sure, like he was launching into one of his sermons at Calvary, "you're talking a mile a minute. Let me get a word in. I want to tell you I'm willing to make a deal here. Find us a way we can both be happy. I want you happy, too."

She folded her hands in her lap. "Talk, Lem," she said, watching a fish jump and the ripples spreading out from the center of the lake.

"I've been thinking," he began, "we ought to move downtown, to the parsonage."

Blindsided, Imo gave a little cough. She could not speak.

"That way I can do lots of my job by just walking over to the church," he continued. "All my committee meetings, my counseling sessions." He looked at her with such an earnest face, and continued. "It's the perfect solution, don't you see? I won't need you to ride me to the church to prepare the chapel for Wednesday and Sunday services, and you won't have to drive me near as much since lots of folks I have to call on are in walking distance of Calvary."

"Oh my," she squeaked, reluctant to even think about his proposal.

"Take yourself a little while to chew on it, dear," he said. "I just wanted you to know I've been pondering what you keep saying." He covered his heart with his hand. "When you first told me I ought to slow down, I was so mad I like to died. Then, I prayed about it. Still am. Now, I know this ain't the perfect plan, but I reckon we'll both have to give a little." He bent over to nuzzle her cheek with his nose, then clasped her hands, pulling one up to kiss it as he stared deeply into her eyes.

Imo smiled back at him weakly. She wasn't quite sure what had just transpired, or if she had agreed to anything, and she would need lots of time to ponder it all.

When they reached home, Imo flew into the bedroom to yank off the offending bra and panties. Bare, she slipped into a cotton work shirt and pulled on a pair of soft old picked double-knit slacks. She took a deep cleansing breath, stretched her arms over-head, and flopped back onto the bed. Hadn't Martha tried to warn her?

She was up there looking out after Imogene. Bet she had tried to tell her about Lemuel's desire to move to the parsonage, and about the grape, but Imo'd been too intent on her own agenda to listen. Probably tried to tell her it was no use carrying Lem fishing. That it was a solitary male type of sport, where she had no business.

Sardines and Vienna sausages, indeed!

Imo stared at the ceiling. "So what *do* you suggest I do here, Martha?" she whispered heavenward. "You know I cannot move downtown!"

No answer.

Imo fought a hint of impatience. Perhaps she was just tired and discouraged and imagining things. Right now what she needed was the solace of tending to the garden. There was something in that soil out there that always helped her work out the hard things.

"It's preposterous!" Imo grunted as she pulled a weed from the squash. "Imagine, me living downtown, in the parsonage!" Bingo perked up his ears at her tone and gazed expectantly at her. "Don't you agree, boy?" she asked him. "You're a farm dog, and you understand."

He lay down and put his chin on his paws to watch her as she worked on, then rose to follow her over to the cucumbers, where she knelt to check for pests. All was clear on the squash bug front and she noted with pride that the cucumbers would soon be ready to harvest. She stepped back to admire them and as she did her heart began to pound so hard she feared it might jump clean out of her chest and land in the cucumbers. She realized that a miracle had occurred at Dillard's Lake. Lemuel had finally opened up to her.

Seven

Rattlesnake in the House

Lou

One Saturday morning in July, just before dawn, when the moon was only beginning to drop into the bottoms and the grass was still wet with the dew, I found Imo sitting at the kitchen table.

"I wake you up?" she asked as I plopped down into a chair across from her.

"Been up," I said.

"And you out so late with Hank?" She shook her head. "I heard you come in at eleven."

I smiled and closed my eyes briefly at the tickly sensation inside. Just the mention of his name did that to me. The night before we'd spent the evening out in his daddy's sorghum field, watching the stars and talking. Hank was even finer than I'd let myself dream; he loved the outdoors, he adored animals, and faithfully he carried his granny to the First Baptist Church in Floyd County. I was in love, and I was pretty sure he was, too.

"What are *you* doing up so early?" I asked Imo.

"Oh, worried myself awake, I reckon. Be time for Lemuel to get up before too long anyway."

"What're you worried about?" I asked.

"Wanda called me yesterday evening . . . ," she said, her words trailing off.

"Well?" I said, searching her face. "What'd she want?"

Imo didn't answer. Sometimes it was hard to get information out of her, as she believed in pondering things a long while before she spilled them out, especially if they were troubling.

"Well, sugar foot, I hate to get you all worried, too," she said at last.

"You won't," I promised.

Imo frowned. "Jeanette's been missing a lot of work."

"But she adores the Kuntry Kut 'n' Kurl," I said, my mind conjuring up a pic-

230

ture of Jeanette lying in bed nursing hang-overs. Still I didn't dare breathe a word about the Honky Tonk Tavern. I would go confront Jeanette privately.

"Jeanette's not skipping work intention-ally," Imo said, cocking her head with the most serious expression. "She gets terrible headaches and has dizzy spells. She passed out at the beauty shop while she was rolling Alice Bickham's hair last Tuesday."

"Oh," I said, my mind racing back to that evening in Jeanette's bedroom when she fainted. I didn't say a word about that either. I had all but put it out of my mind as things were going along so well with Hank, school being out, and my part-time job at Dr. Livesay's summer kennel.

I spooned sugar into a cup of coffee, and all I had to offer Imo were words that sounded pathetic even as I said them. "She'll be okay," I said. "She's tough."

"Well, could be all the chemicals she's around," Imo said. "All those perms and sprays and hair dye can't be good for a body to breathe in all the time."

"Yep. Probably," I said, grasping onto this. "Maybe Wanda should see about get-ting some kind of ventilator put in the salon. Tell you what, I'll run by Jeanette's this morning, before work, and check on her."

"That'd be real nice," Imo said, and I began to see her face soften, the worry lines smoothing out some.

We talked till daybreak spread its tentative morning light into the little kitchen, and when she began to speak of her plans for the day Imo's voice grew lighter. "Surely is going to be a pretty one!" She waved her hand toward the window above the sink and I looked out on a cloudless sky. "Need to pick the squash and cucumbers. Looks like we'll have us a bumper crop of cucumbers, thank the Lord. Plenty for making pickles."

Bingo's happy bark sounded at the back door, his alarm whenever he heard a vehicle heading down the long gravel road from the highway to the house. I rose up to glance out the window. "Felder's here," I pronounced.

Imo sprang to her feet. "Great goodness!" she exclaimed. "Lemuel must be running behind this morning." She scooted back her chair so quick her coffee sloshed out. "I'm running behind this morning!"

She made a beeline down the hallway, hollering at me to let him in. "Fix him fresh coffee and I'll be back to make the biscuits."

I leapt down the back steps just as Felder's rattletrap pickup lumbered to a stop. "How do?" he said, removing his engineer's cap and leaning out of the window to spit a brown stream of tobacco juice. What always made me smile was that he was bald as a baby's bottom on his head, but he had this long, bushy white beard that completely covered the bib pocket on his overalls. I wondered if he grew that as a sort of compensation to himself. He was older than the Reverend, but favored him like a twin through the face.

"Hi," I said.

"Whar's Lemuel?" He narrowed his eyes, peering around the house.

"He's not up yet," I said.

"He ain't? 'At old boy took to sleepin' in?"

"I don't know. Imo's gone to rouse him. She said for you to come on in for coffee and a biscuit."

"Done et this morning. I'll just wait out here." He cut the engine, leaned back, and sighed loudly. "He still got that contraption on his neck?"

"Nossir," I said, walking over to lean back against the pecan tree. I thought it would be rude to leave him out there alone.

"Can't believe he ain't up and at 'em. It's a doozy of a day for fishin'."

I nodded, trying to envision the two of them fishing. Felder I could see, but Lemuel was such a practical man, eschewing jigsaw puzzles, crossword puzzles, reading novels, and most anything else that was purely for pleasure. But he simply loved fishing and it was incredulous to me, too, that he had overslept on his fishing day.

"He ort to get hisself a alarm clock," Felder grunted.

"He has one."

"It ain't workin'?"

"I don't know. He hasn't been feeling too good."

" 'Sides his neck?"

"Mmm-hmm," I said.

"Well, what's ailin' the ol' boy?"

I shrugged. "Arthritis. Tired a lot. Bunions."

Felder snorted. "Ain't nothin' a good day of fishin' won't fix."

A spell later, the Reverend came down the steps with a thermos of coffee and his fishing pole.

Imo was cleaning up the breakfast things

when I returned to the house to get my purse. "Well, time for me to get out there and tend to my garden," she said in a relieved voice. "I was beginning to worry he couldn't wake up."

Driving past row after row of pine trees I thought about Hank, about the way we talked for hours perched on the bank of the Etowah, gathered in by the closeness of the evening air and the songs of crickets and whippoorwills that echoed across the water.

I thought of our words, so sincere and unplanned, weaving themselves together like cloth. And who did I have to thank for this? For walks with Hank down the old logging road to the swamp, holding hands where the earth is covered in moss and clover? I smiled, remembering Jeanette's face the night she made me over. I owed her big time, and I stopped just outside of Cartersville to pick some roadside daisies.

I handed the flowers to Jeanette when she opened the door and her appearance totally shocked me. She wore only a huge T-shirt, her face completely bare of cosmetics. And she had peroxided her hair so that it was almost white.

"Hi Jeannie," I said. Trying to look nonchalant.

"Hi kiddo. What's the occasion for the flowers?"

"Nothing," I said. "Just thought you might like them." I bent to pat the head of a striped yellow cat winding around my ankles.

"Well, come on in. Montgomery's at church and Little Silas is over at his friend's. Don't let that old fleabag in."

"What are you doing today?" I asked as I stepped into the dim foyer. I smelled popcorn.

"Laying out," she said, which explained her bare and shiny face.

"Laying out" meant sunbathing, and when I reached the den I saw her elaborate setup out the back window. One of those cheap plastic deck chairs from Eckerd's, a cinder block turned up on its end with a transistor radio on top, a can of TaB, and a thick gilt-covered romance novel on the Johnsongrass beside the chair.

"Want some popcorn?" she asked. "A shake? I've got vanilla now." She made a sweep with her arm toward the Formica bar in the kitchen where the blender sat.

I shook my head.

"Well, I've got to get on back to laying

out. You can sit in the shade of the house and visit if you want."

I watched her stick the daisies in a tea glass, fill it with water, and set it on the dinette table, and all the while I was wondering how I could bring up the subject of her dizzy spells and follow that with questions about her spiritual walk.

We got outside and I had to suppress a gasp when Jeanette shrugged out of her floppy T-shirt. There was a red spot on her lower back, above her right bun. Standing there, squinting against the sun, I looked closer. It was a tattoo of the Rolling Stones lips!

"Like it?" she asked, smiling at my slack-jawed face.

I was speechless.

Jeanette unscrewed the lid from a brown plastic bottle, shook a puddle into her palm, and slathered oil into all the flesh that her bikini didn't cover, which was most of it.

"What did Montgomery say?" I managed finally.

"Nothin'. He can't cast a stone, now can he? What with bein' covered up with tattoos hisself." Jeanette positioned herself on her stomach on the chair, turning her face toward me. She reached one arm back to swat at a hovering yellow jacket and I saw more marks on her body.

They were not tattoos. They were a line of oval purple stains on the inside of her upper arms, near her shoulders. I suppose it was then, staring at those deep bruises, when I began to understand that Jeanette was very scared about something.

When she was six, newly arrived at Imo and Uncle Silas's, she had lain in the bed at night, wide-eyed with fears she could not name, nursing the insides of her arms. This did not stop until after countless visits with the therapist and lots of love from her new parents.

What was she so afraid of now, I wondered, sinking to a seat, my stomach muscles clenched in a knot.

"Mind rubbing some of this stuff on my back, Lou?" Jeanette's voice pierced my thoughts.

I grabbed the warm bottle of oil and squeezed a puddle into my hand and started rubbing it onto Jeanette, lightly brushing my fingertips over the garish red tattoo.

"Jeannie," I blurted. "You enter that bull-riding contest Friday night?"

"Naw," she said glumly, her voice muffled by a beach towel, "Montgomery's trip to some men's retreat got canceled. Guess I'll be in next month's. Anyway, it'll give me more time to get this blubber off."

"That why you're sucking your arms?" I let myself sink down onto my knees between Jeanette and the sun. She said nothing for a long while and I waited, breathing in the coconut-smelling oil and watching the yellow-striped cat meander through some tall weeds beyond Little Silas's sandbox.

"I'm just . . . ," she said at last. "I don't know . . ."

"You don't know?! Is it those fainting spells?"

Jeanette raised up onto her hands and elbows, gave me a penetrating look, and said, "Look, Lou, I just want to have me some fun. That's all, some fun. Is that too much to ask?"

"Some fun," I repeated, trying somehow to connect erotic bull riding, the tattoo, the cigarette smoking, and the peroxided hair to fun.

"The girls at church, Lou," she said, "all they worry about is *their spirit life.*" She said those last words in a mocking tone. "I asked Marichelle and Theresa did they want to come over and play some poker with me last Wednesday night after prayer meeting let out, and I didn't say one word about drinking or smoking or nothing like that. Didn't say strip poker neither, just plain old poker. Would have been some of that Christian fellowship Montgomery's always harping on. And you know what Theresa said?"

"What?"

"First she looked at me in this high-and-mighty way, and then she said, 'I'd rather have a rattlesnake in my house than a pack of playing cards.' Can you believe it, Lou? I was just trying to make myself some friends in the church!"

I could believe it. Lots of folks figured playing cards was the first step toward gambling. "Well," I said, "I guess y'all could've played Scrabble or checkers."

Jeanette snorted. "The point is, Lou, I didn't *want* to play Scrabble or checkers. I wanted to play poker. Is it wrong to play poker?!"

"I don't know," I answered truthfully.

" 'Course it ain't," she huffed, rolling her eyes at me and flopping straddle-legged back down onto the chair. She sighed and turned her head in the other direction, fiddling with the radio until 96 Rock blasted out.

I crouched there still as a mouse, listening to the Eagles singing "Hotel California," and staring at Jeanette's glistening shoulders. "Take care, Jeannie," I whispered finally as I rose from my cramped position to go.

Driving along to Dr. Livesay's office, I wondered if Jeanette's earlier behavior had been only good intentions mixed with good acting. Maybe when she'd really got out into the waters, walking with Jesus, it had proved to be too much for her.

But then, driving across the dam, I remembered an encouraging conversation between Mrs. Peggy Briscoe and Imo while we were shopping at the Red Dot. It was a couple of weeks before Jeanette's wedding.

"Jeanette sure don't look like no preacher's wife I ever saw," Mrs. Briscoe said. She'd always been a meddler.

Imo didn't take offense, however. She just fastened Mrs. Briscoe with this look and said, "Peggy, God looks on the inside of a person." To which Mrs. Briscoe said, "Now, Imogene, dear, I'm fully aware that God looks on the inside, but I said to Glennis Cobb last week, I said, 'Glennis, there are some things that are proper decency. That girl ought to . . .'"

"You take care now, Peggy," Imo said as

she wheeled away midsentence.

Imo liked to remind folks of the fact that Jeanette had a rough life up until they adopted her, and that she was still a work in progress. "A pilgrim on a journey," she'd say, "like we all are."

Eight

❧

Possum and Taters
Imo

It was early, before daylight on Thursday morning, when Imo heard the phone ringing. She ran to the house from the back steps where she'd been shucking her garden boots. Breathless, wondering who would call at this hour, she picked up the receiver.

"Hello?" she said.

"Well, hello, my dear," a wobbly voice said. "I'm bringing supper to you-all this evening."

"What?" Imo was startled. "Who is this?" Then it dawned on her. "Oh, hello, Aunt Fannie. It's 6:02 in the morning."

"I declare, I certainly am getting a jump start on my day, aren't I?! I got us a possum, freshly dressed yestiddy evenin'.

Warshed him real good and had him soaking in clean water overnight in the icebox."

"What?"

"The possum, honey child. For possum and taters, what else? What I'm bringing you-all for supper tonight."

"Oh, you don't have to do that," Imo said quickly.

"Well, I want to. I'm going to stay and eat with you, too. We haven't had us a good visit since Easter Sunday."

Being the oldest living member of the family had its advantages. You couldn't say no to Aunt Fannie. She would get herself a notion and that was just the way it was going to be.

Aunt Fannie seemed to Imogene to be almost a caricature of herself — with her old-fashioned dresses, petticoats, and button-up boots. She lived in an ancient shack out in the pinewoods of Flinchum's Holler on the other side of Euharlee. Still independent, she didn't cotton much to coddling or to modern changes. Though she did permit herself the luxuries of a telephone and a car, she had no TV, no indoor bathroom and no washer and dryer.

Aunt Fannie lived all alone. It was because of this, and because of being without the outside influence of the television and newspaper that Aunt Fannie had a warped sense of how the world worked nowadays. Imo could no more tell her that they didn't eat possum than she could tell her that women were expected to wear slacks in public now.

"It will be wonderful to see you," Imo said.

Along about four o'clock, Aunt Fannie's car came zipping down the drive and careened to a stop near the well house.

"Whoa, Nellie!" she exclaimed as she eased the door open and the dust settled around her 1969 Dodge Dart. "This old jalopy sure can get away from me sometimes!"

Imo was at the barn with Lou, putting out saucers of milk for Inez and her kittens.

"Come here and tote this critter up to the house for me, girl," Aunt Fannie ordered, holding out a lump in a croker sack.

Lou crept over toward Aunt Fannie, her face white as a sheet.

"Figgered I'd come early and just cook him here. That way he'll be nice and hot when we commence to eatin'. Brought half a dozen sweet taters to bake alongside him, too. I 'spect you-all got a bakin' pan big enough?"

"Yes, ma'am," said Lou, holding the croker sack at arm's length.

Aunt Fannie chuckled. "Don't you worry none, honey child. He didn't come off'n the road. My neighbor, Claude Flannagan, went possum hunting last week, and his dogs tracked this here feller. Scared him up a tree. Then old Claude, he shimmied up that tree hisself and got him in the bag. He give it to me and I been feeding him bread and buttermilk for to fatten him up."

Lou looked like she was fixing to get sick.

"Here, I'll tote it on in," Imo said, and Lou gratefully put the sack in her hands.

"Where's Lemuel?" Aunt Fannie asked, squinting in the sun, and smoothing the seat of her black skirt. Her calves looked like toothpicks sticking up from her boots.

"He's in the house reading," Imo said.

"Didn't you tell him I was coming?"

"Yes, yes, of course I did."

"Why ain't he out here, then?"

Imo shrugged, the possum getting heavy in her hands. "I imagine he thought you'd be arriving closer to suppertime."

Aunt Fannie sighed. "Well, run on in the

house and fetch him. I need for him to take a gander under here." She waved a basket of sweet potatoes toward the Dodge's hood streaked with black pecan tree sap along its power bulges.

Imo headed for the house. It was one thing to be old and venerated and have people do for you out of respect, and quite another to boss folks around. In a flash of blinding insight she married Aunt Fannie off to Toby Outz. What a great couple they'd make! She had half a mind to send Aunt Fannie by the mill with some leftover possum.

Imogene plopped the bag of possum into the kitchen sink. "Yoo-hoo! Lemuel! Your aunt Fannie's here!"

He appeared almost instantly. "The old gal's here, eh?" His eyes twinkled.

"She wasn't joking about the possum, either," Imo said. "You should have seen Lou's face!"

He chuckled and shook his head.

"She's waiting," Imo warned, "so you'd better hop to it."

She stood at the window gazing upon the spectacle of Lemuel raising the hood of the Dodge Dart. He nodded as Aunt Fannie gesticulated wildly, explaining something to him. Imo had heard the car story plenty of times; the original engine in Aunt Fannie's car had blown up in the mid-70s, and she had hired her nephew Randy, who worked at Skelton's Garage, to put a new one in. He dropped in a V8, transforming the Dodge into a muscle car, and now Aunt Fannie zipped around greater Euharlee in fits and bursts, rather like a person in the saddle of a very spirited stallion.

By suppertime, the whole house was permeated with the gamey smell of roasted opossum, and Imo threw open the kitchen window before they were seated at the table.

Lemuel returned thanks and helped his plate to a glistening mound of meat. "Let's dig in!"

At length Imo began to swill tea. She nibbled loaf bread and butter, eyeing her grease-laden plate suspiciously.

"Pass me some more of that delicious concoction," Lemuel said to her.

Aunt Fannie was beaming with pride. "What's the matter with you, girl?" She turned suddenly to Lou. "You ain't even et a bite of your first serving yet."

Lou offered a weak smile. "I'm basically a vegetarian."

"What?!"

"A vegetarian. You know, I don't eat meat."

"Don't eat meat? Why, that's unchristian! God made animals for our nourishment. You cain't get enough protein if you don't eat meat."

"Actually," Lou said, "you can. I eat tofu, and peanut butter, and beans and rice, and cheese and eggs."

Aunt Fannie turned to Imo. "Imogene Peddigrew! You don't mean to tell me you let this girl be a vege-, whatever it is."

To tell the truth, at the moment, Imo was thinking of becoming a vegetarian herself. "She's a healthy girl," she said simply.

"Hmph!" Aunt Fannie crossed her arms. "Why, when I was growing up, you can believe I ate every morsel my dear mama put on our table. I'd have no more turned my nose up at a good possum than I'd have taken the Lord's name in vain."

"Loutishie is a good girl, Aunt Fannie," Imo said, and she looked to Lemuel for support.

"Yes, yes. She's a good girl," he said.

Aunt Fannie sat ramrod straight. "Well, you'd better eat them taters then, girl. Possum flavored 'em up mighty good."

Loutishie forked up a chunk of sweet potato, glistening with opossum grease, and her pleading eyes found Imo's. Imo waited until Aunt Fannie was intent on her meal and she nodded meaningfully at the napkin in her own lap. A napkin bulging with forkfuls of possum meat and potatoes. Lou followed suit, swiftly depositing the potato in her napkin while pantomiming chewing and swallowing.

Lemuel remained intent on his meal, releasing a passionate "mmm mmm mmm" periodically while Imogene devoted herself to instigating conversation. "We've got a fairly new litter of kittens," she said. "Poor old Inez. Has six keeping her busy. Reckon we'll have to tack up a Free Kittens notice at Dr. Livesay's office, or put them in a pasteboard box outside the Wal-Mart in Cartersville."

"I thought we would keep them." Loutishie's voice was a thin wail. "Two of them at least. *Please?*"

"Oh, sugar foot," Imo said, "I just don't know about two more critters . . ."

"Well, I'll be proud to tote 'em all home with me today," Aunt Fannie said. "Tell you the truth, it gets purty lonely out there in my neck of the woods."

"Uh, uh, uh," Lou stuttered, her eyes darting about helplessly. "They're really not old enough to leave Inez yet." She looked down at her plate, blushing from the lie.

Imo rose and went to the kitchen to slip her bulging napkin in the trash. "Alrighty," she sang out. "Time for dessert. Who wants coffee with their pie?"

Aunt Fannie and Lemuel both said yes, and Imo nodded at Lou. "I need help in here, Loutishie dear." Lou scurried to the kitchen, dumping her opossum before she measured out the coffee.

A long, low belch rumbled from Aunt Fannie's lips. "So that's your only advice about my car, sonny boy?" she was speaking to Lemuel. "That I oughter start it up in second gear?"

"Mm-hm," he answered, "thataway it won't accelerate quite so fast on you. Could also put some fatter tires on the back."

Imo supposed that this was in reference to the way Aunt Fannie always scratched out, slinging gravel whenever she took off. "I can hardly believe you're still driving!" Imo exclaimed, setting pie at the old lady's elbow and removing the pan of possum and taters to the kitchen. "I sure hope I'm as spry as you are when I get to be your age. If I *get* to my nineties!"

"Oh, I imagine you will," Aunt Fannie

said. "Healthy as you are." Then she said that Imo's chess pie was the best she'd ever put in her mouth and Imo found herself relaxing a bit, actually enjoying the company.

After a spell, Aunt Fannie turned to Lemuel. "It surely is a blessing to be independent. You back to driving yet, sonny boy?"

"Nope," he said, frowning.

"You *still* carrying him around everywhere, Imogene?" Aunt Fannie asked.

"Yes, as a matter of fact I am. I —"

Aunt Fannie cut in. "Busy as you stay, Lemuel, I bet you're wearing your poor wife out!"

"Well, I —"

"That's a crying shame! Let me dwell on this a spell and I'll figger us out a solution."

There was a quiet moment as everyone finished their pie. At last Aunt Fannie drained her coffee, let out another belch, patted her chest, and turned to Lemuel. "What you need is to move back to the parsonage," she said. "Could walk just about everywhere you need and you wouldn't be such a burden on Imogene here."

"Now, that's what I told Imo I had a

mind to do!" Lemuel practically jumped out of his seat.

Lou's mouth dropped open. Her fork clattered against her saucer.

"A man needs his independence," Aunt Fannie said. "I'll tell you something else, a man has got to keep busy." She leaned toward Lemuel, dotting her words with her spoon. "When your Uncle Cleve was alive, he couldn't tolerate bein' at my mercy. You remember, Lemuel, when he fell off'n his tractor and broke both his laigs? Had to sit at the house for near six months? Like to have kilt the man. Laying up in bed or on the couch, waiting on me to do for him or help him get around. I thought to myself: This man is going to die if he don't get well. I still remember how angry he got whenever I wouldn't drop everything and play a game of checkers with him. Or drive him into town."

"I don't mind one little bit dropping everything to haul Lemuel around," Imo said, taking a weak stand while avoiding Lou's furious eyes.

"Well, other thing is," Lem said, turning to Aunt Fannie, "we could save so much gasoline by living in town."

"You're right on that, sonny boy!" Aunt Fannie slapped her thigh. "Living in town would save piles of money!"

"But still, there's Hope Haven, the old folks' home, and the hospital in Rome that are far away from downtown Euharlee," Imo said, searching her brain desperately.

"We'll work us out a reg'lar schedule," Aunt Fannie crowed, "and I'll swing by the parsonage and carry him to those places in my Dart!"

"May I please be excused?" Lou asked in a strained voice.

Imo nodded.

Aunt Fannie sighed and shook her head. Very solemnly she said, "That beautiful old parsonage is going to seed." She looked Imogene dead in the eye. "Squirrels running around like they own the place. I said to Roy Williams last week, I said, 'Roy, the parsonage is such a purty old place. Almost a historical monument. If only it had folks living in it.' "

Lemuel turned at last to Imo. "Imogene, love," he said softly. "You thought any more about what we discussed when we were at the lake?"

Aunt Fannie looked at Imo pointedly and Imo's stomach contracted. She began to think out loud. "Well . . . I . . . I . . . I've just been so busy, I haven't done too much thinking, and I need, I need some more time. But let me say this, I don't mind driving you atall, Lemuel." She put her elbows on the table and forced a big smile. "We'll make it a habit to run by the parsonage every time we're at Calvary. We'll air the place out. Open the windows, run the water . . ."

She waited.

Lemuel rubbed his chin. "Well," he said, in a voice Imo couldn't read, "I reckon you could have a little bit more time to ponder."

Imo smiled triumphantly.

Aunt Fannie frowned. "Well," she said, "seems to me somebody *livin'* there would be a heap better. Such a purty old place."

Imo tasted the lingering bitterness of coffee on the back of her tongue.

It was late that evening and the glow from a full moon bathed the landscape in an amber light. "What'cha doin'?" asked Lou, standing at the edge of the garden and peering in at Imo, who was kneeling between two squash vines. "Upchucking your supper?"

"No, dear," said Imo, smiling for the first time since supper, noting Bingo's fur sticking up in wet clumps around his neck and Lou's hair hanging in long damp strings. "You two been swimming?"

Lou nodded. "We went down to the bottoms. For thinking."

"I've been doing lots of thinking myself," Imo said. "Was out here fixing to pray."

"I'll leave you be then."

"No, no, no, dear. Misery loves company."

"I'm never leaving this place," Lou said as she crept gingerly along the row and hunkered down beside Imo.

"Never say never, Lou. None of us can see the future."

"Don't say that!" Lou whined.

"Well, sugar foot, I'm just trying to deal with life the best I know how."

"You don't want to leave here, either, do you?"

" 'Course not, child. You especially know it would be a hard thing for me to ever leave this place." She glanced over at Lou's face and reached out to stroke her cheek. "My whole life I've spent here, and sometimes this land feels like it's a part of me. Like my skin almost."

"Yes! That's it exactly! We just can't go, Imo." Lou drew up two palmfuls of crumbly dirt and squeezed them hard until they trickled back to the ground through her fingers.

"But, the truth is, darlin', I do want the

man to slow down a bit. *I want to slow down, too.*" Imo smoothed a damp tendril of hair off Lou's cheek. "Listen, I'm carrying Lem to Dr. Perkins tomorrow, and if Dr. Perkins says he can drive again, like I'm praying he will, then maybe this notion of his to move will just fall by the wayside. No use us borrowing sorrow from tomorrow."

Lou studied Imo for a moment. "Pray hard," she whispered as she rose and sailed out of the garden. "Pray really, really hard."

Alone, Imo first lifted her eyes to the fiery orange ball of the moon. Such a comforting and familiar object, suspended up there in the heavens by God Almighty Himself. Surely what she was going to ask now paled in comparison to making sure the moon reflected the sun's light and that it went where it was supposed to every night.

She sunk her chin to her chest, rounded her shoulders in a humble posture, and placed her palms together the way she had as a child when she said bedtime prayers. "Lord," she began, her voice a plaintive sound above the buzz of the cicadas, "You know I've been asking You to slow this man down. And You sure enough did slow him down, so I have to say thank You first of all. But Lord, You sped me up! And I am plumb wore out from toting Your servant, Lemuel Peddigrew, around.

"But, now, listen, I'm happy to do it if it means he won't ask me to move to the parsonage! You know he's still entertaining ideas of moving back to the parsonage, and You know he won't quit preaching and tending to the sick and bereaved, either. You also know how I love this land; what this piece of Your earth means to me. And it means even more to Loutishie. It's all she's got left of her Uncle Silas. So, Father, would You *please*, please let Dr. Perkins pronounce him able to drive tomorrow so that our problems are solved. In Your son Jesus' name I pray, Amen."

Imogene sat expectantly and fearfully on the edge of a green Naugahyde sofa in Dr. Perkins's office. In spite of her unceasing supplications to the Lord Almighty, she felt no more full of faith than she did when Aunt Fannie had uttered the terrible words.

She felt just like a wave, her faith rising and then falling every few minutes. Today, any minute, her fate would be determined.

He'd been back there in the examining room for forty-five minutes. That could be bad or good. Perhaps they were just visiting at this point — shooting the breeze about old times.

Please Lord, please Lord, she pled silently as she looked out the window, watching a sparrow hopping along, his russet-colored breast plump with insects. For a moment Imo wished she were a bird. An oblivious creature who could fly off at a moment's inspiration.

Checking her watch, she drew a deep breath. After a bit she fished her checkbook out and balanced it, organized the coupons in a side pocket of her purse, and gathered up the loose change on the bottom. She rearranged her driver's license, library card, and Social Security card.

By the time she heard the squeak of a door opening down the hallway, Imo's heart was beating so hard her chest shuddered. Dr. Perkins led Lemuel toward her and she pasted a smile onto her face, rising and fumbling with her purse handles.

"Pretty day we've got out there, huh?" Dr. Perkins said. She looked up to nod, and she admired his head full of wavy white hair and the tiny silver spectacles which sat in front of deep blue eyes; eyes which seemed to peer right into a person's very soul.

"I've placed an order for a shoe stretcher," he continued. "One that comes with a bunion component."

"A bunion component?" she said stupidly.

"Yes, indeed. Lots of my patients swear by them. Be here in several weeks and you can stretch all the Reverend's shoes to accommodate those bunions of his."

Imo cast an inquisitive look at Lemuel's face. She could read nothing. "Sure make walking a lot easier," he said.

"Walking?" Imo said, her mind jumping in several directions at once.

"Certainly will be an improvement in mobility," said Dr. Perkins.

Imogene stood up. Pointedly she dug for her car keys, jangling them in her hand a bit. "Well," she said, *"reckon I'd better drive you on back home, Lemuel.* Thank you kindly, Dr. Perkins. I'm sure the shoe stretcher will be a wonderful thing." She turned on her heel.

As she reached the front door and laid a hand on the cut-glass knob, Dr. Perkins called out, "Why don't you let the old boy here drive home."

"He can drive?!"

"He can drive. Good day to you both."

"He can drive!" Imo practically shouted. Forsaking all modesty, she ran to kiss Lemuel a loud *smack* on his cheek and pressed the keys to the Impala in his hand. Matter-of-factly, as though he'd expected no less, he strode purposely down the walkway to the car and opened the driver's door. She frolicked across the gravel lot, tossed her handbag through the open window to the backseat, sat herself down in the passenger seat, and slammed the door.

She did not utter a word when he ran over the curb as they were pulling onto the street. Instead, she laughed out loud. She leaned back and closed her eyes to enjoy the ride.

In July temperatures soared past the hundred-degree mark, forcing folks to do their gardening in the early hours of the morning, before the sun was at its fiercest, or else late in the afternoon when it was a sinking orange ball. Loutishie took to rising early and working with Imogene before she and the Reverend left on their rounds.

The feel of the soil was like therapy to

them and they never allowed themselves to talk of how close they'd come to leaving the farm.

One morning, as they were in the middle of plucking armloads of pink-blushed beefsteak tomatoes and carrying them to the picnic table in the shade for ripening, Imo paused a moment to look at her wrist.

"Oh my." She drew in a little surprised gasp of breath. "It's time to get on back in the house and fix Lem's breakfast and his tonic. Then we'll commence our plan for the day. I swannee, hon, it's always something."

"You wish you could just stay out here and work, huh?" said Lou. "And just eat a bowl of cornflakes when you took a notion?"

"That doesn't sound so bad." Imo smiled.

"You ever wish you were still single?" Lou asked.

Taken aback, Imo fumbled with her thoughts. "Look at me! Spoutin' off at the mouth like I haven't got a brain in my head!" She chuckled unconvincingly. "I didn't mean that. Reckon my brain's just not awake good yet."

As a matter of fact, she supposed she really had meant what she'd said, and those were thoughts she should press down after her deal with God! Plus, it was nothing she should ever let on to a seventeen-year-old girl. What did that teach the child about love, marriage, commitment, and selfless-ness?

Imogene had a sudden disheartening feeling of letting God down with her negative words and thoughts. Here she had been given what she'd asked for, and these ugly thoughts were most likely canceling it all out.

Lou cocked her head and studied Imo for a moment. "How 'bout I go fix the tonic and the biscuits this morning? You keep working out here a bit longer."

"Dear child," Imo said, "it's my row to hoe. You're young and you don't need to have to worry about things like this. Your day will come before you know it."

Lou nodded, rolling up her shirtsleeves. She took a swallow of ice water from a plastic milk jug and handed it to Imo. "Cucumbers need picking bad," she said, nodding at the far corner of the garden.

"Yes indeed," said Imo. "Now, that's one thing I need to stay on top of, isn't it? You don't harvest them every couple of days and they go to seed."

"I'll make sure to gather them this

morning," Lou said. "I don't have to be at Dr. Livesay's till eleven. I'll also pick the rest of the tomatoes down at the end."

Imo looked at the splattering of freckles across Lou's nose. She was such a good girl. "Thanks for your help, sugar foot," Imo said robustly. "I hope your day's good. I know I'll have a nice time with my Lemuel today. That new shoe stretcher Dr. Perkins ordered is in and it's a literal miracle!"

"It is?"

"Yes, indeed! Worth its weight in gold. I don't know how we ever managed without it."

Imo glanced across the back pasture, at the sky growing brighter with dawn, her face beatific at the memory of Lemuel's satisfied smile when he slid his feet into his newly reshaped wingtips.

Nine

❦

Betrayal
Lou

One sunny afternoon in July I was standing in the waiting room at Dr. Livesay's veterinarian office holding the leash of a German shepherd mix named Rex. His owner had called and was on his way to pick the massive dog up.

I was feeding him one of the bone-shaped dog treats from a plastic bucket marked "Good Patients" when Wanda Parnell walked in with her fussy little shih tzu, Bitsy. The moment Rex caught sight of Bitsy, with all those red bows stuck on everywhere and her tiny toenails clattering on the linoleum, the dog biscuit dropped to the floor and the fur on the back of his spine stood up like a mohawk. I reckoned

265

he might gobble the tiny dog up before she had her appointment, so I leaned my weight back into my heels and hung on to him for dear life.

"Howdy, Lou," Wanda said in that breathy singsong voice of hers. "Looks like you got your hands full." She giggled and her wrist full of skinny gold bracelets tinkled as she set a red handbag down on the counter.

I said hello, eyeing her clingy gingham print blouse and barely there miniskirt that showed off legs tan as a pecan shell. Today Wanda was a dead ringer for Dolly Parton; lots of makeup, big bosoms lifted high, and blond hair piled atop her head.

"You enjoying your summer job here, hon?" Wanda asked as soon as she signed Bitsy in.

"I love it," I said, yanking Rex over toward a vinyl bench in the front window so that I could sit down and brace myself to pull even harder against his leash. He was salivating like crazy, quivering with desire to chomp Bitsy, and straining me so hard my neck muscles ached.

"Well, good, hon. You must be in heaven then, because Jeanette tells me you've got yourself a boyfriend. That Hank Dollar is just precious!" Wanda winked at me. "If I was thirty years younger, I believe I'd take a shine to him myself."

I nodded, stroking the fur over Rex's ribs, relieved that he was finally settling down a bit.

"I imagine Imogene's just crazy over him," Wanda said. She walked over to a display of leashes. "Speaking of Imogene, I'm worried about her."

"You are?"

"I surely am. Did her a wash and set Friday week and she like to wore my ear out." Wanda bent to pick Bitsy up, cradled her against her bosom, and sat down directly across from me and Rex. She tilted her head and looked directly into my face, all serious like.

"Imogene said there's talk about y'all moving to the old parsonage." Wanda paused, shaking her head in an exaggerated way. "She was what I call beside herself."

"Well," I replied, "that was a thought a long while back. But the Reverend's driving again, you know."

We sat quietly for a minute or so while I read a poster on heartworms for the jillionth time.

"Well," Wanda said finally, shaking her head. "All I know is it's still weighing

267

heavy on the poor woman's heart."

The words left me feeling like the sky had just darkened and rain was pouring down onto my parade. Was there something brewing I didn't know about?

"Oh, Lord a mercy, Lou. I didn't mean to get you upset." Wanda leaned forward to pat my knee.

I listened to a dog howling way back in the kennel area, and then another and another starting to bark along to form a shrill chorus. I stroked Rex's warm back till at last a blue van pulled up and Rex's owner climbed out. I jumped to my feet, hastening out to the parking lot to meet him.

Back at the kennels I measured out dog kibbles into a stack of thick plastic bowls and I told myself over and over, "We can't be moving, we can't be moving. I'll never move downtown." I backed Imo into a corner when I got home.

"Oh Lou dear," she said, taking a deep breath, licking her lips, and hunching forward over the crossword puzzle she'd been working, "I was just venting to Wanda about the fact that sometimes the Reverend still talks about *wanting* to move there." After a little spell she raised up, caught my eye, and added, "Now, don't you go worrying yourself one little bit about it, sugar foot." She smiled assuredly. "I'm sure we'll never actually have to do it."

I guess I really wanted to believe Imo because by the end of July those words from between Wanda's big red lips seemed like only a bad dream.

Things were good; I was sublimely happy working at Dr. Livesay's office, and even more so when Hank and I hung out together. Our favorite thing to do was paddle an old johnboat out into the placid waters of the Etowah, jump in for a swim, then crawl up onto the banks while we dried in the hot summer sun. Hank was a good bowler, and I was not, which didn't seem to matter at all. We went to the movies and sat on the back row to cuddle and kiss.

There was no more mention of Jeanette's headaches, or her fainting spells, either, and I put that unpleasantness out of my thoughts as well.

And Imo seemed happy. This was her season. Her season to enjoy the bountiful fruits of her labors. Our table was laden with squash, okra, snap beans, sweet corn, butterbeans, bell pepper, tomatoes, and our most plenteous vegetable of all, cucumbers! We ate a ton of those things, and to Imo's delight there were plenty to pickle. She made sweet pickles, bread-and-butter pickles, dill pickles, and sweet mustard pickles. She was so proud of the shelves in the pantry lined with rows and rows of green-filled Mason jars.

Our second most plenteous crop was tomatoes. We had so many Imo had finally begun toting bushel baskets to give away just about everywhere she and the Reverend went: the post office, the library, the shut-ins, the filling station.

One sweltering Wednesday afternoon when the squirrels moved languidly on the branches of the pecan tree and Bingo draped himself like an inanimate object in the shadows, Imo dipped her head at four pasteboard boxes full of bright red beefsteak tomatoes. "Help me get these into the pickup, Lou?"

"Yessum," I said, figuring she was planning to pass them out to the folks at Calvary's prayer meeting.

After supper the three of us climbed into the truck, the Reverend carrying his tall glass of iced tea along on account of how stifling it still was even at seven.

"Reckon we'll get rain anytime soon?" Imo asked as she situated herself in the center of the cab. "I never thought I'd say it after our wet spring, but things are just drying up around here. Would surely cool us off if it would rain."

"They say these dry days are just going to keep on," the Reverend answered, settling the tea between his legs and fastening his seat belt. "How're things looking down at the bottoms, Lou?" he asked me as we passed the mailbox.

I was startled by this question. Why should he care? He hardly ever went anywhere on the farm other than the house. Only occasionally would he make a trip out past the barn to stargaze, and never, to my knowledge, had he traipsed through the woods. I scratched my head trying to remember how many times he'd actually been down to the river bottoms. Only twice I could recall in the whole two years he'd lived there.

I had to ponder things a moment before I answered. The fact that our part of the Etowah was below the dam meant that we didn't experience the same drastic effects from the long drought as those above the dam, but the fact I couldn't ignore was that now many of the boulders which once were totally submerged by the water stuck up like rocky vertebrae down the river's back.

The weeds growing beside the dirt to the bottoms were dry and spiky, the red clay bank along the river cracked on top like a pound cake. Leaves on the hardwoods leaning out over the water were wispy and sun-bleached. "It's dry down there all right," I said.

"Well, I reckon we'll just have to pray us down some rain tonight at prayer meeting." He smiled.

"That's a fine idea," Imo said, touching his sleeve.

I watched her turn her head then and smile at him tenderly. He took his right hand off the steering wheel and placed it on her knee. They sure seemed happy. To look at them, you would think they'd been married for fifty years.

As we pulled onto the highway I was thinking about my buddy Tara. I was really looking forward to seeing her at prayer meeting. Much as I loved her and enjoyed spending time with her, lately the desire to spend all my free moments with Hank Dollar was more potent, and so I planned to catch up with Tara at prayer meeting, enjoy some soul-satisfying girl talk.

We rode along, the Reverend and Imo chatting away about this and that. At the four-way stop where Cedar Street intersected the highway, the Reverend slowed and put his blinker on.

"'Bout there," said Imo happily. "I surely do hope Odessa's coming tonight. I've got a little article on making watermelon molasses I found in the *Market Bulletin*." She patted her purse on the seat between us.

"Look out!" I cried suddenly, flinching as the Reverend turned much too sharply, propelling us over the shoulder of the road.

My head flew forward at the impact of the front bumper and the far side of the ditch.

"Lemuel!" Imo hollered loudly in a delayed reaction after he'd cut the engine.

Our back wheels spun in midair as the truck was tilted at a thirty-degree angle. This caused all three of us to brace ourselves against the forward pull.

"Well, I be dog," the Reverend said at last, shaking his head.

"What happened?" Imo asked. "Is everyone okay? Lou?"

"I'm okay," I said.

"Lemuel?" she asked.

"I reckon," he said softly under his breath, lifting his glasses and rubbing his eyes.

"What happened?" Imo asked again.

"Near as I can figure it's the steering column," he said in a befuddled voice. I stared hard at him.

"We'd best get on out, Lem," Imo told him. "I've heard of vehicles blowing up after a crash."

The Reverend made a pshawing sound. "Gas tank's in the back," he said.

"Still, we'd better hop on out." Imo eased her door open and set one tentative canvas Ked into the ditch. "C'mon, Lou," she said, "least the ditch is dry."

"Why, lookahere," the Reverend said, still sitting in the driver's seat, "it's Jack and Maudine." He swept an arm out the window at a silver Buick which had pulled to the side of the road. "Had us a little fender bender," he called to them. "No one's hurt, praise the Lord."

Maudine nodded. "We'll ride on to the church and call Sheriff Bentley. He can call Johnny." Johnny Swain was the sheriff's brother-in-law and he owned a wrecker service called Here's Johnny.

Imo and I stood in the ditch waiting. "This had nothing to do with the steering column," I finally whispered to Imo.

"I know, dear," Imo whispered back through her teeth, one eye on the Reverend. "I don't know what happened.

Maybe he blanked out or nodded off for a bit. Maybe he just can't see good anymore."

"It's tore up," I said, pointing at the front end of the truck.

"Sheriff Bentley will take care of it when he gets here."

"We'll be late for prayer meeting," I said.

"They'll have to wait on the preacher, now won't they?" Imo made a lame little smile.

Sheriff Bentley arrived in his official patrol car, the blue light revolving in an officious manner. He pulled off the road, cut the engine, and eyed the scene before he swaggered to the driver's door, bent and spoke a few words to the Reverend. Then he swung the door open, hooked his arm through the Reverend's and hauled him out. I saw a huge wet spot on the Reverend's crotch and at first I thought he'd peed himself, then I remembered the iced tea.

"So, you say you were making a right-hand turn from the highway and your steering column did what?" the sheriff was asking.

The Reverend just shook his head, trying to cover the wet spot on his pants with his hands. He looked deflated, like half the air had been let out of him.

The sheriff radioed his brother-in-law, then waved the three of us into the patrol car. "I'll carry you on to Calvary," he said, pulling out onto the road. "Looks like you won't be too late."

"Wait!" Imo threw up her hands. "My tomatoes!"

Sheriff Bentley slowed to a stop and Imo and I dashed back to the truck bed. On tiptoe to peer over the tailgate, I saw that the tomatoes were now in a great big jumble, their skins split and juice splattered everywhere.

"Ohhhh my stars," came Imo's plaintive moan. "Just leave them be, Lou dear."

That following Friday, which would prove to be one of the worst days of my life, began happily enough; me sitting on the front porch with a lap full of newspapers piled high with just picked half-runner beans.

Stringing beans didn't bother me one bit since I knew what we'd be having for supper: fresh beans, sweet corn on the cob, humongous hot-off-the-vine Brandywine tomatoes, fried chicken and tender, flaky buttermilk biscuits. Perhaps some blackberry cobbler for dessert.

The Reverend was sitting in the kitchen working on his sermon, Imo was snipping the fuzzy rocket-shaped okra pods in the garden, and Bingo was licking bacon drippings from a skillet on the steps and then rolling delightedly in the dewy grass. I peered out at the wash of morning sun as it was slowly dissolving into the light of midmorning across the back pasture.

We weren't dwelling on the Reverend's wreck. His truck was back in the shop getting a new front end, and Imo was letting him drive the Impala on all their errands. If she'd said it once, she'd said it a thousand times — "Thank the blessed Lord in heaven no one was hurt" — and she'd shake her head and smile like we'd just won the lottery.

Today I was looking forward to my four hours at Dr. Livesay's and my paycheck. Hank was getting paid, too. He worked for his daddy, flying a battered silver biplane to crop-dust the cotton fields against boll weevils. We were planning a celebration: a late movie in Rome, Georgia, followed by a midnight walk down the old logging road to the swamp, then right through the swamp on account of the long drought, to a nice, high clearing. This was our favorite place to spread out Uncle Silas's old army sleeping bag, twine our fingers together, and gaze at the full moon. "I love you, Lou," he'd always say, kissing the inside of my forearm, his warm lips and rough whiskers sending shivers up my spine till I almost fainted in pleasure.

This is what I was daydreaming about when the phone rang.

"I'll get it!" hollered the Reverend. Through the open window I could hear his "yell-o," then one short "you got him," and some "mmm hmms" and nothing more for the longest time until I heard him utter a gruff "good-bye" followed by the click of the receiver.

I swear I felt something like a shroud descending over us then. I remember wondering who had died as I sat there mechanically stringing beans and waiting. I didn't know what I was waiting for, I only knew that it was no good.

The Reverend stepped out onto the porch and scanned the backyard for Imo. Spotting her in the garden, he went slowly down the steps and across the grass.

I watched them talking for a long time, his hands moving in animated gestures and her head shaking, then nodding. I couldn't make out their faces from that far to read grief or shock or something terrible.

Cicadas began their continuous buzz from the acuba bushes and Bingo barked at a small critter moving in the weeds at the mailbox. *Get ready, Lou,* I told myself when I saw Imo trudging back toward the house.

She climbed the steps, her mouth pressed into a grim line. I worked furiously on my pile of string beans.

Imo smelled of bitter marigolds as she stepped closer to me. "Lou," she said, twisting the hem of her work shirt. "I'm real sorry to have to tell you this, but we're going to move into town. Real soon. They've taken Lem's license away. I don't want this as much as you don't want it, but the time seems to have come."

I sat there, still not looking at her, aware of a red-hot fury eclipsing my rational thoughts. Imo patted my wrist but I would not meet her eyes.

"We'll still have the farm, sugar foot," she pled. "You can come back to visit anytime."

Bingo streaked across the lawn, and a bird warbled from the branches of the pecan tree. I saw the Reverend slumped down on an overturned bucket at the garden's edge.

I remained a statue for several minutes, then folded my newspaper carefully around the beans. I was amazed at how Imo could stand there, so serene. Didn't she feel the world being yanked right out from underneath us?

I laid the newspaper full of beans on the floor, smoothed back my hair, held it in one hand, and took off for the river.

You gave me hope when there was no hope, Imo! I shrieked inside as I ran, *I cannot leave this place. I will not.*

The farm was much more than what was held in by the barbed wire fences, and reasons we could not leave were woven through every fiber of my being. I ran headlong down the trail beside the Etowah and my bare feet felt reasons in the warm red banks that held the water in. I smelled them in the sunlight falling on leaves and I heard them in the long, low hoots of owls calling across the waters, the slap of a beaver's tail on the surface. I could see the reasons in the water itself, in its deep shades of sapphire and jade, in the image of a hawk circling overhead, and the cornstalks stretching proudly skyward in the surrounding fields. I tasted them in the salty tears which stung my cheeks.

Late that evening I sat with Hank in the back row of the theater. I had not unburdened myself to him yet. Maybe I was still numb from the shock, or maybe I was afraid that speaking the words would give them power, make them more real somehow.

Anyway, I knew that words would never be adequate to describe the way I felt. But Hank could tell that something was bothering me and he put an arm around me and held me extra close to him, his other hand reaching over to squeeze mine. I laid my head on his shoulder.

I found this position very comforting, and I let myself sink down into Hank, consciously trying to follow the movie and drown out the echo of Imo's words in my brain.

Toward the end of the movie, I heard the sounds of rain on the roof. A gentle patter at first, then a massive storm with thunder that shook the building. I didn't know whether to laugh or cry. We were desperate for the rain, but I needed that moonlit walk with Hank so bad.

Driving home through the torrential downpour I was still angry. I was scared. I was sad, and I felt betrayed.

We rolled into the brightly lit parking lot of the Dairy Queen and still my struggle seemed such a private thing.

"I think this great rain calls for a banana split!" Hank said, knowing this to be my weakness. "You stay put, Lou babe. We're gonna have us a private party."

Moping in the front seat as Hank ordered the ice cream, I tried to pray, but instead merely saw red like an angry bull. Soon he was back, cradling one glorious banana split and two long spoons. With great ceremony he scooped up a cloud of whipped topping and held it to my mouth. Dutifully I parted my lips, but it tasted like cardboard and I could hardly swallow.

"Lou?" Hank whispered, "what's the matter? You haven't been yourself all evening."

I was so relieved to let it spill out. I told him the whole awful story — about the impending move, Imo's lie, and my fury. My betrayal.

"Aw, Lou," he said, setting the melting banana split onto the dash to hold me close. "She didn't mean to lie to you. Probably just wishful thinking on her part, too."

He was right, I knew, but still I was not at peace, for I had come to realize somehow, during the course of things, that life doesn't always go as a person desires.

Ten

❦

Jealous Bone
Imo

Imo wished she could think of a way to cheer Lou up. She'd tried almost everything since The Big Decision. First there'd been the long, hot month of August, with Lou wearing a continual hangdog expression as she wandered slump-shouldered throughout the old farmhouse, across the fields, and down to the river bottoms. Even starting her senior year at Euharlee High with Hank had not changed things. Then October came and the two kids were inseparable, but still the most notable thing about Lou was her slumped shoulders and her protruding lower lip.

Now, here it was, a cool, overcast Thursday morning during Thanksgiving break from school, the day of the move. Lou shuffled out of her bedroom, dark circles under her eyes, and her hair a ratty tangle. She flopped down on her back on the couch in the den, folded her arms across her chest, and sighed, long and loud.

"I absolutely will not move," she ventured at last.

Imo tensed in the kitchen where she was packing the contents of the freezer into a Styrofoam cooler. She didn't know just what she'd expected from Lou, but this blatantly defiant behavior was not it.

God knows, she'd felt that way herself at first. Her mind went racing back to that fateful morning; "They've taken my license away from me, Imogene sweetheart," Lemuel stated glumly as he trudged between rows of sweet corn to her side.

Startled, Imo cried out, "They can't!"

He nodded. "It's time to move."

Her skin drew up tight and the earth beneath her trembled. Desperately she wanted to stamp her feet on the ground and curse. But somehow, by an act of will, she managed to keep herself together. Holding her breath and gazing heavenward, she breathed a silent prayer: *Lord God Almighty, have mercy on your ser-*

vant. Direct my steps. Not my will, but Yours be done.

Then she heard a voice. A still, small voice, calling to her from inside herself. Actually, it was more like a film of her wedding day, rolling through her mind. "Whither thou goest, I will go," she heard herself saying as she looked into Lemuel's acorn-colored eyes . . . "to love, honor and obey . . . for better or worse."

Did God really just say what she thought He did?!

Really?

But maybe not, she argued with herself. This was actually feeling more like a dream, wasn't it? Yes, like a surreal and hazy dream. Maybe her blood pressure had flown sky-high from the shock and caused a disconnect from reality. Surely, this was all a dream.

She bit her bottom lip hard. "Ouch!" she squawked. No, not a dream. A nightmare was more like it. She kicked a clod of dirt. This, this was her land! She couldn't just up and leave it and move to town.

She could not believe God was telling her to leave the homestead. How could she leave her beautiful garden? And poor Loutishie! She would be absolutely devastated.

Dumbstruck, her heart in her throat, Imo went to the house to tell the girl.

With the next morning came an almost mystical peace. Though Lou had become, as Imo imagined she would, hysterical over the news, Imo also figured that her mad dash down to the river would begin to salve her wounded spirit.

Imo hadn't expected to get over the shock and the indignant anger so quickly herself. It seemed to be a miracle, as now, in a strange sort of way, it felt almost like relief to be leaving. Threats of leaving had been hanging over her head like a lead shoe for what seemed like ages now, and to have some sort of final decision took the constant wondering out.

Perhaps it was that Lemuel's feelings were rubbing off on her. Despite his gloom over losing his license, he seemed almost ecstatic. Come that next morning, Saturday, he'd bounded out of bed early, oblivious to his bodily aches and pains, made a delicious batch of cat-head biscuits, stuffing them with piles of salt-cured country ham.

"This afternoon, I'll have myself a little talk with Lou, Lem," Imo promised him as they sipped coffee together at the kitchen table. "I'm sure she'll come around."

He looked at her with seriousness and said, "I'm going to make sure you're real happy on Cedar Street."

After lunch Imo found Lou sitting in the hayloft of the barn, her arms wrapped around her legs and her chin on her knees.

"Hello, sugar foot," Imo said softly as she climbed the rickety ladder up to the loft.

"Hi," Lou responded, still staring straight ahead with glassy eyes.

Imo settled herself beside the girl in a warm nest of hay, watching dust motes swim in the light from the high window at the front of the barn. She placed a hand on Lou's thin shoulder. "Tell me how you're feeling," she said, letting the words fall all around them.

"Rotten," Lou answered after a long spell. "Sad clear down to my bones."

"Well, of course you're sad. And believe me, Lou, I understand. I was heartbroken, too."

Imo told Lou about the supernatural peace. "Change is hard for all of us, sweetheart," she finished, "but we'll both be stronger over this, and it'll all make sense by and by."

"How do you figure that?" Lou hissed from between clenched teeth. "Just give me one good reason I should want to move to town. I won't move to Cedar Street."

"Well, it's in walking distance to the high school."

"So. I don't care. I'm not going."

"You're not eighteen, honey child. I cannot leave you here. And even if you were old enough, I wouldn't want you staying out here in the sticks by yourself."

Lou shrugged Imo's hand off.

"Let's just make the best of it, dear heart. Please," Imo pled. "Look at the bright side, we're not *selling* the place. It'll stay in the family. We can visit any time our hearts desire, like I said. Come next spring, you better believe I'll still have my garden here. I'll drive out twice a day to see to it if need be."

"That's not the same thing atall," Lou said. "Now is it?"

It seemed unreasonable to insist that it was. Imo searched her brain furiously, and at length she pictured Lou as a young girl, six or so, her face in evening lamplight, enrapt as she sat listening to Imo read from her big Bible storybook. "Lou, dear," she began, "I have this feeling, call it faith, but I just know things will work out for the best."

Lou did not look convinced.

"When I said my vows, I said 'for better or for worse.' I said I'd follow the Reverend wherever he went. And I said all this standing at the altar rail of Calvary. I said it in God's presence. You can surely understand that, can't you?"

Lou wound the ends of her hair around her fingers.

"I have to honor my vows," Imo said, "now don't I?"

Lou's brow wrinkled in thought. She closed her eyes, raised her chin, turned her head, opened her eyes, and looked directly into Imo's soul. "Yep, I guess you do," she said.

Imo paced the hallway of the parsonage that first morning, pausing intermittently to unpack a box of linens and to peer out at the overcast sky. "Ahhh," Lemuel sighed happily as he sank down into a faded green wing chair in the west parlor of the parsonage. Imo paused, searching his face. She would have to say that he looked the happiest she'd seen him in ages.

She herself felt displaced, very closed in. The old farmhouse was a rambling, spacious structure, sprawling haphazardly atop the highest knoll of the upper forty acres, and the parsonage on Cedar Street was a tiny cottage on less than three quarters of an acre, tucked between thick boxwood hedges.

Built in the 1840s, it was a one-story structure in the country Greek Revival style, with whitewashed lapboard siding and surrounded on two sides by a picket fence. There were two little porticos, one along the front and one along the west side. If you entered through the front door, you would find yourself in a central hallway that also doubled as a breezeway. This hall adjoined front rooms, referred to as the east and west parlors.

The parlors had a fireplace apiece, and flooring, walls, and ceilings made of knotty pine. The east parlor was a bedroom for Lou, as well as a formal dining room, and the west parlor was a bedroom for Imo and Lemuel, as well as a sitting room.

A narrow passageway from the west parlor led to a spacious kitchen, lined with old pine cupboards. Along this same side of the house was Martha's treasured perennial flower garden.

Imo stacked half a dozen empty pasteboard boxes in the breezeway and checked her watch. Eleven a.m. Time for a break.

She made her way outside to the flower garden, settled herself on a cement bench, and folded her hands in her lap to rest.

I wish it were spring, she thought. *This whole move would've been hundreds of times cheerier in the spring.* She raised her head to gaze over the leafy expanse of trees between the parsonage and Calvary Baptist. Trees slowly turning to fiery oranges and reds. Fall was such a fragile season, she mused. It seemed that almost the instant the trees turned their breathtaking hues, they began to lose their foliage. The ginkgo leaves would flutter like golden fans to the ground and the maple leaves like red mittens would gather into piles. The branches would turn stark and black against the sky.

Well, maybe it was better to do it now, when the steely grasp of winter was on its way. The old homeplace would be harder to leave in the springtime, heartbreaking in its beauty, dotted with pink flowering dogwoods and fields of daffodils.

The moving had not been physically difficult, as the parsonage was still fully furnished. Besides packing foodstuffs, clothing, books, and the contents of the bathroom, all they'd had to worry about was plugging up mouse holes and securing homes for Dusty Red, Inez, and her kittens. Finally Lou had the bright idea to give all the creatures, except for Bingo, to Hank. Bingo had slunk into the backseat of the Impala and seemed relieved when they did not end up at the vet's office. He was fastened up on the back porch now, watching her through the mesh screen.

She had done her best to play the part of an obedient and cheerful wife this first day, smiling and humming as she swept down cobwebs, and opened up all the doors and windows to air out the dusty, unlived-in smell.

She spent that first late afternoon trying to bolster Lou's spirits. For starters she rustled around in one of Martha's trunks and sprinkled a thousand-piece jigsaw puzzle across the table. Then she put a pot of hot cocoa on to simmer. Reluctantly Lou seated herself and hunted the corner pieces of the puzzle, which was a giant picture of the Eiffel Tower.

"Isn't this exciting, sugar foot?" Imo said. "Our first night here!"

Lou shrugged. "Where's the Reverend?" she asked.

"He went over to the church to get some things ready for Sunday's service."

"When can we go back home? For a visit, I mean."

"Well, turns out I left a few things behind that we'll need. I'm making a list. May have to go as early as tomorrow afternoon."

Lou's face brightened a bit. "I'm taking Bingo with us."

"Well, I know he'll enjoy that," Imo said, glancing at the dog lying at Lou's feet. He looked as bad as Lou, melancholy and uncomfortable. Keeping sagging spirits bolstered was going to be hard. Well, she reassured herself just as quickly, at least Lemuel was happy as a rooster in a henhouse.

By suppertime, Imo had acquainted herself with the kitchen fairly well. She browned porkchops in a skillet and while hunting for a potholder, she discovered an apron hanging on a wooden peg beside the stove. She tugged it down and draped the neck loop over her head. Startled to see that it read KISS THE COOK, she quickly pulled it off to hold it at arm's length, thinking *Martha wore this. Lemuel probably gave it to her one birthday and when he caught her in it he pulled her into his arms and laid a big one on her.*

A feeling of Martha swept over the kitchen and Imo felt an uneasiness in the pit of her stomach. "Ah well," she said aloud to herself, "you really shouldn't let it bother you. Just put it down in the bottom corner of the cupboard there and forget about it.

"It really doesn't bother me a bit," she said to Bingo. "Out of sight, out of mind, as they say."

That night, she dreamed she was standing at the mailbox, thumbing through the day's mail. It was a sunny spring day and the yard of the parsonage was in full and glorious bloom, the scent of roses sweetening the air. A long gleaming black hearse glided to a stop and the window went down. Imo glanced up to meet the driver's eyes. It was Martha.

"I thought you were up in heaven," she said. Martha narrowed her eyes, pointing at Imo's chest. Imo was wearing Martha's KISS THE COOK apron. "On no!" she cried, "I didn't mean to!" She dropped the mail and her hands quickly fumbled with untying the apron's sash. "So, my husband wasn't enough, huh?" Martha whispered. "Now you're even taking over my house and my clothes." "No, no, no!" Imo countered.

"You've got to believe me! I was only . . ." but her words died in a cloud of exhaust from the hearse.

Imo sat bolt upright in bed, clutching the covers. It was still pitch-black dark, so she lay back down till the alarm clock went off.

"Ahhh," Lemuel said as he awoke, stretching languidly, then spooning against Imo's back. He kissed her shoulder.

"Feel good?" she asked him.

"Feel like a million bucks," he said. "Had myself such a lifelike dream I'm surprised I didn't wake up chewing on my pillow." He chuckled.

Imo did not mention her dream, and after a bit, Lem began to nuzzle her neck. "Dreamed about the first time I ever tasted blackberry jam cake," he said, adding "mmmm" and sighing happily at the memory.

"Pardon?"

"Jam cake. Was Martha's grandmother's recipe. Hundred-year-old recipe. I was just courtin' Martha, had gone to her folks' house in Pell City, Alabama, and her grandmother was living with them, and she fixed us a jam cake for dessert. She didn't even have the recipe written down!" He shook his head. "Made it by heart. Must've been twenty-leven different ingredients. Good thing she wrote it down for Martha before she passed away."

He used his hands to roll her over to face him. Pale morning light from the window bathed his face. "Let me tell you something, Imogene, that blackberry jam cake was just about the closest thing to heaven I'd ever put in my mouth." His eyes rolled back in his head in mock ecstasy.

Imo's mind was spinning. She couldn't remember ever making a jam cake, or tasting one, either, and if there was anything other than gardening which spoke to her soul, it was cooking. *I'll find the recipe for that hundred-year-old blackberry jam cake he's crowing about, then I'll make one, too. I'll make Lemuel think he's in heaven.*

Thoughts of this plan helped Imo to put her own uncomfortable dream out of mind as she boiled grits for their breakfast. When she called "Ready!" Lemuel practically sprinted to the table. He was dressed to a tee. Already in his overalls and wingtips. He'd asked no help from Imo.

"Feeling good, huh?" She smiled at him.

"Fit as a fiddle," he said. "Ready to conquer the world. Or at least Euharlee."

"Looks to be a pretty day for conquering

Euharlee, now that those clouds are gone," she said, smiling and setting the cream and sugar on the table. "You planning to work at the church most of the day?"

"I imagine. Be home for lunch, though. Isn't it nice to live right next door to Calvary?"

"Mmmmm," she said noncommittally. It was too early to tell, though Lemuel certainly seemed to be a different man. She hadn't heard a peep out of Lou yet, which was unusual for a girl who used to be the first one up out of bed, who loved the earliest part of day.

It might not be so bad to be here, Imo reasoned. Living in the heart of downtown would certainly be nice in the social department, though no one had dropped by to call on them yet. It looked like she was going to get a good share of alone time. Time she could use to drive to the old homeplace come spring, come gardening time. But now, in the fall and the coming winter, she could spend her time concentrating on being the Garden Club president, on social events, and on cooking. She was still burning with curiosity and she pictured herself finding the jam cake recipe that very morning, gathering the ingredients, cooking it up, and sliding it from the oven, nice and hot.

Lemuel left and rustling noises came from the east parlor, Lou's bedroom. At this, Bingo rose with hopeful eyes and eased out from underneath the table. He scampered to her door, his tail wagging like crazy. *Thump! Thump! Thump!* went his tail against the door.

"Good morning, Lou," Imo said as the girl shuffled into the kitchen, Bingo at her heels. "How was your first night?"

Lou shrugged as she plopped down at the table.

"Biscuits, grits, and scrambled eggs?" Imo asked.

Lou nodded.

"Well, good," Imo said. "Looks like we have a pretty day to finish unpacking and settling in." She gestured at the window.

Arms folded, Lou shrugged. Imo could see that no cheerful chitchat would come from her this morning, but she smiled patiently as she set a cold glass full of orange juice before her. Surely the girl would come around given time. You could not expect her to bounce immediately into city life.

Waiting for the skillet to heat, Imo bent to search a low shelf in one of the cupboards for Martha's recipes, all the while silently pleading with God to let Lou be happy with living there. She found nothing but placemats, napkins, and a stack of crocheted doilies. She stood up, hands on her hips, to consider other possible places. She rummaged through each drawer, the other cupboard, the pie safe, and all of the cabinets.

"Here we are, dear," she said at last, setting a steaming plate of eggs on the table in front of Lou. Lou did not speak, but she began eating hungrily. Imo noted that she wore an old sweatshirt, faded denim overalls, and sneakers. Out of the bib of the overalls sprouted one of her uncle Silas's threadbare white handkerchiefs. It stood out like a flag in the light from the overhead light. Clearly she was trying to make a statement.

Imo only smiled. "My goodness," she said, "I have looked just about everywhere I know to look. Reckon where Martha keeps her recipes?" she startled herself by speaking of Martha in the present tense.

Perhaps a little time would change this, Imo mused, allow her to make her own memories here and make the constant feel of Martha's presence but a memory.

One week later, in early December, Imo

was folding the laundry while listening to a radio station out of Atlanta. There was a definite chill in the air and visions of a warm blackberry jam cake swam in her mind.

She had searched high and low for Martha's recipe collection; left nothing unturned. The hardest thing about the search was that every nook and cranny held reminders of Martha, had a story to tell. It was while hunting through the secretary that Imo decided she'd had just about enough. She closed the drawer against stacks of old postcards, faded letters, bills, and address labels.

"This is my house now, Martha!" She felt her powerless words echo through the breezeway.

A sense of Martha was still in the air that evening as Imo pulled a sour cream pound cake from the oven. She felt Martha's presence behind her, felt Martha's hand on her shoulder, and saw her shaking her head disbelievingly, or was it a superior shake? She fancied she heard Martha saying, "It's my granny's famous hundred-year-old recipe he loves, Imogene."

Another week passed and the presence of Martha became palpable. While at first the phantom houseguest Martha, lurking in the corners like a silent witness, was only mildly disturbing, now it had turned into a major annoyance.

Radically rearranging the interior of the parsonage was all Imo could think of to do. She set to work, busily moving rugs, mirrors, chairs and tables, and bit by bit, the heavy love seat. When Lou was home from school, she had her get on one end of the looming secretary and help turn it to face the wall. Then they inched it down to the dark corner of the east parlor.

"Whew!" she blurted when they'd finished, "certainly feels better in here now, doesn't it?"

"Sure," Lou said. "Mind if I take the Impala for a couple of hours? I'm going to carry Bingo to the homeplace. The leash law here in town makes him nervous."

"Oh, I'm sure it does." Imo nodded, smiling. The truth was that Lou thought up a different excuse for visiting the farm daily. First it was to get various and sundry personal items, then it was to check out things like pipes, though it had not gone below freezing yet, and then to see if there were any pumpkin stragglers. There were not.

"You'll miss Wanda's visit," she said as

Lou was slipping out the door. "I invited her by to chat." She was also planning to ask Wanda for the jam cake recipe. She wanted to give Lemuel a little taste of heaven herself.

Wanda did not knock. She sashayed in, perched herself on a parlor chair, looked around with her brow furrowed and her bottom lip poking out.

"Hello, dear," Imo said, hastening in from the side yard. "Come on in the kitchen and I'll start us some coffee."

Wanda rose, walking slowly and taking inventory with narrowed eyes. She was silent as she settled herself at the kitchen table.

"How're things going at the Kuntry Kut 'n' Kurl?" Imo chirped.

"Oh, moving right along, I reckon," Wanda said, giving Imo a sideways look. "You've changed things around in here. Where's Sister's secretary at?"

"Oh, I moved it down the hall," Imo said.

"But it caught the light best right where Sister had it."

Imo blinked, gazing out the window as she hunted a new subject. "Such a lovely day, isn't it? Lou drove to the old homeplace to let Bingo run around. I know she'll be sorry she missed seeing you."

Wanda was uncharacteristically quiet and Imo could see she was in a snit over something. She decided pound cake would sweeten her up and she got the cake plate from off the top of the Frigidaire and sliced two pieces.

Setting these on the table, Imo sat herself down. "How's my Jeannie?"

"She's good," Wanda said, brightening a tiny bit. "We've gone and decided to add doing acrylic nails at the salon. Also a tanning bed. Both her ideas."

"Well, isn't that lovely," Imo said, rising to pour coffee.

"Yep," Wanda conceded. "She really knows how to bring in the business."

"This is so nice, Wanda, dear, not having to worry about Jeannie anymore," Imo said, "settled down, married, working at a steady job she loves. Thanks to you for that. And Lemuel is certainly happy to be here," she continued, "doesn't have to depend on me to drive him so much. Still have to carry him on his visiting rounds, but he's a man in control again."

Wanda nodded, distractedly lifting a mug to her bright pink lips. "Listen, Imo, it was real sweet of you to invite me over, and I sure did enjoy our little visit, but I've got to be going."

"But you just got here! I was hoping for a nice long visit together. Aren't y'all closed on Wednesdays?"

"I need to run to Atlanta and get me some beauty supplies from my wholesale place." Wanda rose and gathered her huge straw bag from the floor. "Toodle-oo."

"Wait!" Imo said, standing and leaning forward to grasp Wanda's sleeve. "I need to ask you about something."

Wanda turned to face her.

"I need a recipe. It's for hundred-year-old blackberry jam cake."

"You talkin' about my granny's recipe?"

"Uh-hmmm. I can't find Martha's recipe collection anywhere. I've turned this house top to bottom."

"That one's a family secret," Wanda said, winking as she climbed into her car.

Imo was momentarily stunned, her chest daggered by Wanda's words. She stood at the front portico watching Wanda's orange VW bug with its plastic daisy fastened to the antenna till it was out of sight. *But I am family now,* she mused as she went inside to tidy the kitchen. *Aren't I?*

Eleven

Faith Lift
Lou

Times of testing our faith come to everyone,
I guess. We've all heard those little reminders about how diamonds are formed
after many years of intense pressure and
pearls are the result of an irritation inside
the oyster. These oppressions cause beautiful things.

I awoke that first morning in the parsonage with the feeling that God desired to
do some sort of work in me. However, this
realization did not make me happier or
things any easier. I didn't get down on my
knees to echo Jesus and say, "Nevertheless,
not my will, but Yours be done." I fought it
kicking and screaming.

Just as I figured, living downtown was

awful. Being pent up between those narrow walls, almost on top of one another, with the sounds of cars constantly in my ears. No Dusty Red to crow me awake. No moonlit walks down to the banks of the Etowah. No fields of goldenrod or sorghum stretching away to meet the horizon. In fact, that was it! There were absolutely no wide open spaces to be had. There was no way to even breathe properly.

I was not happy. If Imo was dismayed by leaving the old homeplace, she had too much resolve to show it. She pasted on her *God has a higher purpose here* face and listened to my complaints with an infuriating smile. "I know, dear," she'd say. "It's not easy. But we weren't promised a life of ease. This is where I feel we're supposed to be right now." Then she'd quote that irritating little verse — "Into each life some rain must fall. Some days must be dark and dreary."

I told myself to just quit mentioning it to her. To take it up with God. And I did. I wrestled in prayer, as they say. Literally prayed without ceasing.

After two weeks on Cedar Street, I had established a morning ritual. First I made a quick trip to the bathroom, then the kitchen for a glass of orange juice, then back to my bedroom to dress and pull my hair back into a ponytail. Finally I slid the chain at the front door and turned the dead bolt. This was Bingo's signal to trot happily to my side, his leash dangling from between his teeth. "Morning, boy!" I paused to rough up the fur underneath his collar and tickle his rib cage as he closed his eyes in ecstasy. Clipping the leash onto his collar we were out the front door and down the tiny front walkway to Cedar Street.

It was downright cold and our breath made white puffs like smoke as we followed the sidewalk a quarter mile. We always began in the opposite direction of Calvary so that our first stop was the covered bridge in the heart of downtown, where we liked to pause and admire the steam on top of Euharlee Creek. It was no Etowah River, but we had grand hopes for wading and catching crawdads there come warmer weather.

From one end of the bridge, I peered out at the dark windows of city hall and the Dixie Chick Restaurant. It gave me an enormous thrill, to be the only ones up and about, wandering the sleepy town.

Someone had transformed the heart of Euharlee with Christmas lights on every telephone pole: some shaped like wreaths and some like candles, alternating on both sides of Main Street, from the clinic to Dub's Filling Station.

Christmas. As far as I was concerned, there wasn't going to be anything to celebrate as long as we were still held captive on Cedar Street. I clucked to Bingo and he fell in step with me as we crossed Euharlee Creek, making our way up the hill toward Shiflet's Grocery for our next stop. Shiflet's was a tiny wooden structure of clapboard in the center of a crumbling rectangle of cement. What had once been fresh signs proclaiming Merita Bread, RC Cola, and Sinclair gas were victims of time and weather, and the store had been permitted to run down to a comfortable state. There was a long wooden bench in front of the store and after ten o'clock it usually held two to three older retired gentlemen, who drank coffee, shot the breeze, and napped.

I took a seat on the worn bench, leaned back, crossed my legs, and wedged my icy hands between my thighs to rest a spell. Bingo snuffed around in some patchy weeds till it was time for the last leg of our daily journey, the hike to Calvary Baptist.

We always looped through town, passing

the clinic and the U.S. Post Office and ending with a pause at the church, usually pausing a moment in the cemetery. Moseying along we spied a handful of blue-black crows pecking in the ground out front of the post office. Bingo pulled me into their midst and they scattered to the sky. I thought about Dusty Red at Hank's house. Hank had laughed and told me he was a crazy little rooster, crowing at all hours of the day and night. "He's probably just confused," I said, "being in a new place and all."

When we reached Calvary's yard, I paused and reined Bingo in close to my side. No matter how mad I stayed at the Reverend or impatient with the Lord, Church remained a sacred place to me, a place of reverence, and I would not allow Bingo to lift his leg on the sides of the sanctuary or the tombstones. I glanced at the wheeled marquis. November's saying was still up:

IT'S HARD TO STUMBLE
WHEN YOU'RE DOWN ON YOUR KNEES.

I considered this just as I did each morning. I sure enough felt like I was stumbling along through my life at that exact moment. But, figuratively, at least, I *had* been down on my knees. I'd been praying like crazy.

"Are you even listening to me, Father?" I asked aloud, my eyes on Calvary's steeple against a lightening sky. "This is your servant, Loutishie Lavender, again. Please, You've got to make a way for us to get back to the farm."

Bingo looked up at me with concern in his eyes. He pressed his snout into my thigh and I crouched down to cradle his head. "I'll be okay, sweetie," I crooned, stroking the fur behind his ears. "I've always heard that faith can move mountains, and that all things are possible with God. I just have to figure out a way to get my faith stronger."

I paused for a moment to think about what I'd just said. If faith came from God, and I believed that it did, then who better to ask for more of it? I rolled forward so that I was on my knees and tucked my chin to my chest. "Show me, Lord," I said. squeezing my eyes shut tight. "Show me how to get more faith and also how to use it." Then I felt selfish for focusing on myself so much. "And Lord," I added, "please bless the teaching and hearing of Your word here at Calvary Baptist. Pour out

Your spirit of wisdom on the Sunday school teachers and on Reverend Peddigrew."

I felt really sanctimonious at the last part of my prayer, as I could not hardly stand to look at the Reverend anymore, but still a ray of hope nestled in my heart as we scampered back to the parsonage for some breakfast.

On Saturday evening, I sat in the front parlor sipping a cup of hot spiced tea and reading. There was a knock at the back door and I heard Imo opening the door and then Little Silas's breathless voice saying "Mi-moo!" Then I heard Imo grunting as she swept him up in one of her massive hugs.

"Jeannie, darlin'," Imo said, "come on in out of that cold."

"Hi, Mama," Jeanette said. "I can't stay to visit." Her stiletto heels rapped on the kitchen floor. "Think you could keep an eye on the little man for a spell tonight? I've got to go visit a friend who's feeling poorly."

"Well, now. I surely can. Who's ailing?"

"Oh, a girl you wouldn't know," Jeanette said, a desperate tremor beneath the surface of her voice. "Montgomery's gone till

312

tomorrow, and I packed up Little Silas's night things in case I'm real late tonight . . ."

"You need me to call Dr. Perkins and let him go with you?" Imo's voice reached that high pitch of concern. "He keeps late hours if need be."

Jeanette laughed. "Mama, she's got the medicine already. Just needs me to sit with her."

Curious, I made my way to the kitchen. I smelled her strong perfume before I even saw her.

"Hi, Lou," Jeanette said. "You ain't got no date tonight?"

"Hank's coming by around eight."

"Don't you need to go and start fixin' yourself up then?" she asked, eyeing my ragged jeans and bare face. "Just 'cause you snagged him don't mean you don't have to work at keepin' him."

I smiled. The place where Hank and I were going didn't require more than coveralls, work gloves, and a pair of boots. Earlier that day he'd called and said that one of his mares was getting ready to foal, and we planned to spend most of the evening out at his daddy's barn, with occasional treks up to the house for hot drinks. There was a perfectly cozy stall full of hay where we could nestle together and wait.

"We're going to hang out at a barn," I said, smiling.

She looked at me like I was crazy.

"Listen, Jeannie," I said, "I would give *anything* to be a vet and do this all the time, and also, I'm hoping this'll be a feather in my cap when Dr. Livesay chooses his intern for this summer."

"I thought he had half a dozen of you crazed animal lovers shovelin' crap for him this past summer." She shook her head in disbelief.

"This is different," I told her. "In this job it's like you're an actual vet. You help Dr. Livesay in the examining room and also you accompany him on barn calls. And he chooses only one person a summer. One senior." Although I did not like to admit it, even to myself, I thought I would just die if he didn't pick me.

Imo and Little Silas wandered off to the sitting room and Jeanette patted my shoulder. "Whatever floats your boat," she said as I took in her midcalf length winter coat, buttoned up tightly, with a snug scarf and a floppy knit hat. Glittery blue eye makeup and a meticulously drawn-on red mouth made me wonder where she was really off to. Made me wonder what was *un-*

derneath that coat.

"Ain't none of your beeswax," Jeanette said. She looked very sly, standing there smiling.

"You're not going to the Honky Tonk, are you?" I whispered.

"Heaven only knows," she answered, whirling on her heel and heading toward the door.

I ran after her. "Jeannie," I pled, "you really oughtn't —"

She turned toward me a bit, her eyes flashing as she stood in the open doorway, freezing air rushing in on my bare feet. "Listen here, Saint Loutishie, I don't need nobody telling me what to do, least of all my little sister!"

The way she flared up so quick I could tell something else was bothering her. "How're those dizzy spells?" I asked softly.

Jeanette tensed. "My what?"

"They're worse, aren't they?"

She nodded, growing quiet. "Left cheek's gone numb," she admitted finally, and her face said *and I am so scared.*

I reached up to touch her cheek. "Jeannie," I said, "you really ought to see a doctor about all this."

"Maybe I will, Lou," she said, placing a hand on top of mine and pressing it hard to her face. "Maybe I will."

Back in the parlor, I curled in a chair, holding my novel open, listening to the happy banter of Imo and Little Silas as they made brownies. I could not read one word. I smoothed the afghan across my thighs, and my chest tightened with concern. A numb cheek? It had to be something terrible if her own fear of it was so apparent.

I could only take comfort in the fact that she said she'd see a doctor now.

That next morning, the first Sunday of December, I awoke to the sound of heavy rain against the window. It was cold and pitch dark as I climbed from my bed and pulled an old blue sweater over my flannel nightgown.

Bingo met me in the small sliver of light as I emerged from the bathroom, his leash between his teeth and his paws dancing excitedly on the hall rug. "Sorry, boy, no walk today," I said as I made my way to the kitchen to get the space heater fired up and to fix a cup of orange spice tea.

At dawn I did walk Bingo briefly out into Martha's perennial garden so he could relieve himself. The day was going to remain overcast and cold, that much I could tell, and the morning air smelled of wood smoke from fires in the homes up and down the street. Quickly we returned to the kitchen where I dried Bingo's fur with a bath towel before he curled up on a blanket by the heater. Enjoying the warmth, I sank beside him and we stayed this way until I heard stirring from Imo and the Reverend's bedroom.

Imo had hardly got the coffee going before the Reverend came shuffling into the kitchen frowning, wrinkling up his nose, and saying, "What's that awful smell?"

Before anyone could say "wet dog," I gulped the last of my tea, clucked to Bingo to follow and beat it back into my bedroom to get ready for church.

"No breakfast, Lou?" Imo called. "Got ham today."

Though my stomach grumbled hungrily, I called back, "No, ma'am." I was not feeling particularly charitable toward anybody right then, but especially not the Reverend, who had insulted Bingo. If I let myself, I could feel all sorts of hateful thoughts about the man and I was worried that this type of behavior might annul my prayers for faith. Removing myself from his presence seemed the best way to suppress those evil tendencies of mine.

We ended up driving to Calvary, the rain against the windshield blurring our view as we turned down the cracked concrete driveway of the church that ran underneath a tin overhang at the side door.

I wasn't in the mood to go to Sunday school or sit through one of the Reverend's long sermons. I had too much on my mind, and I wished I had taken Imo up on breakfast. *Ah well,* I encouraged myself, *at least you'll get to see Tara. You can sit in the back pew and pass notes to each other.*

We were there early so that the Reverend could get the place cozy, and I took a seat in a cold, empty Sunday school classroom, thinking about the wee hours of that morning when Hank and I had delivered a foal. The mare's nostrils were flaring wildly and she lay heaving on her side. Talking softly and stroking her flank to soothe her, we helped usher a newborn colt into the world. "He's anything like his brother," Hank said, holding me in a nest of warm hay afterward, "he'll be a real hellion." I let my eyes wander to a stall where her first progeny, Chieftain, stood. Chieftain was a wild-eyed stallion and Hank was the only one who could ride him, and that, unsaddled, with only a rope halter. Absolutely no bit. Though they'd tried and tried to break him, Chieftain remained an independent and unpredictable creature.

Jeanette was like Chieftain. Wild and unwilling to accept a saddle, bit, or bridle. She was an unbroken colt, resistant to reins that could turn her. She thought she could control her own destiny, and in my innermost heart, I knew she was struggling with the Holy Ghost. God wanted the reins to her life, and she hadn't learned that she'd finally get some peace when she submitted to Him, that she would finally feel the security she longed for, the peace that passed all understanding.

Behind me, I heard someone opening the door. It was Miss Mattie Hembree, close to a hundred years old and the self-appointed Sunday school teacher of the teenagers. In her gnarled hands she clutched a bag of candy — butterscotch discs she passed out to reward us for righteous answers. "Good morning, Loutishie," she said in her quavery voice. "How are you on this Lord's day?"

"Fine," I mumbled.

"That's nice, dear." She placed her Bible and the butterscotch discs down on a folding chair, standing prim and straight, a large ivory cameo at her throat, her sparse hair in a tiny bun.

I'd often mentioned to the Reverend that we should get a more youthful teacher to guide the youth of Calvary. One who could identify more with our lives. "Wisdom comes with age," he'd always say. "You listen to Miss Mattie's every word. They are pearls of wisdom."

Well, I listened, usually. Answered questions to receive the candy to suck later during the service, preunwrapping them before entering the sanctuary. But I never felt that shiver, that mystical feeling of spiritual enlightenment down deep in my soul when Miss Mattie instructed us on our spiritual journeys.

More youth began to trickle in, but as ten o'clock came and went, there was no Tara. Disappointed, I hunched down in my seat, crossed my arms and prepared to endure. Miss Mattie uttered the opening prayer asking God to bless the words of her mouth and the meditations of our hearts. Solemnly she opened her Bible to a large crocheted bookmark in the shape of a cross. Smoothing a parchment-thin page, she cleared her throat.

"Neither he who plants is anything, nor he who waters, but God who gives the increase." Her eyes scanned the tiny half circle of us teenagers. "Who knows where this verse is found?"

Blank faces stared back at Miss Mattie, some mouths open in exhausted stupors from late Saturday nights.

"It's from First Corinthians," she reproved us. "Paul is telling folks at the Corinthian church not to place too much faith in their own abilities, or too little in God's. Some were praising Paul's seed-planting ministry, and others favored the seed-watering ministry of Apollos. Here Paul is reminding them that it's God who brings the seeds to fruition." She fingered a butterscotch disc, rustling the cellophane pointedly. "But still, boys and girls, Paul is not saying the efforts to plant and water were wasted. They're part of God's plan, too.

"You all just imagine a farmer sitting lazily on his back porch looking out over his cornfield. 'What're you doing?' you call out to him. 'I'm farming, by golly,' he says. 'Well, what are you growing?' you say, staring out at the barren unplowed field. 'Corn,' he says. 'But, you haven't even plowed or planted any seeds,' you say. 'You are correct,' he says, 'I'm farming by faith. I'm believing in the Good Lord for my harvest.' 'Don't you think you should be doing something?' you argue. He answers, 'I am doing something. I'm praying and believing.'"

Miss Mattie looked piercingly at each of us. "You can have faith and you can pray," she said slowly, "but God won't do your work for you. You've got to plant and water and weed and mind the insects. Then trust Our Heavenly Father for the crop."

At that moment all the dark clouds in my brain disappeared. I felt a warm ray of mystical sunlight shining down on me as the words tingled up and down my spine.

I didn't catch much of the sermon, stood up only to hold my hymnal aloft during singing. After the benediction was said, I floated to the front door of Calvary. The rain was over and I decided to walk on back to the parsonage.

Stepping outside, I turned up the collar of my red wool Sunday coat against the bone-chilling wind. Hands stuffed into the pockets, I felt one last butterscotch disc and popped it into my mouth.

Kicking clumps of wet leaves I made my way slowly to Cedar Street, Miss Mattie's words still ringing in my ears. I paused a moment to read December's saying on the marquee and as I did, a tentative finger of butter-colored sunlight broke free from a cloud overhead and lit directly on the ground at my feet.

PRAYER IS ASKING FOR RAIN.
FAITH IS CARRYING AN UMBRELLA.

"You don't have to knock me over the head with it, Father," I whispered, smiling heavenward.

Twelve

❦

Welcome Wagon
Imo

The long evenings were Imo's favorite time of day come mid-December. At five-thirty p.m. the last rays of the sun disappeared and Lemuel laid a fire in the kitchen hearth. As the flames leapt and crackled Imo prepared supper, looking forward to kicking back, warm and cozy in her rocker, to work her nightly crossword puzzle once the dishes were washed and put away. Some evenings she addressed Christmas cards or did a bit of quilting.

The mood in the house was lighter now. It seemed Loutishie was finally coming around. There was a new spring in her step and an almost flippant undertone to her speech. This offered irrepressible hope and

Imo was thankful. If it had to do with Time being a healer or the girl finally seeing The Light, Imo did not know.

This evening, as Imo worked the last bit of her crossword, the air was laced with the sweet aroma of banana bread from the oven. "What's an eight-letter word for false sense of security?" she asked Lem, tapping her pencil thoughtfully against her temple.

Lem closed his eyes to think for a moment. "Sorry, dear," he said at last, "I can't get it."

She continued to stare at forty-five across, telling herself she could eventually fetch Lou's thesaurus, but only as a last resort. She never let herself cheat by turning to the final page of the paper where they printed the answers. Several minutes later she put the pencil down and turned her head from right to left with a puzzled expression on her brow. "Did I just hear a car pull up?" she asked.

"Didn't hear a thing myself," he said from behind his newspaper.

Imo shrugged and went back to her puzzle. The last letter was *n,* she knew that much.

"I *know* I hear something out there," she said, rising to make her way to the front window, furtively looking out toward the mailbox. "Don't see anybody," she called to Lem. Then from the backyard she heard a car door slam. "Who do you suppose?" she asked, tucking her blouse in neatly and smoothing her hair. "Must be somebody we know good to come around to the back of the house like this." She sailed through the house and squinted through the peep-hole in the door.

It was Dewey and Lillian Puckett. Lillian had a spry step and a handbag hanging from her forearm, and was carrying some type of plant. Dewey followed, holding her elbow.

Imo swung the back door open. "Evenin' " she called.

"How do?" bellowed Dewey as they neared the glow of a lightbulb at the steps. He paused, nodded, touching the brim of his felt fedora. "Right purty evenin' out, ain't it?"

Lillian, an energetic and stout woman in an emerald coat and big gold earbobs, pulled him right up the steps.

"It surely is," Imo said, swinging the door open wider. "Won't y'all please come in?"

"Good evening, neighbors," Lemuel boomed, coming from behind Imo to pump Dewey's hand vigorously. "Long time no see."

"I know we're a bit late in officially welcoming you to the neighborhood," Lillian said, "but we've been out of town for an entire month! Dewey's sister, Janie, had herself a stroke and we've been in Chattanooga tending to her." She set a scarlet poinsettia down on the table, nodding at Imo's crossword there. "Just did finish mine," she said.

"That's nice," said Imo. She gathered the puzzle and her pencil and set them on the counter beside the sink. "Sit yourself down, Lillian, dear," she said, patting the back of an oak chair at the table.

"Smells mighty good in here, Imogene," Lillian said. "And I must tell you those nandinas along the fence out front are gorgeous. Took my breath away yesterday when we were getting home."

"Well, thank you, dear," Imo said, and she felt almost guilty, like she was accepting Martha's praise. Years ago, Lillian had been vice president of the Euharlee Garden Club, and had won numerous awards at flower arranging shows across the state. However, she dropped out at forty-two, when her first and only child, Dusty, was born. He was twenty-eight now, married with two small children, and still Lillian acted as if he were her full-time responsibility.

"How's Dusty?" Imo asked.

Lillian's face lit up. She opened her mouth to speak, but before she could utter a word, Dewey had turned on his heel to face Imo.

"Boy's finally getting his head on straight!" He slapped the worn fabric of suit pants across his thigh. "Beats all I ever saw. Seems last time he come forward to rededicate his life at Calvary, he meant it."

"Well, hallelujah!" the Reverend said. "He give up drinking, then?"

"Yessiree. Angie said he's been stone-cold sober ever since. A mite grumpy, she did add, but walking the straight and narrow." Dewey removed his hat and held it reverently over his heart.

"Have a seat, Dewey," Lemuel said, nodding at the chair next to Lillian.

Imo slid the steaming banana bread from the oven, measured out coffee, and turned the coffeemaker on. Dusty and his reckless drinking binges, his DUIs, and his car wrecks were legendary around Euharlee. They were also the reason for the Pucketts' constant prayer requests. What amazed Imo was how Dusty always managed to come through those crashes alive. The car could be literally crumpled, look just like a smashed Pepsi can, and

Dusty Puckett wouldn't have so much as a scratch on him. Some folks maintained it was because Dusty stayed wholly inebriated and therefore pliant that he came through unharmed each time. Lillian said it was because of her fervent prayers.

"Bet Angie's tickled," Lem said.

"She sure enough is," Dewey said. "She told Lillian here that it looks like we can all relax now. Used to, girl was packing up little Brittany and Ricky every other day and running home to her mama's house up in Boone. Dusty'd come out to the house to eat and he'd just lay up on the couch with the phone in his hand, begging Angie to come on back home. Tellin' her he'd quit drankin' for sure if she'd come back."

"That must've been hard," Imo said, setting a napkin and a steaming cup of coffee in front of Dewey.

"Hard," said Lillian.

"Yep, boy's on the good road now," Dewey continued, leaning back in his chair and clasping his hands over his potbelly. "Thank you, Reverend, for standing in the gap all these many years, praying for my boy."

"You think nothing of it. It was my delight."

"Lillian and me, I don't know what we'd

have done if that boy kept on going the way he was. If Angie'd left him like she threatened, and carried our grand-young'uns off." His eyes grew misty.

Imogene looked politely away. "Who'd like warm banana bread?" she asked.

"Why, that's one of my very favorites!" exclaimed Lillian.

"Why, it's Lou's, too," said Imo. "And this reminds me, you don't happen to know Martha's recipe for hundred-year-old jam cake, do you, Lillian?"

"No, dear, I don't."

There was a pause as everyone dug in, forks clinking.

"Mighty dee-licious, Imo, dear," Lemuel said, dabbing a napkin to his lips. She waited for him to add "best I ever put in my mouth," but apparently he was on to other thoughts.

"Been thinking of adding a little addition off the back of Calvary, a new Sunday school wing," he said to Dewey. "We need the space."

"Yes indeed," Dewey said. A carpenter, he loved to talk square feet and two-by-fours, and he especially loved to tell the story of himself at seventeen, when he'd hung out a shingle at a little shop front in downtown Cartersville, and folks had looked quizzically at him and said, "Dewey Puckett, how come you not to follow in your father's footsteps and work down at the tractor dealership? Your father makes himself a good living." He would smile, point up to heaven, and say to them, "Oh, but I *am* working in my father's business. Didn't you know Jesus was a carpenter?"

Dewey rubbed his chin. "I'll be retiring come January and I reckon I could do the addition."

"Well, praise the Lord!" Lemuel bellowed. "I been cogitatin' on how to get that done."

"When are you retiring, Reverend?" Lillian glanced at Lemuel.

"Not till the good Lord tells me it's time," Lemuel said. "I'll keep going till I hear Him say 'stop.' "

"He talks to you like that?" Lillian asked, her eyes wide.

"Indeed He does."

"Oooo." Lillian set her fork down and squeezed herself. "That's spooky. *How* does He say things to you?"

The Reverend paused a moment. He cocked his head and smiled benignly. "He speaks to me in a still, small voice."

"Bet He sounds kind of like Imogene," Dewey remarked, and everyone laughed.

"Dewey here just up and decided to re-tire himself," Lillian said. "Going on fifty years since he started his carpentrying."

"Wait a minute here," Dewey said. "I be-lieve I had myself some help in deciding to retire." He looked pointedly at Lillian.

"Well, a bit, I suppose." Lillian smiled and patted his arm. "Now that Dusty's doing so good, I figure we can even get away every now and then. Go down to Panama City Beach for a weekend."

"Maybe so," Dewey turned to the Rev-erend. "You're keeping busy, eh?"

"That I am. Busier than ever, it seems. There's always work to be done for the Kingdom."

"Like living back downtown?"

"Yessireebobtail," he answered proudly. "I walk to Calvary every morning. Walk home for lunch, walk back to work . . ."

Imo got up and began to clear the plates. "Well, I for one wish he would slow down," she said. "He goes nonstop." She stood at the sink running water over the plates.

Lillian rose to help her. "Amen, sister," she said as she dumped the coffee filter into the trash can underneath the sink. "I know just what you mean. We're not sup-posed to work ourselves down to little nubbins, then turn right around and jump into the grave. Dewey's work is hard. It's physical labor. We deserve some time off now. Some fun. I cannot wait for January to get here."

Imo was watching Lemuel's face. He was talking away to Dewey, oblivious to it all. Well, she thought, so was Lillian, for that matter. Building a new Sunday school wing would be a full-time job. At least for a good while. But surely Dewey must realize that. Why of course he did! Paying lip service to Lillian was all he was doing when he said he was retiring and then offered to work on Calvary's new addition. Some men could not slow down. Didn't know their own limits.

"Enough about us, Imo," Lillian said, leaning in closer to Imo and lifting her crescent-moon glasses to her nose. "You simply must fill me in on your girls."

Imo smiled. "They're good. Jeannie's still in Cartersville and Lou's a senior now."

"She can't be." Lillian shook her head. "Why, seems like she was just born yesterday."

"Practically grown now," Imo said.

"She taking the move well?"

"She surely is," Imo said, "it's just a miracle. If you'd have seen how contrary she was when all this first came up."

"And your Jeanette is happy?" Lillian asked.

"Being married is good for her. I don't have to worry, because Montgomery takes care of her."

"You look like you're ready for Christmas," Lillian said, glancing toward the mantle where Imo had arranged magnolia leaves and red candles. "Bet Jeanette's boy is just about beside himself with waiting for Santa Claus. I know my Dusty's two can't hardly stand to wait."

"Little Silas is mighty excited," Imo told her. "Two and a half weeks may as well be eternity in his eyes."

"Loutishie out of school yet?"

"She doesn't get out till the eighteenth, and poor Bingo, he waits right there for her to come home whenever she goes anywhere." She gestured at Bingo, who was sprawled out in front of the door. Lillian smiled.

"Well, I'd say you're doing fairly good if it's only the dog who's complaining."

Imo bit her lip. "There's one more soul who doesn't seem delighted to have us here."

"Pray tell," Lillian breathed, leaning forward.

"Wanda Parnell."

"Martha's sister?"

"Mm hmm. I just get this feeling when I talk to her. Listen at this, I recently asked her for the recipe to that hundred-year-old jam cake I mentioned to you, the one my Lemuel raves about. It was passed down from Martha's grandmother, you see, and she all but said *you must be out of your mind to even ask me for that.* What she actually said was, 'It's a *family* secret.' Like I'm not family. I was so startled, Lillian."

Lillian shook her head. "I declare," she said gently, patting Imo's hand, "that was ugly of her. But the fact of the matter is Wanda has her a selfish side. Baby of the family and all. So, if I were you, I wouldn't take it personally."

Imo relaxed a bit. Leaning her elbows on the table. "I guess she doesn't hate me then."

"Goodness, no. Wanda's just high-strung. She's done worse to me."

"Really?"

"For sure." Lillian took a breath before sipping her coffee. "Back when she was between her second and third husbands, recently separated from Ervine Womack, I believe, Wanda set her cap for Dusty. Well, he was already going with Angie at that point, and I just flat out had to tell her not to keep calling or coming around stalking my boy. Oh, he was flattered, he was, but being a good twenty years younger than Wanda, I had to step in."

"You did?"

"And do you know what that girl said to me?" Lillian asked, eyes wide. "She said 'First of all, Miz Puckett, dear, I hate to have to tell you this, but twenty years is not that much when you consider women live longer than men, and second, all's fair in love and war. And if he prefers me over that mealy-mouthed little Angie Skinner, then you don't have a thing to say about it. Dusty is a grown man, and you've got to learn to cut those apron strings!' "

Imo shook her head. "That was not a very respectful thing for her to say to you." She thought for a moment, then continued. "I guess Wanda *is* used to getting what she wants. I know she misses Martha. Martha practically raised her the way I raised Vera, you know, and maybe it's hard for her to see me in Martha's old role."

"I bet that's it, hon!" Lillian patted Imo's hand. "Anyhow, don't you fret, I bet I can get my hands on that jam-cake recipe for you."

"You're not serious."

"Absolutely. Old Miss Verner down in Acworth was close as she could be to Martha and Wanda's grandmother. She may be old as the hills, but still got herself a mind sharp as a tack. I'll ask her for the recipe."

"That would be wonderful, Lillian!" Imo smiled as she rose to freshen everyone's coffee.

They ate warm banana bread, laughing and talking in front of the crackling fire. Lillian regaled Imo with stories of past Christmases and Imo liked her good-natured, down-home philosophy about life. Imo's days way out on the farm had not included many impromptu social visits from neighbors, and as she looked at Lillian, she was thankful. She felt soothed and connected and warm down in the very center of her being.

Toward nine, Lemuel yawned as he rose to punch up the fire and add another log. Dewey stood and offered his hand once again. "We better get ourselves on back home, Reverend."

In spite of Lemuel's invitation for a nightcap of spiced cider, he protested, saying he had to rise at the crack of dawn to complete a carpentry job. Imo walked

Lillian outside to their car.

"I'm so proud your Dusty's doing good now," Imo said.

"And your girls, too," Lillian answered. "We're very blessed now, aren't we? There's no more peaceful feeling than to know your young'uns are safe and happy. And don't you worry about Wanda. She won't stay in a snit forever. Keep on being kind to her, and she'll come around."

"Thanks, Lillian."

"Well, take care," Lillian answered, "I meant it when I said to drop by anytime. My door's always open."

"Same here," Imo said. "Let's do keep in close touch. Thank you for the lovely poinsettia."

Imo walked back into the bright kitchen and stood at the counter to swallow the last of her coffee. Her eyes caught a quick glimpse of forty-five across. A false sense of well-being, a false sense of well-being, an eight letter word for a false sense of well-being. She rolled the words around and around in her brain. She closed her eyes to think.

At last, she picked up her pencil and filled in *d-e-l-u-s-i-o-n*.

The next afternoon Imo returned from

the Red Dot Foodstore, her arms laden with a ten-pound turkey, mincemeat for a pie, and a box of Whitman's chocolate-covered cherries to carry to Lillian. When she reached the kitchen, she paused a moment.

She set her groceries down and looked hard at the pine table beside the hearth. Hadn't she removed that little saucer on top there? The one Martha made in a china painting class?

She distinctly remembered smoothing her fingertips over the tiny purple forget-me-nots encircling the plate before swathing it in newspaper, and placing it on a low shelf in one of the cupboards. She remembered collapsing the tiny golden easel it sat upon and laying this across its top.

She knew for certain that Lou didn't put the plate back out. The girl had no interest in that type of thing. She began to imagine Lemuel rustling around in the cupboard, extracting the little painted plate, looking down at the gold script reading Martha Peddigrew, and pressing it to his heart.

Would he do something like this? He'd never mentioned missing the plate or any of the other pictures, photos, or knick-knacks that Imo had wrapped up and stored out of sight. He did not seem to care that Imo had rearranged the furniture to suit herself. He was good about letting her do as she pleased, and did not even raise an eyebrow when she changed the drapes in the front rooms.

Unless, she thought, he was one of those silent brooders. Those people who stored up feelings and resentments until they came to a head. Imogene picked up the phone to dial Calvary.

Lemuel answered promptly. "Reverend Peddigrew here. Smile, God loves you and so do I."

"It's me, dear," Imo said. "Listen, I have a quick question."

"Okay."

"Did you, by any chance, move that little china plate with the forget-me-nots back onto the table near the hearth?"

"What?" he asked and by his confused tone, she could tell he had no inkling of the plate.

"Oh, nothing," she said. "What time did you say you need to leave for your visiting rounds?"

"Three o'clock, sweetie pie. You mind just swinging by to pick me up here?"

"Not atall. Bye-bye now."

Imo hung up and sank down into a chair

at the table. She couldn't shake the creepy feeling; it was like Martha was right there. Her very presence hovering in some other dimension, yet from which she could affect things in the earthly realm.

The plate had to be Martha's doing. She must not be in a peaceful state up there yet. Perhaps she was having second thoughts about Imo and Lemuel.

Imo sliced a giant wedge of pecan pie and fixed a cup of Sanka with lots of heavy whipping cream, sat down, and looked suspiciously from side to side. "I may not can see you, Martha Peddigrew," she warned, "but I'm on to you!"

The creamy coffee went down smooth and she followed it with a crisp, chewy bite of pecan pie. She leaned back, sighed, and tried to think about the upcoming holidays. She was determined to fill her mind with peaceful thoughts of baking and entertaining and gift giving, but it was not to be.

"Oh, mercy me," Imo whispered, "I'm not alone here, am I, Martha, dear? Much as I want to, I cannot put you to rest."

Imo had never pictured herself as a person who believed in ghosts, or not ghosts exactly, but spirits. The only other time she'd even entertained the notion of interaction with someone deceased was when her Silas died. Imo remembered the day they lowered him into the ground, a cold winter day made colder by the fact that they all stood atop the high rocky spot that was the family cemetery. Martha was there, dispensing tissues and squeezing Imo's hand in a comforting manner.

Imo remembered Martha saying that she sensed Silas up there watching them from heaven. As Imo returned home, so grief-stricken that just breathing was an effort, it had been an enormous encouragement just knowing she had him up there, battling with her in the struggles of this world. Imo remembered how comforting it was as she trudged through those awful first months. The way she would speak aloud to him as she went about her daily tasks, just to say his name.

"Imogene," Martha used to say to her when she was despairing, when she was missing Silas so bad, "you two spent forty-eight years together as man and wife. You don't think he's going to just disappear from your life now, do you?"

Imo shook her head and stood up quickly from the table, from the memory. For a moment there she had felt the lines between fancy and reality begin to blur and she wondered if she was going off the deep end. Anxiety stalked her as she walked down the breezeway to her bed-room. Perhaps you just imagined that you tucked that little saucer away, Imogene, she fussed at herself; your imagination is running away with you.

Just as she was beginning to calm down, she noticed that the secretary was back in its original position. She stopped and took long, deep breaths to clear her head. She patted her chest. She was not imagining things! She distinctly remembered moving that with Lou. Her gaze traveled the entire hallway. On the wall opposite the secretary was a picture of Tiffany that she definitely remembered putting out of sight. In the bedroom, an armchair was returned to its original position, and an afghan she'd stored in the linen closet was back on the foot of the bed.

I am most definitely not imagining *all this,* Imo thought, the hairs on her arms alert and insistent. When I left to go to the grocery, everything was as I had moved it and when I got home, the door was still locked.

Rocked by a shiver, Imo recalled how Martha liked everything just so when she lived in the parsonage.

When Lemuel came home for lunch, Imo sat with him to eat a tuna salad sandwich and a cup of tomato soup.

"I need to talk with you, Lemuel," she said plaintively after the blessing. "About the dead."

"Alrighty," he said.

Imo considered coming right out and saying it had to do with Martha, but decided to use a more generic approach. "When believers die," she began, "can they . . . well, what I mean is, do they . . . can they visit us here?"

Lemuel placed his napkin in his lap. He looked at her over his steaming soup. He lowered his voice to a preacherly tone. "What you're wanting is a minicourse in eschatology."

"What?"

"That branch of theology concerned with what happens to a person after death."

"Yes! That's what I want to know."

"It's a fascinating subject, my dear," Lemuel said. "When a believer dies, he or she goes immediately up to heaven, where they wait for the resurrection of their body. You know, 'the dead in Christ shall rise

344

first: then we which are alive and remain shall be caught up together with them in the clouds, to meet the Lord in the air: and so shall we ever be with the Lord.' " He paused to drink some tea.

"So, they're just up there in heaven waiting, right?" she asked, expelling a long breath. "They're stuck, waiting on everlasting life."

"Actually, Imo, dear," he said matter-of-factly, "everlasting life starts the moment a person is born. And at death, the righteous one does not go into a dormant, unconscious state." He paused to drink some tea and she put her elbows on the table, staring at her soup, and looking so serious that he reached across the table to stroke her forearm. "Can you recall what happened with Jesus?" he asked. "How after He died and was resurrected, He came down here?"

"Yes, yes," Imo said, waves of frustration hammering her thoughts.

"Well, He was not a ghost or a spirit. He had hisself a body. He was flesh and bones. He could walk through walls, however. He was unrestrained by earthly boundaries."

"But that was Jesus!" Imo said, her eyes wide. "Can the departed saints come down here like that now?"

Lemuel smiled. "Well, you've got to realize, Imogene, that some substances are of a higher type than others. Though all are visible in their own realms, some may not be visible to others of lower realms. Spirit beings are of higher substance than us flesh and blood beings down here, and they're not limited to ordinary substance as we know it. So, spirit beings can go through closed doors, walls, or other material objects. Like Jesus did."

This sent shivers up and down Imo's spine. "Can *regular* dead folks up there come down here?"

He chuckled and took a bite of his sandwich. Once he'd swallowed, he said, "Can they leave heaven and come down here? Hmmm. I really can't say, dear, as I don't rightly know. What I do know is that a believer can get so set in their mind, uh . . . what's that word I'm looking for? Dogmatic! Yes, that's it. A person can get too dogmatic in conclusions about life in the hereafter. I say that because not all has been revealed to us yet." He slurped a spoonful of soup. "What I do know, however, is that the Bible does talk about going in and out of those *pearly gates*." He looked pointedly at Imo. "Now tell me, Imogene Peddigrew, if there were no movement in and out of the city of heaven, there wouldn't be no need for pearly gates, now would there?"

She shook her head.

"Well," he continued, "with that in mind, we'd all do well to keep ourselves some *open* minds — if it doesn't conflict with what the Bible already makes clear about eternity, that is."

Lemuel left for Calvary and Imogene sat quietly, her hands in her lap, looking out at bits of sky between the branches of a cedar.

The first few days of February were bone-chilling, and the sky stayed overcast, so you'd feel like it was constantly dusk outside. Imo tried not to dwell on Martha or the random things that kept moving around inside the parsonage, but it seemed that every other day a piece of furniture, or a picture, or a throw rug returned to the place where Martha used to keep it.

When Imo told Lillian her suspicions about the moving things, Lillian had only laughed and said, "Well, I swannee to Pete, Imo, I've heard of ghosts moving stuff around, but to have one in my very own neighborhood!"

Imogene had grilled Lemuel, Lou, even Jeanette and Montgomery, about the continually moving items so many times they'd gotten annoyed with her.

Her coping mechanism now was the elaborate art of denial and a swift return of things to her preferred positions. She decided that if she didn't think about the troubling matter too hard, it would not exist. This gave her a small measure of peace and she made no more mention of the various disturbances to Lillian as their friendship progressed.

They'd begun to meet each morning for coffee, alternating being the hostess. Imogene talked of her girls and the weather and new recipes. She was deeply grateful to Lillian, who had managed to secure the authentic recipe for hundred-year-old blackberry jam cake. Lillian's conversations were centered around her son, Dusty.

"I always knew the boy would turn out all right," she gushed this morning. "Even wild as he was from the moment he was born, I still knew God would get him headed down the right direction."

"I know you and Dewey are proud," Imo said, nodding and studying Lillian sitting there in the carved oak chair at her kitchen table, her fingers laced peacefully on the floral placemat.

Imo began to talk of that night's potluck at Calvary, the meat loaf and carrot salad she was planning to bring.

"Wait a minute, Imo, dear," Lillian said, slapping her knee, "you've just got to tell me how your Lemuel liked that jam cake!"

Imo's eyes lit up. "Oh, he adored it," she said, smiling at the memory of Lem's face as he had walked in the door late one evening and spied the three-layered cake sitting atop a crystal cake pedestal.

He walked closer to eye it, leaned in to smell it. "Jam cake?" he asked, his eyebrows high and hopeful.

"Yes," she said triumphantly. "*Hundred-year-old* blackberry jam cake. Like a slice, dear?"

"Yes, I would," he said. "Before supper?"

"Certainly."

He sat down quickly, resting his elbows on the table, and she sliced a giant slab of moist cake smelling of allspice, cloves, and nutmeg. She poured a tall glass of sweet milk and set it down next to his cake.

After several bites, he let out a sigh. "Imogene, love," he murmured, closing his eyes in ecstasy, "this is absolutely divine. Better even than I remembered."

"Shhh," Imogene said, placing a finger on his lips. There was no point in getting Martha all riled up.

Lillian jolted Imo back to the present. "You use blackberry jam like old Miz Verner said to?"

"Yes, yes, I did. 'Cept I couldn't come up with but a cup and a half, so I ended up substituting a half cup of my fig preserves," Imo said. "And I do believe Lem liked it even better that way. Listen, Lil, I sure do appreciate you hunting that recipe down for me."

"Oh, you think nothing of it. Was my pleasure," Lillian said, leaning forward to pat Imo's hand.

Imo smiled at her friend. She smiled at Lillian's calico cat, who was curled on the floor at her feet. A warm fuzzy of pleasure tingled up from the base of her spine to settle in her heart at the memory of Lemuel's happy face.

As she walked back home that morning, the sun peeped out from behind the clouds and lit up leaves on the magnolia trees lining Cedar Street. Living downtown was not so bad after all.

The days, the weeks, and the months in town began to have a comforting rhythm to them. Each morning Imo tended to Lemuel before he traipsed across the grass and through the bushes to Calvary. She did her morning chores, then took off for Lillian's house or waited for Lillian to come to the parsonage. The flexibility of their life downtown allowed Imo to plan her days, at least till it was time to tote Lemuel on his rounds.

When she opened her eyes on March fifth to see bright skies hanging over Euharlee, she thought it was spring come early. She crawled out of bed and stood looking out the back window at the lifting haze of dawn pierced by golden rays of sunshine. Tiny lemon-green tendrils of leaves on the dogwoods inspired her.

March always awakened in her this rest-lessness to get her hands into the soil and she was enticed almost beyond her resis-tance. She felt an overwhelming urge to leave Lemuel a note with a bowl of cornflakes, call Lillian about having lunch instead of coffee, jump in the Impala, still wearing her nightgown, floor it and head straight for the farm. She felt a little thrill as she considered this possibility.

Well. It would still be waiting after her nice little visit with Lillian. She would turn a blind eye to housework and hurry out to the old homeplace before it was time to carry Lemuel on his afternoon rounds.

"How are you on this lovely day, dear?" Lillian asked as she stepped into the sunny kitchen and settled herself at the table.

"Oh, pining away to start my garden," Imo said. "Did you see that gorgeous day out there?" She set a plate of warm cinnamon rolls on the table. "How 'bout you, Lil?"

"Well, Imogene," Lillian said, sipping her coffee, "Dewey and I have come to a decision."

"A decision?" Imo asked, curious at the resolute, delighted lilt in Lillian's voice. "Y'all heading down to Florida like you've been dreaming of?"

Lillian shook her head. She smiled. "We are going to devote ourselves wholly to God."

Imo looked hard at Lillian. "Hm?" she said, her eyebrows raised high.

Lillian folded her hands together and gazed beatifically toward heaven. Then she tucked her chin, humbled.

"What?" Imo said. "Do tell."

Lillian lifted her face to Imo's. "Dewey and I," she began, "we are so grateful to God, so happy for Dusty's transformation, we are going to give our all to Him." Her eyes were bright. "As you know, Dewey's been just waiting for the right moment to begin adding that new Sunday school wing at Calvary, and frankly, he's been right bored sitting around the house with me all the time, so, starting today, he's going to begin working on the wing and I'm going to be the secretary at Calvary. The full-time volunteer secretary, that is. Get the phone, type the letters, see to the Reverend's appointment book. That means you and I'll have to do our morning coffees down the street at Calvary."

Imo studied Lillian's fervent face. She wasn't quite sure what to say. "That's mighty generous," she said at last.

"Well, it's the least we can do in thanks for our Dusty!" she cried. "I will be grateful to God forever, as He is my witness!"

To Imo, Lillian's joy seemed so fragile, like a tiny glass figurine perched in a precarious place. The pitch of her fervor sent a shiver up Imo's spine. Here was a person made utterly vulnerable. She wanted to say to Lillian not to set herself up like this. She wanted to ask: What if Dusty falls off the wagon next month? Next year?

A part of Imo began to feel guilty for not offering to do the secretarial job, and she felt a ripple of annoyance toward her friend. Just as quickly she scolded herself: If Lillian wanted to do this thing, then who was Imo to rain on her parade? She should support her friend. Imo reached across the table and patted Lillian's arm. "I think that's wonderful, Lil," she said. "I know Lemuel will be beside himself when he finds out."

Imo was back and forth to the farm many times over the next week, tilling the garden to get the rows ready for planting her spring vegetables. She figured this was what was meant by "having the best of both worlds." It would be a triumph to her, to have a bounteous harvest and a happy husband.

Loutishie was at her side for the weekend journeys, talking away about Hank and school. She never complained about living at the parsonage anymore.

Jeanette did not visit at the parsonage often, only dropped by quickly to leave Little Silas while she ran errands. She'd been losing weight, Imo could tell, and her cheekbones were beginning to show again. She was pensive these days, the way she'd been as a little girl.

"Things going okay with you all,

Jeannie?" Imo had asked late that Saturday.

She had said little, only smiled absently, and Imogene put this out of her mind, dismissing it all as female hormones.

That next Monday Imo was sitting in a wing chair in the east parlor, fixing to sew a button back onto one of Lem's dress shirts. It was almost ten o'clock in the morning and the air was just beginning to lose its nighttime chill. The skies were clear and everywhere there were daffodils and narcissi blooming. Today was Aunt Fannie's day to tote Lemuel around and Imo relished the thought of an entire day to herself. At the old homeplace, the garden was ready for seeds and seedlings, and Imo was carrying this anticipation around with her like a new baby.

The phone rang and it was Montgomery. By his somber tone she knew it was not to be a happy conversation. He told Imo that he had carried Jeanette to the ER after a fainting spell the week prior, and it turned out that this spell had been one of many, but only the first that he'd been aware of. After a battery of tests and a CAT scan, they'd sent Jeanette to a neurologist, who ordered an MRI.

"We heard from the neurologist's office

today," Montgomery said. "The doctor says there's a tumor, a tumor on Jeannie's brain."

Imo stopped breathing and the phone slid from her hand to her lap. His words went on, muffled by the fabric of her skirt. *No,* thought Imo, *no,* somehow retrieving the phone with a trembling hand, to hear more words about how they hadn't told her earlier because they didn't want to worry her if it turned out to be nothing.

Montgomery was not using his authoritative, confident minister's voice. He had a tremulous tone that snatched Imo's breath out of her. After a spell, she sat up straight and set her mending on the floor. Her words began to tumble out. "There's things they can do for tumors," she said. "The medical world is just amazing nowadays."

"We don't even know if it's operable yet," he said.

"It must be," she said, rising with the phone to glance out the window. She focused on the red nectar in a hummingbird feeder hanging from the eaves and tried to keep from crying. "We'll need to get a second opinion."

For a moment, Montgomery did not respond. When he did, his voice was hushed.

"All we've got to do is remember that underneath are the Father's Everlasting Arms, and we'll understand it all by and by."

Imo had been aching for him to say something like this. Something ministerial and comforting in the Big Picture sense. She had experienced the peace and healing of the Everlasting Arms, as he called them, many times over the years. Buried her Silas, and Fenton Mabry, and her dear friend Martha, and then her mama. But on the other hand, this brain tumor inside Jeanette's head was a whole different animal!

To lose a spouse, even after forty-eight years of marriage, and to lose a new fiancé, and a parent, was hard. Yes, it had taken the sowing of many tears to reap the peace she now carried, but for harm to come to one of her girls or Little Silas? Oh, that was unthinkable. She cleared her throat, hoping he would continue.

"Got to pray and keep the faith, you know?" he said.

It wasn't such a simple matter. She had lived her entire life believing in the power of faith and prayer. Well, not in those things, exactly, but in a Heavenly Father who was gracious and merciful and abun-

357

dant in loving-kindness, and whose ear was ever attentive to his children's pleas.

At the same time, however, she also believed in what was referred to as "A Higher Purpose." *God's ways are not our ways* had been drilled into her brain from an early age. She had not forgotten the look on people's faces over the years, members of the congregation, as they mourned children lost to sickness or mishap. "There was a higher purpose here," someone would always declare solemnly.

"Imogene?" Montgomery said, "you still there?"

She stared outside.

"Imogene, answer me, please."

His words registered with Imo at last. She hesitated a moment, transfixed on a leaf beginning to unfurl on the maple tree just outside the window. She felt a panicky surge of fear mixed with a mother's longing to hold her child spreading through every vein like blood.

"I'm on my way," she said, her heart battering against her rib cage.

Thirteen

Here Comes the Rain
Lou

I came home from school one day to find Imo sitting on the queen-sized canopy bed in the east parlor in hushed grayness. The light was off and the curtains were drawn. She was sitting there in her gardening clothes, holding a mud-encrusted spade. I sat down beside her and we talked some about the garden. After a bit she dropped her voice so low I could barely hear her, and she told me in one terrible instant that Jeanette had a brain tumor.

A brain tumor!? How could that be true? But immediately I knew that I had known all along. I also knew this was not something to leave to fate. This was serious. I went to my room, climbed into bed and burrowed myself in my blue corduroy bedspread to pray down an umbrella of faith for Jeanette's healing. I intended to pray straight till school that next morning, but by five I was hungry and had accumulated a measure of peace, and so I climbed out to fix oatmeal cookies and milk for our snack.

As we ate Imo was quiet and contemplative, a shaken woman; I was calm by comparison. I knew God would act. It wasn't hard for me to figure out what was going on with Imo; she could not get a firm grasp on that childlike hope called faith.

I carried my own faith, the substance of things hoped for and the evidence of things unseen, deep inside myself in a private, sacred place. I felt confident that Jeanette would be well, and I knew we would move back to the old homeplace. I gave myself absolutely no wiggle room for doubt in the matters.

When I mentioned faith to Imo later that evening, she looked dazed and she twisted her hands together. I said, "Imo, don't worry. Pray. The Reverend will pray, too, and you said you and Montgomery prayed about it already."

"Lou, I'm trying not to worry," she said. "I really am."

"Well, good," I said, nodding my head emphatically. "Then don't worry anymore. Prayer is asking for rain, faith is carrying the umbrella."

"Oh, Lou," she said, taking my hand between hers and squeezing it. "God bless you, child."

On the first Saturday in April, Imo and I sat watching the news when the weatherman reported there was going to be rain, and also that temperatures would dip below freezing that night. We didn't have to say a word, we just jumped into the Impala and rode out to the farm. We were in a hurry so we'd have enough time to cover the germinating seeds and the seedlings of our frost-tender crops.

We didn't say a word as we drove along. I could tell Imo was thinking about Jeanette again, and I felt like we were in total role reversal; like I was the calm, seasoned adult and she was the terrified youth. She just wasn't the same confident soul who had once tried to convince me to see our move to town from a spiritual viewpoint. And I'm not the same Loutishie, I thought.

I was pondering all this as we jounced along over bumps and ruts in the yard,

361

pulling right up beside the fledgling garden, and shining the headlights so we could see to work. A full moon hovered low over the earth, the sky still painted with bits of day. I cracked the window a mite to close my eyes and listen to the sounds of an early spring night in the country — peepers tuning up, mingling with the tapping of raindrops on pecan leaves.

"We'd better hop to it," Imo said, tugging on gloves as she stepped out of the car.

I was hopeful. Being in the garden was a heap better than anything else for chasing Imo's dark clouds away. She had run the wheels off the Impala for close to a month at that point, so eager to get the garden in, and in her fervor she had risked planting before the last chance of frost was officially past. Good Friday, our usual date for getting the young seedlings in the ground, was still a week away.

I jumped out and opened the trunk; there were stacks of old newspapers and ragged bedsheets, along with a bulging trash bag of pine straw.

Imo was walking along the edge of the sweet corn. "Let's start with the pine straw, Lou," she said. "When it gives out, we'll use the bedsheets and newspapers."

"Yessum," I said, hefting it out and carrying it to her side.

"First let's cover the sweet corn," she said. "They're the most unhappy in cold weather."

We shook the pine straw along over the corn rows in the darkening garden, then did the same for the watermelon. The rain got heavier and the air got colder, and we worked steadily, not talking. I was fairly oblivious to the discomfort of it all, picturing myself back on the farm permanently as I tented newspapers over the germinating okra seeds. So how will God manage it? I wondered. How will He line everything up to get us back here for good? However He would accomplish it, it was wonderful for me to contemplate, as I knew His ways were higher than our ways. I smoothed back my wet bangs, smiling inside with my blessed assurance.

"Looks like we got everything," Imo said to me finally when we'd covered the squash.

Several days later I drove to Cartersville after school. Jeanette lay facedown on the couch while I stroked her back. "Imo told you, didn't she?" Jeanette's words were garbled by tears and a throw pillow. She raised her mascara-streaked face to me. "Did she tell you it may not even be operable?"

"No," I said, a ripple of alarm beginning in my knees. I'd overheard a dozen phone conversations between Imo and her Garden Club girlfriends, relatives, and Lillian Puckett, and not one word about the fact that it might not be operable.

"Well, Lu-lu, this might be it for Jeanette Lavender Pike."

"Stop talking like that! When will they know if it can be operated on or not?"

"Few days."

"What does Montgomery say?"

"Oh, he says, 'Pray and leave it in God's hands,' and stuff like that, but I can tell he's scared spitless."

I swallowed hard. It was one thing to have faith about a tumor when there was something doctors could do and quite another when they couldn't. I could feel fear nipping and yapping at my heels like vicious little dogs. *You're not getting your teeth into me,* I spoke to that monster inside, *I will cling to my faith.* I rehearsed all my litanies about how victory is in the Lord and He is the answer to all the problems we face in life, and I determined I would not let my mind dwell on the problem, when I could think about the Answer.

I had come to realize that thoughts and words had power, and I just had to believe it would be okay. I had to pray and have faith. I would carry the umbrella for everyone.

"Everything's going to be fine, Jeannie." My voice sounded high.

Jeanette's lusterless eyes stared at a soap opera on the television screen, but I could tell her mind was miles away. Her hair was a frizzy mess with a long stripe of dark brown at the roots. "They think it might even be malignant," she said, reaching over to the end table for a pack of Virginia Slims.

"Might not," I said, my blood literally running cold at the mention of cancer in this person who seemed so indestructible.

We sat listening to birdsongs carried in on a breeze through the screen door. Jeanette leaned forward to light another cigarette, then sank back into the couch. "Know what's crazy, Lu-lu?" she said at last, her eyebrows knit in puzzlement as she inhaled deeply.

"What's that?" I said.

"When I found out about the tumor,

well, in a way it was a relief, you know? To finally know what's going on with me. But, that's not what's crazy. The doc says it's pretty normal to feel that way. What's crazy is when I found out how serious this thing is," she paused and put an index finger against her forehead, "and that I might croak, you know, what's so crazy is that now every little thing is so precious to me! My little runty house in my little runty town, and the way the trees look. Trees!" The ashes from her forgotten cigarette drifted to the floor. "Heck, Lou, I mean, there I was, before all this. So unhappy, you know?"

I nodded.

"Now I wouldn't trade this average little life I have, *had,* for anything. Every minute I'm begging the Old Boy in the sky for just another ordinary day down here. Another day with my heart beating next to Montgomery's when we're laying up in bed together, for Little Silas climbing in between us when he's woken up from a bad dream, for scrubbing that blasted skillet in the kitchen after I fried us up some hash browns, for . . ." Her voice trailed off and her eyes grew shiny with tears.

"Dernit, Lou!" she said, standing up finally to stub out her cigarette and cross her arms.

She said she's praying, Lou, I reminded myself.

"I can't even *drive!*" she screamed out, pacing the tiny den, tears glistening on her cheeks.

I didn't cry because I couldn't even take a breath. I stood up to drape my arm across Jeanette's shoulders. "It's good you're praying," I told her, zipping up my tone with enthusiasm.

"Well," she said, "I'm praying. That's for sure. But I don't really feel like anyone's listening." She laughed.

Jeanette's laughter didn't fool me; she was a desperate woman. She needed more faith. Suddenly April's marquee saying at Calvary popped into my mind:

ARE YOU WRINKLED WITH A BURDEN?
COME TO CHURCH FOR A FAITH LIFT.

"Let's go pray at Calvary," I said in a burst of inspiration.

Jeanette kept snuffling, her gaze straight ahead, but she nodded ever so slightly, and it looked like a little light came on in her eyes. I could see it gleaming when she turned to me. "Okay," she said.

I wanted to shout "Praise Jesus!" but I also understood that that type of thing didn't sit well with Jeanette. "Good," I said in as toneless a voice as I could muster.

I wasn't exactly sure what I would say to God once we got to Calvary, like make it operable or make it benign or make it gone, and it scared me, how serious things were, but somehow, that bright flash of hope in Jeanette's eyes made me feel energized and capable.

The loud mewling hit my ears sometime before daylight on a Monday, and I sat bolt upright in bed like I'd been struck by lightning. It sounded like a baby crying at first, then the keening grew too throaty for a baby. I had no idea what I was hearing. Bingo gave a low growl and stood tense at my bedside. "What is it, boy?" I whispered, my hand reaching out to touch the fur along his back standing stiffly at attention.

I felt for the switch on my bedside lamp and a puddle of yellow light fell across my chest. Four a.m. The yowling got louder, making me wince and shut my eyes. "Reckon we better go check it out, boy."

He moved his rigid body to the door as I groped for a flashlight I kept under the bed. We crept out into the hallway, following its white beam.

"Must be coming from outside," I whispered, fastening Bingo's leash to his collar. I opened the front door and we crept out into the yard, where he darted to the forsythia shrubs, sniffing wildly and pulling so crazy I had to drop the flashlight and hold on to him with both hands. "Hold on, easy now," I breathed, racing around behind him, squinting through the dark.

He stopped short at the foundation of the house, barking shrilly and digging furiously with his front paws so that stinging bits of earth pelted my bare shins.

The porch lights came on, and I could make out the Reverend's form in the doorway. He held a shotgun.

"Reverend?" I whispered. "It's okay. It's just me and Bingo."

"What's going on out here, Loutishie?"

"I don't know. We heard something. There's something under the house."

He padded down the brick steps in his slippers, a robe cinched tightly at his waist.

"Some type of critter," I said. "First it sounded like a baby. Like a baby screaming."

"Thought I was dreaming," he said, squinting, "dreaming about a cat fight."

Now that I thought about it, it did sound

like a cat fight. Imo appeared at the Reverend's elbow, rubbing her sleep-swollen face. "Lemuel?" she said.

"Some type of varmint's carrying on up under the house," he said.

Another shrill yowl pierced the air and I saw Imo's eyebrows fly up. She crept closer to me and Bingo. I put Bingo's leash in her hand and went to root around near the steps for the flashlight. I cast the flashlight's beam along the house at ground level. After a minute or so, Imo burst out with "Look a yonder! Shine the light over that a way, Lou!" She gestured frantically toward the cellar door.

I turned and the flashlight threw wavering black shadows as a shape lumbered out and stopped, paralyzed for a split second in the light's beam.

"Mercy!" Imo gasped, clutching the fabric of her nightgown at her neck. "A skunk!"

We all stared with mingled amusement and shock, at a lunky black-and-white creature slinking off into the shadows. Suddenly a second creature appeared out of a hole next to the cellar door. I shone the beam of light on him. An orange striped tomcat with a mangled right ear and a definite limp. *"Rowrrr,"* he fussed, blinking at us a moment before he, too, departed.

"Well, I be dog," the Reverend said, rubbing his chin in a dazed sort of way.

"I hate to say it," Imo said then, "but I'm catching a whiff of something right potent."

By daylight an awful odor had permeated every square centimeter of the parsonage. We didn't even bother to put on our daytime clothes. We just grabbed some sandwich fixings and a couple of things to put on later and jumped into the Impala to head for the old homeplace.

When we got there we left the car doors standing open to air the car and put our extra clothes out in the sun on the picnic table.

The dusty, stale, closed-up interior of the farmhouse smelled like heaven compared to the skunk's fragrant expulsion. "Come nine o'clock I'll drive to the Red Dot and get us some provisions," said Imo, striding over to the bare cupboards. "Laundry powder, too. I 'spec I'd better wash those clothes we brought before we wear them."

"It's up to you, dear," the Reverend replied. "I hope we'll go back home before too long. You can drop me off at Calvary on your way to the grocery."

"Lemuel! We'll just let Lillian know you're here and you can take today off. She can surely hold down the fort. If I remember right, skunk smell takes several days to be tolerable."

He was nervously pacing the den. "Several days?!"

"Several days," Imo affirmed. "May as well get settled in here for a spell." She was smiling. "The world will keep right on going."

"I've got things I need to tend to at Calvary!"

"Oh, sweetheart, it'll keep. Anybody could understand if you tell them you had a skunk do his business up under the parsonage."

"I'll call the extension office," he said. "I'll ask an expert."

"You do that, dear."

The rise and fall of Imo's and the Reverend's voices were so familiar to me that I tuned them out. The poor Reverend's voice was kind of quavery. He was angry, or sad maybe, to be at the farm.

But I was in hog heaven, deliriously happy. *My prayer has been answered,* I kept shouting to myself internally, the enormity of this gift making me buzz from toe tips to hair follicles. Bingo was ecstatic, too. When we pulled up, he tore out of the car and ran zigging and zagging around the yard, the barn, the well house, and then down toward the bottoms.

After I helped Imo crank open the windows and turn on the attic fan, I went after him. I would have called it a perfect day, even if I weren't getting to spend it where I loved best. Blue skies and sunshine, a sprinkling of Shasta daisies blooming just beyond the fence. I could smell the Etowah when I got close. How do you hug a river? I wondered as I ran along its banks.

I dawdled a ways upriver. Across the water spread a bank of lilies in full glory, their trumpetlike blooms swaying in the breeze. As I pondered the mystery of God's ways, something inside dropped me to my knees, to give thanks. I lived in the moment. I did not even let myself consider that eventually the skunk's odor would be gone.

I stayed outside that whole afternoon. Imo carried the Reverend to Calvary and then went to do her shopping. She also consulted with Miss Luckasavage, our county extension agent, who told her to open all the windows and doors in the parsonage, and to spray three parts water to one part bleach all up under the house. Then she was to sprinkle generous amounts of lime all over the ground.

"Hank rode by the parsonage looking for you while I was there, Lou," she said, "and he helped me tend to things, so I invited him out to eat supper with us tonight. Brought some of last summer's squash, green beans, limas, okra, and tomatoes. How does vegetable soup and cornbread sound?"

"Fabulous," I said.

"I'll call Jeanette and her crew to come out, too," Imo said, "when I run back to Calvary to pick Lemuel up."

I nodded, hesitant to ask the question that hovered over us constantly. We did not dare call the tumor a tumor aloud to one another and still we had no word on it being operable or not.

Imo set a bag of cornmeal on the counter. "Tell you what, Lou, let's eat a quick sandwich and work in the garden some before I have to go."

We sat down at the pine table in the sunny kitchen. That table was worn to a smooth, almost silky patina over the years; I knew every knothole and line of wood grain on it like the back of my hand, and it was beautiful. That bologna and mustard sandwich on white bread was the best thing I ever put in my mouth.

I could tell Imo was in a euphoric state as much as I was. She patted her lips when she finished, leaned back, folded her hands in her lap, and closed her eyes, a half smile on her lips. "Sure is nice to be home, isn't it?" I said.

I could see Imo struggling to maintain her preacher's wife demeanor. "We did what we had to do, Lou, dear," she said in measured words. "We have a lot to be thankful for." But as we headed out the door, her eyes caught mine, and they said, *Yes, it is. It is wonderful to be here.*

Outside, we weeded, mulched, and made third plantings of snap beans and squash. Imo squinted in the sun as she tied the tomato vines to their stakes. "Looks like we did indeed save them from that late frost last month, doesn't it, Lou?" she said.

Imo's eyes were smiling as she pointed out some irises blooming proudly amidst a patch of spearmint along one side of the barn. "I believe this is the prettiest I've ever seen it here."

Later as we were putting our tools away, rounding the corner of the shed, she gasped at the bright orange heads of her

Oriental poppies waving above their woolly leaves and stems.

"Did you ever," she murmured, stopping to stroke one of the flowers.

"It's gorgeous," I admitted. "A whole lot prettier than at the parsonage."

We sat down to supper at six o'clock sharp.

"Take two and butter 'em while they're hot," Imo directed, passing round a basket of biscuits. Seven glasses of ice tea and seven steaming bowls of vegetable soup lay on the dining table.

Hank was seated at my left, with Jeanette and Montgomery directly across from us. The Reverend was at one end of the table and Imo was at the other, with Little Silas at her elbow.

After the Reverend said a long blessing we all dug in. "Tastes like summer itself, Miz Peddigrew," Hank said, smacking his lips. "And these biscuits are superb. How do you get them so light and fluffy?"

Nothing made Imo happier than a compliment on her cooking, and she lit all up. "Well, the vegetables I put up from last year's garden and the biscuits are from Mama's buttermilk recipe. This year's garden promises to be good, too. Lou and I were out there this afternoon and everything is just coming along so nicely."

Montgomery reached for the sorghum syrup. "Playing hooky from school to garden?" he teased.

"I'd say a skunk's a good excuse," Imo said. "I don't think anybody would've wanted Lou in school before she got all washed up."

Everyone was laughing but Jeanette. I noticed her stirring her soup in a distracted sort of way. I was gobbling mine, however, its hearty taste mingling with all the good feelings of being home.

"So, how long y'all going to hang here?" Montgomery asked as he spread sorghum on a biscuit.

"Oh," said Imo, "Miss Luckasavage said it will most likely be till late Wednesday afternoon."

"But you'll be at school tomorrow and Wednesday, won't you, Lou?" Hank asked, placing his hand on my knee underneath the table.

"Sure," I replied, flushing warm at this intimate act in front of Imo and the Reverend. Funny thing was, I had been kind of flirting with the idea of laying out of school for a couple days, of spending time down at the river bottoms with Bingo, in the garden with Imo. But I knew it was useless to torture myself with this kind of thinking. Playing hooky was not in my nature.

I sized up Jeanette as she ran her finger through the condensation on her tea glass. Had she heard more news about the tumor?

I had to bite my tongue against the urge to bring up how nice it was to be staying on the farm. I kept hoping Imo would bring the subject up herself, on account of how happy she was. Surely the Reverend could figure it all out. He wasn't a stupid man.

I knew the skunk deal was God's doing, giving us a foretaste of bliss, and I had taken to stepping up my praying, every cell of my mind and body crying out in supplication that we could just stay on.

"Pecan pie for dessert," Imo sang out when she heard spoons scraping bare bowls.

The Reverend made a pleased grunt.

"My absolute favorite, Miz Peddigrew," said Hank. "Pecans off your trees out back here?"

"Why, yes, they certainly are," she replied. "Lou harvested them last fall."

Hank squeezed my knee and shot me a look that said *We'll have to get some alone time later this evening.* I got the tickly sensation I always did when I thought of us together.

I was feeling pretty good until I saw Montgomery trying to coax Jeanette to eat more of her supper. "No more." She shook her head and clamped her lips together.

"But you've hardly eaten a bite," Montgomery pled, aiming a spoon toward her mouth the way you do with a child. "For me?"

I tried not to watch as they were engaged in what was clearly an intimate and on-going struggle. Jeanette had lost a good deal of weight; the pounds she'd fought against for so long were now gone, along with quite a few more. She'd stopped fixing her hair and she didn't wear makeup anymore either. A baggy old gray sweatsuit hung on her gaunt frame, something she wouldn't have been caught dead in before.

I rose to follow Imo into the kitchen. I watched her slice the pie into wedges. "So have you heard anything about Jeannie?" I whispered. "She looks awful."

"Well, sugar foot," she said after a long moment, "Montgomery says they'll most likely hear something one way or the other in the morning." Her eyes were shiny.

"Imo," I said, "she'll be fine. You'll look

back at all this one day like a bad dream."

Imo smiled wanly and I reached over to cover her hand with mine. "Jeannie's so *young*," she said, a few tears escaping down her cheeks.

Late that night I rolled over into that wonderful gully in my old mattress. I could smell Imo's bath powder floating down the hallway and I heard night birds stirring beyond my window. I knew I was going to sleep great. I wanted to fall asleep recalling Hank's face, his slow, broad smile, luminous in the moonlight as we stood in the clearing alone.

He held me in his arms. "The fact that we're here, on the farm, is a pure miracle, Hank," I whispered into his ear.

"Too bad it's just till Wednesday, huh?" His breath was hot on my neck.

"Don't be so sure," I said, nibbling his ear. "Did you get a load of the Reverend after supper? Him sitting up beside Imo on the glider, holding hands and watching the sunset? They were happy," I insisted. "Happier than they are at the parsonage. They never sit together holding hands like that at the parsonage."

"Yeah," said Hank, "sure." But I heard a note of hesitancy in his voice.

"They *are,*" I maintained, watching the fabric of his T-shirt as it rose and fell at his neckline. He pulled me against him and bent to cover my mouth with his.

He'll see, I said to myself, walking beside him back to the house. God will not let me down.

I carried my umbrella stubbornly.

"Good news," Imo said, as she opened the door for me when I returned from school that next afternoon. "I heard from Montgomery and he said it's operable! They've scheduled the surgery for May twenty-first. Three weeks."

"Thank the Lord!" I said. "Why are they waiting so long?"

"Well, he figures it's because they want to put a little bit more weight on her."

A wave of relief swept through me. "Operable," I breathed out, floating into the den to drop my backpack and collapse onto the couch. "But earlier didn't they say it was growing?"

"Yes, growing, but three weeks will be okay, Lou. That's what they say."

I felt an overwhelming sense of relief. Whatever little bits of unbelief I'd unknowingly held were now gone.

"It's still a real risky surgery, the doctor

told Montgomery." Imo's body language communicated a still lingering stronghold of fear. "Being near her brain where it is. He doesn't think it's malignant, but we're not totally out of the woods."

"But operable is good," I told her. The sky beyond the window was pure blue, the leaves of the magnolia trees reflecting sunlight. "I'm going outside," I announced.

I cut through the pasture and into the woods, running beneath towering red oaks, their big trunks rising like the pillars of a cathedral, spreading out to form a sunlit canopy of branches and leaves. With two answers to prayer under my belt, I felt invincible.

That evening Imo was absorbed in her crossword puzzle and the Reverend was reclined in the La-Z-Boy, listening to WPCH, a station out of Atlanta that played what Jeanette called old fogey rock.

Now, that's a picture of contentment, I thought as I did my calculus homework at the kitchen table with a Pepsi at my elbow.

"Walked over to the parsonage today during my lunch hour," the Reverend said.

"You did?" Imo answered him, and I saw her stiffen a bit.

"Smell's really clearing out," he said.

"Is that so?" Imo dipped her head toward her crossword so I couldn't see her face. I pressed my pencil against my temple. No big deal, I kept telling myself. That doesn't mean anything.

"It is indeed," the Reverend said after a moment, sounding extremely happy. " 'Bout time to be getting ourselves on back home, isn't it." He did not phrase this as a question.

He does not want to stay here, I acknowledged in a silent panic, and you, Loutishie Lavender, will be going back with them. This is no dream you're going to wake up from. This is reality, and your umbrella has been blown inside out. Rain is pouring down on your head.

At last Imo looked up from her puzzle. "You're certain, dear?" she said to him. "Clearing out?"

"Be fresh as springtime tomorrow."

I sat motionless, looking to Imo in silent appeal, though I knew I would get no backup from her. She was Pastor's wife, after all, and she did seem to be taking to life on Cedar Street better than I was.

Then he dropped the biggest bomb of all.

"I been thinking, dear," he said. "Ever since we got out here I been thinking.

Maybe it'd be nice to sell this place. Taxes the way they are."

Stunned, I drained my Pepsi, looking at them but not hearing a word they said. Right then and there I made a decision. If Imo even considered selling the farm, I would not stand by for it. I would not be their compliant, sweet-natured girl anymore!

What scared me were the things I was willing to do to keep that land. I felt a burning, stabbing sensation in my chest as I looked up to the heavens, thinking, "I will stay right here. I will fight that man. Even if he is a man of God, I will fight him tooth and nail if he tries to make Imo sell this place."

And I knew just how to start.

Fourteen

My Dusty!
Imo

That first night back in the parsonage
Lemuel fell asleep as soon as his head hit
the pillow, snuggled up cozily to Imo's side.
She spent the night tossing and turning,
thinking of Lou all alone out at the old
homeplace.

It had certainly been an ugly scene. After
Lou heard Lemuel's suggestion she
marched up and screamed right into
Lemuel's face. "Just who do you think you
are?! You are out of your ever-loving mind
if you think you can sell this place! Do you
hear me? This land was my Uncle Silas's
pride and joy, and you aren't half the man
he was!" Then she turned abruptly, ran
into her room, and slammed the door so

hard the whole farmhouse shook.

"She didn't mean that," Imo said after a spell, reaching over to touch Lemuel's cheek. He did not respond.

"She's never done *anything* like this before," Imo said, working hard to sound convincing. "Lou's a good girl. She's just, just . . ."

"Willfully defiant," he said, slumping down into the La-Z-Boy in aftershock. "Back in my day, young'uns respected their elders. I would no more have raised my voice against my father than —"

"But you're not her father, Lem," Imo broke in. "Silas was her father. Well, he raised her like a father. And she worshiped the ground he walked on. Still does."

"Apparently so," Lemuel said in a preacherly tone.

Imo felt a twinge of resentment at that comment, though she bit her tongue. Only the steady buzz of the cicadas filled the next minute.

She'd not been prepared for his words about selling the place, either, and they had caused a thick blackness to come rushing down on her. She could not say a thing with that cloud on her, and even when the shock wore off a little bit, she was still at a loss for words.

Much later she served Lemuel another piece of pecan pie and hesitantly approached the subject again. "Lem, dear," she said, "about your comment, about selling this place — you know, I believe I want to hang on to it."

He sat there, smiling, watching her nervously toying with the pie server. "Maybe when you hear what I have to say you'll change your mind," he declared.

Her heart skipped a beat. She shook her head. "But this place feels like part of me."

"Well . . . ," he said, "place is going to seed with no one here."

His words were a jackhammer in her heart. "Won't be long till Lou will be able to keep it," she pled breathlessly. "I know what! I'll ask Jeanette and Montgomery to move here now!"

He laughed, reaching for his milk. "I can't see Jeanette living out here in a million years, Imo, and Lou will be four, maybe eight years in school still."

"I couldn't possibly say yes," Imo said in a small voice. "There's a lot to think about. I cannot imagine selling it."

"It's just dirt," he said, wiping his mouth on a napkin. "Don't worry, I got a feeling that a year from now you won't even think about it. You'll be so happy."

How could he sit there talking like that? What was going on in that man's mind?

She shook her head harder. "I can't say yes."

Lem reached out and took her hand. "We could use the money soon," he said, squeezing her hand.

His voice was still strange and she studied him. "Do we need money?" she asked. "I thought we were fine in that department."

He looked up at her and his eyes grew all moony. "I believe I've heard His voice. It's time," he said. "Time to think of retiring, and I aim to show you a good time, Imo, love — time of your life. We'll use the money to take us some trips. Cruises."

"Oh my." Imo felt the ground shifting. Careful now. Did he really just say what she thought he did? Saying retirement in with all this talk about selling the farm bewildered her. She didn't know what to say back. Her idea of retirement, of living out her final days included being right here.

She looked out the window and tried to focus on the stars beyond the darkness. The heavens stretched away, engulfing the ball of earth they stood on, and she could not comprehend it all. Shakily she rose to put his dishes into the sink. *Lord, help me do what's right in Your sight,* she prayed fervently. *I cannot think through all this right now. And please, wrap Your loving and protective arms around my little Lou.*

Imo mixed biscuits while occasionally peering out the window at the morning sun, pale through thick gray clouds. The first pot of coffee she poured into a large thermos to carry to Calvary for her visit with Lillian. She began another for Lemuel and put water on to boil grits.

She stuffed some of yesterday's blueberry muffins and some napkins into a hamper and settled the thermos next to this, added a pint of half-and-half, two coffee cups, and two spoons. She set Lemuel's breakfast before him when he appeared, excusing herself to go get a bath.

Steam rose as she lay back in the tub, letting her shoulders submerge, feeling the silky water cradle her tired bones. She floated blissfully, climbing out only when she heard Lemuel's chair scraping back after his prayer time. Hastily she dressed, buoyed by the relaxing bath and the prospect of an intimate chat with Lillian.

The short walk to Calvary was laced with the fresh, cheerful faces of daffodils and the soft warble of bluebirds. It was comforting to see Dewey's long white pickup truck pulled alongside the church, with its bed full of ladders, sawhorses, and two-by-fours. A fading door panel on the truck read: FOR A JOB DONE RIGHT CALL PUCKETT'S BUILDING & REMODELING.

Imo could send herself into spasms of guilt if she added up all the hours Lillian and Dewey put in at Calvary. Between the two of them, it was well over sixty a week. Dewey had already framed the new Sunday school wing, and Lillian had organized Lemuel's jumble of files. She had also tidied the Sunday school curriculum from pre-K to seniors, added a wall poster with a little table underneath which held a spiral pad for folks to volunteer for each Sunday's pulpit flowers, and scrubbed the dirt from years past off of all the play pretties in the nursery.

The two were certainly offering themselves wholly to God, and Lillian's reports on Dusty's sobriety were still laced with overwhelming gratitude and breathless wonder.

Imo lugged the hamper through the front door and into the anteroom of the church office. A profusion of purple irises and yellow forsythia sat in a vase beside Lillian's typewriter. "Good morning," said

Imo. "What lovely flowers!"

"Mornin' darlin'!" Lillian beamed. "Those are fresh from my yard this morning."

Imo sat down on a tufted burgundy love seat against the wall, underneath a picture of the Last Supper.

" 'Don't Wait for the Hearse to Take You to Church,' " Lillian said, smiling.

"What?" Imo stared blankly at her.

"Catchy, don't you think? It's next month's saying for the marquee outside. Think the Rev will like it? It's either that or 'Kmart's Not Your Only Savings Place.' "

"Oh," said Imo, "I know he'll love it. You sure are making life easy for him these days."

"Well, it's my pleasure, you know," she said, lifting her eyes from Imo's face to Jesus' in the picture above Imo's head.

Imo patted the hamper and smiled. "Ready?"

Lillian smiled and cleared her desk. "How are things with you today? Bet you're glad to be back home. Glad for all the fresh air." She chuckled.

"Well, yes, no, I don't know . . . Lou's still at the farm, Lil. She wouldn't leave."

"Wouldn't leave?" Lillian's voice rose.

"Wouldn't budge when we packed up

and left. Giving Lemuel the silent treat-ment."

"Are we talking about *your* sweet little Loutishie?"

"Yes."

"You don't say."

"Mm hmm. She's all torn up because he mentioned selling the farm."

"You all didn't drag the child back with you?" Lillian asked, her eyebrows high.

Imogene sighed. "She's big as I am, Lil. Plus, if you'd only seen her face. She's ab-solutely crazy about the place. I've never seen the like." Her voice trembled. "Unless you count me, that is."

"Oh, hon," Lillian said, moving to the couch beside Imo and covering her hand with her own. "What did you tell Lemuel?"

"Nothing really, not yet anyway," she said with an exasperated sigh. "On the one hand, the man's talking about retiring, and I have to say, that would be the best thing ever. He's got to retire, Lillian, and I'd do almost anything to get him to retire. But on the other hand, he acts like he'd have to go on cruises if he retires, and so he thinks we have to sell the farm to get some money. He gets an idea about something and . . ."

"You just tell him you won't sell it,"

Lillian said, squeezing Imo's hand for emphasis. "You just tell him you won't sell it."

"But what if he says he won't retire if I don't?" Imo said. "Or maybe I will sell. I don't know. I'm torn in two. Oh, I'm talking to myself now. I'm so awfully tired I can't even think straight."

Maybe that was it. In all the excitement of the skunk and moving to the farm, and moving back to the parsonage, and Lou's rebellion, there had been moments when Imo couldn't think. She could only react. It didn't help that she was so worried over Jeannie.

"I can't believe little Loutishie," Lillian said, shaking her head and going "mmm mmm mmm."

Imo laughed shakily, fidgeting with the antimacassar on the arm of the love seat. "I'm going to check on her every single evening. I'm going to save my gardening for the evenings."

"You're a good momma," Lillian said, standing to open the hamper. "Now, let's have us some coffee." She pulled everything out and arranged it on the desktop. Dragging a metal folding chair from a stack in the corner, she set this up directly across from her own. "Here we are, dear."

Imo moved to the cool seat of the chair

as Lillian poured two cups of coffee. She was so efficient, you could easily imagine her as a secretary for one of those large firms in Atlanta. Some busy, important office.

Imo felt a bit of responsibility to offer some cheerier conversation. "I've got some good news," she said at last.

"Pray tell, dear heart," Lillian said.

"Jeannie's tumor, it's operable."

"Why, that's wonderful news, Imo!" Lillian exclaimed. "I was scared to ask if there'd been any more news. Didn't want to upset you if it was bad." She raised her coffee cup and held it toward Imo. "Let's make a toast! To God with thanks that He's paved our children's paths with blessings!"

Imo forced herself to smile and clack her cup to Lillian's. "Listen, Lillian," she said after a steaming gulp, "it's a mighty serious surgery nonetheless. So close to her brain and all. Doctor doesn't think it's malignant, but he won't know definitely till he's in there. Surgery's good, but he said there're no guarantees."

"Oh, Imo," Lillian said, easing out from behind her desk and bending to engulf Imo in a hug. "It's the waiting that's so hard, isn't it? Sometimes I wish the Lord didn't make us learn patience."

"Patience," said Imo weakly.

"Now, drink up," Lillian said, returning to her desk to peel the liner from a blueberry muffin.

Imo drank her coffee and in her mind was an ever-present picture; Loutishie out at the farm, willfully defiant, staking her silent claim. How pitiful the girl was, to be waging a war against someone who didn't even know he was fighting, who couldn't know how much that land meant to them. He could not fathom Lou's anger, her *righteous* anger, as Imo thought about it now, and how could he? Was it even fair to expect him to understand their feelings?

The phone rang and Lillian chirped a happy "Good morning, Calvary Baptist." She kept the receiver to her ear as she nibbled her muffin, nodding occasionally and saying, "Yes, yes. I know the Reverend will want to know all about that. I'll be sure to pass it along." She hung up and for a while it was quiet as they finished their muffins. They had second cups of coffee and began to talk of spring and the coming bazaar Calvary held each May.

They laughed over Sheriff Bentley's new buzzed haircut. He was a giant man and the style made him look like one of the wrestlers on TV by the name of Abdullah the Butcher.

"Well, I imagine I'd better head on back to the house," Imo said, standing abruptly to gather the breakfast things. "Lillian, it's been a real treat, as always."

"It'll all be okay, darlin'," Lillian said, searching Imo's concerned face as she stood at the door.

Imo sighed deeply. She felt like doubting Thomas, like a fraud of a preacher's wife. "Lil," she confessed, scarcely able to get the words to come out, "just when it seemed things were looking up all around, they've taken a turn for the worse." Thankfully she managed to blink back the tears.

"Just trust in the Lord, Imo, dear," Lillian soothed. "If He can deliver Dusty from the bottle, He can surely handle Jeanette. And Lou. And your beloved homestead."

Imo nodded, though she felt a million miles away from God at that moment. "Bye, Lil," she said with a tight-lipped smile.

As she walked out the door, the sun emerged from the clouds, striking magnolia leaves along Cedar Street so that they lit up golden yellow. Imo studied the sky. It would be a nice day for digging in her garden.

That Sunday, stepping into the empty church fellowship hall ahead of Imo, Lemuel flipped the light switches as usual and went straight to his tiny office to pray over the upcoming sermon. She went around opening all the window blinds and morning sunlight poured in, dappling the floor. She checked her watch — still a good half hour till folks began arriving for Sunday school.

She didn't mind the solitude, but it put her in mind of the fact that usually she waited with Loutishie. Dear Lou. Her behavior of late still bewildered Imo, and her open animosity toward Lemuel was so uncharacteristic it was almost frightening.

On impulse Imo made her way to the still darkened sanctuary, sliding into a pew at the back. She'd pled with the girl at length over things. In her mind, the first step was just getting Lou to talk to Lemuel. "When can you come to the parsonage, Lou?" she asked often as they worked together in the garden.

"Never."

"Couldn't you just call him on the

phone, then, and have a civil discussion?"

"Nothin' doin'."

"Can't you just try and understand? Bend a little? Forgive him enough to open up the channels for a *discussion* on the matter? I don't want to sell the homestead either, and if you'd just come for supper one night, when he's in a good mood, we could all sit down and communicate; why, then, Lou, dear heart, perhaps he'd listen. Perhaps . . ."

"Imo!" Lou's face was bright with indignation. "I'm staying right here, and if he tries to sell the place, he'll have to do it over my dead body!"

Imo looked up. To the sun shining through the stained glass window behind the pine lectern and the choir loft. The window held a picture of Jesus, sitting on a boulder, His arms outstretched to a group of barefoot children running toward Him. Their faces were joyful at His invitation, His acceptance. She stared hard.

She wanted to feel that way. Feel that there was a big pair of all-knowing hands there to lift her up, to hold her protectively and minister peace unto her. She wanted those same hands to enfold Jeanette, and Loutishie, too. Tears threatened and Imo shook her head mutely, trying to imagine Jesus' arms around her. How would it feel to have the Son of God hold you? She hugged herself. She felt bruised and sore.

She closed her eyes, bowed her head. "Father God," she whispered, "I am so weary, and I feel so far away from You. Please put Your everlasting arms underneath me and hold me up. Amen."

When she opened her eyes the sanctuary was full of a pearly gray light. So gently she felt this mystical tingling begin at her spine and spread throughout her whole body, like a mild electric wave. Every nerve stood at the alert.

A holy shock treatment? She wondered, looking to the left and right in wide-eyed wonder.

With it came a peace, a stillness inside that wasn't a brash loud "who the heck cares what befalls me" sort of peace, but a still, quiet voice susurrating through every fiber of her being, saying, "Have no fear, my child, everything is in My hands."

Sunday school and the service both passed in a blur for Imo and it was with a lighter heart that she walked home to prepare ham, escalloped potatoes, and English peas for their Sunday dinner.

Friday's sun and high temperatures felt like a damp sheet after a solid week of rain. Imo left close to noon to do her weekend grocery shopping. She planned to get a pretty graduation card for Lou and some gourmet coffee beans along with the usual fare.

She was backing down the tiny drive when she saw it. Someone had moved the cement birdbath back to the midst of a circle of liriope in the center of the front yard. That was where Martha had liked it. Imo preferred it just to the left of the steps, nestled among ivy. She mashed the brake pedal and stared in astonishment. "Oh, my goodness gracious" slipped from her lips.

Well, well, well, Imo thought, now she's taken to rearranging my yard. For a moment, she considered going back in the house and calling Lemuel, but she dismissed that thought almost immediately. He would just look at her quizzically, suggesting by his expression that she was the crazy one.

She toyed with giving Martha a good what-for, but she had made up her mind lately to ignore Martha. She would not give her the satisfaction of being fussed at.

Imo pulled onto Cedar Street and floored it, lowering the window for some fresh air.

At the Red Dot Foodstore, Imo waved at the owner, Mr. Justice, in his snow-white apron. He sat up on a swivel chair behind a low bar where you could buy stamps or pick up one of the weekly sales flyers. She made her way first to the tiny revolving greeting card rack at the rear of the store. It seemed she was the only customer in the place and she took her time at the cards, finally selecting one with an owl wearing a mortarboard that read: Whooo's headed for great things?

The sight and smell of some chicken planks and corn dogs under a heat lamp next to the pastries made her hungry, so she grabbed the tongs and nestled eight chicken planks and four tater wedges into one of the collapsible cardboard boxes. *This will make a nice lunch for Lemuel and me,* she thought, popping a piece of crust into her mouth. Her fingers were shiny with grease as she wheeled her buggy over to the dairy section to gather eggs, butter, and half-and-half.

At the coffees, she lingered, torn between one flavored with hazelnut and one called French Vanilla Nut. "Let's try us something new, hon," Lillian's voice echoed in her head. "Something exotic. So we can feel like we're at one of those fancy coffee shops in Atlanta."

I'll get both, Imo decided. *I'll make a batch of my apple scones, and I'll carry it all to Calvary tomorrow.* Their morning coffee hung gleaming like a ripe peach in her mind and she felt herself begin to relax.

Mr. Justice was shelving a humongous carton full of Pampers when Imo was ready to check out. He was a young, auburn-haired man, very trim, with what Imo thought of as smiling blue eyes. He had moved to Euharlee from New Jersey just six short months ago when his grandfather, Homer Justice, had passed away quickly and left the Red Dot Foodstore to him in his will. No one really knew the younger Mr. Justice yet, though it was rumored Wanda had been out to the drive-in with him. It was also said that he'd never heard of fatback, boiled peanuts, chitterlings, pickled pig's feet, or muscadines before arriving in Euharlee. Imo had been relieved to find that he still offered these items in the store.

"Find everything you needed?" he asked Imo, his unusual northern accent still a shock.

"Yes. Even the grits," she added with a smile.

Stepping outside, Imo caught a whiff of new-cut grass. She rolled the windows down in the Impala and cruised slowly home, enjoying the clear blue sky stretched above and the sounds of songbirds all around. She ignored the birdbath and parked haphazardly, hurrying inside to put away the groceries and get lunch fixings on the table before Lemuel appeared at twelve o'clock sharp.

It seemed that she hadn't been home for more than five minutes when a loud boom shook the parsonage. Imo shuddered along with the plates in her china cabinet. She wasn't sure exactly what had happened, but reverberations of it were still pulsing through the air.

She reached for the phone, but then she paused and held a hand to her open mouth as she glanced out the window to see a black mushroom blooming toward the west. It filled the sky quickly. Her eyes widened and she ran to open the front door. At that exact moment the long wail of a siren began and all the neighborhood dogs began to howl. Many human voices lifted up, too, strained and loud. Imo staggered back, blinking and gripping the doorposts with images of Armageddon and nuclear war flashing through her mind.

Lemuel came toward the house, waving his arms frantically and hollering something she couldn't make out. Rushing to him, she saw folks tearing out onto their lawns up and down Cedar Street.

"It's Lamar's," he said breathlessly when he got closer. His words confused her. Lamar's was a large fuel storage warehouse on the outskirts of town. A place where tanker trucks full of propane gas regularly pulled up to the loading dock near several large holding tanks. Lamar's was where Dusty Puckett had been hired as the plant manager.

"Dusty?" she ventured.

"I don't know," Lemuel breathed. "No one knows anything at this point. Tank exploded."

She was painfully aware then of Lillian's figure emerging from the dark shadow of some crepe myrtles at the edge of the parsonage's lawn. She came toward them, hands flying in a commotion of nervous energy.

"Lillian!" Imo said, rushing forward to grasp her hands.

"No . . . no!" she pulled away, continuing her frantic trek toward Lamar's, where the sky was now engulfed in gray clouds.

"I'll go with you," Imo said.

"Not safe!" Lemuel barked. He shook his head. "They don't need the whole town there rubbernecking."

They were at the mailbox when an ambulance came streaking down Cedar Street, lights spinning. Lillian stopped to watch it pass, wailing, "Dusty, my Dusty . . ."

When it was out of sight, she lay down on the liriope between the sidewalk and Cedar Street, her body trembling. Lemuel knelt beside her. "Is my boy okay?" she whimpered into the earth.

"Let's get you inside," Lemuel said, beckoning Imo to get on the other side of Lillian and shepherd her into the house.

"My boy, my boy," Lillian keened steadily, gripping both their hands with urgency as they laid her gently down on the couch. Imo threw her arms around her, hugging her tightly.

Finding herself at a loss for words, Imo stared at a sympathy card on the table in front of her. There were already some flowery phrases printed inside, but they were so generic, insubstantial, and unable to convey what her very soul wept over.

With all you've shared, Lillian, it almost feels like Dusty was my own child, my own flesh and blood. She tapped her pen on the table. Ever since news had come that Dusty had lost his life in the explosion at Lamar's, Imo could not think straight. She missed Lillian terribly. She had seen her only once in the three days since the news came.

Unshaven and red-eyed Dewey Puckett had come to the door the last time Imo tried to speak with Lillian. "She won't talk to a soul," he said.

But still, he let Imo creep in, carrying a vase of yellow mums. "Lil?" she said hesitantly, rounding the corner into the Pucketts' parlor. The sideboard and the dining table were laden with gifts of food and flowers and cards, all untouched as far as Imo could tell.

"She's in bed," he said.

Imo made her way down the short hallway, wearing what she hoped was a loving and concerned expression. Lillian lay prostrate in her bed, still wearing the white blouse and green skirt she'd worn the morning of the explosion.

Imo stepped closer to her and set a hand on her shoulder. "Oh, Lil," she said, "my heart is just broken for you."

There was no response and Imo swallowed hard. Lil's eyes said it all; her stricken eyes were vacant holes. She looked as if her very soul had been plucked right out of her body. Gently Imo set the flowers down and held her breath as she tiptoed back out the front door.

Driving home Imo saw that Lemuel had changed Calvary's marquee to:

SOUL FOOD SERVED HERE.

"Considerate of him," she murmured to herself, still feeling empty and dazed. Maybe she should stop in at the church and let him offer the healing balm of hope to her. It was what she needed. She had no more reserves of hope left at the moment.

The worst of this would be facing Jeanette's surgery without hope. Just one more week. Inconceivable, really, that the peace she'd taken for granted just days ago was gone. She pulled into the gravel lot, hesitated. It was a terrible feeling to know Lillian was not just beyond the front door there, efficiently taking care of business and brightening Imo's life with her friendship.

She cut the engine finally, and as she made her way toward Calvary, she set each footstep down carefully, as if to keep herself from stepping off the edge of the earth.

Fifteen

Funeral Dirge
Lou

"You've got to come with me to the funeral tomorrow," Hank told me as we stood barefoot in the creek late one afternoon, water rippling around our ankles. I sat down on the bank and dabbled my fingers in the cool water as sunlight fell on us through the leafy sweet gum branches stretched overhead. Hank was biting his lower lip and giving me one of those concerned looks of his.

The things happening in my life lately seemed to belong in the Book of Job. What I really needed was some mothering after hearing about the explosion at Lamar's, but I was too stubborn to call Imo. It felt weak to admit that need even to myself, me holding myself a hostage at the farm like I was. "I didn't really know Dusty that well," I said, but this left me feeling even worse, feeling childish and mean.

I thought about the war I'd been waging; that first battle where I swore I'd never talk to the Reverend as long as I lived. Shouted I never wanted to see his face again, all the time hearing that annoying little voice in my head going "Never say never, Loutishie Lavender. Just as soon as you do, you'll be eating your words."

Of course, I knew I would say it again in a heartbeat if it came down to it. Imo rode out to the farm almost daily and once she said she thought the Reverend might be wavering a little bit on the matter, but I did not believe her. I felt betrayed by her, bewildered by her seemingly easy surrender to him. I was mad with her for an entire week when she moved back to the parsonage with him after he made that awful comment. Had she forgotten how much even *she* loved the land?

Now when she would say to me, "Lou, I did say a marriage vow to Lemuel Peddigrew," I felt nothing but fury and impatience.

"Great," I'd answer sarcastically, wanting desperately to spit, "but you don't have to

410

let him talk about selling this place! You could stand up for us! Have you ever thought of that? Tell him you're not letting it out of your life. Convince him it's in his best interest to keep it. Use your feminine wiles. Have you tried that even?"

And she'd just stand there looking at me and I'd know that she had tried everything she knew to do and that she could offer no guarantees.

"I'm sorry," I told Hank. "I just cannot go and face that man. He'll preach the funeral."

He sat quietly beside me for a few minutes. Then he reached his arm around me and held me like he'd never let go. "I hate to see you like this," he said finally.

"I know," I managed. "But I'll be okay. I just need some time."

Hank studied the sky and I looked at his free hand resting on his knee. I thought his hands were beautiful, just like the rest of him. They were big and square and brown from the sun, and when they held me they gave me goose bumps up and down my spine. Hank was staying nights at the farm with me.

After two nights alone I came to understand that while Bingo was the ultimate dog — a vigilant guardian, as well as a

411

wonderful listener and friend — he could not offer stimulating conversation. He could not give me sage advice or a warm embrace. He could not calm my irrational fears over axe murderers and escaped convicts. Plus, Bingo had the outdoors in his blood and he would come and go, slipping away constantly, unfettered, following the scent of a rabbit or the faraway howl of a bobcat.

To both my and Hank's surprise, he managed to convince his parents we would keep ourselves pure. When he arrived, carrying a big black duffel bag, he set it down in Imo's old bedroom without a word. There was not even a question as we'd had this implicit agreement from the very start of our relationship that there would be nothing below the neck till we were married. Sex was a mystical, sacred, deep, dark, warm place and we both vowed we would not spoil it in a heated moment. I would make it my gift to Hank. I would be his alone when the moment was right. I would lose my virginity on our wedding night.

I'll admit sometimes it was hard for me to find the strength to stand by our decision, like when we sat talking and holding one another late into the night on a

412

blanket in the yard, surrounded by cool night air and the songs of cicadas, and whippoorwills calling up from the river. Times like those I felt very weak and a part of me knew that if Hank had ever ceased to be the gentleman he always was, if he had touched me in that frantically throbbing place, my animal nature might have gotten the better of me and I would have been powerless to stop myself.

I was completely powerless over what the Reverend called my "willful disobedience." To be honest, I did feel a little guilty about it, but usually I was able to squelch those feelings by telling myself that what I'd done was truly justifiable.

It was easy to just ignore it out of existence most of the time. I kept busy with school and studying for final exams. Every afternoon I was outdoors, working in the garden or ambling across the fields and along the river. I have to give Hank credit for not ever mentioning my feud with the Reverend. He gave me space and listened thoughtfully to my ravings, and today he offered the quiet warmth of his company to the part of me that felt so vulnerable. "Let's go down to the river bottoms," he said after a spell. "See if we can find any arrowheads." He stood, stuffing his hands in his pockets.

I squinted up at him. "Okay."

We followed the creek a ways, then cut across the lower pasture to a wide place in the Etowah. Red Georgia clay and decaying plants dyed the water there a café au lait, and save for the occasional harsh squawk of a great blue heron, all was silence and reflection.

Hank skipped a stone across the river's width, and he looked so handsome and vital I could hardly stop staring. Then for some reason, I thought about the funeral again. "Must be hard to lose a child," I blurted out. "Someone you love so much."

He turned to look at me. "C'mere," he said. I did and he enfolded me in his arms. I melted into him, breathing in the mixture of sweet hay and sweat that followed him.

There was a ragged, painful place inside of me; part of my problem was overwhelming sadness for Lillian and Dewey Puckett, and part of my problem was guilt and feeling selfish over saying I would not go to the funeral. But the stubborn part of me found it hard to even imagine being physically near the Reverend anywhere, much less being at Calvary Baptist, close enough to look on his face, to hear him speak.

Hank pulled back a bit and his eyes met mine. "I'm not going," I said firmly. "I'll pray for Lillian and Dewey Puckett here. I'll light a candle in Dusty's memory." I stood there feeling lower than a pissant, all the tranquillity sucked from my spirit. Hank only nodded and enfolded my numb self in his arms again.

"I know what!" I exclaimed after an uncomfortable spell. "Let's go see if any of the squash or cucumbers are ready for picking!" I wanted to blot out my pulsing conscience, and if anything could help me sidestep this troubling issue, it was the garden. Every single plant in it was literally thriving. It had been the best spring in my memory in terms of weather. Every time it looked like it might be dry enough to haul out the hoses and the sprinkler, the skies would open and deliver just enough to give things a good drink. When the weather turned warmer, weeds began to sprout in all the bare patches, but this did not dampen my joy. I took great delight in ripping them, roots and all, from the earth. I knew these violent acts were therapeutic for me.

"Sure," Hank said, but something in his glance told me I wasn't fooling him. We started back through the woods and the fields toward the house, Hank leading as usual, to clear spiderwebs and snakes out of the path. Everything was lush and green and overgrown. The fields needed a good mowing, but the purple wisteria and the pink dogwoods along the clearing for the power line were breathtaking. Fragrant honeysuckle vines covered the fence rows. I thought the most beautiful thing in the world must be the farm in May. "It's really spectacular here this time of year, huh?" I called to Hank as I jogged along, feet sunk in blooming clover, trying to keep pace with his long-legged strides.

"Yup," he said, loping along.

At last we ducked underneath the strand of barbed-wire fence that led to the backyard proper. I jogged to the garden and stood between the sweet corn and the snap beans. Sundown was fast approaching and the evening sky was pink on the horizon behind him. Crickets rang out from the yard like bands of tiny maraca players.

I watched Hank as he ambled through the garden, peeking under prickly squash and cucumber vines. "Aha!" He smiled after a bit, lifting a good-sized cucumber up like a trophy. Eventually he also found two tender yellow squash big enough to pick. "The fruits of your labors," he said to

416

me, cradling the three vegetables in his palms.

It made me feel like a proud parent, hearing him say that. But I knew it wasn't only *my* labor. Thoughts of Imo led to thoughts of Lillian Puckett and the funeral. Feeling a tiny pain begin in my chest, my eyes suddenly watered. "Look," I said, gesturing quickly at the tall vines. "Imo's growing a couple types of heirloom tomatoes over this a way." He saw me trying to suck it up, to keep my face turned away until I could blink the threatening tears out of existence, but he did not call me on it.

"Well, what are they?" he asked.

"One's Tangella and one's Opalka," I said, recalling Imo's face as she pored over the *Market Bulletin*, perusing the pages of various seeds for sale. "Imo's crazy about trying new seeds."

"She gave that love to you, Lou."

I shrugged. "Maybe."

"Not maybe. She *did.* I can see it," he said. "Seeds produce after their own type."

That was a quote from Mr. Gruner in ag-tech class. I knew those words were true. You reaped what you sowed in life, too. Everyone knew that. "Sow your seeds wisely," Uncle Silas used to say. "For they will sprout up soon enough. It's just a matter of time. . . ." I stood there, marveling at how a tiny brown seed could turn into a fresh green plant, and simultaneously wondering at the inextricable tangle of all our lives.

Had I lost all sense of community? Was I just plain selfish? Had I somehow mistaken my so-called righteous anger against the Reverend for a worthy cause? I certainly didn't want to be a sour old shrew barricading herself from others. I refused to admit it, but I missed being in the thick of my family, such as it was. It was as if I were retreating farther and farther into myself.

Being there for Imo was my duty, I thought, as I began to entertain the notion that I might attend Dusty's funeral. That small voice in my own heart would not be quieted and I trudged across the yard to the glider. I watched Hank bend to pick a marigold at the edge of the garden. His eyes made a silent appeal as he knelt down beside me and placed the flower on my knee.

"I'm going with you," I said to Hank finally in the gathering darkness, looking at him and thinking, *This is one of the many reasons I love you so. You can see things that I can't, and you have this incredible gift of teaching me to know myself.*

It seemed every soul in the city of Euharlee, the whole county even, had turned out for Dusty Puckett's funeral. Many folks lived in walking distance, and cars were jam-packed in Calvary's lot, then end to end down Cedar Street and Jessamine Street, also angled sideways on the shoulder of the adjoining highway.

The day was balmy, the sky a dazzling clear blue and what lawn there was at Calvary freshly cut. A new sprinkling of alabaster marble chips iced the parking lot.

I held Hank's hand, walking a bit unsteadily on my unfamiliar heels, the panty hose ensconcing my thighs making little *swish-swish* noises as we trekked toward the sanctuary. It was early still and a good number of people were in clumps outside, talking in low tones. It startled me to see the long black hearse parked at Calvary's side door.

"I doubt there'll be an open casket," Hank said when he saw my face. "Heard he was so badly burned you couldn't even recognize him."

I shuddered. That was the kind of thing nightmares were made of. I hated funerals. I never knew just what to say at them. Or how to act. "Just listen to your heart," Imo always told me. If I'd listened to my heart at that moment, I'd have been hightailing it for the hills. Besides looking on the bereaved countenances of Dewey and Lillian Puckett, I had to face the Reverend. Mustering the courage to swallow my pride had been hard enough, and now that I was close enough to see the whites of his eyes, I was having second thoughts.

Truth was, I still couldn't forgive him. No amount of praying over the matter had changed the fact. *If I can just get through the service and rush on back home without having to speak to him,* I thought, *I'll be okay.*

Unfortunately, I saw that he stood on the brick stoop of Calvary, greeting folks as they entered the building. I gulped. "Can't we just wait out here a little bit longer?" I whispered to Hank, grabbing his arm and pulling him around the corner. "Maybe the Reverend'll head on inside before too long."

We stood and watched people dressed in somber blacks and browns mingling in small groups on the lawn. Some of them wore corsages and boutonnieres and we figured they were Puckett relatives of some sort. A man with a booming voice said,

"It's a hero's funeral, actually."

"I should say so," answered Miss Beula Weaver, clasping her white-gloved hands at her throat. "Lillian should be proud of her boy. He saved so many lives!"

My curiosity aroused, I turned quickly to Hank. "What happened that day at Lamar's?"

"You haven't heard the story?"

I shook my head.

He went over the details of the explosion: A tanker truck full of propane gas caught afire while it was parked at the warehouse. Flames shot forty feet out the back of that truck and then spread to the loading dock. Several large tanks nearby were in danger of exploding. Dusty, after helping to rescue the badly burned driver, jumped into the cab and drove the blazing truck away from the warehouse. His quick action cost him his life and saved dozens of others.

I had goose bumps when Hank was finished. "He really is a hero," I breathed. I felt grief and compassion for the Pucketts, but I also felt pride. Pride at Dusty's selfless act and a simultaneous shame at my own big pity party. Emotionally, I was pretty much a roller coaster at that moment.

I stood speechless for a minute or so, gathering myself together. It was getting on toward three o'clock, the appointed time for the funeral. I peered around the corner. The Reverend was still standing there.

"Ready?" Hank asked. "Let's go get us a seat." He grabbed my hand and with my heart banging in my chest I managed to stroll casually in his shadow.

"Afternoon, Preacher," Hank said, releasing my hand as he stopped to pump the Reverend's hand. He stepped inside.

Okay, Lou, breathe, I coached myself as I stepped in front of the Reverend, *remember, you're only here to honor Dusty Puckett, a hero.* The Reverend clasped my hand and looked at me intently. I felt a flash of my old resentment and I could hardly look at him.

"Hello, Loutishie," he spoke very gently. "Your mother and I were hoping you'd be here. Come by the house after the service, won't you?"

I said nothing. I didn't realize how bright the sun was until I stepped inside the dim vestibule and the melancholy aura of the church. The walls were literally lined with flowers. More flowers than I'd ever seen in one place in my life. I walked carefully between them toward the sanctuary.

I slid into the smooth oak pew next to Hank just as Miz Sylvia Turner began playing a low hymn on the organ. A myriad of perfumes and aftershaves assaulted my nose, and I heard sniffles here and there over the music.

Dusty's widow, Angie, began to make her way down the aisle to sit at the front. Her hair was matted and she wore only one gold hoop earring. There was no white in her eyes at all, and tears ran down her cheeks in two glistening lines.

But that was nothing compared to Lillian Puckett, who followed her. She was not crying, she was *weeping,* and I got lost inside the inhuman sound of it, my stomach tangling up in knots. Beside me, Hank's comforting presence was like God's.

The Calvary Baptist choir filed into the choir loft in their filmy gray satin robes. Below them I glimpsed the metallic sheen of a casket, closed as Hank had guessed. Literal cascades of flowers, mostly mums and red roses, encircled the choir loft, the casket, the altar rail, and the pulpit.

Lillian Puckett had quieted herself, and I saw Dusty's two children wriggling around between her and Mr. Dewey Puckett. His face was drawn and his eyes had taken on a haggard look.

I looked around at row after row of stricken faces. It seemed that Dusty's sacrificial death had touched the whole community in an unfathomable way. I found Jeanette's gaunt figure, her face unadorned by cosmetics, and Montgomery beside her, his eyes closed and his eyebrows furrowed in concentration. Was he deep in prayer or imagining what it would be like if this were Jeanette's funeral?

I noticed Imo's head bent in the front pew. Suddenly, she turned around and her eyes found mine. A warm smile crossed her face and I felt five years old again, like I needed to go and sit beside her. I made my face go lax and unresponsive, not wanting her to get her hopes up and think I was giving in on the matter of the homeplace.

The sanctuary grew quiet, except for random throat clearings, the shuffling of feet, and the *swoosh-swoosh* of Hardigree Funeral Home cardboard fans slicing through the air. Engrossed in my own thoughts, I was startled when the choir stood and reverently began to sing "Lead Me to the Light."

When they finished the Reverend somberly made his way to the lectern. He was quiet a moment as he put on his glasses, which made his eyes look really big. With one elbow resting on either side of a big black Bible, he cleared his throat.

Then, to that wounded congregation, he gave a mercifully short sermon; about the uncertainty and the brevity of life on this earth, about life beyond the grave, and about holding on to your hope and your faith. As he looked toward the Pucketts, he uttered a verse from the Psalms, something about as you sow in tears, you will reap in joy.

He also said that he was utterly convinced that Dusty Puckett was with Jesus in His mansion in the sky, and that angels were rejoicing to have him there, singing "Welcome Home." That if we kept our feet on the straight and narrow path, we would get to see Dusty Puckett again in the Life to Come.

"The floor is now open," the Reverend was saying, "for those who would like to say something about Dusty Puckett."

There was a pregnant pause, until at last Wanda Parnell stood. She looked stunning in a long gauzy dress of deep lilac that sucked in at the middle and curved out bodaciously above and below. Her shining hair was piled spectacularly high. She had what she called a "native tan" on account of the tanning booth they'd added at the Kuntry Kut 'n' Kurl.

"Dusty Puckett," she began, in the deep throaty timbre of a smoker, turning her head this way and that to comb the crowd, "a man cut down in the prime of his life. He woke up on Wednesday and he didn't have no idea what that day was gonna bring his way. I'm bettin' he kissed his lovely wife and his beautiful children and he whistled as he left for Lamar's, toting his lunch box." She paused and the whole congregation sat perched on the edge of their pews.

"And I bet he figured on coming home that night, folks. Maybe he planned to eat a big old juicy steak for supper, to read the paper, watch his favorite show, and to tuck his children in bed. We may never know.

"Dusty was a good man. A man tortured by his own private demons. A man who struggled with his biggest demon, drinking. Now, don't you all sit there, looking all righteous and holier than thou, pretending you don't have some of your own. We all do. I do." The widened eyes all around me made it clear that the congregation was under some giant cosmic microscope.

"And when I heard he was gone from this world, my world turned upside down. Where is Dusty Puckett's soul? I asked myself." Wanda's shoulders shrugged dramatically. "He's free, I tell you. Free of his struggles. But we," she waved her bejeweled and manicured hands, "still struggle. Now, I firmly believe that Jesus loves you where you are . . ."

Folks were nodding, encouraging this vein of words. No doubt feeling the stinging nettles of conviction.

"But I will be the first to admit that I ain't perfect." Wanda ran down a list, naming off her flaws and foibles, things like taking drunk and longing after multitudes of men. She confessed her long string of husbands and extramarital affairs. She told about her fixation with outer beauty at the expense of her soul. "Many Sunday mornings I have laid abed with a hangover." She wrung her hands, shook her head in self-disgust. "I thought only of this life." She cast her eyes downward and you could've heard a pin drop.

"And I pray to God today," she said, "to forgive me."

I began to feel mighty uncomfortable. Was this a funeral or a confessional? What if everyone began to air their dirty laundry? We'd never get out of there. Just when I thought Wanda was fixing to hush and sit down, she turned herself in a forty-five degree angle.

"What we've learned from Dusty is to honor others in our community, and I have failed there, too." She paused breathlessly, "Imogene, honey, it is you I've failed. I'm sorry, but I've been the meddlin' haint what's been messin' around at the parsonage. Please find it in your heart to forgive me." Wanda sank down in an exhausted and dramatic flourish.

I wasn't altogether certain what Wanda meant by that last comment, but I saw first shock, then knowing, register on the Reverend's face. He beckoned again with his arm to say, "Anyone else?"

Several men rose, fumbling with words to give unremarkable speeches about what a fine boss or coworker Dusty had been, how he'd saved their lives or the lives of a loved one or friend. Things grew quiet and I thought we were home free until Lillian Puckett stood and turned to face everyone.

She literally stared us all down for a moment as she blew her nose and sucked in a deep breath. "The hardest part of all this is saying good-bye," she said in a quavery voice, and then more softly, "good-bye to someone you love more than life itself."

The crowd was eerily silent and there was not a dry eye in the whole place.

"Words seem woefully inadequate," she went on, shaking a fist toward the stained glass picture of Jesus and the children. "All those sweet promises of heaven seem woefully inadequate, too. I have just one thing to say to you — don't go getting your hopes up!"

Was this blasphemy? Was I imagining it or did she look pointedly at Imo when she finished her ranting?

I sat thoughtfully in my pew as six pallbearers hefted Dusty's remains and the Reverend said the benediction. We filed out into the balmy afternoon. The burial was right there in the church cemetery and we moved as a mute herd next to the fresh mound of red Georgia clay beside a dark hole.

"From dust I was made and to dust I shall return," the Reverend uttered, which didn't sound very comforting. Beside me Hank's head was bent in reverent thought. I lifted my head to look beyond the casket, to more flowers, a stretch of tombstones, and over the treetops at the roof of the parsonage. The Reverend's invitation to come there after the service echoed in my brain.

Should I go? I wondered, praying silently for wisdom. I did not want to take the chance of seeing the Reverend anymore. I considered that I'd done my duty already.

Suddenly, as I looked up at the church's steeple, it began to glow white-hot. It was like a fire, growing brighter and brighter until I could see nothing else. "Go, Loutishie" came His voice, resonant and full of love. "Go and share your tears. Sow a seed, for one day you, too, will need a community of tears."

Pausing for a deep breath, on the steps of the parsonage, I saw Imo and several members of the Garden Club standing like waitresses behind the sideboard, and a line of borrowed card tables which groaned under more pies, casseroles, and hams than I'd ever seen in one place before.

"Y'all come on in and get yourselves a plate!" Maimee Harris called to me and Hank. "Tea's in the kitchen. Coffee, too."

I was surprised to find myself so hungry for real cooking. We'd just been making do out at the farm, living on peanut butter and jelly or bologna sandwiches and an occasional bowl of cornflakes with milk. Hank and I both filled our plates to overflowing and squeezed through the packed hallway to look for a seat outside in the backyard.

I had been relieved to notice that the Reverend was sitting and eating in a corner of the kitchen, surrounded by folks. It would be easy to avoid him in the large crowd.

Settling onto a lawn chair, I perched my food precariously on my thighs and settled my tea in the fresh-cut grass at my heel. Hank and I spent a few minutes in serious eating as folks spilled in and out of the house. We were on our coconut cream pie when Miz Fiona Gantry and her husband, Eb, came to sit across from us.

Mr. Gantry worked at Lamar's and Miz Gantry was a guidance counselor at Euharlee High. Miz Gantry had a hawk-nosed face with penetrating blue eyes beneath a wiry pageboy of snow-white hair. She was a concave-chested chain smoker and she painted up her lips so red she left startling blood colors on her cigarette butts. Smoking was prohibited at the high school, but Miz Gantry's seniority, along with her orneriness, afforded her the right to smoke in her corner office. Each time I was there to get her wisdom for applying to colleges, she narrowed her eyes and blew smoke into my face as she spoke.

"Sure is a purty day out, isn't it?" Mr. Gantry said. He was a cheerful, plump, apple-cheeked man, balding on top. His sprightly good nature was just the opposite of his wife's.

"Yessir," I said, "sure is." I watched Miz Gantry. She hardly touched her food. She smoked and sipped tea with her pinky finger aloft.

"Loutishie," she finally said, waving a red-tipped cigarette. "I hear you're living out at your uncle's old place."

I exchanged quick glances with Hank. "I sure am," I said, my voice faltering. I did not know my life was common knowledge.

"You staying out there all alone?" she asked.

I studied the chicken bones scattered on my plate and I felt naked beneath Miz Gantry's scrutinizing gaze. Before I could respond, Mr. Gantry said, with overexuberance, "Was a lovely service, it was! We're naming a part of the new building at Lamar's after Dusty. Got a nice metal plaque. Why, I wouldn't be sitting here today if he hadn't done what he did."

"Yeah," agreed Hank, but Miz Gantry sulked in her chair and said nothing. After this, Mr. Gantry and Hank struck up a conversation about baseball. It was getting hot and I excused myself to get more tea, offering to bring seconds for whoever else wanted anything.

"I'll come with you," Miz Gantry said, startling me. I felt strange walking elbow to elbow with her into the house. Folks were getting seconds and thirds from platters of ham and fried chicken, and there were now more desserts than you could shake a stick at. As soon as I'd refilled my tea, Miz Gantry pointed toward the breezeway with a cigarette. "Look! Yonder's John Franklin Wells." She nudged me forward a bit.

"Yes, it is him," I said, feeling her angular chest at my shoulder blades, wondering why she was so excited. John Franklin was a senior, too, in FFA with Hank and me, but it was no surprise to see him standing there between his folks.

"I think I should waste no time in telling you this, Lou," Miz Gantry said, and I turned to face her in puzzlement at her strange tone.

I could see bad news in the set of her jaw. "You aren't the one Dr. Livesay's considering. John Franklin's his favorite. Boy's been lending him a hand after school every single afternoon. And you know, being neck and neck at the top of the senior class alongside you doesn't hurt either. And being a man. There's just some things a man has the edge in. Particularly with the larger animals, like the . . ."

I went mute with shock. All through my fury at the Reverend and my fear over Jeanette, the job at Dr. Livesay's had stretched before me like a lush green oasis in the middle of a desert. Now I saw it blip and fade away, and an endless summer appear in the gap.

I didn't really want to repeat the terrible conversation, but when Hank and I were back at the farm, sitting in the glider watching daylight fade, I felt my mouth opening up, saying, "Miz Gantry said John Franklin's going to get the job at Dr. Livesay's."

"You think that old biddy knows anything?" he said, smiling. "She just has a bad case of meanness is what it is."

"But he could," I said. "It's possible."

Hank squeezed my hand. "Listen, Lou," he said, "You're not thinking straight. It's been a long day and we're both tired. I think what we need's a race down to the river!"

And without warning he took off running. I followed, Bingo at my heels, desperate to gain back his unfair advantage.

But he held a good lead on us all the way to the edge of the Etowah, and when I reached him, panting and holding my side, he grabbed me around the waist and carried me right out into the water where it was knee-high and set me down like a sack of potatoes. He sat down, too, and we started laughing and splashing each other till we were soaking wet.

Climbing the hill back toward the house, I looked out across the pasture bathed in moonlight. Hank could act so sure, but I knew it wasn't certain. There were lots of things to consider when it came to picking an intern. Sure, I loved critters and I'd had plenty of experience, but John Franklin was on the wrestling team as well as the FFA, and his daddy owned a horse farm. I desperately needed to see Imo, nestle myself into a corner of the sofa, and have her smile at me and tell me things would work out fine. I thought of asking Hank to drive me to the parsonage, but I did not, because I didn't want to face the Reverend again.

Sixteen

Soul Rainbow

Imo

"Made my flesh crawl," Lemuel told Imo. "Mary Bean flounced in to the Pucketts' this morning while I was there visiting and you know what that woman said?"

"What, dear?" Imo looked up from folding the laundry.

"She said, and I quote, 'Well, Lillian, God just needed Dusty in heaven more than He did down here. I reckon Dusty finished his work, and so God called him on home.'" He pounded the counter as he looked at Imo and shook his head incredulously. She imagined she could see steam coming out of his pink ears.

"I looked at Lillian and Dewey and those two young'uns of Dusty's huddled up on Dewey's lap and I wanted more than anything to grab Mary Bean around the neck and holler right in her face, 'No! Don't you go blaming God for this! Maybe someone carelessly tossed a match, maybe an engine got too hot, maybe something was wrong with the wiring, but I will not stand for you blaming God for these folks being without a son, and these young'uns here without a father!' "

Lem took a hankie from his trouser pocket and dabbed his forehead.

"People sometimes have funny notions," she told him. "You know how it is. And some, they mean well, but they just don't know what to say."

"Well," he said, "it just rankles my hide."

Imo patted the pile of towels.

"Some folks think God is like this great big old Santy Claus in the sky," he continued. "You've heard it all, too, I know. They say, 'Where was God when my child, my husband, my wife, whatever, was killed?' I used to be speechless when they asked me that, Imogene. Now I just tell them God was in the exact same spot He was in when His own Son died. And I also tell them He is right there with them in the midst of their grief."

Imo cocked her head, considering. "How is Lillian today?"

"No better."

"No better?"

"Catatonic, I'd call her. Laid up in bed. Won't eat, Dewey says."

"I'm planning to go back over there again this evening," she said.

"Don't get your hopes up. This morning marked my fifth visit and she hasn't said a word to me yet."

"She has to get herself together one of these days."

"Some never do," he said. "Folks handle their grief different. I've seen some can't make it. The weight of sadness is just unbearable and they're done in. But there's some that don't get bitter or resentful toward God. Take Dewey, for instance, he's taken all he is and he's still pouring it into God's kingdom. Shows up every morning, bright and early, at Calvary to work on the new Sunday school wing. In fact, he's working harder than ever since Dusty passed on. Did you see he came to Sunday school and service alone yesterday?"

She nodded. "Does he really leave Lillian to come work at Calvary every day?"

"Her sister's there. Sitting with Lillian

and minding the grand-young'uns."

"What about poor Angie?"

"I hear she's trying to pull herself to-gether."

"I'll fix two of my sour cream pound cakes, you hear?" Imo said. "Carry one to Angie, and one to Lillian with some of that beef stew in the freezer for their supper. I bet Lil's sister is just worn to a frazzle with those two wild kids. Bet they're living on frozen dinners."

"Well, I tell you what, Imo, dear," Lem said. "This evening I'll ride back over there with you. I have a book I found for Lillian."

"I'll get to baking right now," she told him. "Probably help Lil out a lot to get some nourishing food down her." But even as she spoke, Imo heard how desperate and uncertain she sounded, and she saw how Lemuel raised his eyebrows in doubt.

She set the butter out on the counter to soften and she measured flour into a mixing bowl. While rummaging through the cabinets for the vanilla, mace, and cream of tartar, she spied a bag of minia-ture pastel-colored marshmallows flopped in the back corner. She patted it. Still tender and soft, so she unfastened the twist-tie on the bag and popped several into her mouth. It took her another palmful and a minute to recall why she had such an unusual item among her baking things. She'd made Easter cupcakes for Little Silas's Sunday school class! White cakes with lemony yellow frosting and a sprinkling of marshmallows.

Of course, this was all back during simpler times. Before they had any inkling of Jeanette's tumor and before Dusty's death. Mostly she tried to suppress thoughts of Dusty's death, just as she did those of Loutishie out at the farm, still angry and noncommunicative with the Reverend. Her great hope had been that Lou would mend things with Lemuel when they were eye to eye at the funeral. But for some reason Lou had dashed off in a huff, the first to leave, though Lemuel claimed he hadn't said a contrary thing to her.

The funeral. Wanda's confession had given her a measure of peace, but it made Imo feel awful to recall Lillian's words there in Calvary's chapel — "Don't go getting your hopes up." Now, almost two weeks later, they were still a thorn in her flesh. They jabbed holes in Imo's faith even though she knew they were spoken in extreme grief, in anger at God. They pulsated like her heartbeat, sending shock waves of fear through her as she contemplated Jeanette's surgery.

This had turned into one of the busiest times of Imo's life. Still she visited Lou in the evenings, though she felt somewhat better with Hank being there. She also felt responsible for keeping in touch with Lillian, and in addition to this, in all the chaos of Jeanette's illness, she volunteered to keep Little Silas a part of each day, cooking enough supper for both families, and sending some back to Cartersville every afternoon.

She was thrilled in those rare moments when Jeanette would actually talk with her as she sat down to visit. Generally she lay there on the couch, staring vacantly at the TV, or else sleeping. She ate next to none of Imo's good home cooking. "I love you, sweetheart," Imo said, squeezing Jeanette's hand each time she left, and each time it was harder and harder to keep the brave smile on her face.

Imo sat down then and put her elbows on the kitchen table, her face in her hands. So much pressure on a pastor's wife to keep her chin up, her faith strong. There seemed little guaranteed in the world; children died, children rebelled, folks got tumors, folks were perpetually facing hardships.

In a perfect world these things would not happen. This world was definitely not perfect. It had its good moments, however. Good moments made even more precious when you considered the rest. She recalled with no surprise the new saying Lemuel had put on Calvary's marquee.

THE SOUL WOULD HAVE NO RAINBOW,
HAD THE EYE NO TEARS.
— JOHN VANCE CHENEY

It made her think of Lillian as being in the eye of some monstrous storm, where lightning, thunder, and torrents of rain raged mercilessly. *Lord, calm the storm,* Imo prayed fervently, squeezing the flesh on her cheeks until it hurt.

After a while she seemed to feel a little bud of hopefulness beginning to bloom inside, and she stood up, scraped back her chair and crossed to the sink for a glass of water. Her eye caught a glimpse out the window of a pink dogwood close to the septic tank. It was splendid in the morning sunlight, and the forsythia hedge beyond it was a brilliant yellow cloud. Pleased, she sipped her water and realized with a puzzled wonder that the yard there, the parsonage itself, now felt like hers.

Maybe it was Wanda's confession at the funeral that had released her from the perpetual feeling that she was trespassing in Martha's home. Gone as well were the fears that Imo couldn't measure up to Martha's memory. Things were blessedly peaceful in that department.

Oh, at times Martha seemed to hover in the house and yard still, but it was more of a friendly feel. Imo knew intuitively that Martha dwelt at peace beyond those pearly gates, in that realm she could not touch, though sometimes she still spoke aloud to her.

"You're one of the first people I'm going to look up when I cross over Jordan, Martha, dear," she'd chuckle. "Reckon I'll see my Silas first off, then Mama and Daddy and Vera, too. But then, girl, you and me are going to have to find a nice place where we can sit down, relax, and have us a good, long chat about Lemuel Peddigrew!"

When Imo and Lem set out for the Pucketts', clouds had begun to darken the late afternoon sky. Imo nestled the steaming pot of beef stew on a towel in the middle of the Impala's front seat. The pound cake was tented in foil on the back floorboard.

Lemuel eased into the passenger seat with a small white book in hand.

"That a Bible?" Imo turned the key in the ignition.

"Nope. Book on dealing with loss from a biblical perspective." He offered it to her. "Here, take a look."

She stroked the faux leather cover with the words "Good Grief" embossed in gold. She opened to the first page, where a little prayer was printed in italics. *Lord, when sorrow dims our eyes along the path, help us to see with eyes of faith.* "You think Lil'll read this?" she asked with lifted eyebrows.

"Might," he said wearily. "It's worth a try anyway."

They rode slowly along to the corner of Cedar Street, and turned onto Main Street to go the quarter mile to the Pucketts'. Feeling apprehensive, Imo pulled to a stop beneath a little clump of magenta crepe myrtle trees in the Pucketts' backyard. "Ready?" she asked, peering through the waning light of day at the steep shingled roof, an iron eagle lightning rod stretched high beside the brick chimney.

They walked up a short cobblestone

path to the front porch, and Imo gave a tentative knock. Dewey opened the door and beckoned them into the dark parlor, switching on a lamp so that they saw with no surprise that the house was a total mess; newspapers everywhere you looked, socks and sofa cushions and toys and Pop-Tart boxes strewn from corner to corner. Some of Lillian's cherished Hummel figurines lay in a corner with a one-legged Barbie doll.

"Imo fixed y'all some supper," Lemuel said in a hushed tone.

Dewey nodded. "I know Betty'll be real tickled to hear that." He led them into the kitchen and turned on the light. "She's carried the kids into Cartersville to see a picture show," he said, "so Lil can rest."

Imo set the pot of stew down on the stove. "Can I see her, Dewey?" she whispered.

He rolled his lips inward and stared blankly at her for a moment. "Aw, may as well," he said finally. Lemuel pressed the white book into Imo's hand as she turned to go down the hallway.

She found Lillian in bed, holding, of all things, a bronzed baby bootie, the stiff high-topped shoe so popular in the 60s. Imo stood in the doorway, waiting for

Lillian to acknowledge her, listening to the faint *tick-tick-tick* of the bedside clock and the rustle of the covers as Lillian shifted positions.

"We all miss you at Calvary," Imo blurted after a bit. "I mean it, we really do." She smiled as she tiptoed forward and placed the book on the corner of the bed. "I'm praying for you," she added, leaning closer.

Minutes passed. Long, uncomfortable minutes where Imo twisted the hem of her blouse and cleared her throat. At last she lifted the book and set it on the covers across Lillian's knees. "Here," she said.

Her answer was a dubious look and a shake of Lillian's head. Every now and again Lillian would sigh deeply and close her eyes for one brief moment.

This was all so heartbreaking, so frustrating, having to stand there at Lillian's bedside pleading for a smile she knew the woman didn't have. *Lord,* Imo asked in desperation, *bring the rainbow to Lillian's soul.* She picked up the book, then opened it to the flyleaf. "Let's pray together," she said to Lillian, reaching for her limp hand. "Lord," she began, reading the poem printed there, "when sorrow dims our eyes along the path, help us to see with eyes of faith."

Suddenly, like a fierce wind had ripped it from Imo's hand, the book went flying across the room and hit the wall with a dull thud. Imo knew from the fiery glint in Lillian's eyes to say no more.

Over the next days Imo felt a cloud hovering over her own soul. There was no hiding from Lillian's face; she'd look up from the dishes or the laundry or the garden and see her lying there — always wearing the same bitter face.

And each morning, more out of a sense of duty than anything else, Imo went back for a brief visit with Lillian. She was careful not to mention Calvary or God or faith. Careful not to look at the bronze baby shoe sitting on the bedside table. Instead she sat stiffly beside Lil's bed chatting about the weather, the neighbors, anything she thought might cheer her.

Sometimes Lillian would talk. She talked about the rosebush just beyond her window, the butterflies and bees hovering there. However, one day she balled up a painfully frail fist and smacked it into the palm of her other hand.

"What? What?" Imo gasped, surprised at this show of emotion.

"Today is Dusty's birthday," she whispered.

"Oh, hon, I'm so sorry," Imo said, watching Lillian's chin tremble. "I'll say a special prayer for you today."

"Don't bother," Lillian spat. "I cannot believe in a God who would deny me my only child."

Imo bent to awkwardly embrace Lillian's raging figure. "There, there, now," she soothed, "let it come on out."

The next day Imo brought a steaming carafe of hazelnut coffee and two mugs. Lillian was sitting up in bed this time, a bit more color to her face. She was eager for the coffee now and also to let loose on her favorite subject — her familiar lament against God. Her blasphemy was shocking, but Imo let her rage on and on, squelching her impulses to defend Him.

Each time she left the Pucketts', Imo felt rather shell-shocked, and the spiritually disastrous aftermath of these visits lingered into the early afternoons, until Lemuel came home for lunch and relayed Dewey's latest accomplishment on the new Sunday school wing. Then a hopeful little spurt of faith would struggle to rise up in Imo's soul.

But sometimes Lillian's rantings allowed a certain fatalism to undermine Imo's faith and she felt powerless to stop this. Faith, she knew, was the critical factor as they approached the date for Jeanette's surgery.

Imo's first thought when she woke before Thursday's dawn was that today was the day. She spent another half hour in bed, snuggled up to Lem's shape, trying desperately to return to the blissful escape of sleep.

Finally she gave up, swung her legs out from the covers, and padded through the darkness to the kitchen. Lowering herself gently into a chair at the table, she nudged her hands deep into the pockets of her robe and tried to hear God's reassuring voice telling her that underneath were His everlasting arms. But all she could hear was the plaintive hoot of an owl somewhere and the shifting gears of a truck slowing as it reached the turnoff from the highway to downtown Euharlee.

Today they would know. Today Jeanette's future would be revealed one way or the other. The surgeon's words tumbled around and around in Imo's brain — ". . . a very risky surgery . . . nothing guaranteed . . . better than not operating, however, Mrs. Lavender. Without surgery, her death would be certain . . . very skilled team here at Emory Hospital."

She had to get stern with herself. She renewed her fierce vow to fan the flames of her faith and to block out those thoughts that undermined her confidence. Every time the fear reached its spiny tentacles toward her heart, she got her hands or mind or both busy. She worked crosswords, she cleaned every inch of the parsonage till it shone, she baked, she needlepointed, she sewed.

She rose to start the coffee, comforted by the steady and familiar gurgling of hot water through the filter. She made biscuits with a fierce *whack-whack* of her rolling pin, sending flurries of flour everywhere. This would give her more to clean. She fried patties of spicy sausage. She set the butter and the fig preserves and the strawberry jam onto the table.

At last a faint haze of morning light shone above the gingham curtains on the window above the sink. Sweeping the curtains aside, Imo took in the day. There was a spattering of raindrops on the holly bushes below the window and the skies were a gunmetal gray. Dark clouds huddled together in the east. A storm, she thought, would be here before noon.

Now, wouldn't that be appropriate? A storm to ride through to Atlanta, to sit through during the surgery? Imo had been hoping for clear blue skies. For some idyllic late spring day to enfold them like the backdrop of a movie set.

Imo poured two cups of coffee just as a figure darkened the doorway. Lemuel strode in, and without a word he sat down, picked up the steaming cup, and guzzled half of it.

"What time we need to head out?" he asked.

She glanced at her watch, calculating the hour's drive to get to Emory Hospital. "Nine," she said. "Montgomery's there with Jeannie. Spent the night. I told him we'd arrive an hour or so early to see her before the surgery."

"Alrighty." Lem sliced open a steaming biscuit and slid a sausage patty inside. "Did I tell you Felder's coming? Aunt Fannie, too. You heard from Loutishie?"

Imo glanced at the telephone. She sighed. She had not heard from Lou in days. Even on her numerous trips to the old homeplace to work in the garden, the girl had been nowhere about. Maybe she was at the library, snowed under preparing for her finals. Maybe she wouldn't be able to get away today as it was the last day of school. Watching Lem, she twisted her hands together in her lap and then said in a weak voice, "It's finals week at the high school."

"You and I both know she'll be there, love," he replied with a gentle nudge of his knee against hers. "No doubt about it."

Now her heart swelled. She smiled and looked into the eyes of this man, who seemed at moments like this, a solid rock, a bastion of faith and surety. Someone she could lean on.

Montgomery sat on a sofa in the hospital's waiting room, his head in his hands, and when he looked up at Imo and Lem, his face looked washed out in the fluorescent light.

"We're going to speak to Jeannie," Imo said. "Be back in a jiffy."

"She's not s'posed to have anybody but medical personnel with her now," Montgomery replied.

"But we hurried," Imo said, her hands clutching the fabric of her blouse at her neck. "I drove seventy-five all the way to get here. Can't we just see her real quick?" She had to see Jeanette, touch her, before this risky surgery.

Lemuel placed his hand on Imo's forearm. In a gentle voice, he said, "I'm sure they'll let us see her. Let's go talk to them."

Then his hand was under her elbow, steering her along to the nurses' station. When they reached the horseshoe-shaped counter, Lemuel put one arm around Imo and spoke in pleading tones as he gestured with the other. At last, after a dazed nod, a plump nurse with fiery red hair led them down a long hallway smelling of antiseptic, her rubber soled shoes thudding along steadily on the linoleum till they came to a pair of silver doors.

The doors swung open, into a cold room that seemed to be entirely silver and white. With each step, Imo concentrated on putting a peaceful smile on her face, though she felt fear rising in her like a tidal wave.

The sight of Jeanette lying beneath spotless white sheets with all of her hair shaved off was almost more than Imo could bear. She had an overwhelming urge to enfold the girl in her arms, to press her cheek against Jeanette's vulnerable scalp showing through the stubble.

The nurse held up a hand in warning

and Imo stood paralyzed, clutching her handbag, listening to her own heart thudding in her ears. "How're you today, sugar foot?" she asked in a soft breath.

"Oh, same as any other day," Jeanette said with a wry smile. "One day giving a perm and one day having brain surgery."

Somehow these were just the words Imo needed to hear. "Well, good," she said. "I love you and we're all right here with you." She trilled her fingers in a little wave as the nurse ushered them from the room.

When they returned to the waiting room, they found Felder, Aunt Fannie, and Wanda sitting in a corner, chatting loudly. Dewey Puckett was standing at the window, looking out at the dark storm clouds.

"And how are we? How's our Jeannie?" Wanda asked, galloping over to Imo. She took Imo's hands and squeezed, her loud perfume enveloping them in an almost visible cloud.

Imo glanced back down the long hallway. "Mighty quiet," she said, and then on impulse, "She's bald."

Wanda sucked in a breath and held a red-tipped nail to her mouth. "You don't say!"

"Yes."

"No!" Wanda insisted. "You're not serious!"

Imo nodded. On the other side of the room a vending machine glowed brightly. The silver doors of the elevator next to that opened, and she tried to concentrate on what Wanda was saying as she watched a skinny elderly man with a walker clattering out. She wondered if Lou would show up.

"Look, babe," Wanda was saying, "no hair, no problem. Being in the beauty profession does have its benefits! I just remembered I've got this wig catalog with some gorgeous hair pieces! She'll even get the wholesale rate."

"That's good," Imo said, patting Wanda's arm, preoccupied, uneasy.

"This one client of mine, Missus Violet Turley, she lost every one of her hairs due to old age," Wanda said. "Was ninety-three years old. She came in to the Kuntry Kut 'n' Kurl and we sat down and flipped through the wig catalog. We found her a blond Farrah Fawcett do, in addition to this dark little pixie thing. When the wigs came in, we had the best time playing around with those things! And let me tell you, she looked like two entirely different people! Later, I ran into her at Dub's, with her dear little old husband, and you know what he did? He ran up and gave me the biggest hug and he said, 'Thank you, Wanda Parnell, you are an angel. Thank you for giving me two new wives,' and he had hisself a twinkle in his eye, too."

Dewey Puckett appeared at Imo's elbow. He held a vase of pink tulips. Imo turned to look behind him for Lillian. "I'm alone," he said. "These are for Jeanette."

"They're just lovely," Imo told him. "I'll be sure she gets them."

Dewey nodded. He found a seat next to Aunt Fannie, whose eyes bulged as she leafed through a tattered *People* magazine.

"So, anyhow," Wanda continued, "hair is important, but losing it isn't the end of the world. When she gets back to the salon, we'll go through the catalog and see what we can find. Fix the girl right up. I'll find the perfect hair for her. They've got these computer dealies now, these things called virtual makeovers, where you can plug in your face and try on all these hairpieces on the computer before you plunk your money down."

"What? Well, I declare!" Imo said, turning as she heard the elevator opening again. Three nuns stepped out.

"Hard to fathom, huh? Next thing you know, you won't even need salons. Folks can just click a button on what they want and this robot will do their hair. Heaven forbid!" Wanda giggled. " 'Cause then me and Jeannie'd both be out of jobs."

As Wanda chatted on and on, Imo found herself wondering if Wanda was clueless as to the serious nature of this surgery (why, didn't she know Jeanette could *die* in there?) or if she were just a naturally optimistic person. Imo peered at her glossy magenta lips. Maybe Wanda possessed a childlike sort of faith. Maybe she herself could learn a little something from Wanda.

For a moment Imo said nothing. She just let Wanda's words sweep over and in her along with the cool air of the hospital. At last she managed a small smile and said, "A wig sounds like a lovely idea, Wanda."

Just then, a white-coated figure came into the room. Imo's breath caught in her throat as she recognized Dr. Rajgarhia, the doctor who would perform Jeanette's surgery. Dr. Rajgarhia was a small, dark, finely boned man with jet-black hair that shone like it was coated with shellac. He laced the brown fingers of his slender hands at his waist.

Lemuel turned away midsentence from talking with Montgomery and crossed the room with his hand outstretched. "Hello, Doctor," he said.

"Hello," Dr. Rajgarhia responded, shaking Lemuel's hand. "We will begin soon. I just wanted to speak to the family before."

"We're glad you're here," Lemuel said. "You're looking mighty perky this morning."

Dr. Rajgarhia's brow knit up in puzzlement. "Perky?"

"Yes, yes," Lemuel said. "That's a good thing. Listen, Doc, we'd like to lay hands on you and pray over you before you commence."

Dr. Rajgarhia's eyes popped open wide.

Aunt Fannie was elbowing her way to Lemuel's side. "Lemuel?" she said, grabbing him by the ear, "don't you know nothing? This here's one of them foreigners what worships foreign gods. I reckon he ain't Baptist." She turned to Dr. Rajgarhia. "You Baptist?"

He shook his head.

"See? I reckon he don't want you praying over him neither."

There was a lull and Imo held her breath as she looked from Aunt Fannie's scowling face to Lem's startled one. Would he acquiesce to his beloved aunt like he usually did?

Lemuel slowly reached into his pocket and drew out a small silver cross. He fingered it a moment before sliding it back in. He cleared his throat. "Let us pray," he said firmly, beckoning to everyone.

Montgomery was already there, standing at Lemuel's elbow, and Felder got to his feet. Dewey stepped into the circle between Wanda and Imo. At that moment the elevator doors glided open and there stood Hank and Lou holding hands.

"Come join us in prayer," Lemuel urged them.

Lou scowled at the sight of him, but Imo held out a hand and waggled her fingers until Lou and Hank joined the circle. At last Aunt Fannie grudgingly stepped in next to Felder.

Placing one hand on Dr. Rajgarhia's back, the Reverend Lemuel Peddigrew bowed his head and commenced to pray. "Our gracious Heavenly Father," he intoned, "You are the Great Physician and we are gathered here to ask that You anoint Dr. Rajgarhia's hands with Your skill as he operates on our Jeanette. Guide his every move and by Your marvelous compassion deliver Jeanette to us whole. In your Son's name we pray. Amen."

"Amen," Montgomery echoed.

Dr. Rajgarhia turned quickly and left the waiting room with his hands laced behind him and his head bent forward.

"Sleek little feller, wasn't he?" Wanda said. "Reckon he's married?" Everyone laughed, breaking the tension in the room.

Hank was talking to Dewey in the corner and Lou looked lost and unsure of herself, standing in front of the magazine rack. Imo stepped next to her. "Glad you're here, darlin'" she managed, giving the girl a brief hug.

Lou nodded.

"Was worried you couldn't get out of school."

"I got to exempt all my exams."

"I'm so proud of you and your good marks, Lou," Imo said. "I know you're at the top of Dr. Livesay's list for his summer internship."

Lou glanced down at her shoes, "I . . . I don't know," she said, swallowing hard.

Imo tipped Lou's chin up with an index finger. What would lift the girl's sad countenance? Perhaps her emotions were on the surface on account of Jeannie's surgery.

Like she read Imo's mind, Lou said, "How's Jeannie? I wanted to get here in time to see her before her operation."

"She's okay," Imo said, reaching her hand out to stroke some wispy hairs off of Lou's forehead. She seemed so small, so fragile and haunted, Imo knew, with more than Jeannie's plight. She often thought of the heavy load Lou's thin shoulders held, particularly her desperate battle over the farm.

When she was small, Lou had trailed her Uncle Silas all over the farm, like his constant shadow, helping him mend fences and feed cattle and harvest corn. She often said "I'm going to be a farmer *right here* when I grow up." She had spent more time along the banks of the Etowah River than anywhere, and Imo could not explain to anyone just how much she knew that land meant to Lou. There was something vital in the soil of the farm that worked its way up through the soles of the girl's feet and reached her heart. Something the girl could not turn her back on. Imo swallowed and it felt like a spiny sweet-gum ball going down.

"How's the garden coming along?" she asked. "Didn't get the chance to get out there yesterday."

"Good," Lou said in a high, thin voice. "Been getting a good little mess of squash."

"Is that a fact?" Imo smiled. "It's right early, but I imagine with all that TLC you've been lavishing on the plants, it's really no wonder. Now's the time to plant our sweet potatoes, isn't it?"

"Couldn't do a thing out there early this morning," Lou said. "The way it was raining and all."

"I know, I know," Imo said. "Wish this storm would go on and play itself out."

"Pole beans are running real good. Retied them yesterday evening. Okra and the lima beans are both blooming, you know." A slight smile crept across Lou's face.

"Come sit down, sugar foot," Imo said, looping her arm through Lou's and tugging her over to the cool vinyl couch. She noted that Montgomery and Wanda were engrossed in a deeply philosophical discussion about the Baptists' stand on "once saved, always saved," with Wanda maintaining you could backslide clear to hell itself and still get through those pearly gates long as you'd accepted Christ as your savior when you were twelve. Montgomery's heated protestations clearly amused her as she sipped a Diet Coke.

It seemed that Felder and Aunt Fannie were engaged in scintillating conversation, too, with Aunt Fannie yapping away and

Felder nodding every so often.

"Want some hot chocolate?" Imo asked Lou, happy when the girl nodded yes. Relieved to have something to do, she rustled around in her handbag for three quarters and officiously made her way to the vending machine. She wrapped her fingers around the hot paper cup and glanced at the clock hanging next to the elevator. Eleven o'clock. Dr. Rajgarhia had been at it for one hour so far. She did not want to imagine the scene in surgery. She sank back against her cushion, envisioning Jeanette's shaven and vulnerable head. She snatched up a thick issue of *Architectural Digest* and thumbed absentmindedly through the pages and she hoped, she prayed, that Dr. Rajgarhia had had himself a restful night and eaten a healthful breakfast.

Ah, but wasn't he reputed to be one of the best in the Southeast? Still and all, he was human. It was impossible to concentrate on any of the articles in the magazine and her mind flitted to the garden. She would be grateful for a long sunny morning in the garden when this was all over.

Imo turned to look out the window at the dark sky and the sheeting rain. She sighed deeply.

"What?" Lou said, turning to her.

"Nothing, dear." She fought to put a smile on her face. Then she looked from one waiting face to another. These are good people, she thought, family and friends clinging together in the eye of an insidious storm. But Lillian is not here, she admitted to herself. She is in shambles and could not scrape herself together enough to come. But if she had come, Imo wondered, wouldn't that have made it harder? Harder to hold on to the shreds of faith she was grasping so frantically even now?

Yes it would have, she admitted, feeling herself sliding into the uneasy and numbing world of waiting.

When one-thirty came, Hank stood and announced he would drive to the nearest McDonald's to pick up lunch for everyone. He took orders on the back of his hand. "Come with me, darlin'," he said to Lou, who hopped up quickly.

The conversation in the waiting room was all chitchat and small talk at that point. Talk of no real substance. Imo noted that Montgomery was biting his nails and Wanda was twisting her hair. Aunt Fannie was asleep, her chin on her chest, and Lemuel, Dewey, and Felder were discussing antifreeze.

Lunch arrived and Imo found herself with no appetite for the cheeseburger and apple pie she'd ordered. She peeled the flabby pickle from the bun and ate that, wrapping the burger back up to keep it warm. Aunt Fannie roused herself and began eating noisily. "Where's *my* pie?" she demanded when she'd polished off a Big Mac and a large order of fries.

"Here, have mine," offered Imo. She leaned back and crossed her arms while everyone finished eating.

"Man, I'd about kill for a cigarette," Wanda said, dabbing her greasy lips with a napkin, looking steadily at Aunt Fannie. "Want to step outside with me, Frances babe?" The two women linked arms and slipped into the elevator.

Imo glanced at the clock. Two-thirty p.m. There had not been word one from any of the doctors or nurses who zipped past the waiting room in their antiseptic shoe covers. Everything had all sounded so simple, so quick, when Dr. Rajgarhia described it. Imo fidgeted in her seat. She tried to focus on the world beyond the hospital walls, because this was getting to be really unnerving. There were millions of things going on out there, and millions of lives moving about, at work, at play, eating and sleeping with no cares, and here she was sitting, waiting while someone cut into her precious child.

She pressed her fingertips against both temples, closing her eyes to stare at the unnameable color of the insides of her eyelids. It all bewildered her — this life. She didn't know what to think, to pray anymore.

Well, if only Jeanette would pull through, then nothing else would hurt, certainly not this pounding of her heart from the terrible fear. Never mind losing the farm, her precious garden. Why, those were only things! To heck with them. She would not care a fig.

She would be delirious with joy just to see Jeanette's face, alive. With this realization came a fresh twinge of pain at Lillian's loss. Her stomach knotted as she unwillingly imagined herself in Lillian's shoes. *No, no, no, don't go there,* she begged her brain. Eyes closed, she murmured a frantic prayer that God would bind up the gaping wound that was Lillian's heart.

She turned her attention to a TV in the corner, where a very pregnant anchor girl with frosted pink lips was talking about the storm. A commercial for Dentyne gum came on and Imo rose to buy herself a cup of coffee from the brown machine she'd been staring at for hours.

The bitter liquid scalded her throat going down, but she hardly took notice. She unwrapped the cold burger and ate half before she wrapped it back up in its greasy paper. Outside the storm still raged. At the moment no one was talking. Lou had moved beside Hank and Lem had settled in next to Imo. His warm fingers in her palm were comforting.

Thunder rolled continuously, sounding like a train station. Imo leaned her head on Lem's shoulder and closed her eyes, though she did not sleep.

At three o'clock, Lem rose to use the restroom and when he returned Imo noticed that he kept the conversation light, far removed from anything that would upset her. He told her about one Christmas during his childhood when his parents had brought home a balsam fir tree too tall for their tiny house. His mother would not cut the majestic tree again, so she decorated it with strings of popcorn and cranberries and put it out in the yard for the birds. Cardinals came and they looked like ornaments.

The whole time he talked Imo kept her

eyes on the clock. Five hours! She wanted to shout, "It's been five long hours!"

At long last, close to four, an eternity in Imo's mind, Dr. Rajgarhia appeared. She could read nothing from his face. Everyone rose and encircled him like filings to a magnet.

"It is done," he said, his eyes cast modestly down. A long, streaking lightning bolt zipped outside the window and silenced him for an instant.

"It went as well as could be expected," he continued. "She is in recovery. You will be happy to know that it was not malignant."

"She's all right?" Imo breathed, standing on tiptoe. "Everything went along okay? When can we see her?"

"The immediate family can see her shortly," he said, thumbing a black wing of hair to his temple, "soon. Half an hour. We'll talk more then." He strode from the room.

A sense of relief swept through everyone. Hugs and tears made their way around. Before long Dewey, Wanda, Felder, and Aunt Fannie gathered their things and left for the long drive home.

Exhausted and impatient, Imo scooped up her handbag and walked to the nurses' station to wait. Jeanette was alive! *Thank you, Lord,* she breathed, *it was not malignant. How could I ask for more?*

When it was time Imo stormed into the recovery room, then stopped dead in her tracks at Jeanette's colorless face, her head swathed in pure white bandages like clouds. Behind her Lem breathed a prayer that sounded like *Lord, God Almighty,* and Montgomery circled quickly around the head of the bed to kneel at Jeanette's shoulder.

"She's awake now," a nurse said softly, arranging the covers over Jeanette's feet. "I'm going to try to get her to suck on this cloth." She stood patiently, tickling Jeanette's lips with a piece of gauze.

At last Jeanette parted cracked lips and clamped them down on the gauze. Her brow knit up in puzzlement and her eyes fluttered open for only a split second.

The nurse stroked her forehead. "Jeanette, honey," she trilled, "wake up and try to suck this for me. Your folks are here to see you."

Startled, Jeanette blinked and cut her eyes to the left and the right. Her face remained expressionless.

"Don't worry. It's the anesthesia," the nurse said, looking at Imo's startled face.

"Dr. R will be in directly."

Jeanette's eyes sought Montgomery's face.

"Hi there, love," he crooned. "You look like you're ready to go riding on the back of my Harley with that new haircut."

Jeanette's eyes smiled up at him, but her mouth remained slack. Moving close to her side, Lou bent and pressed her cheek to Jeanette's. "You look beautiful, Jeannie," she murmured.

Dr. Rajgarhia appeared after another twenty minutes, briskly professional.

Shifting her eyes to him, Jeanette said, "I need a mirror." Her right hand fumbled at her mouth.

Dr. Rajgarhia nodded at the nurse, who bent below a cabinet for a small hand mirror. She held it at Jeanette's face.

"Oh!" a little noise of shock escaped Jeanette's lips. "Is my mouth always going to be like this?" she asked, shock registering in her eyes.

The fluorescent lights overhead seemed unusually strong to Imo as she let her eyes travel to Jeanette's mouth. Half curled up in an animated expression and half lay lifeless.

"Yes," Dr. Rajgarhia replied. "To remove your tumor, I had to sever a nerve that controls the muscles of your mouth. You're a lucky woman. I believe I got it all."

Jeanette flung the mirror away like it was disgusting. She looked as though Dr. Rajgarhia had punched her.

Imo did not know what to say. Quickly, Montgomery dropped to a squat at Jeanette's bedside so that his face was level with hers. "Hey, Motorcycle Mama," he said softly, tickling her chin till she gave a lopsided grin, "I think it's kind of cute." Then he leaned forward and twisting his own lips to match hers, he kissed her.

A soft dusk was falling on the city of Atlanta when Imo and Lemuel left for home. The rain had stopped, and a stunning bow of pastel colors arched over the earth at the horizon.

Epilogue

Lou

On what would prove to be the last afternoon Hank and I would spend at the farm by ourselves, I worked out in the garden, getting a second crop of sweet corn in the ground. The backyard was filled with the scent of freshly turned earth and the soft guttural cooing of doves swooping in and out of the dovecote, a small shelter Uncle Silas put up near the shed in another life. Every now and again I looked up to watch their bluish-gray wings catch the late sunlight.

Hank, after fishing all morning, then scaling the whopping catfish he'd caught as Bingo looked on, had disappeared into the kitchen to try his hand at skillet-frying the catfish and making cornbread hush puppies. He came out to inform me of his progress fairly often, looking achingly sexy in only jeans and one of Imo's paisley bib aprons. I could stare for hours at his golden biceps and his muscular shoulders.

I sure had plenty of time for things like that, and for gardening, too. It had been five long days since Jeanette's surgery. Long on account of school being out and also because I still hadn't heard a word about Dr. Livesay's decision.

Though I had not spoken a word to the Reverend at Dusty's funeral or at Emory Hospital, I knew he was still talking to Imo about selling the farm because whenever I mentioned the matter to Imo, she hemmed and hawed and would not meet my eyes.

My future, my very life, hung in the balance, and it seemed everything was just a hair's breadth away from collapsing.

I was still hoping fervently, to the point of misery, that I would be Dr. Livesay's choice — that old Miz Gantry's prophecy was wrong — and still praying without ceasing about the land, begging, beseeching God to change the Reverend's heart and mind. I lay in bed night after night, holding only myself, my thoughts a tangled mixture of hope and fear for the future. A fear so deep it threatened to pull me under.

I tried desperately to keep ahold of the faith umbrella. I'd shut my eyes tight and try to conjure up a picture of me at the farm as I turned twenty, thirty, forty, and then sixty. In my hopes and dreams I ran through the pasturelands sucking up the scent of sun-warmed fescue.

I tried to think of nothing except staying there for good, but sometimes I could see nothing but my own doubt glittering like a pair of fox eyes in the night. I knew my own palpable disbelief and I bit my nails till my fingertips bled. I literally tasted my fear, my doubt.

I got to thinking about the time Uncle Silas and Jeanette and I came up on a cottonmouth snake down at the river. I was seven and Jeanette was ten and when we'd finished with supper — cold tomato sandwiches and sweet tea in front of an oscillating fan — Uncle Silas said he was going to go and dip us in the river to cool us off. "Full moon and river water," he said to Imo, chuckling. "An old Indian cure for heatstroke."

It was dusk on a summer day, night was coming and the stars were out. A round orange moon hung in the sky and an owl called from the woods. The day had been hot as fire, close to a hundred degrees, and no amount of lemonade or watermelon or playing out in the shade of the pecan tree had eased our irritability.

Practically falling all over ourselves in excitement, Jeanette and I pulled on old tank tops, cutoffs, and flip-flops, and we raced ahead of Uncle Silas, down the dirt road to the bottoms, laughing and patting our hands like Indians over our mouths as we called out "Wooo-woo-wooo-woo."

At the water's edge we slid out of sandals and plunged headlong in up to our necks, our toes squiggling down into deliciously cool silt and muddy slime on the bottom. The big moon kissed our bare shoulders and we dove and splashed each other happily.

Suddenly, as I reached to get a stick floating along on a current of river water, I spied the slim coil of a snake. I froze. My heart pounded so hard I was afraid it might jump plumb out of my body, goose pimples rose on the backs of my arms.

"Snake," I whispered to Jeanette, backing away ever so slowly.

Uncle Silas called from the bank. "What's wrong, gal?" and instead of answering I pointed to the orangey brown snake floating there on the river. He narrowed his eyes to see through the murky dusk.

"Yup," he said, his voice high with fear, "cottonmouth. Stay still, girls. Don't move."

Jeanette looked over her shoulder at me, then at the snake. "Big whoop-tee-do," she said airily, grabbing a slender twig from a birch tree on the bank and advancing on the snake, saying "En garde, Mr. Snake. One of us has got to beat it."

"They're deadly," I breathed.

Uncle Silas waved his arms on the bank at us. "Stay still," he warned again.

I opened my mouth and watched in surprise as the snake silently slipped under the surface and moved away. Jeanette giggled and dove down into the water.

Uncle Silas marveled for months over that incident. "I cannot believe that girl," he'd say. "Cottonmouths chase folks! One of the most dangerous snakes I've ever heard tell of."

I wasn't sure why Jeanette felt no fear and I always did. I didn't know how she could laugh in the face of danger like that. But with all that had happened the past months, I realized she wasn't as invincible as I had her figured to be. When I saw her face following surgery, when she looked in that mirror, I could tell that the old sneer at life was gone from her eyes.

I paused to lean against the handle of the hoe and look down toward the bottoms. Wisteria was blooming in purple profusion, and the late sun threw long shadows across the smooth dirt road, worn to a sheen by years of feet and truck tires. It looked like a painting, a work of art.

A mental image of myself thrust from the farm gave me a wistful catch in my throat. My mood lowered and I grabbed the hoe and began to strike hard at the dirt again. When the corn was in the ground and watered, I began to retie tomato plants to their stakes.

By and by Hank stepped out onto the back porch, waving a hot mitt. "Yore aunt called, Lou," he hollered.

"What'd she want?"

He shrugged. "Said she and the Reverend are coming out directly."

That really threw me. Imo never called when she was coming out and the Reverend never came with her. I worked myself into a mild state of panic over the purpose of Imo's visit. Maybe it was bad news about the farm — the Reverend had convinced her to sell it. My brain numbly rehearsed the words I'd conjured up on one of those nights I lay tossing and turning in bed. Words I prayed would convince him not to sell.

Please, God, I prayed, *let this blind man see the light. Cast the scales from his eyes.*

I let myself get lost again, in the rhythm of mulching the beans, listening to a small chunky brown bird perched on the telephone pole as he whistled a clear *bob-WHITE, bob-WHITE.*

"Chow time," Hank said a spell later, wearing a wide smile across his lumpy cheeks as he chewed on a mouthful of something. In his hands was a tray heaped with golden brown catfish, hush puppies, and a huge bottle of ketchup. His idea of fine dining. He set this down on the picnic table.

"Looks delicious," I said, running my hands underneath water from the hose. He looked mighty proud, and I smoothed a napkin across my thighs and began to eat with exaggerated gusto, though I had no appetite.

The moment seemed so fragile then. The man I loved beside me, the land I loved beneath my feet, the late May moon above us. I suppose I managed to exclaim enough over Hank's cooking because he looked pretty content as we finished eating and sat nursing our ice tea in the soft evening air.

Soon a car nosed around the corner of the house and I saw a solemn-faced Imo and the Reverend in the front seat. This did not look good. I flinched as Bingo rose stiffly to greet them. Hank laid his napkin on the picnic table and crossed the yard to the Impala. Reluctantly I followed, scuffing the toes of my sneakers in the grass.

I knew immediately when I saw Imo's face that she had something serious to discuss. "Howdy," I said in a fake cheerful voice, my fingernails digging into my palms hard.

"Hi, sugar foot," Imo said, "lovely evening, hm?"

I nodded and Hank said "Sure is" in a hearty voice, pumping the Reverend's hand. That's when I noticed the white envelope in Imo's hand. I could still hear the *bob-WHITE, bob-WHITE* of the busy little bird, but vaguely, far away, like it was not real. Imo's face had a pensive expression.

"Loutishie," she said when we finished our hellos. "This came for you today. From Dr. Livesay's office, it says."

And then it seemed even more surreal as

she held that envelope out to me and I slid it from her hand with everyone's eyes drilling into me. "Thanks," I said, turning it round and round in my fingers. My heart was beating a mile a minute when finally I slit the flap and pulled out a piece of folded white paper. In one terrible second I allowed my eyes to scan the words. *Pleased to inform you . . . my pleasure . . . please report to my office by eight o'clock on June 1st . . .* I read, the last line before Dr. Livesay's sprawling signature.

I raised my head, eyes squinched tight. "Yes, yes!" I breathed.

Everyone crowded into me for one big group hug and I did not even flinch as I felt the Reverend's stubbly old cheek against mine. "Lou," Imo gushed, stepping back from me a bit as she held my shoulders. "This is wonderful! You should be so proud."

"Congratulations," the Reverend said, and I nodded, relief flooding through me. I was still lost inside some kind of delirious dimension when I heard Hank offering Imo and the Reverend some leftover catfish.

They all moved eagerly to the picnic table, laughing and talking a mile a minute. "I knew she'd get it" was what

Hank kept on saying. "I told her over and over, I said, 'Lou, you're going to get it. Nobody else on God's green earth can handle a critter the way you do.' "

They ate and I stood there with that letter in my hands, thinking to myself that if only the farm were secure in my future, too, then I'd be wholly at peace with the world. Pluckiness rose up in me as I told myself I just had to have that conversation with the Reverend. If I could just get the man down to the river that night and talk to him, how could he say no?

You can do this, Lou, my frantic brain said as I edged my way to the Reverend's side and sank down next to him on the very edge of the bench.

"What else can I get for you, Reverend?" Hank was saying.

The Reverend, still chewing, held up a hand and shook his head to say he was fine.

Taking a deep breath, I laid a hand on his shoulder. "Want to take a walk with me?" I asked him.

I saw surprise in his eyes as he turned to look at me. "I do believe I could use an evening constitutional," he said.

"To the river?" I asked as he rose from the picnic table.

"Fine idea," he said.

I pretended not to notice the way he was hobbling along, each step so obviously painful. I almost felt sorry for the old guy. On his feet were those shiny pointy-toed wingtips. I stayed at his side, going achingly slow, as frogs and katydids made a racket along the roadside. I was rehearsing my spiel, feeling a little nervous about pleading my cause.

We walked along in silence until the Reverend blurted out, "You still sore at me, Loutishie?" When I didn't answer, he added, "I know we don't see eye to eye on everything, but believe me, I try to look at things from every angle." I did not believe him, but I nodded anyway, biding my time as we inched along closer to the river.

We didn't talk the rest of the way down to the edge of the Etowah, then I led the Reverend downriver a ways to where I decided it was at its most beautiful. A slow, shallow part embraced by tall hardwoods leaning out over the water to gaze at their own reflections. Unhurried, the amber water moved like honey between its banks.

I looked eagerly at the Reverend's face. He stared flatly at the water, saying nothing. "Don't you think it's heaven on earth right here?" I urged. "And that reminds me, I've got this really great idea. I wouldn't be surprised if it was divinely inspired. A revelation!"

He turned to me, blinking and studying my face. Ever so slowly he nodded. "Tell me, Loutishie," he said.

"I firmly believe that this land should be kept in the family." My words spilled out crazily. "Set aside for the Lord's use. Turn it into a summer camp for Baptist youth. No, for undeveloped youth. Mentally and physically challenged youth. A year-round camp!" I'd meant to say underprivileged, but it didn't seem that the Reverend had noticed my blunder. "Can't you see it?" I went on breathlessly. "A place where kids can come to recreate and to feel closer to God! Would you just *look* at this river? It's like the veins of God!!

"And there's other things, ideas," I went on without hardly a breath. "We could build cabins. Let the kids learn gardening. Horseback riding. Hey, we could have minister conferences here, too, and I could keep the grounds. Make sure things run well." I did not say that I pictured this camp to be years down the road, that I would be an old woman when this happened. I took a deep breath and held it, closed my eyes.

I watched him hobble over to a knee-high boulder and lower himself wearily down on it. I was disappointed to see the pained expression on his face.

"Reverend," I said, "what do you think about all I just said? I mean it, it's definitely divine inspiration! It's got to be! I know God's been talking to me."

"My feet hurt," he said finally, his face contorting in pain.

Watching him pick up each leg in turn, transferring his weight, something clicked in my mind. Hadn't I overheard him a million times, moaning plaintively to Imo that in heaven surely everyone went barefoot? I smiled. I slipped off my sneakers.

"I was thinking of naming the camp Barefoot Farms," I said, thumping my big toe fetchingly on the soft silt of the bank. " 'Barefoot Farms, where it feels like heaven.' Catchy, huh?"

He thrust his hands into his pockets, hunched forward, and for a few minutes stared out at the waning light of the sun on the surface of the water. There was no doubt he was engaged in a sort of personal quandary. But I wondered if it was over slipping out of his shoes and exposing the indignity of his feet or my proposal. He sat and he sat and it seemed that all was lost until finally he sighed and bending forward he grunted as he pulled off his wingtips and set them carefully, toe-to-toe, on the boulder beside him.

And so I eased out into the shallow edge of the river, pretending I wasn't watching him, the water swirling around my shins. *Please, please, oh please,* I murmured noiselessly through clenched teeth.

At last he rolled his socks down like donuts to his ankles and over his heels till they popped off at the toe tips, exposing a pale stringy collection of bone and sinew. Angry red bunions glared and pulsed at the sides of his feet.

"That does look painful," I said, not able to help myself.

"Yep," he said, sighing. "My cross to bear."

"But I thought you had that wonderful shoe-stretcher thing that accommodates your bunions."

"Did," he said wearily.

"Did?"

"Okay. I lost it again," he said, "third time, I admit it. Was totally my fault." He stood tentatively and eased forward, letting the oozing mud along the riverbank squish over his bunions. I stood in place, looking nonchalantly downriver.

Wallowing happily, the Reverend rolled up his pant legs and moved a bit farther out into the water and stomped around a few minutes. There was a beautiful sound of sucking mud as he raised each foot in turn, black with mud. "Ahhh, oohh, oohh," he moaned in a voice I'd never forget. Then he became silent and still for several seconds, rolling his eyes and looking somewhere beyond the treetops with this fierce concentration. At last he cleared his throat meaningfully.

"You know," he said, almost to himself, rubbing his hands together. "I reckon I really oughter start slowin' down a mite. Spending some time at Barefoot Farms, wading in God's artery." He regarded me for a long moment with something like relief in his eyes. "I can just about see myself rocking on the back porch of the farmhouse with my sweetie, watchin' God paint the sunset." He looked at the pink and orange glow hanging in the sky to the west.

I almost burst into tears of joy. "You mean it?" I gaped at him. I was the picture of bewilderment as he stood out there in the edge of the Etowah for the longest time, transfixed, with his feet thrust in the healing mud.

Slowly he nodded his sparse-haired old

head. "Now, Loutishie," he said, rubbing his palms together, "I reckon we're going to hafta lay out some plans for dividing our time between the parsonage and the farm, here. Till I get myself fully retired anyway. Like to tore Imogene's heart out when you didn't come home with us. I been missing you, too."

Before I even realized it, I was over there hugging the Reverend, and it felt like being baptized, when you come up out of the water all clean from your trespasses.

Hank and Imo and Bingo came loping along toward us, and when they got close I heard Imo laughing and calling out, "Lemuel Peddigrew? Why, I never!"

I gazed downriver at the water moving slowly round a distant bend, and I felt a huge welling of thankfulness as I listened to doves crying in the trees.

That turned out to be the finest summer of my life. When I'd glimpse my reflection in the glass of the front door at Dr. Livesay's veterinary practice, I saw the face of a deliriously happy girl. In the evenings, weary in a good sort of way, I'd go sit out in the backyard, in the old iron glider, and watch the sunset over the bottomland.

One evening in early July I thought I'd carry my notebook along with me and jot down a few things for posterity. I wrote about how the tomatoes and cucumbers were ripening so fast it was all Imo and I could do to keep them harvested, and how the Reverend took it literally when he retired. For weeks after they moved back into the old farmhouse with me, he went around barefoot. He lived to fish and nap and read. Calvary Baptist hired what he jokingly referred to as "a young whippersnapper" as the new minister. The Reverend's only contribution was to write something on the marquee he figured would reassure folks during the change:

UNDER SAME MANAGEMENT
FOR OVER 2,000 YEARS.

I'll write about Imo and the Reverend's quirky little relationship, I thought, how they are truly enjoying themselves now, acting like a couple of teenagers in love.

But I glimpsed Inez then, slipping out from beneath the barn, and her bulgy sides put me in mind of Jeanette. For weeks after her surgery, Jeanette would not be seen in public. She certainly would not smile her lopsided smile for anyone.

But one evening she called the house and she said, "Lou, you're not going to believe this, but I'm pregnant!" and I could hear some of the former Jeanette's joy of life as she went on about how absolutely thrilled Montgomery was. He was painting the nursery as we spoke.

She told me she was planning to get back involved in singing with the praise squad at her and Montgomery's church. I managed to bite my tongue before I blurted out, "Are you sure?" It was common knowledge that Jeanette didn't have a musical bone in her body. But it didn't matter. Wanda had also convinced her to return to her job at the Kuntry Kut 'n' Kurl, though Jeanette refused to wear the long blond wig Wanda ordered, preferring instead her chic postsurgery buzz cut and the new tattoo of a cross on the nape of her neck. "Heck," she said, laughing. "May even have to head to the Honky Tonk for next month's bull-riding contest!"

It wasn't till I expressed grave disappointment in this idea that she said, "Relax, Saint Loutishie, I was just pulling your leg. Even if I did want to enter, wouldn't nobody let a preg on the bull." I had to laugh. Jeanette was still throwing sticks at snakes after all.

Imo, of course, was mighty tickled with all of this. The only thing that still burdened her soul, as she called it, was knowing that Lillian Puckett did not have peace.

Then one Saturday afternoon I was outside relaxing in the glider when a car pulled up, and dear God, it was Lillian, pale as a turnip and waving a piece of paper.

"Lou," she said breathlessly, "your aunt here?"

"She's in the house. I'll run fetch her."

Imo came out of the house on my heels, wide-eyed like she'd seen a ghost. "Lillian?" she said. "Sit down. Let me fix you some tea or something."

"No, no, dear," Lillian said, flapping that folded square of paper. "I want you to look a here. I was going through some of Dusty's things to donate to the Salvation Army and I found this."

"Let me see." Imo's trembling hands accepted the paper and she smoothed it out flat.

"It's a speech he was writing on for his AA group," Lillian said.

Imo nodded. Pursing her lips she read aloud:

Dear Fellow AA members —
Nowadays I drink all I want. I smoke all the pot I want. Also, I cheat and I lie all I want. I reckon I got y'all's attention now, don't I? Well, the fact is, I just don't want to do none of them things no more. I mean it, really. It's downright peculiar, but I reckon that the Holy Ghost, my "Higher Power," done got a hold of me and turned me inside out. No one this side of heaven could ever know how absolutely free I'm feeling. I mean, I ain't scared of nuthin'. The devil hisself can burn in hell. Ha ha ha. I guess what I'm sayin' is, I know how the story ends now. One thing I can't figure out is why Believers are afraid to die. After all, when they die they get to be with Jesus all the time, forever, and we know ain't nothin' more better than that!

I watched Lillian Puckett, hugging herself, rocking to and fro. "You cannot imagine how comforting it was to find this," she said, suddenly on the verge of tears.

Imo nodded and pulled a napkin from her apron pocket. "I know, I know, dear," she crooned. "It's absolutely the most beautiful thing I've ever read."

Every time I think of that scene between Imo and Lillian Puckett, a mystical feeling washes over me, like my very own personal river of peace. A river which restores my soul.

I would never look at that awful time we'd all just been through the same way again, because I had finally realized there is always a light waiting around the bend.

I knew without a doubt that Uncle Silas, Martha Peddigrew, and Dusty Puckett were there somewhere close by, and that they were smiling as well.

And if that isn't something to be happy about, then I don't know what is.

Acknowledgments

I am filled with gratitude to:

Amanda Patten, my friend and editor, who encouraged me to write this book and whose tireless input on every draft made it much better than I could have imagined.

Lisa Sciambra, also at Simon & Schuster, a literal marvel at publicity.

Nancy Lambert, who has the tedious task of getting the Euharlee Garden Club newsletter together and out, and who does an awesome job.

Jenny Bent, my wonderful agent, who is as generous with her enthusiasm as her thoughtful advice. She always makes me feel like I've got another story inside.

Joel Spector, the New Jersey artist who

did the gorgeous cover. You sure can paint Southern!

Booksellers all over the country who have shown such devotion to my earlier novels, "hand-selling" them, as they say in the business, so that I have the freedom to write more.

All my readers, many of whom have called, or sent letters and emails from literally everywhere. I hope you enjoy reading this one as much as I enjoyed writing it!

My fellow writer Augusta Trobaugh whose friendship and generous spirit give me faith to believe in all manner of miracles.

My partners in the Dixie Divas: Karin Gillespie, Jackie L. Miles, and Patricia Sprinkle, for their constant encouragement and the good reading material.

My family on both sides, for their many faceted support. Especially my sweetheart, Tom, and our children, who provide the inspiration and the environment that make the actual writing possible, and who give me infinite reasons to live, love, and laugh every day.

My heavenly Father. *I hope I did you proud.*

Reading Group Guide
Those Pearly Gates

1. Despite their ever-widening family circle, the heart of Julie Cannon's *Homegrown* series is Imo, Lou, and Jeanette. Compare and contrast these three women and the roles they play in *Those Pearly Gates*.

2. Imo has raised two adopted girls, one of whom is actually her niece. In *Those Pearly Gates* she is remarried to her late best friend's husband. Jeanette and her husband are raising Jeanette's child by another man. Lemuel, as a Reverend, is often placed in the role of Father to an entire congregation. Discuss the ways in

which "family" can be defined, and how growing up in various family structures might affect a child both positively and negatively.

3. When Lemuel starts to show signs of slowing down, Imo has a very difficult time convincing him to take time out of his busy ministerial schedule for himself and for their relationship. Do you think Imo is doing the right thing? Do you think she is overreacting? How much influence do you think her own weariness of being a reverend's wife has on her treatment of Lemuel? How does one tell the difference between selfishness and self-care? *Is* there a difference?

4. What does Imo love so much about gardening? How does gardening bring her closer to God? Are her feelings about the farm different from Lou's? Why or why not?

5. Were you surprised when the source of Jeanette's headaches and dizzy spells was revealed to be a brain tumor? Why do you think the author chose this particular twist?

6. Imo is convinced that her departed best friend and Lemuel's first wife, Martha, is haunting her. This prompts her to have a conversation with Lemuel about the Biblical opinion on spirits. Do you believe that the ghosts of loved ones can pay us visits? Have you ever experienced this?

7. People in Euharlee refer to their faith in God in very different ways. Discuss the religious views of Imo, Lemuel, Lou, Jeanette, and Lillian and Dewey Puckett. How do they compare to your own?

8. If you've read the two previous novels in this series (*Truelove & Homegrown Tomatoes* and *'Mater Biscuit*), consider how the people of Euharlee, Georgia, have been represented. Do you see characters growing and changing, or do they remain static and constant? How has or hasn't this happened over the course of the three novels?

The employees of Thorndike Press hope you have enjoyed this Large Print book. All our Thorndike and Wheeler Large Print titles are designed for easy reading, and all our books are made to last. Other Thorndike Press Large Print books are available at your library, through selected bookstores, or directly from us.

For information about titles, please call:

(800) 223-1244

or visit our Web site at:

www.gale.com/thorndike
www.gale.com/wheeler

To share your comments, please write:

Publisher
Thorndike Press
295 Kennedy Memorial Drive
Waterville, ME   04901